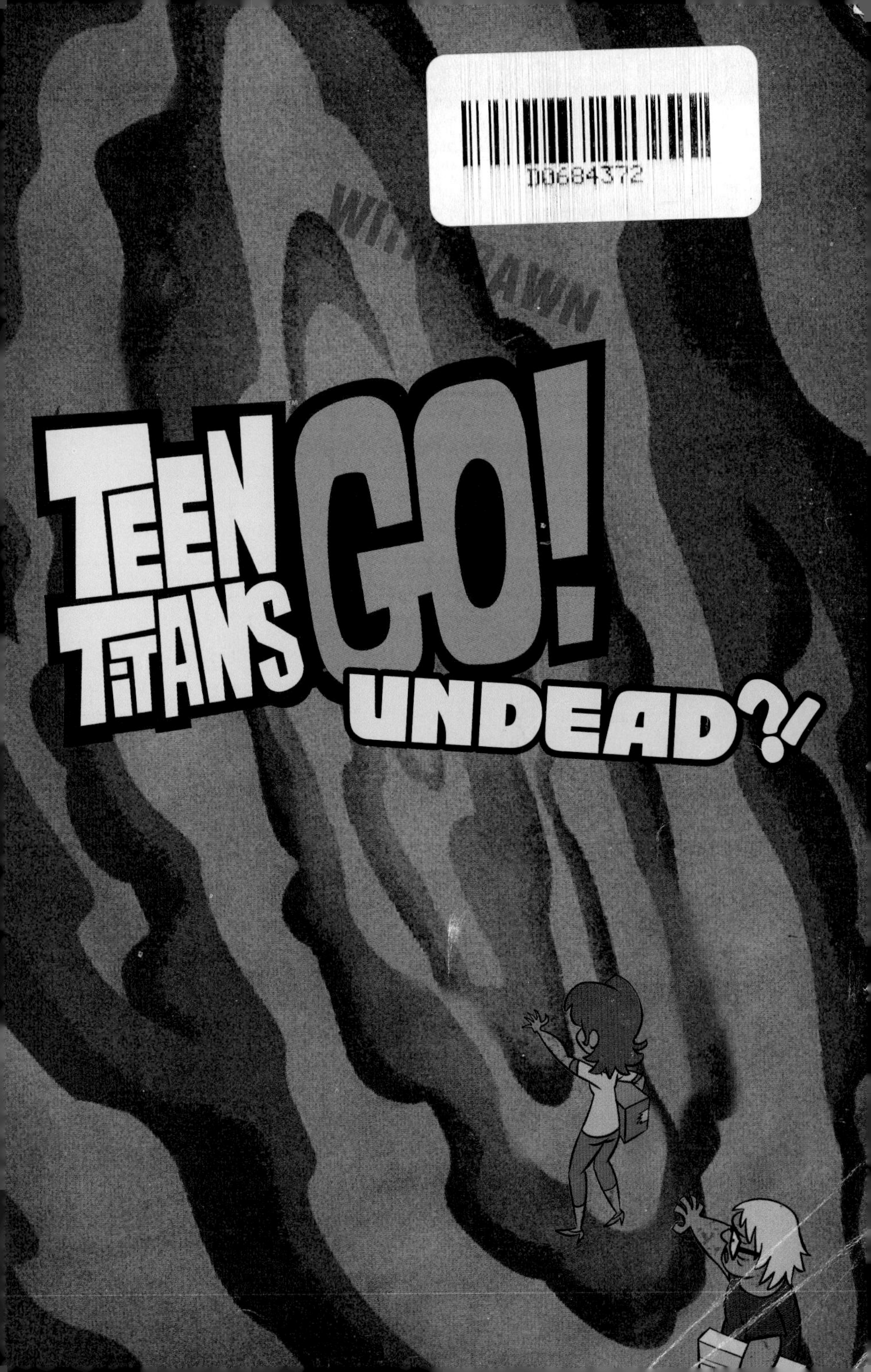
TEEN TITANS GO!
UNDEAD?!

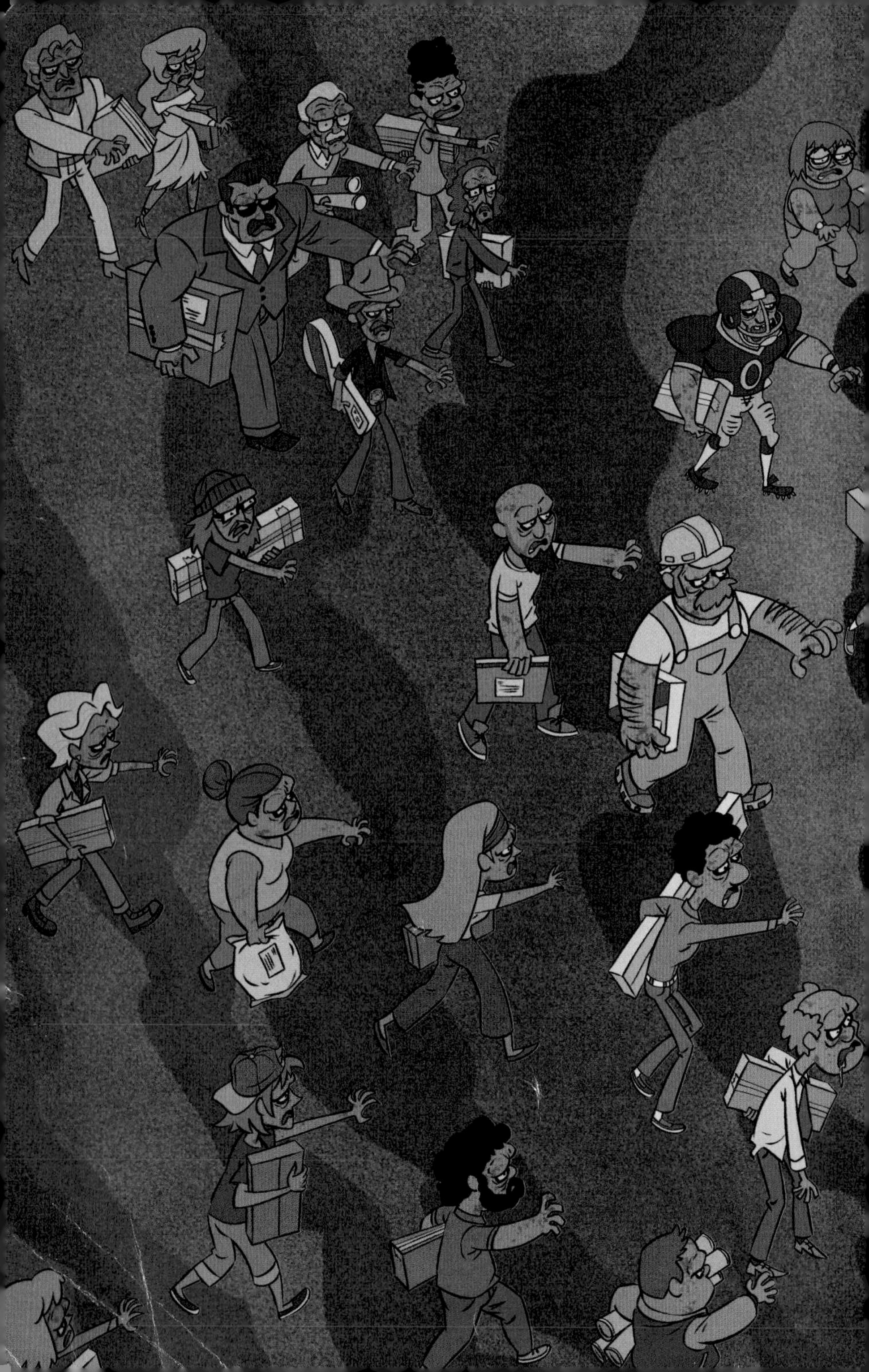

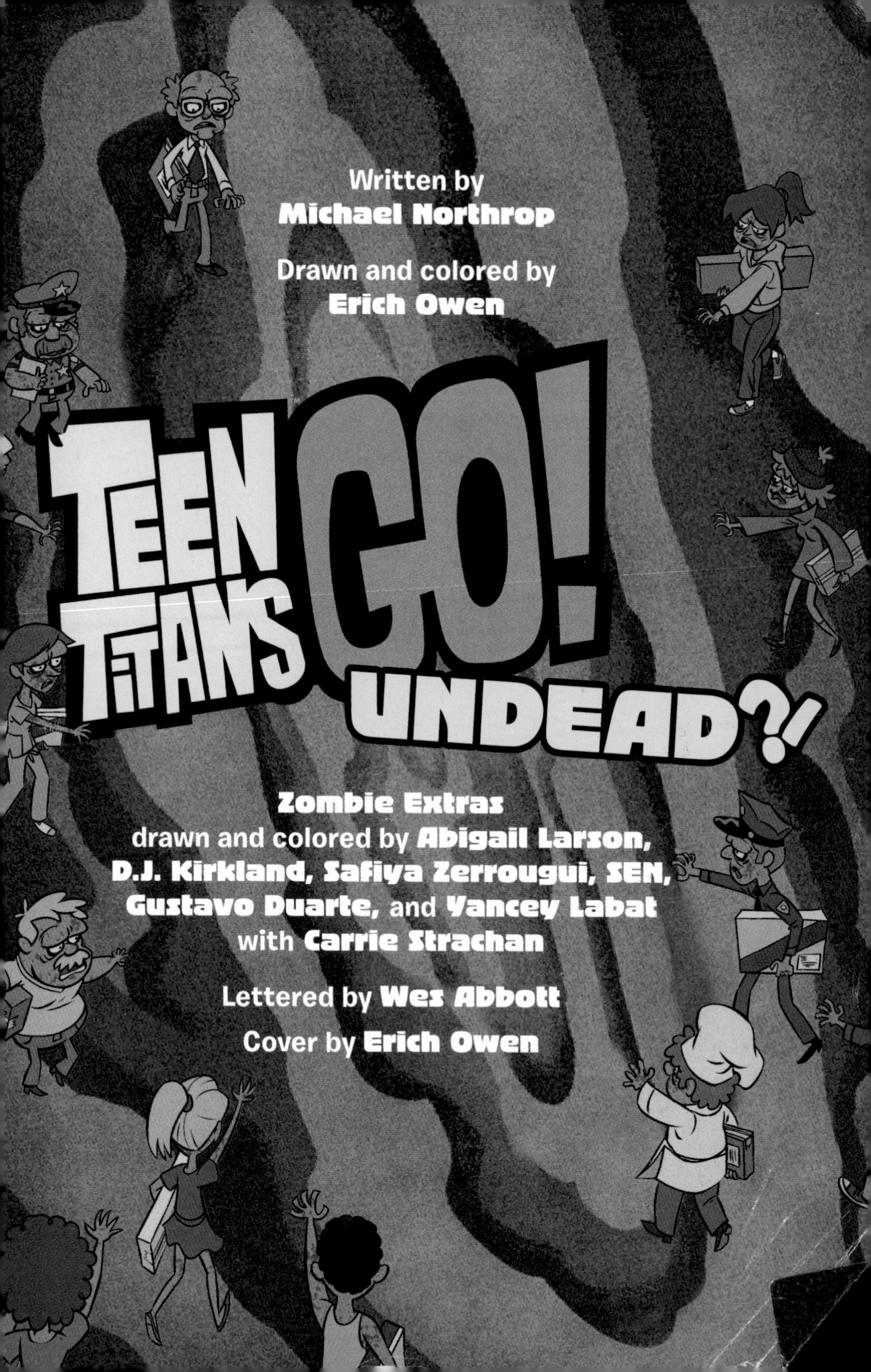

Written by
Michael Northrop

Drawn and colored by
Erich Owen

TEEN TITANS GO! UNDEAD?!

Zombie Extras
drawn and colored by **Abigail Larson, D.J. Kirkland, Safiya Zerrougui, SEN, Gustavo Duarte,** and **Yancey Labat**
with **Carrie Strachan**

Lettered by **Wes Abbott**

Cover by **Erich Owen**

KRISTY QUINN Senior Editor
STEVE COOK Design Director - Books
AMIE BROCKWAY-METCALF Publication Design
DANIELLE RAMONDELLI Publication Production

MARIE JAVINS Editor-in-Chief, DC Comics

ANNE DePIES Senior VP - General Manager
JIM LEE Publisher & Chief Creative Officer
DON FALLETTI VP - Manufacturing Operations & Workflow Management
LAWRENCE GANEM VP - Talent Services
ALISON GILL Senior VP - Manufacturing & Operations
JEFFREY KAUFMAN VP - Editorial Strategy & Programming
NICK J. NAPOLITANO VP - Manufacturing Administration & Design
NANCY SPEARS VP - Revenue

What the heck is that‼

That's an interrobang! It's a punctuation mark that combines a question mark and an exclamation mark that is beloved by designers, including the one that designed this book! It was created in the early 1960s by Martin K. Speckter. Other possible names included exclamaquest, QuizDing, and exclarotive.

TEEN TITANS GO! UNDEAD?!
Published by DC Comics. Copyright © 2022 DC Comics. All Rights Reserved.
All characters, their distinctive likenesses, and related elements featured in this publication are trademarks of DC Comics. DC logo is a trademark of DC Comics. The stories, characters, and incidents featured in this publication are entirely fictional. DC Comics does not read or accept unsolicited submissions of ideas, stories, or artwork.
DC - a WarnerMedia Company

DC Comics, 2900 West Alameda Ave., Burbank, CA 91505

ISBN: 978-1-77950-785-3
Printed by Worzalla, Stevens Point, WI. 5/20/22.
First Printing.

Library of Congress Control Number: 2022935114

FSC
www.fsc.org

MIX
Paper from
responsible sources
FSC® C002589

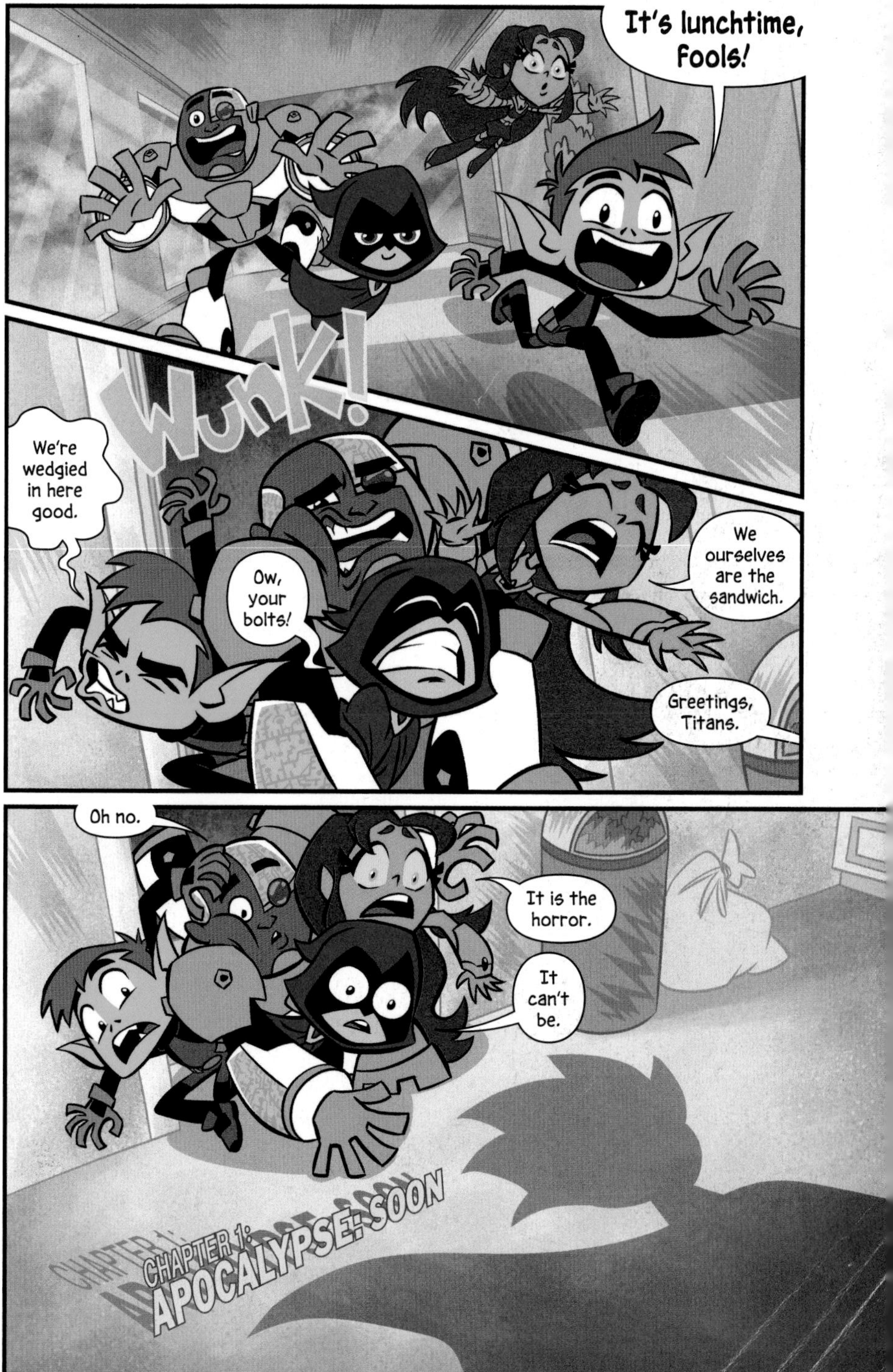
It's lunchtime, Fools!
WUNK!
We're wedgied in here good.
Ow, your bolts!
We ourselves are the sandwich.
Greetings, Titans.
Oh no.
It is the horror.
It can't be.
CHAPTER 1: APOCALYPSE: SOON

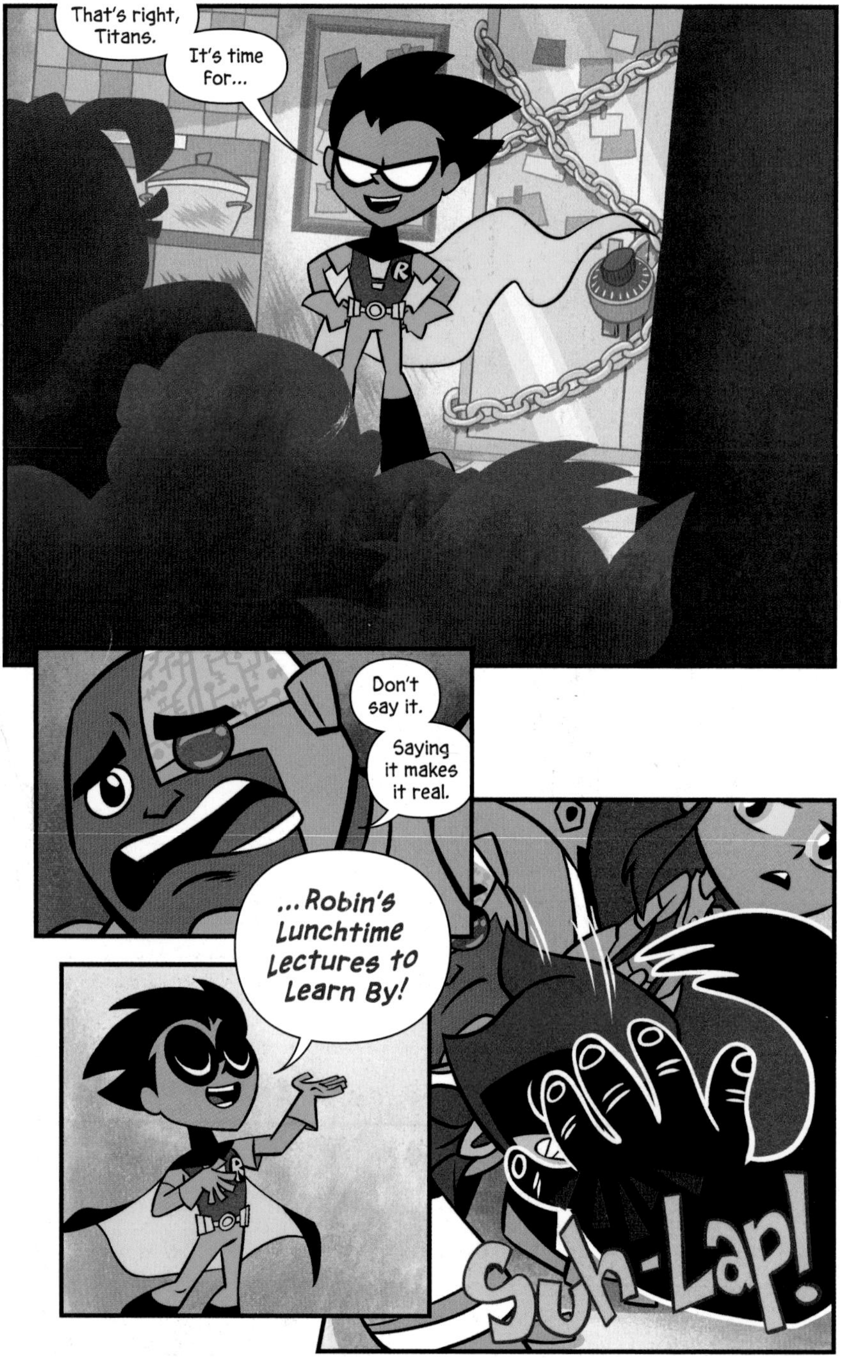
That's right, Titans.
It's time for...
Don't say it.
Saying it makes it real.
...Robin's Lunchtime Lectures to Learn By!
Suh-Lap!

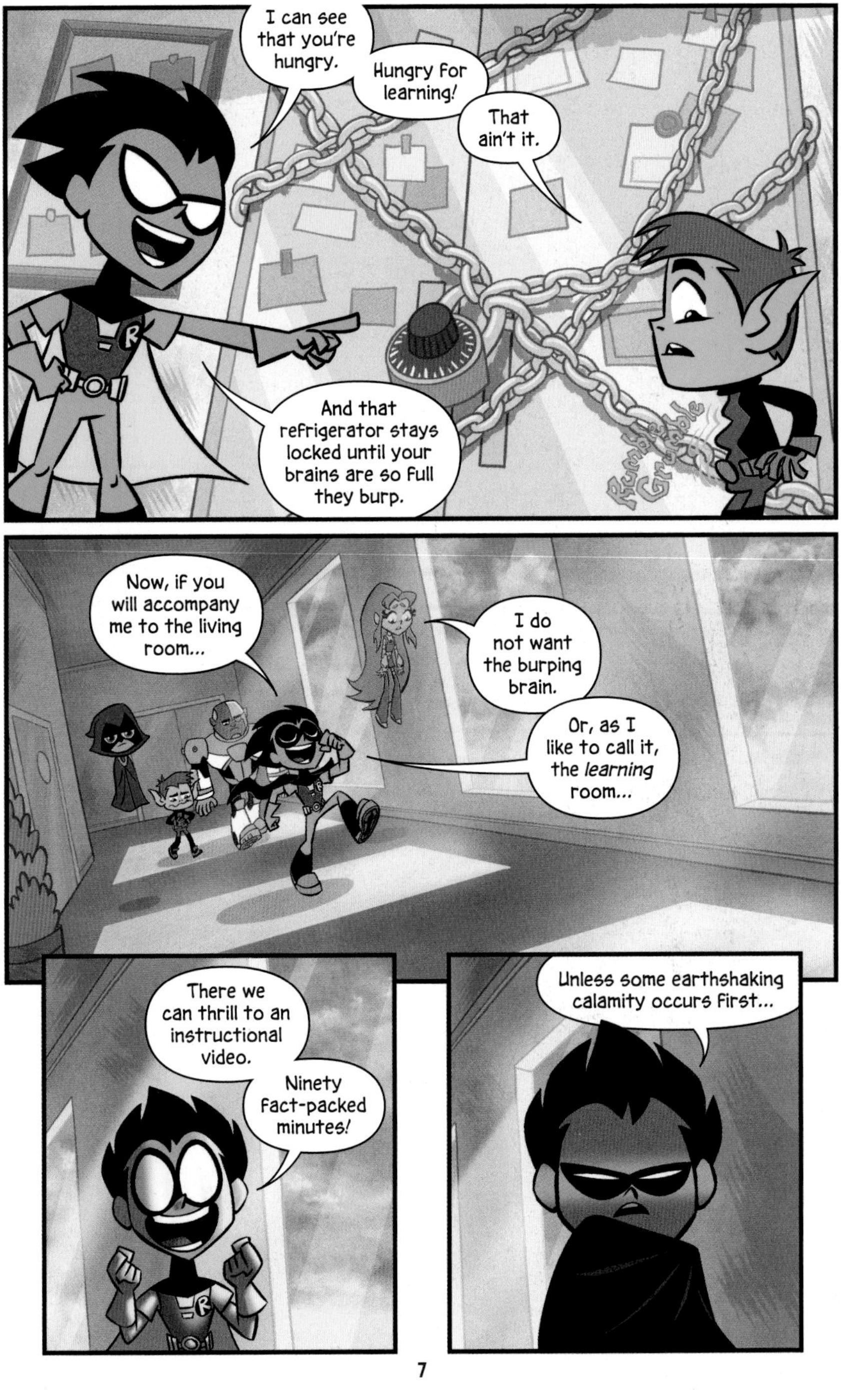
I can see that you're hungry.
Hungry for learning!
That ain't it.
And that refrigerator stays locked until your brains are so full they burp.
Rumble Grumble
Now, if you will accompany me to the living room...
I do not want the burping brain.
Or, as I like to call it, the *learning* room...
There we can thrill to an instructional video.
Ninety fact-packed minutes!
Unless some earthshaking calamity occurs first...

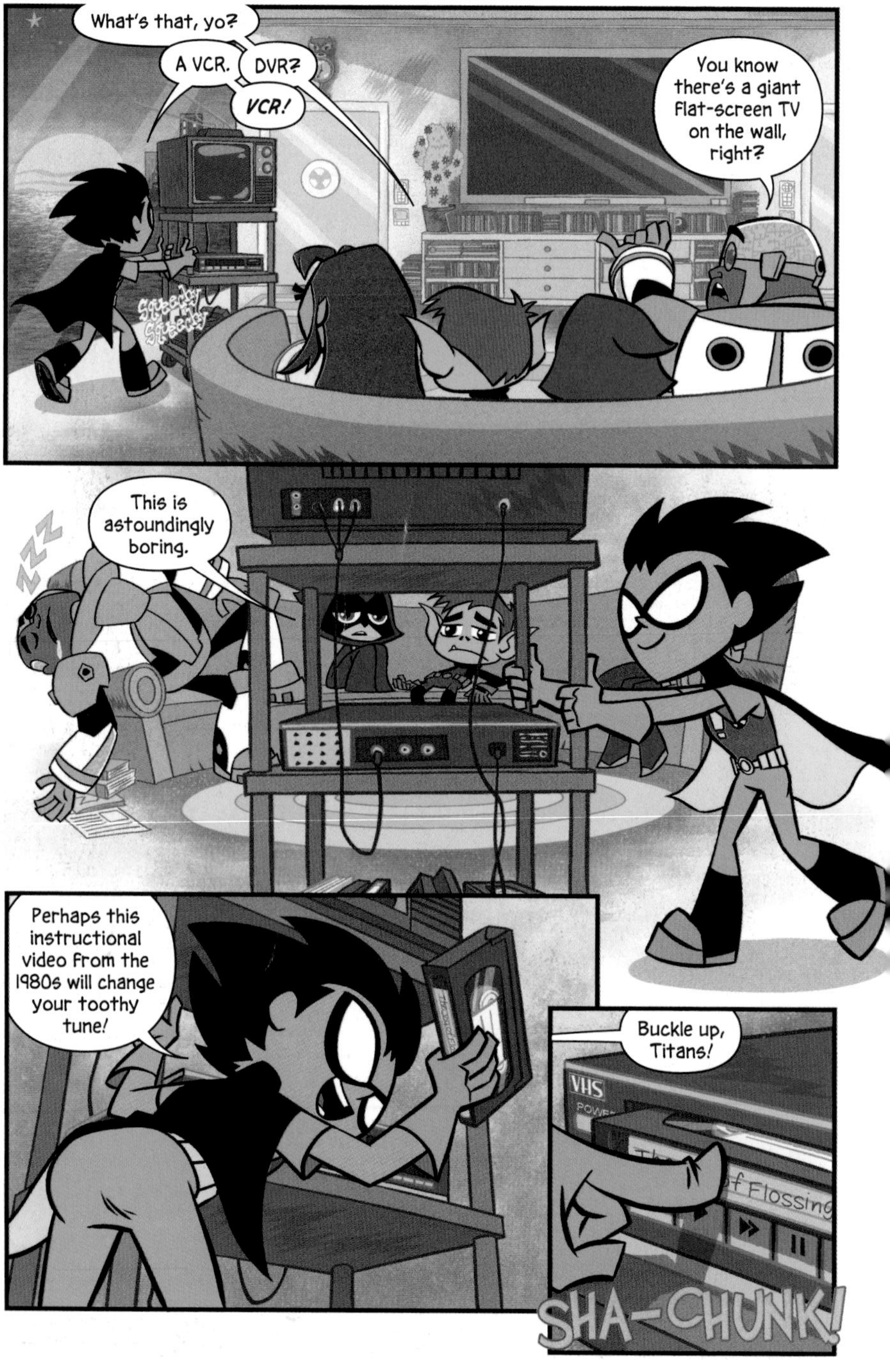
What's that, yo?
A VCR.
DVR?
VCR!
You know there's a giant flat-screen TV on the wall, right?
This is astoundingly boring.
Perhaps this instructional video from the 1980s will change your toothy tune!
Buckle up, Titans!
VHS
of Flossing
SHA-CHUNK!

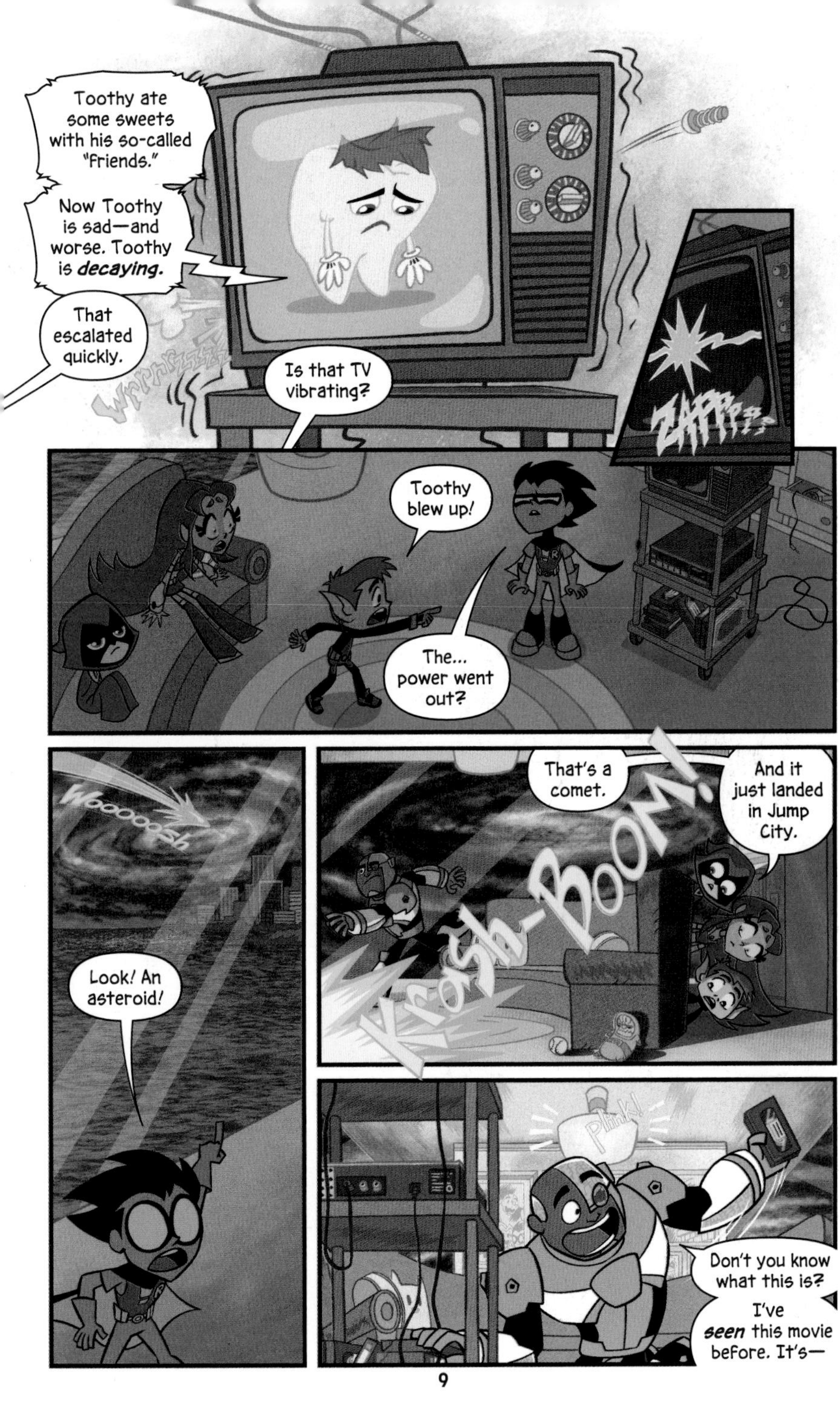
Toothy ate some sweets with his so-called "friends."
Now Toothy is sad—and worse. Toothy is ***decaying.***
That escalated quickly.
Wrrrrzzzzz
Is that TV vibrating?
ZAPPP
Toothy blew up!
The... power went out?
Wooooosh
Look! An asteroid!
That's a comet.
And it just landed in Jump City.
Krash-BOOM!
Plink!
Don't you know what this is?
I've ***seen*** this movie before. It's—

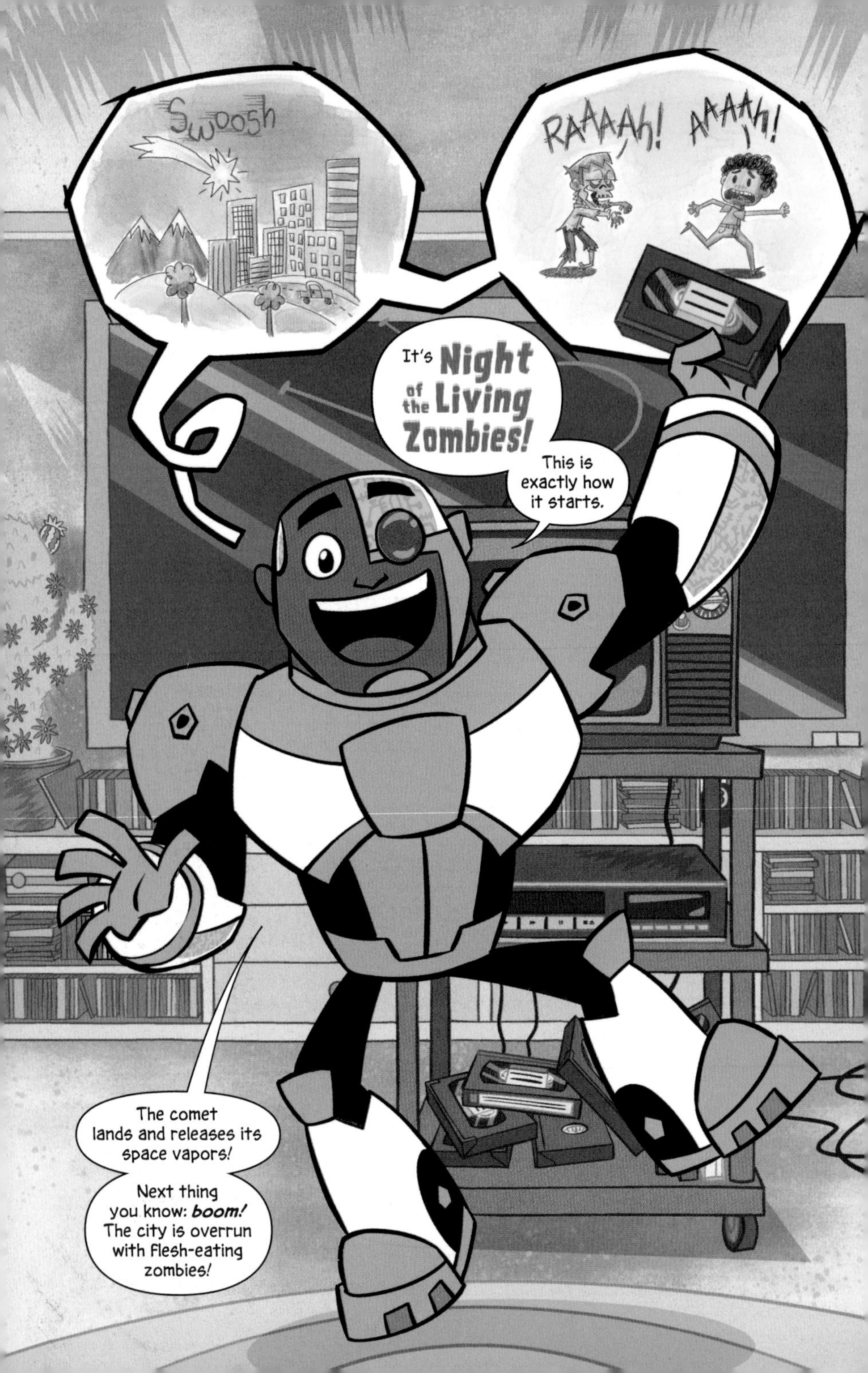
SWOOSH
RAAAAh! AAAAh!
It's Night of the Living Zombies!
This is exactly how it starts.
The comet lands and releases its space vapors!
Next thing you know: *boom!* The city is overrun with flesh-eating zombies!

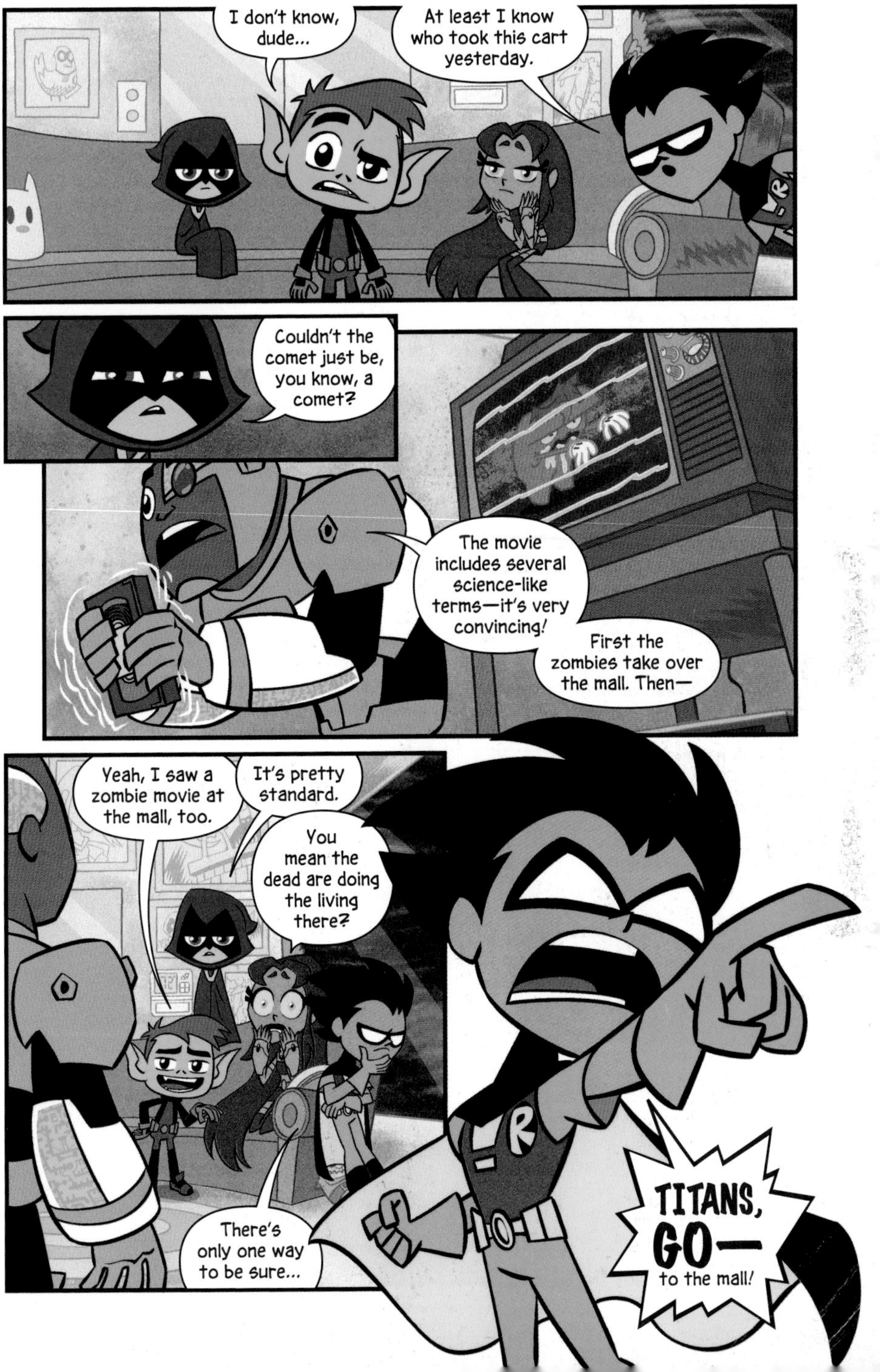
I don't know, dude...
At least I know who took this cart yesterday.
Couldn't the comet just be, you know, a comet?
The movie includes several science-like terms—it's very convincing!
First the zombies take over the mall. Then—
Yeah, I saw a zombie movie at the mall, too.
It's pretty standard.
You mean the dead are doing the living there?
There's only one way to be sure...
TITANS, GO—
to the mall!

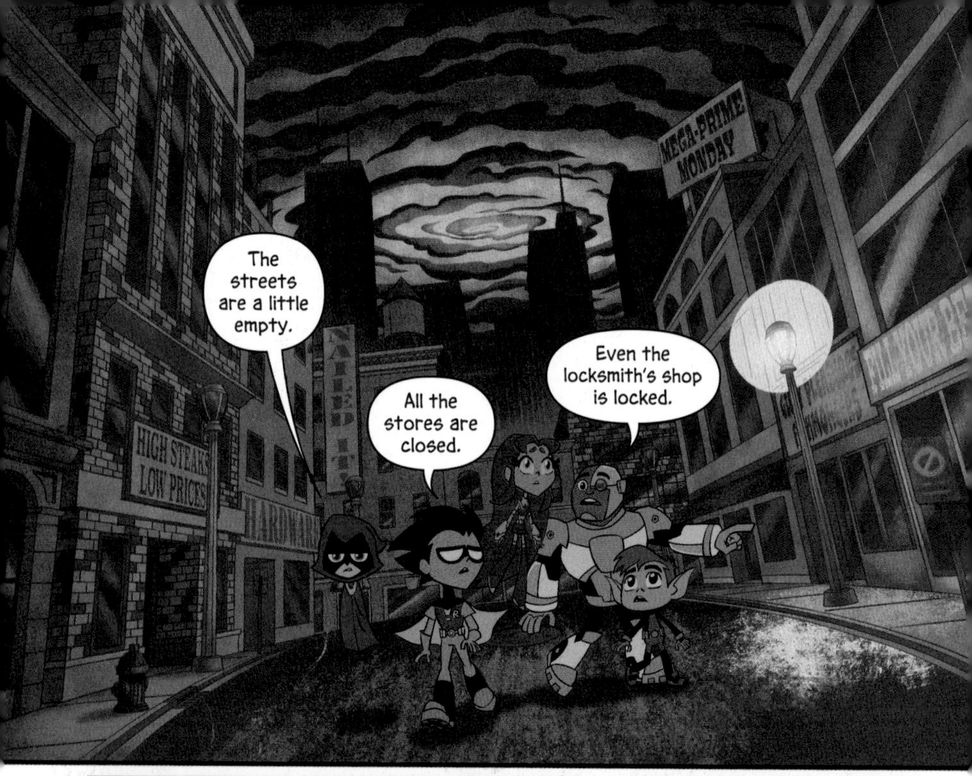
MEGA-PRIME MONDAY
HIGH STEAKS LOW PRICES
The streets are a little empty.
All the stores are closed.
Even the locksmith's shop is locked.

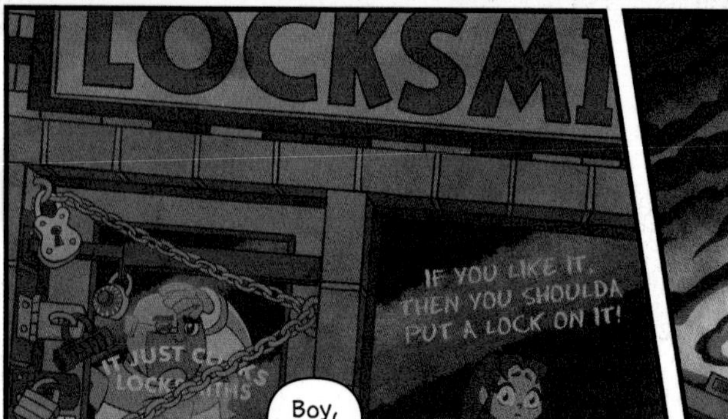
LOCKSMI
IF YOU LIKE IT, THEN YOU SHOULDA PUT A LOCK ON IT!
Boy, is it!

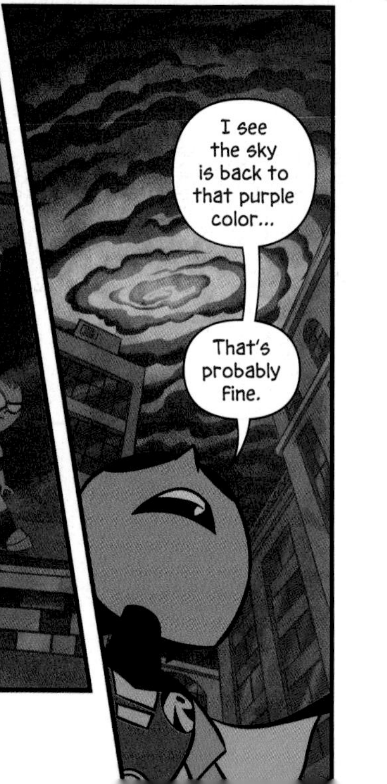
I see the sky is back to that purple color...
That's probably fine.

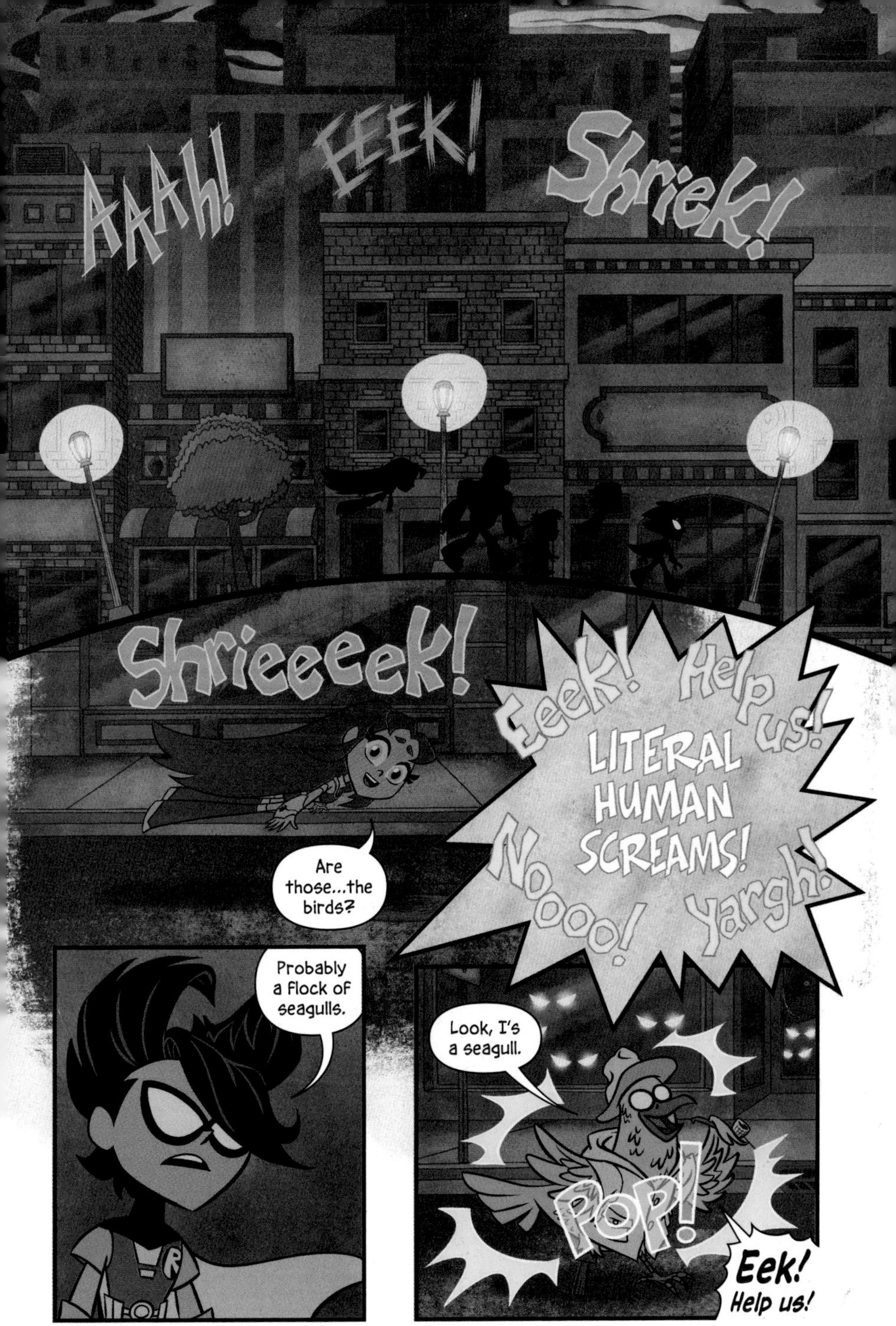
AAAh!
EEEK!
Shriek!
Shrieeeek!
Eeek!
Help us!
LITERAL HUMAN SCREAMS!
Noooo!
Yargh!
Are those...the birds?
Probably a flock of seagulls.
Look, I's a seagull.
POP!
Eek!
Help us!

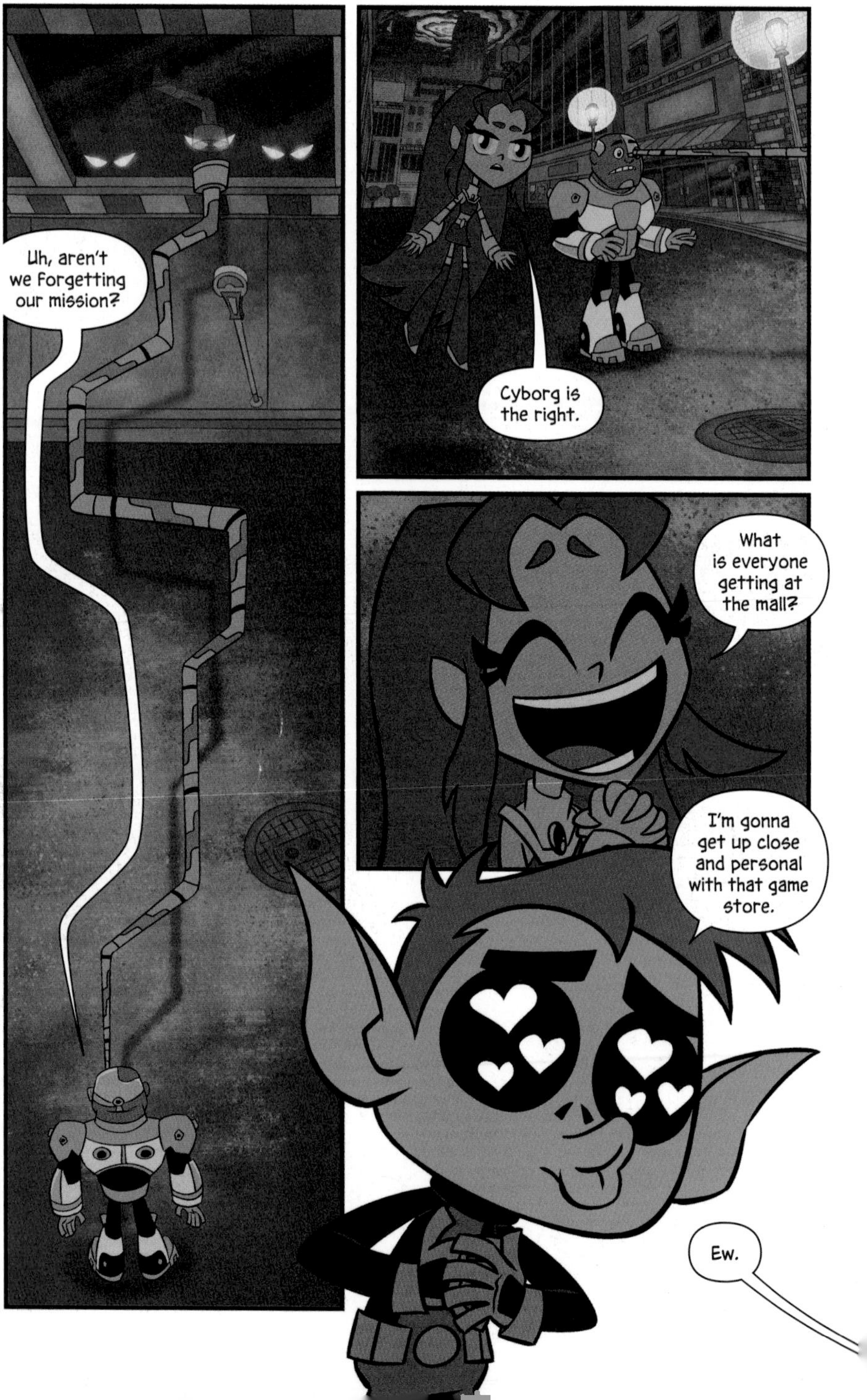
Uh, aren't we forgetting our mission?
Cyborg is the right.
What is everyone getting at the mall?
I'm gonna get up close and personal with that game store.
Ew.

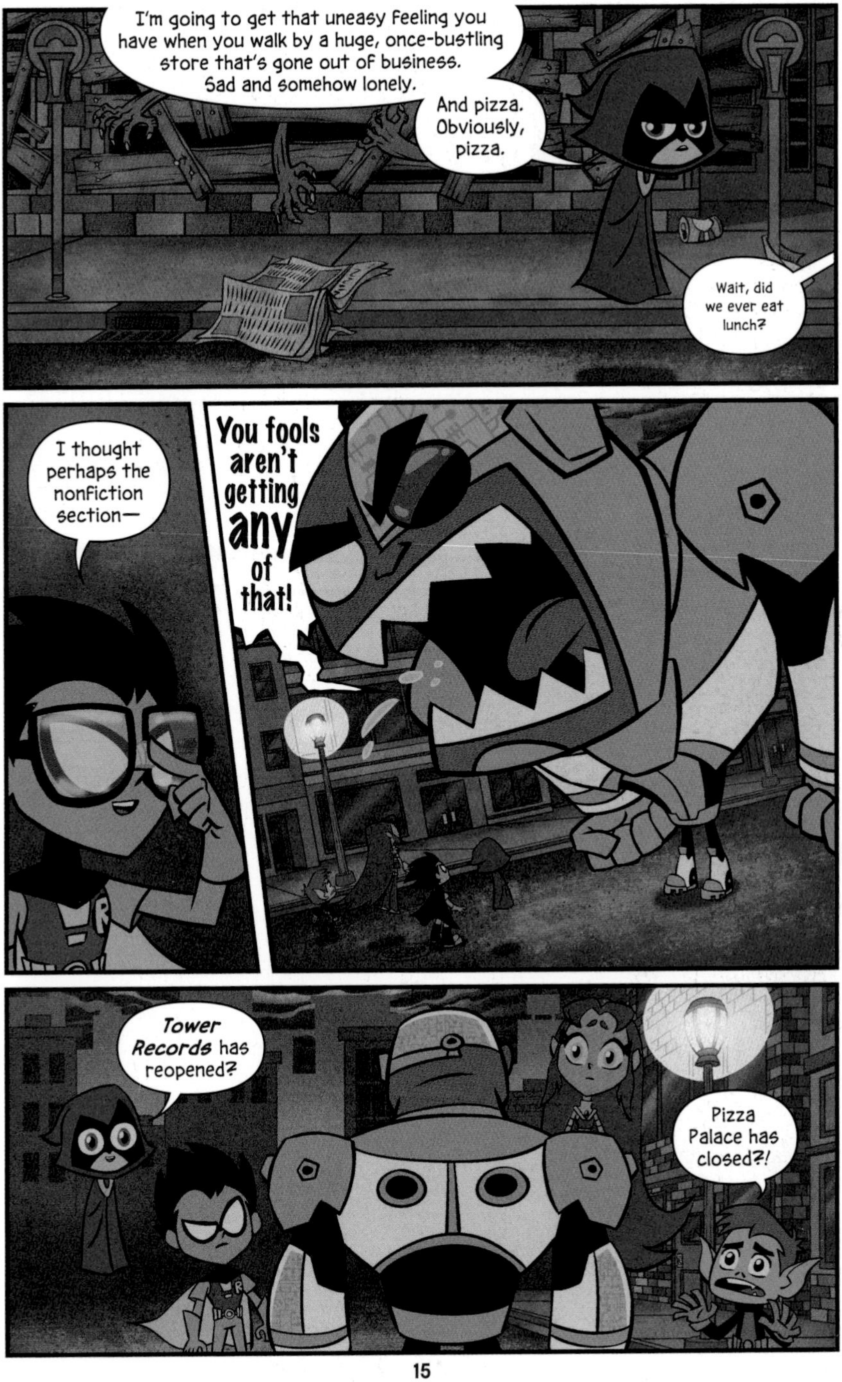

I'm going to get that uneasy feeling you have when you walk by a huge, once-bustling store that's gone out of business. Sad and somehow lonely.
And pizza. Obviously, pizza.
Wait, did we ever eat lunch?
I thought perhaps the nonfiction section—
You fools aren't getting any of that!
Tower Records has reopened?
Pizza Palace has closed?!

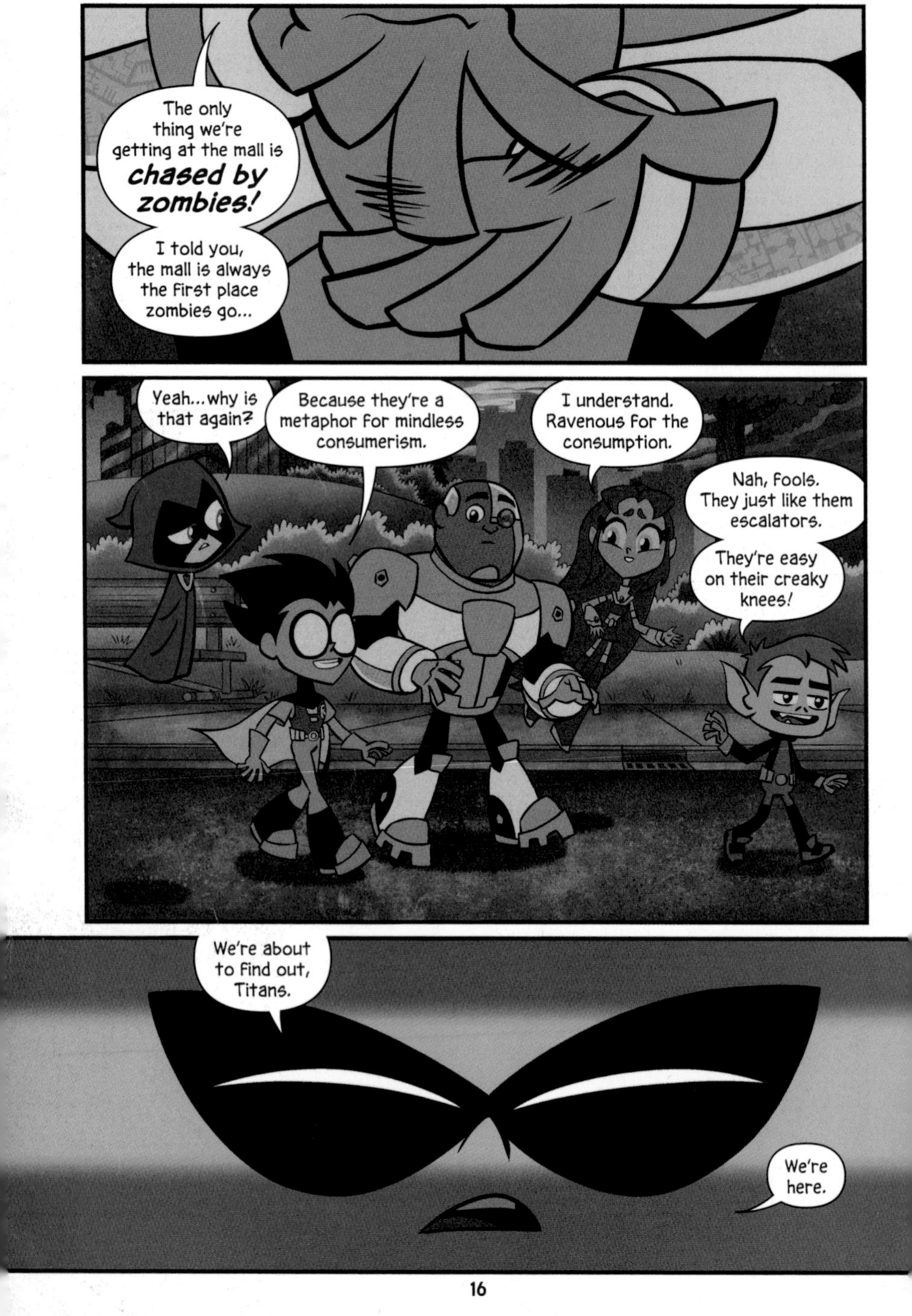
The only thing we're getting at the mall is ***chased by zombies!***
I told you, the mall is always the first place zombies go...
Yeah...why is that again?
Because they're a metaphor for mindless consumerism.
I understand. Ravenous for the consumption.
Nah, fools. They just like them escalators.
They're easy on their creaky knees!
We're about to find out, Titans.
We're here.

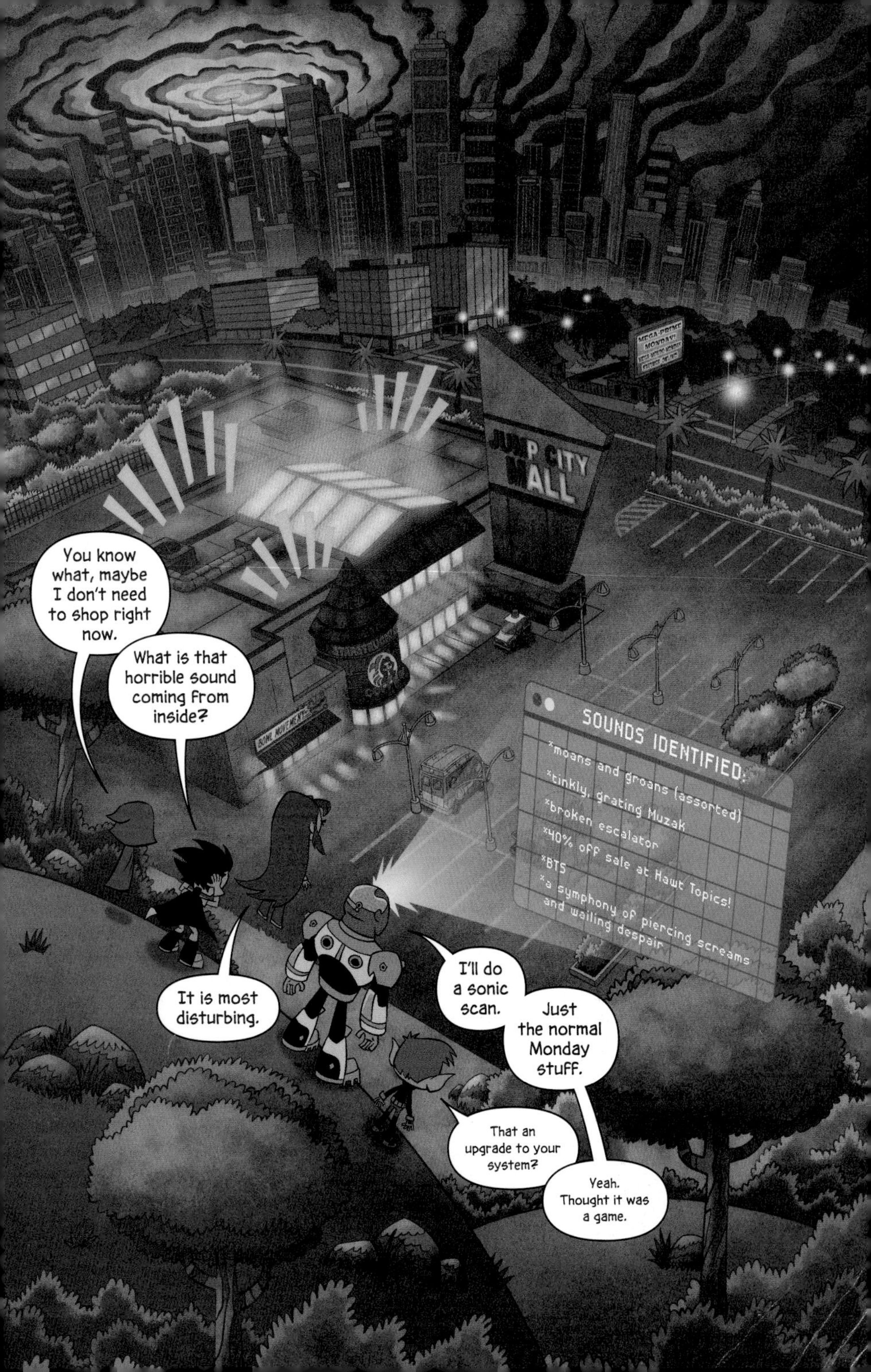

JUMP CITY MALL
MEGA-PRIME MONDAY!
You know what, maybe I don't need to shop right now.
What is that horrible sound coming from inside?
SOUNDS IDENTIFIED:
*moans and groans (assorted)
*tinkly, grating Muzak
*broken escalator
*40% off sale at Hawt Topics!
*BTS
*a symphony of piercing screams and wailing despair
It is most disturbing.
I'll do a sonic scan.
Just the normal Monday stuff.
That an upgrade to your system?
Yeah. Thought it was a game.

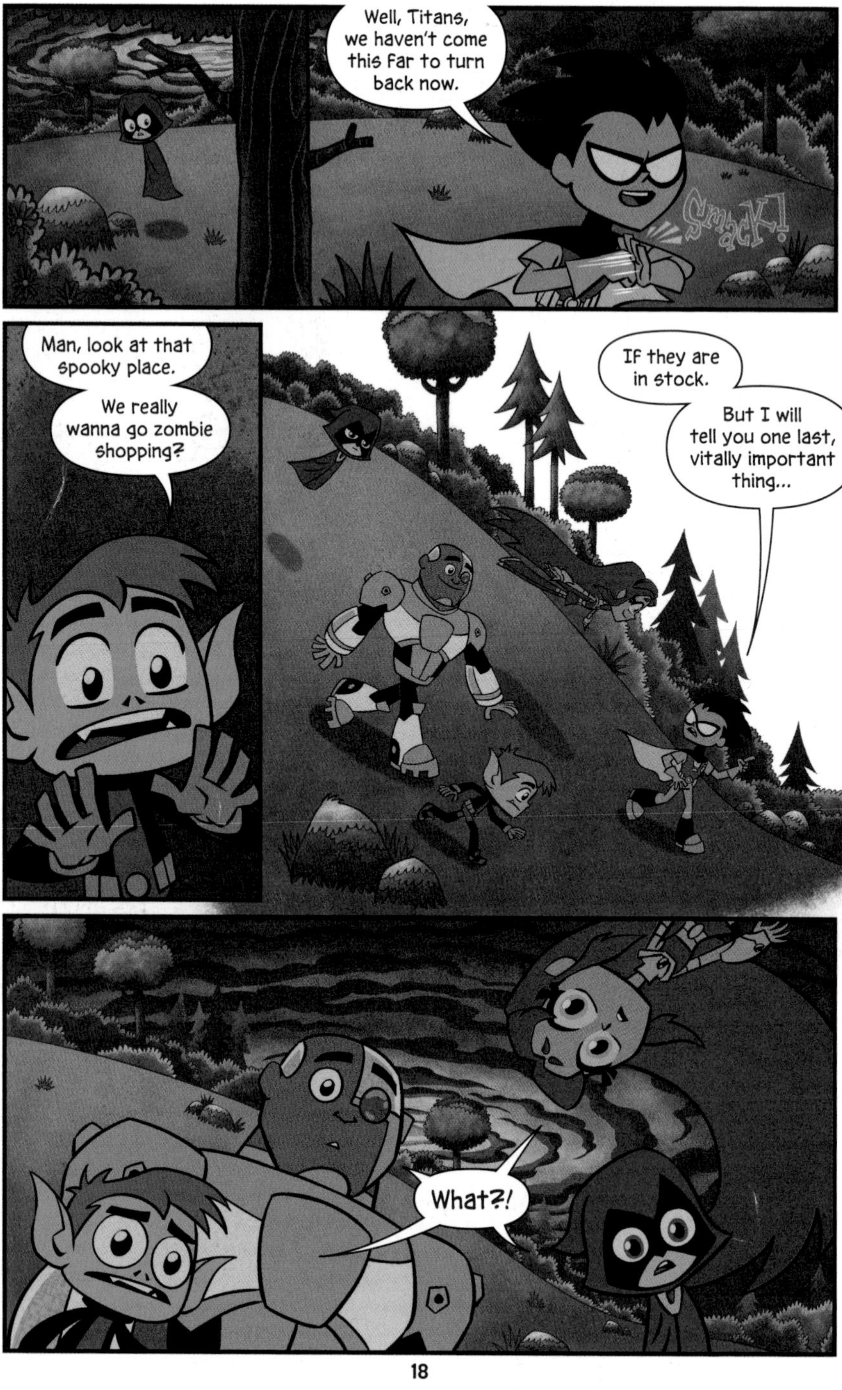
Well, Titans, we haven't come this far to turn back now.
SMACK!
Man, look at that spooky place.
We really wanna go zombie shopping?
If they are in stock.
But I will tell you one last, vitally important thing...
What?!

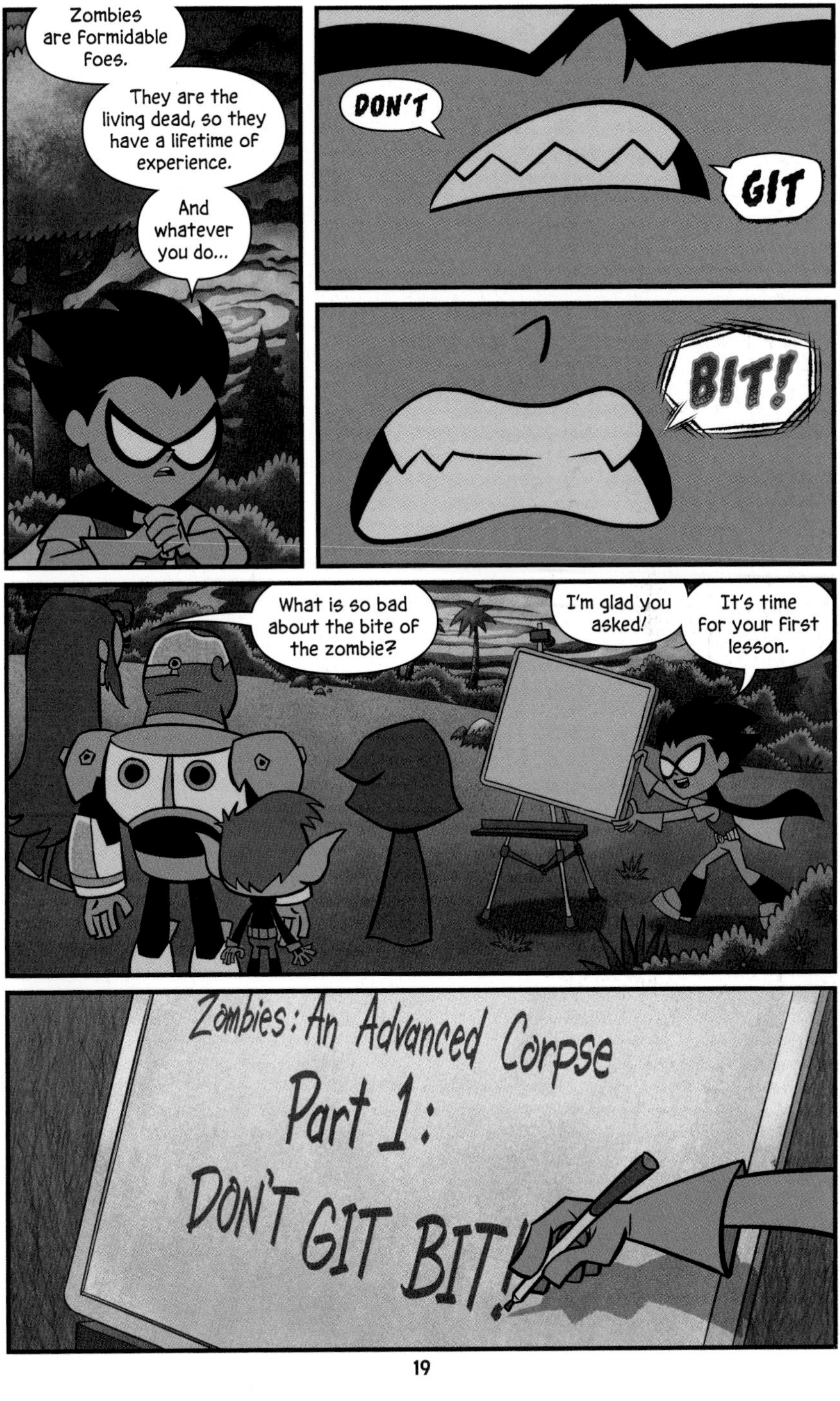
Zombies are formidable foes.
They are the living dead, so they have a lifetime of experience.
And whatever you do...
DON'T
GIT
BIT!
What is so bad about the bite of the zombie?
I'm glad you asked!
It's time for your first lesson.
Zombies: An Advanced Corpse
Part 1:
DON'T GIT BIT!

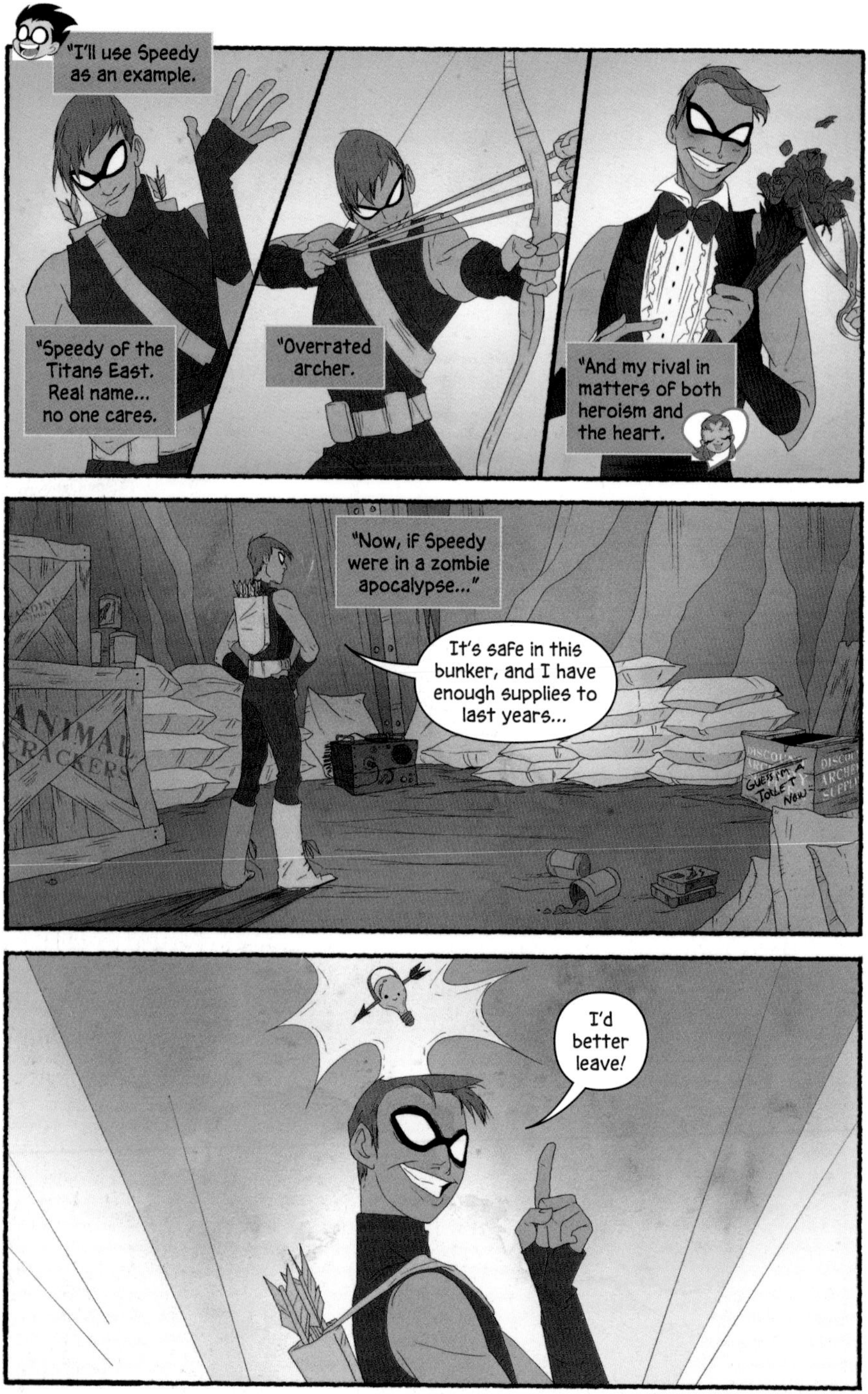
"I'll use Speedy as an example.
"Speedy of the Titans East. Real name... no one cares.
"Overrated archer.
"And my rival in matters of both heroism and the heart.
"Now, if Speedy were in a zombie apocalypse..."
It's safe in this bunker, and I have enough supplies to last years...
ANIMAL CRACKERS
GUESS I'M A TOILET NOW
I'd better leave!

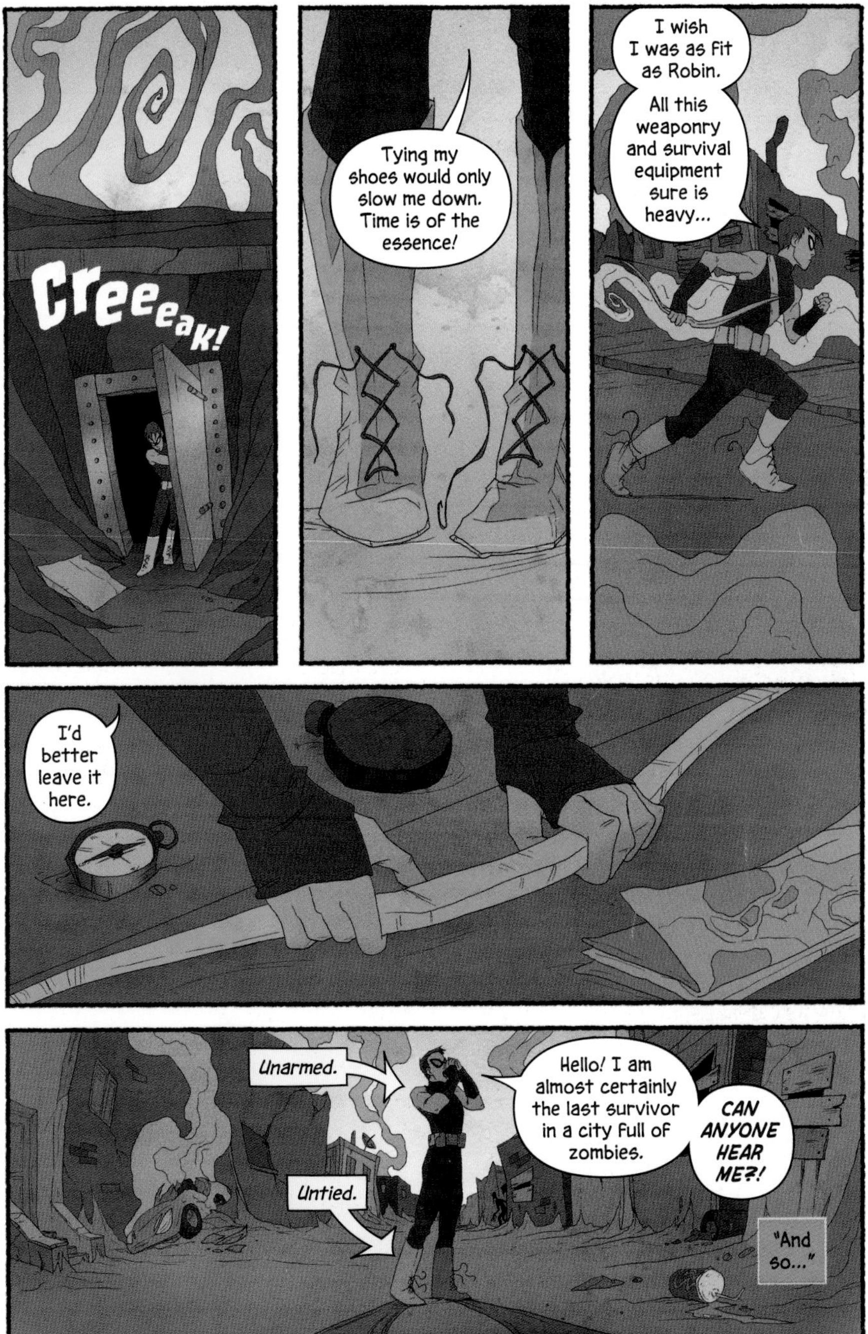
Creeeak!
Tying my shoes would only slow me down. Time is of the essence!
I wish I was as fit as Robin.
All this weaponry and survival equipment sure is heavy...
I'd better leave it here.
Unarmed.
Untied.
Hello! I am almost certainly the last survivor in a city full of zombies.
CAN ANYONE HEAR ME?!
"And so..."

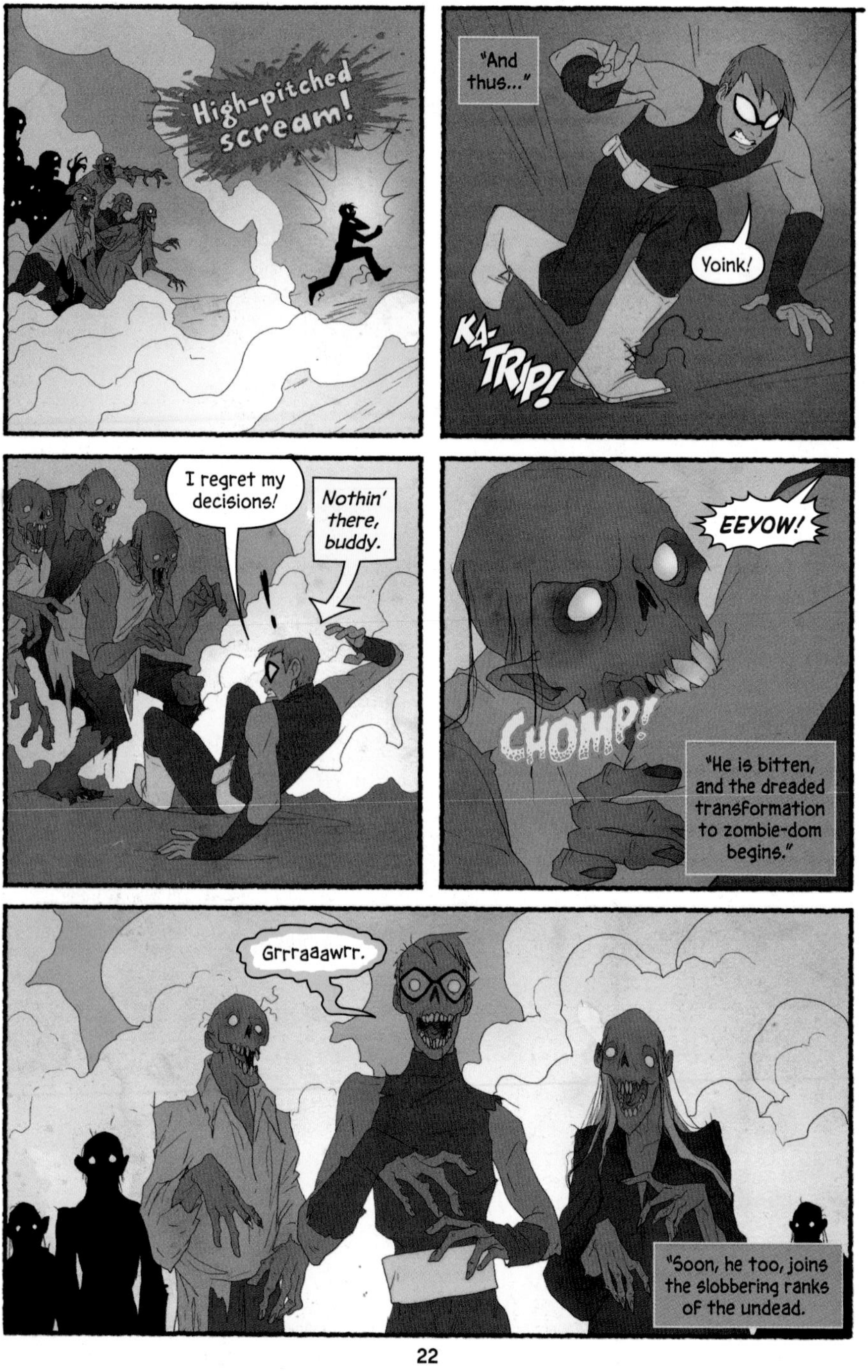
High-pitched scream!
"And thus..."
Yoink!
KA-TRIP!
I regret my decisions!
Nothin' there, buddy.
!
EEYOW!
CHOMP!
"He is bitten, and the dreaded transformation to zombie-dom begins."
Grrraaawrr.
"Soon, he too, joins the slobbering ranks of the undead.

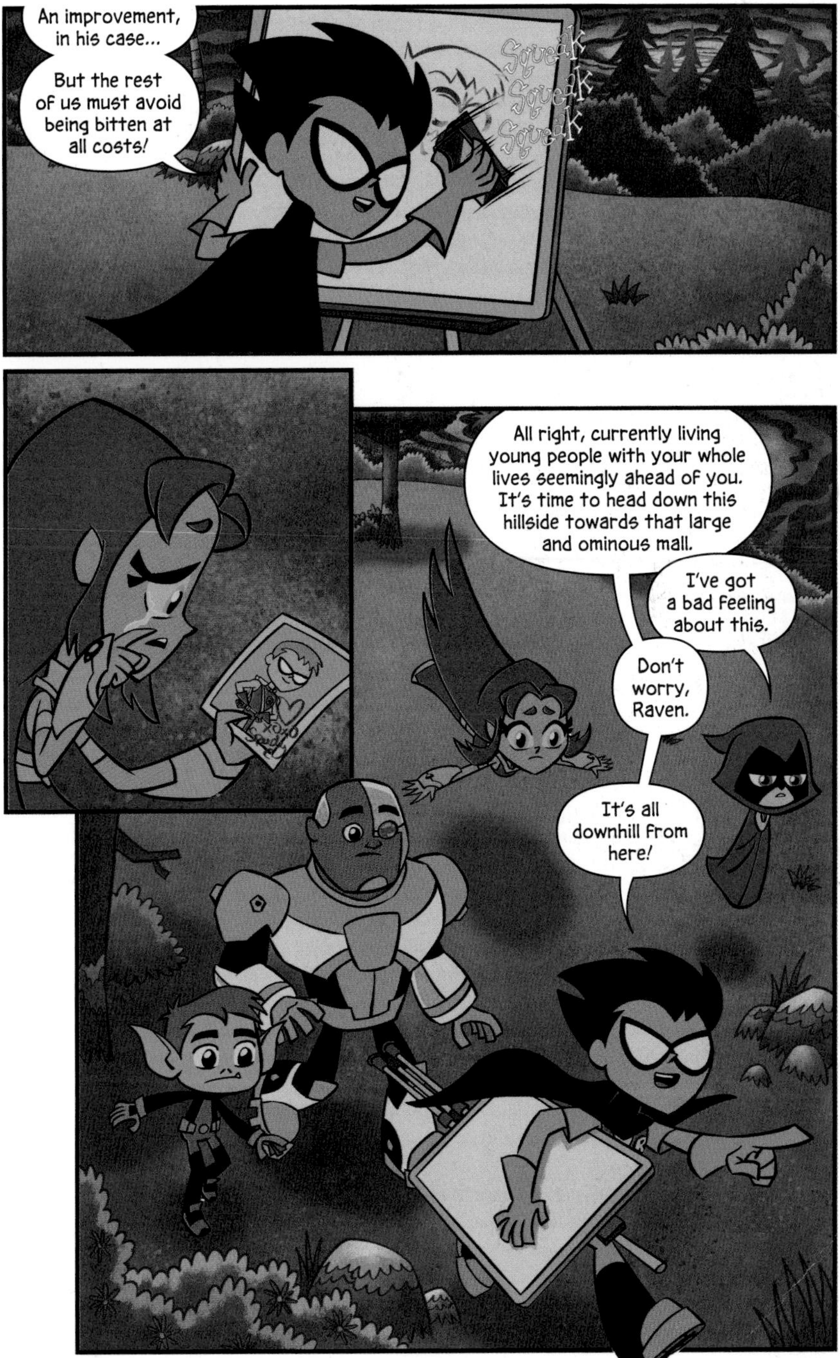
An improvement, in his case...
But the rest of us must avoid being bitten at all costs!
Squeak
Squeak
Squeak
All right, currently living young people with your whole lives seemingly ahead of you. It's time to head down this hillside towards that large and ominous mall.
I've got a bad feeling about this.
Don't worry, Raven.
It's all downhill from here!

Chapter Two

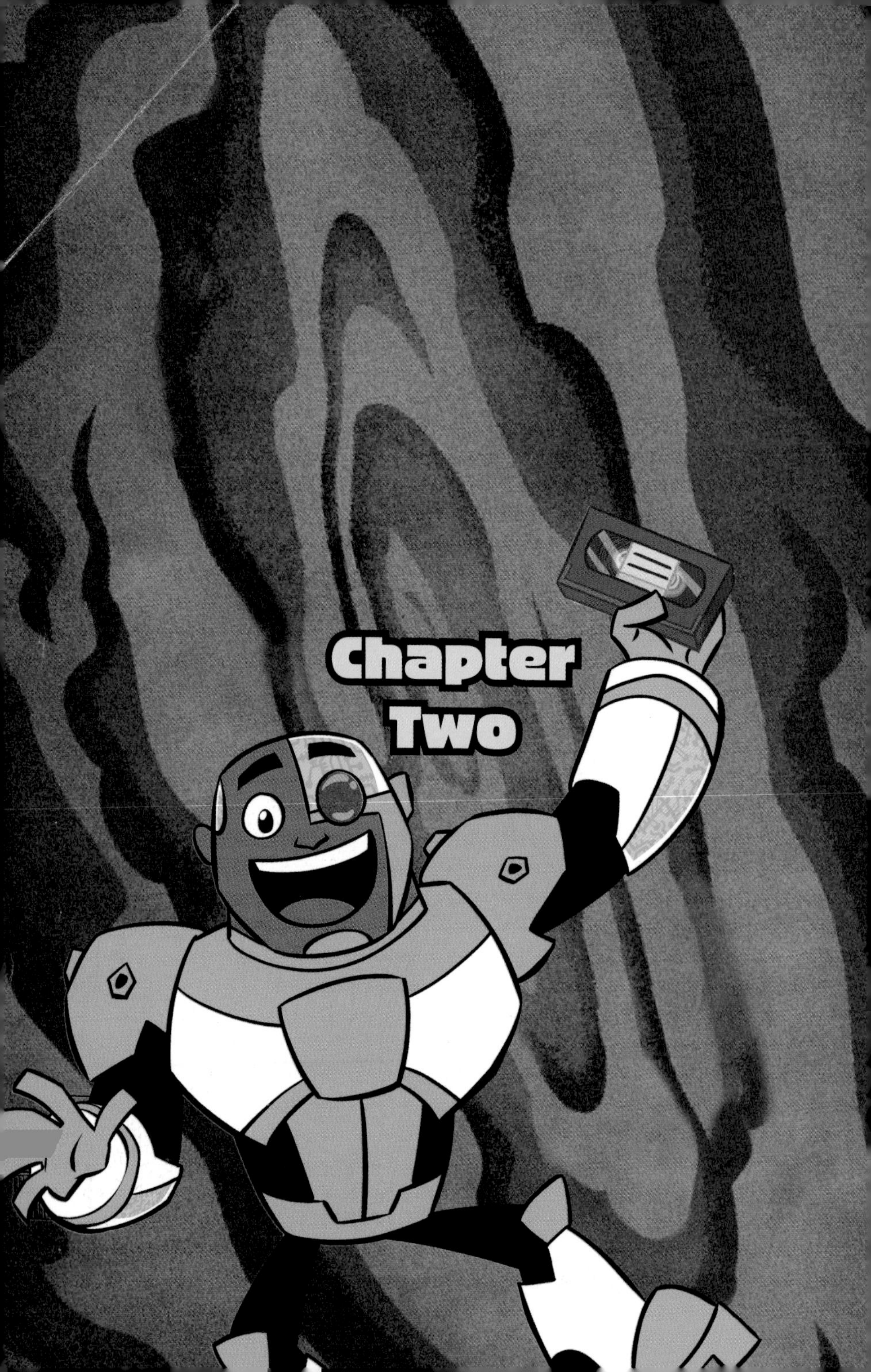

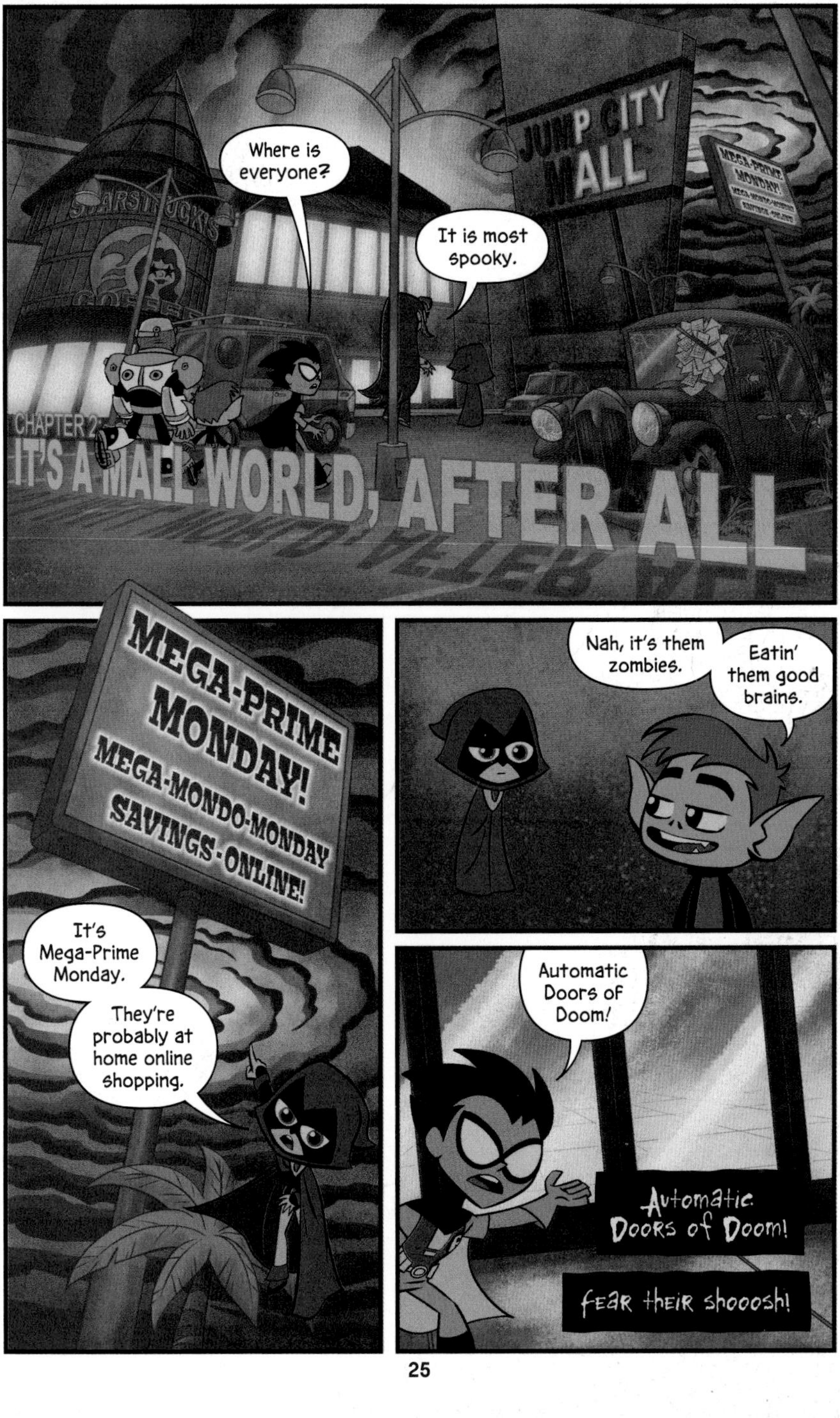

JUMP CITY MALL
Where is everyone?
It is most spooky.
CHAPTER 2:
IT'S A MALL WORLD, AFTER ALL
MEGA-PRIME MONDAY! MEGA-MONDO-MONDAY SAVINGS-ONLINE!
It's Mega-Prime Monday.
They're probably at home online shopping.
Nah, it's them zombies.
Eatin' them good brains.
Automatic Doors of Doom!
Automatic Doors of Doom!
fear their shooosh!

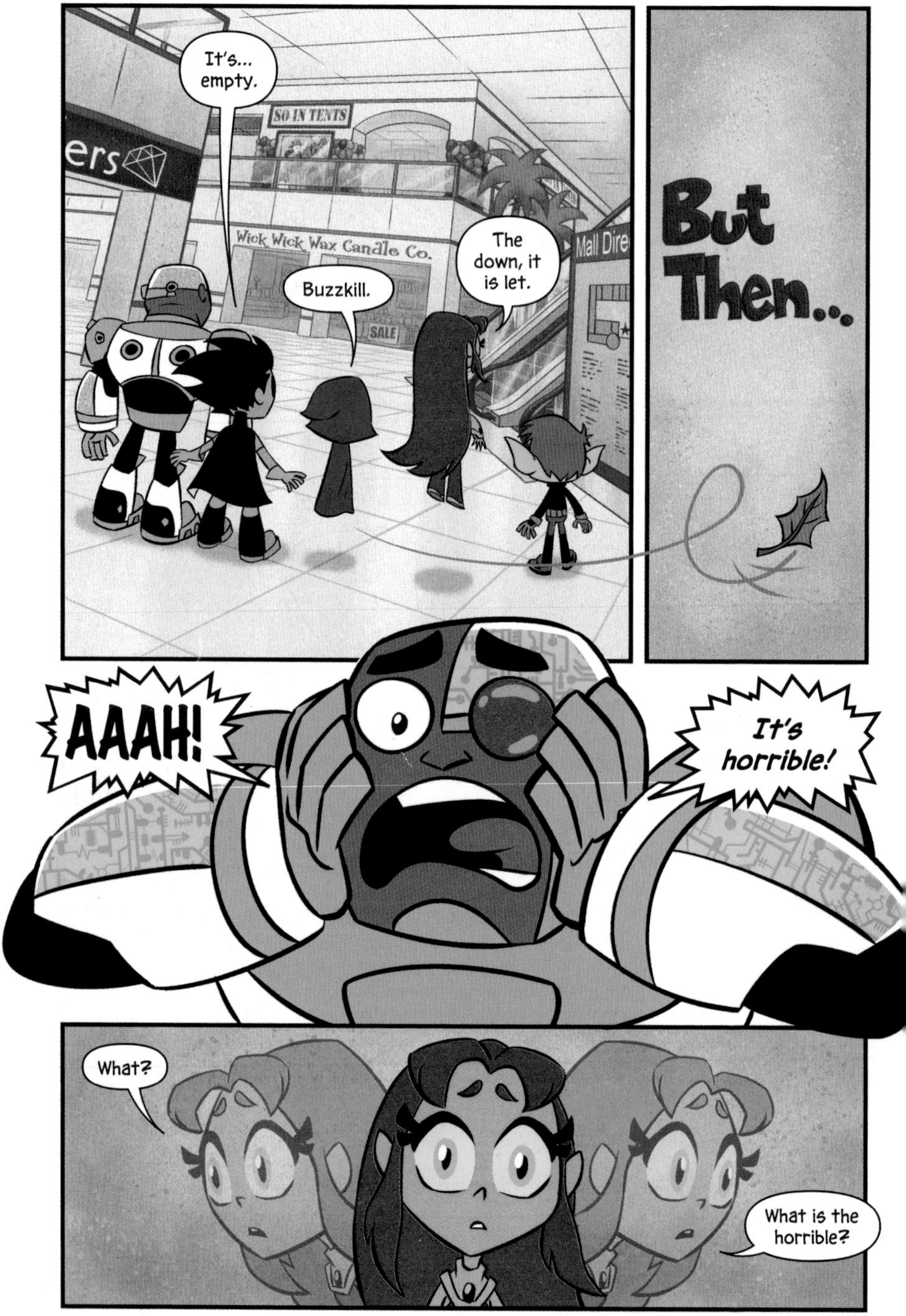
It's... empty.
ers
SO IN TENTS
Wick Wick Wax Candle Co.
SALE
Mall Dire
Buzzkill.
The down, it is let.
But Then...
AAAH!
It's horrible!
What?
What is the horrible?

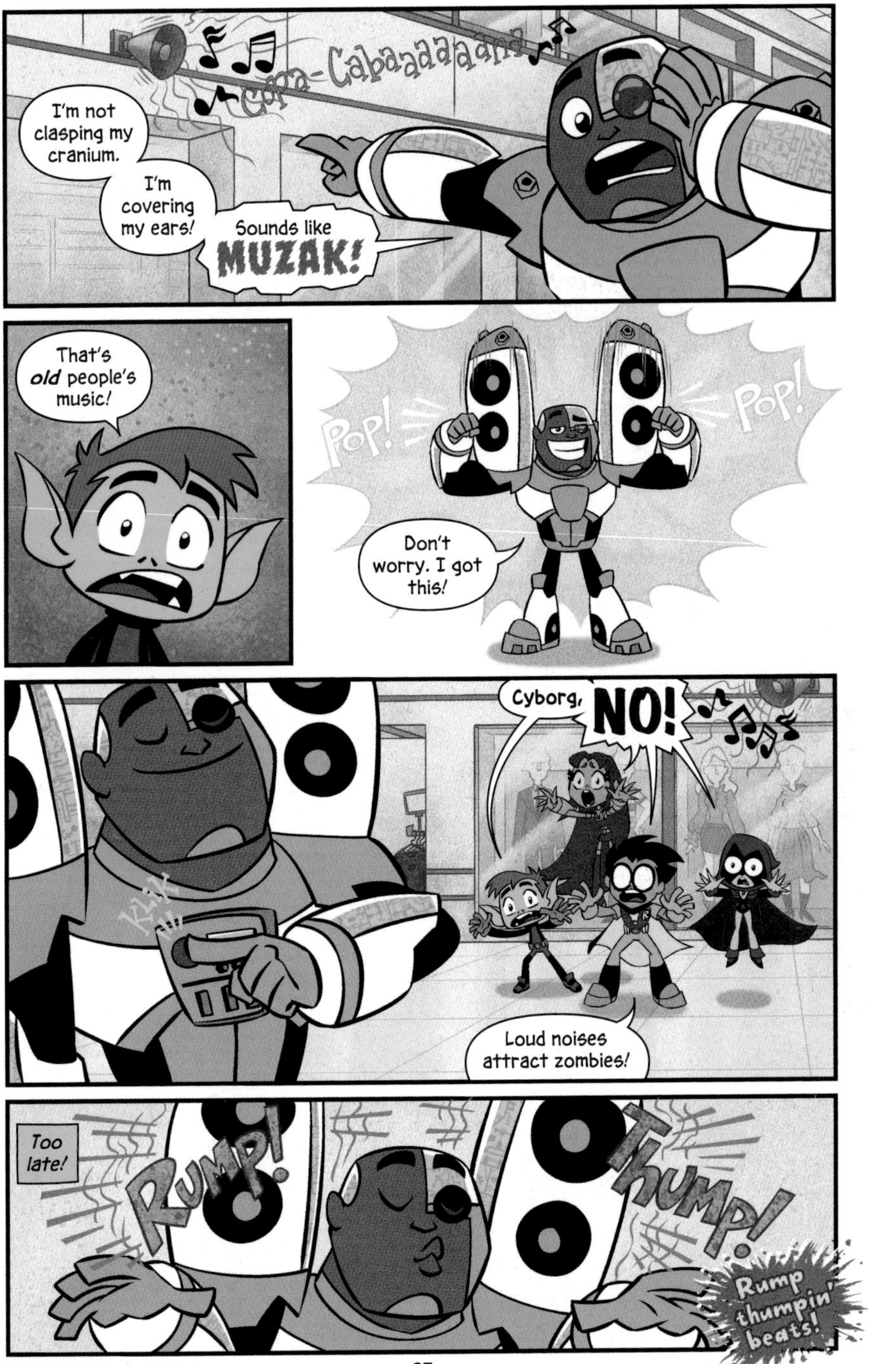
Copa-Cabaaaaaana
I'm not clasping my cranium.
I'm covering my ears!
Sounds like MUZAK!
That's *old* people's music!
POP!
POP!
Don't worry. I got this!
KLIK
Cyborg, NO!
Loud noises attract zombies!
Too late!
RUMP!
THUMP!
Rump thumpin' beats!

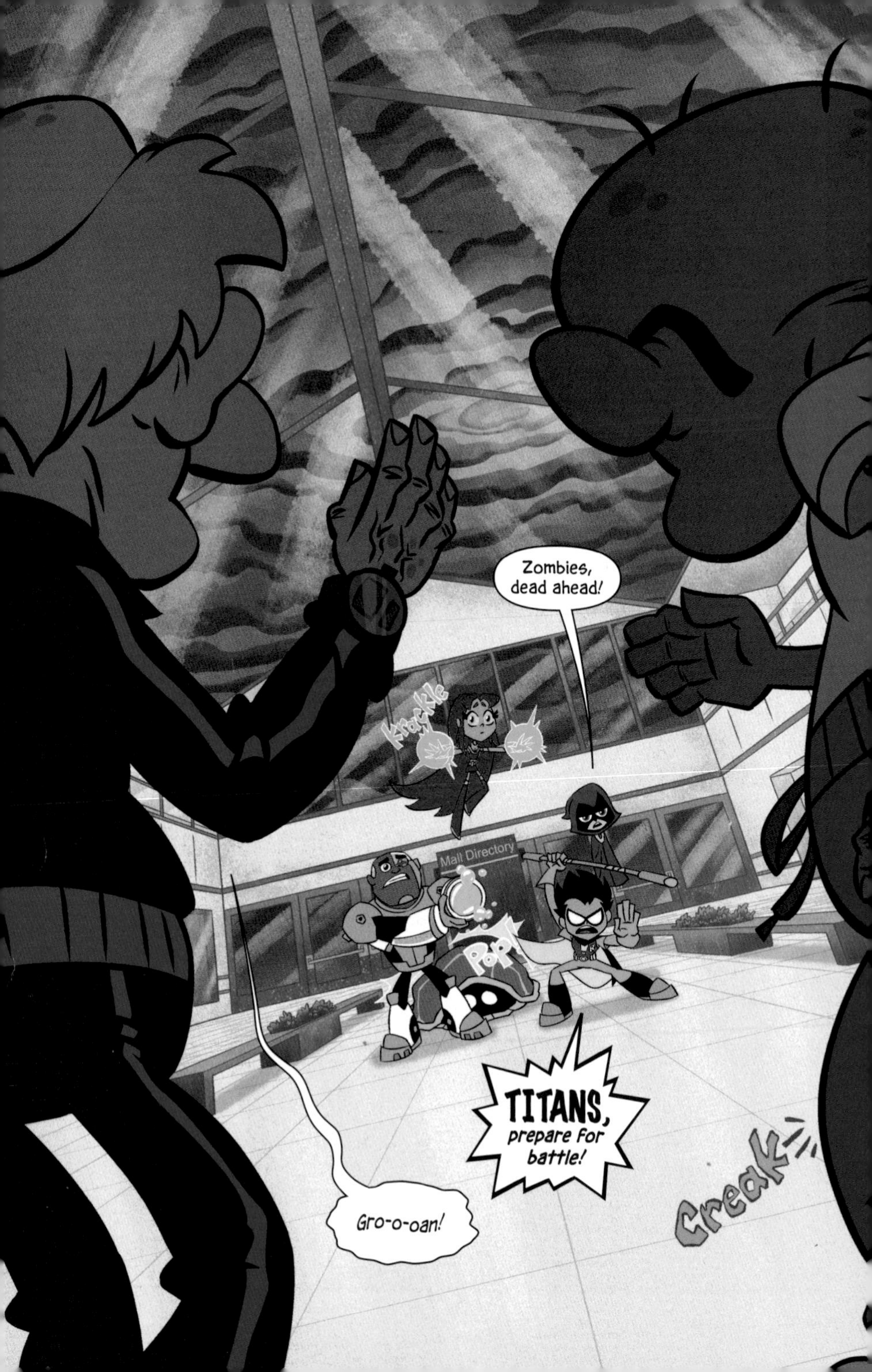
Zombies, dead ahead!
Krackle
Mall Directory
Pop!
TITANS, prepare for battle!
Creak
Gro-o-oan!

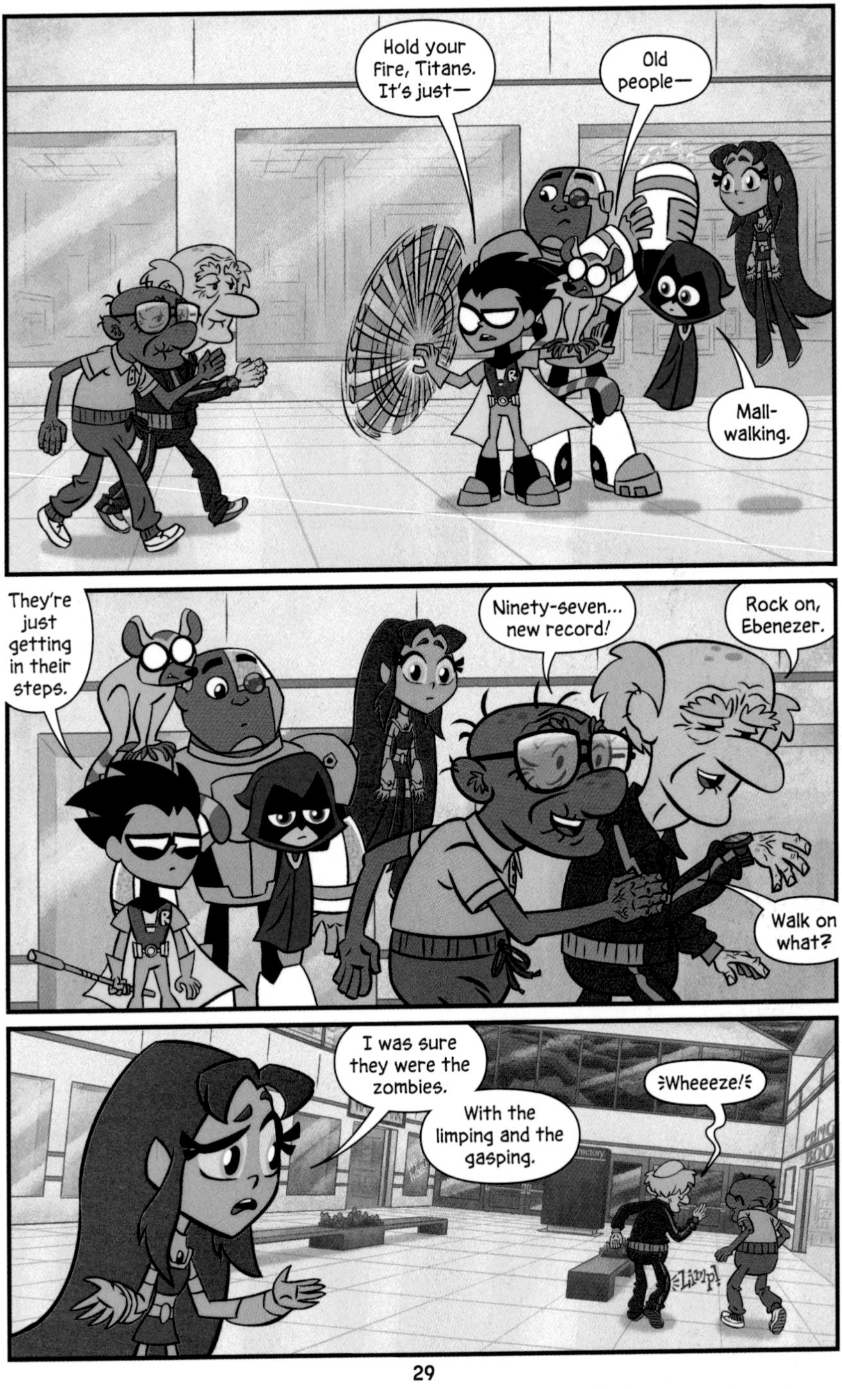
Hold your fire, Titans. It's just—
Old people—
Mall-walking.
They're just getting in their steps.
Ninety-seven... new record!
Rock on, Ebenezer.
Walk on what?
I was sure they were the zombies.
With the limping and the gasping.
Wheeeze!
Limp!

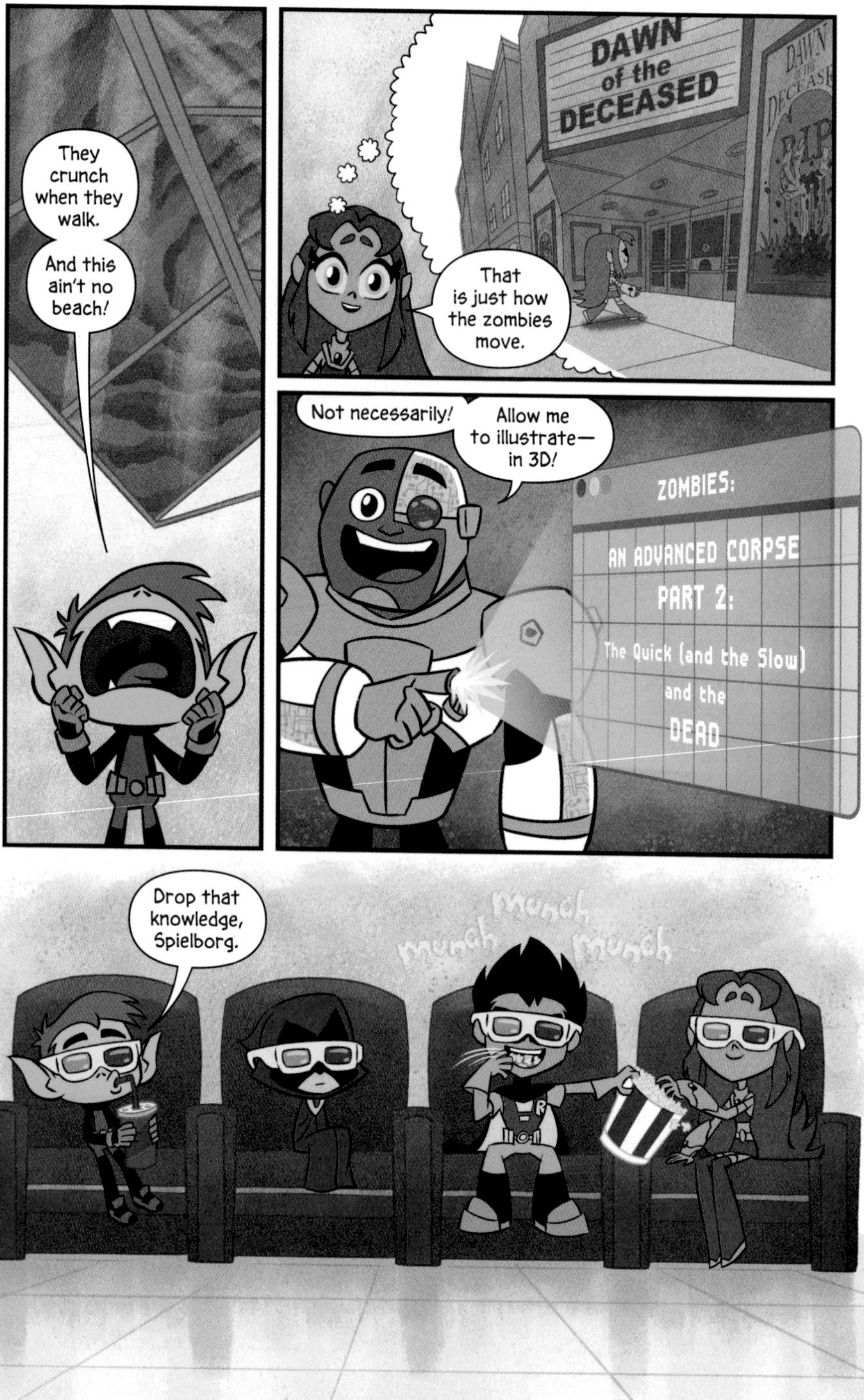
They crunch when they walk.
And this ain't no beach!
DAWN of the DECEASED
That is just how the zombies move.
Not necessarily!
Allow me to illustrate— in 3D!
ZOMBIES:
AN ADVANCED CORPSE
PART 2:
The Quick (and the Slow)
and the
DEAD
Drop that knowledge, Spielborg.
munch munch munch munch

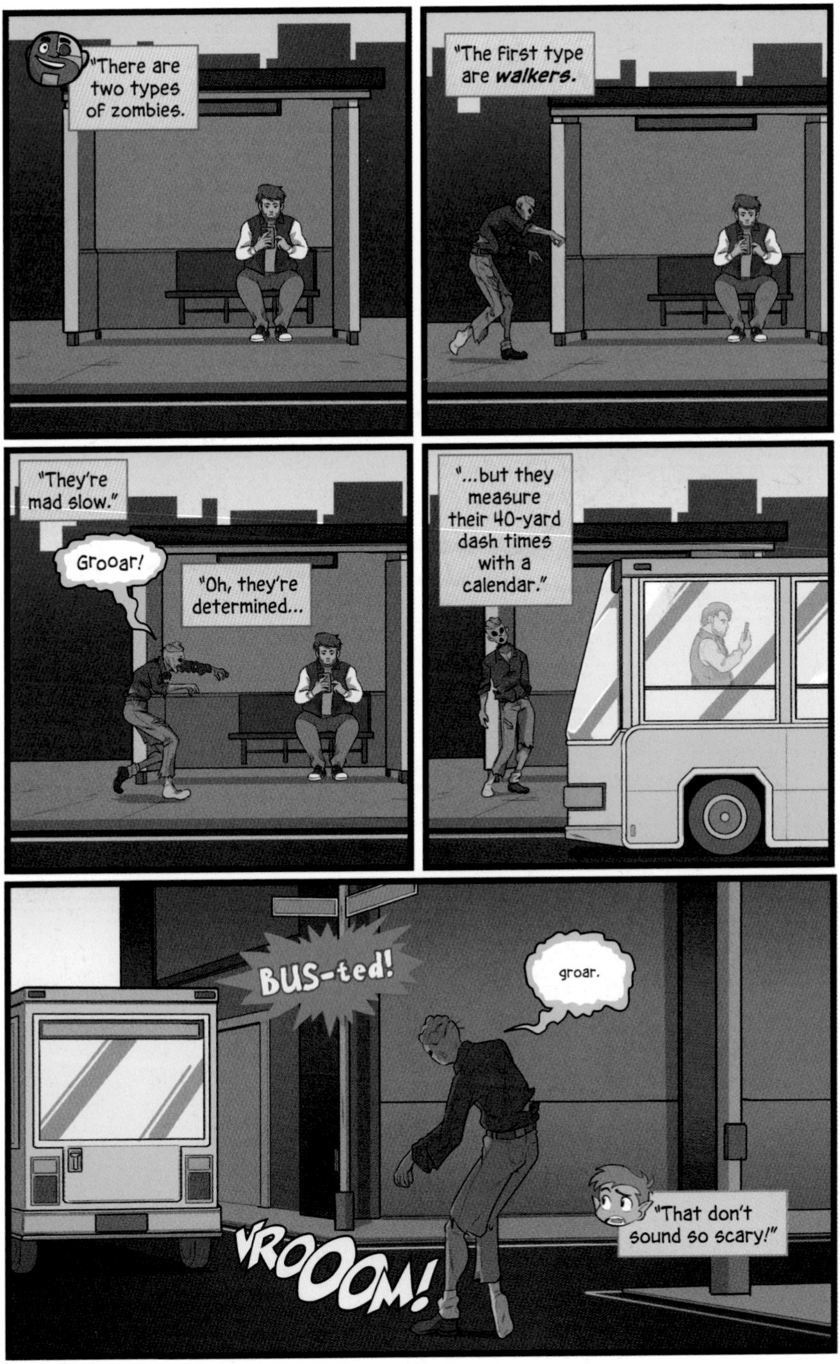
"There are two types of zombies.
"The first type are *walkers.*
"They're mad slow."
Grooar!
"Oh, they're determined...
"...but they measure their 40-yard dash times with a calendar."
BUS-ted!
groar.
VROOOOM!
"That don't sound so scary!"

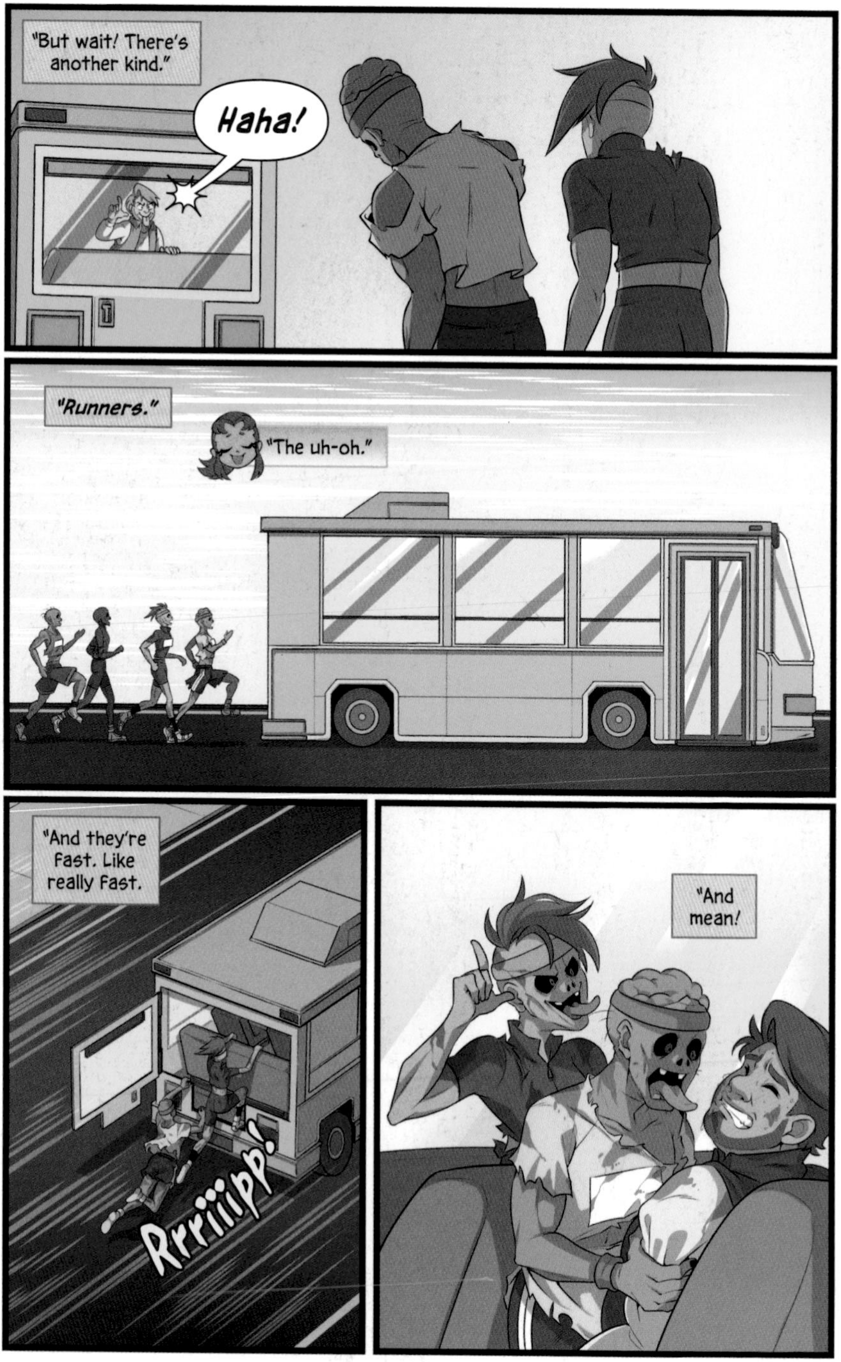
"But wait! There's another kind."
Haha!
"Runners."
"The uh-oh."
"And they're fast. Like really fast.
Rrriiipp!
"And mean!

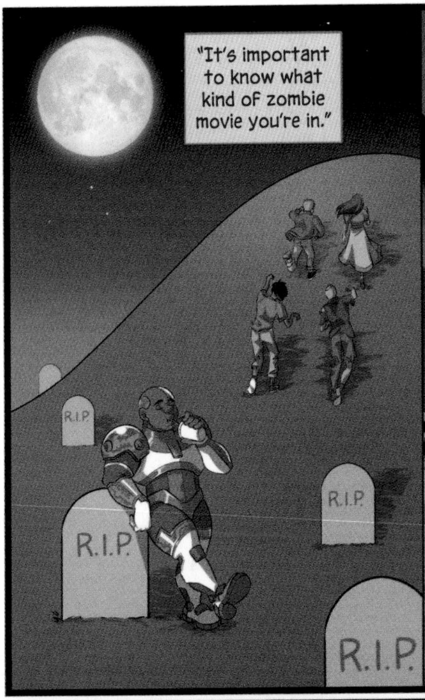
"It's important to know what kind of zombie movie you're in."
R.I.P.
R.I.P.
R.I.P.
R.I.P.

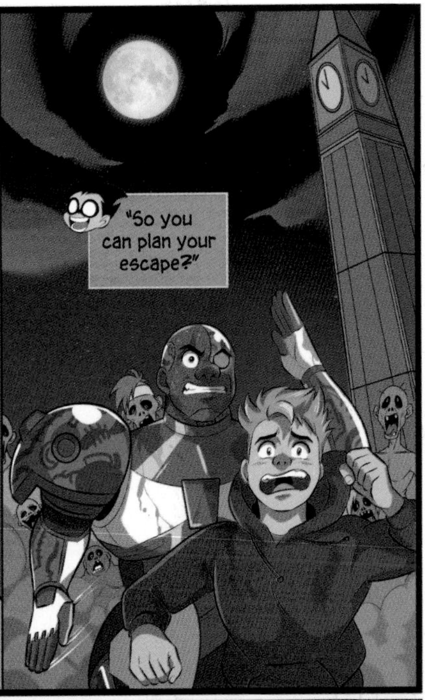
"So you can plan your escape?"

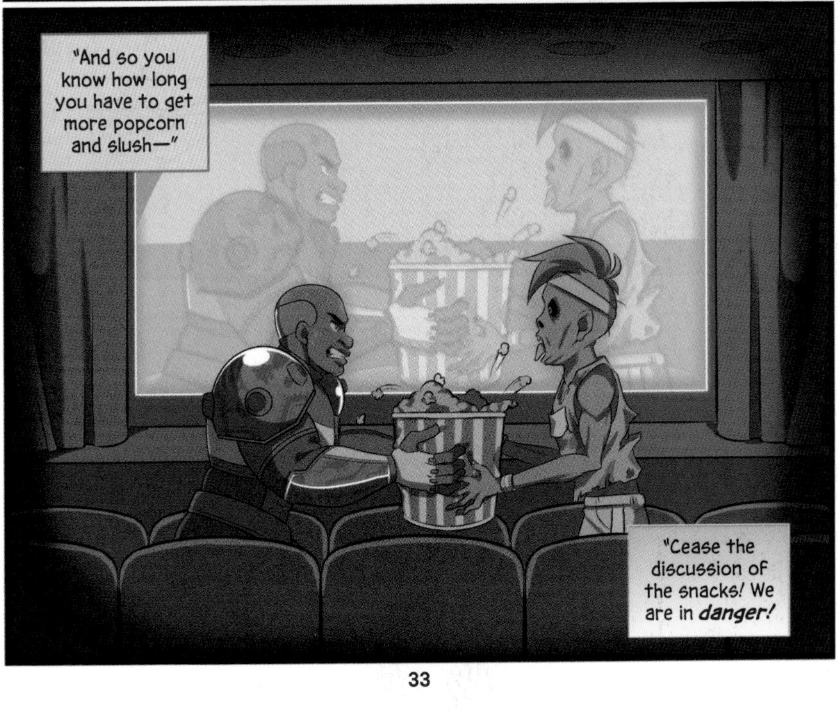
"And so you know how long you have to get more popcorn and slush—"
"Cease the discussion of the snacks! We are in *danger!*

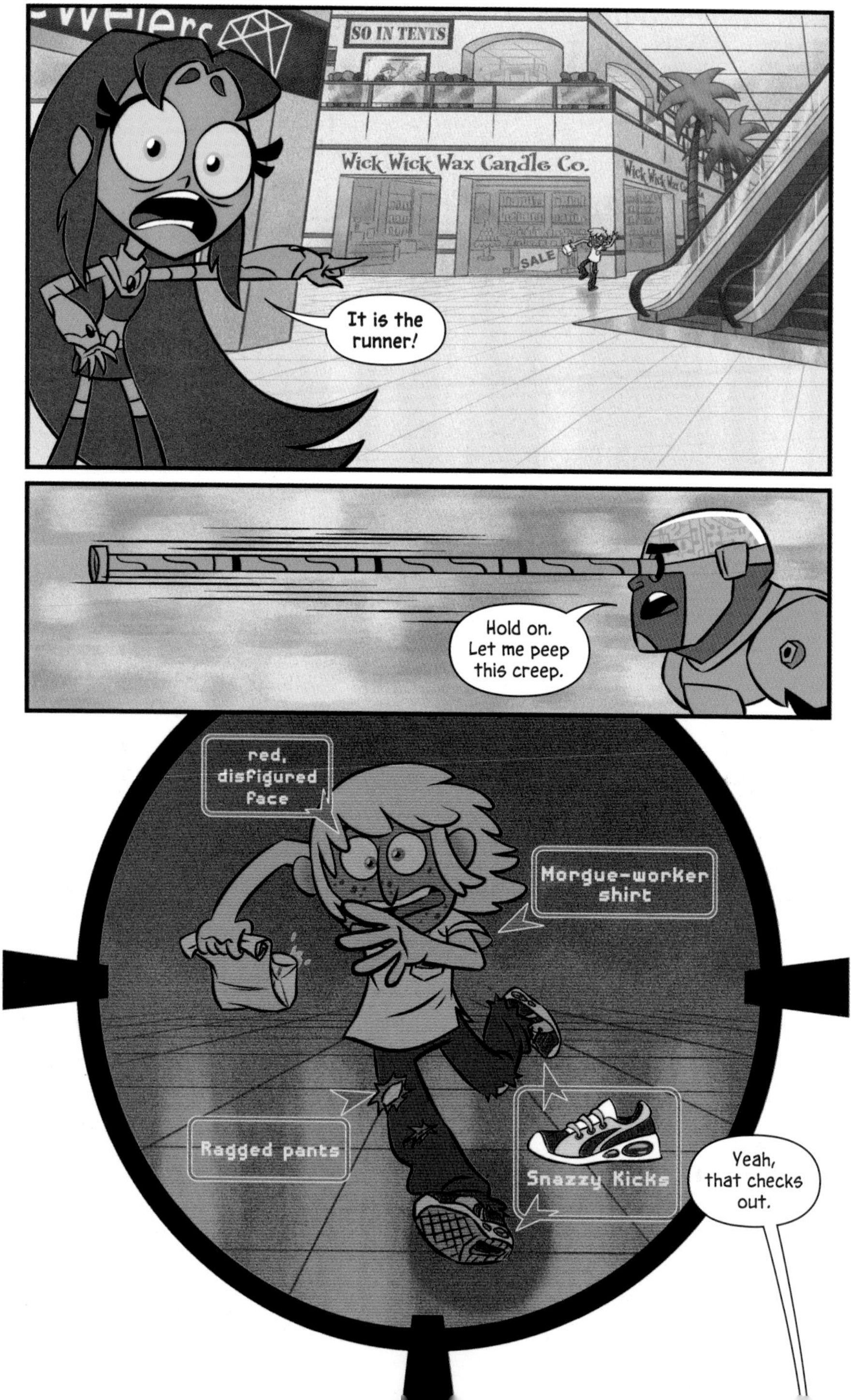

SO IN TENTS
Wick Wick Wax Candle Co.
SALE
It is the runner!
Hold on. Let me peep this creep.
red, disfigured face
Morgue-worker shirt
Ragged pants
Snazzy Kicks
Yeah, that checks out.

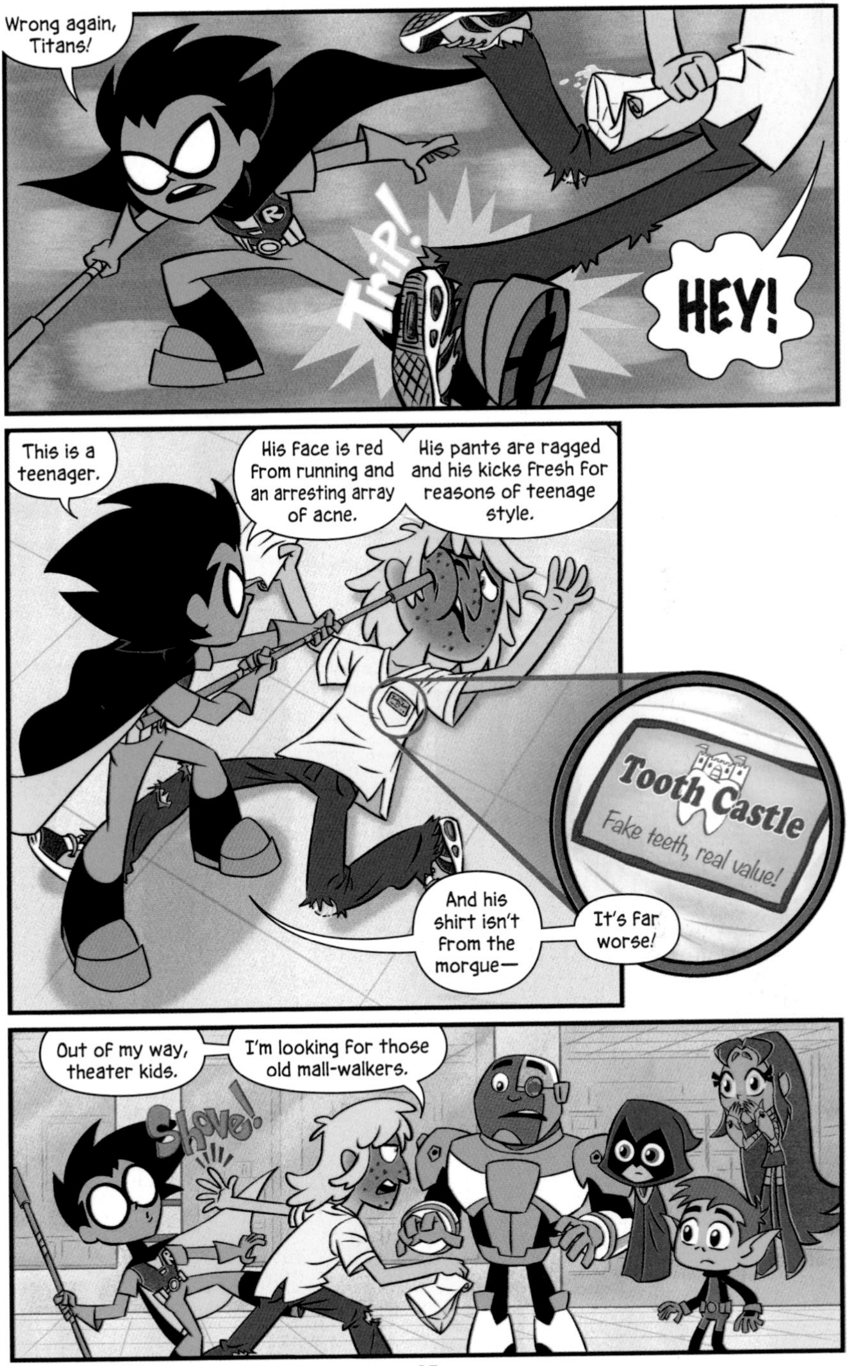

Wrong again, Titans!
TRIP!
HEY!
This is a teenager.
His face is red from running and an arresting array of acne.
His pants are ragged and his kicks fresh for reasons of teenage style.
Tooth Castle
Fake teeth, real value!
And his shirt isn't from the morgue—
It's far worse!
Out of my way, theater kids.
I'm looking for those old mall-walkers.
Shove!

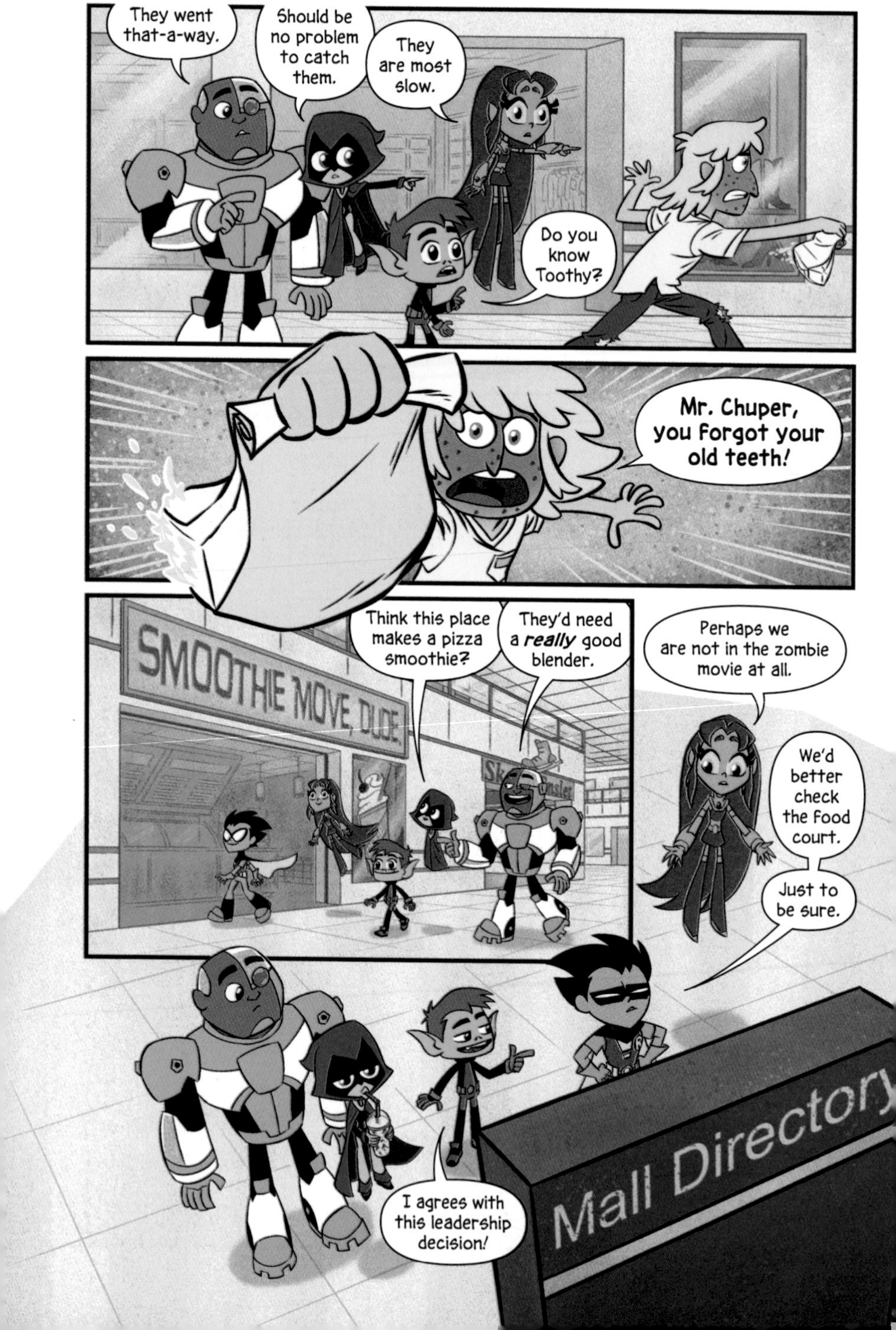
They went that-a-way.
Should be no problem to catch them.
They are most slow.
Do you know Toothy?
Mr. Chuper, you forgot your old teeth!
SMOOTHIE MOVE, DUDE.
Think this place makes a pizza smoothie?
They'd need a *really* good blender.
Perhaps we are not in the zombie movie at all.
We'd better check the food court.
Just to be sure.
I agrees with this leadership decision!
Mall Directory

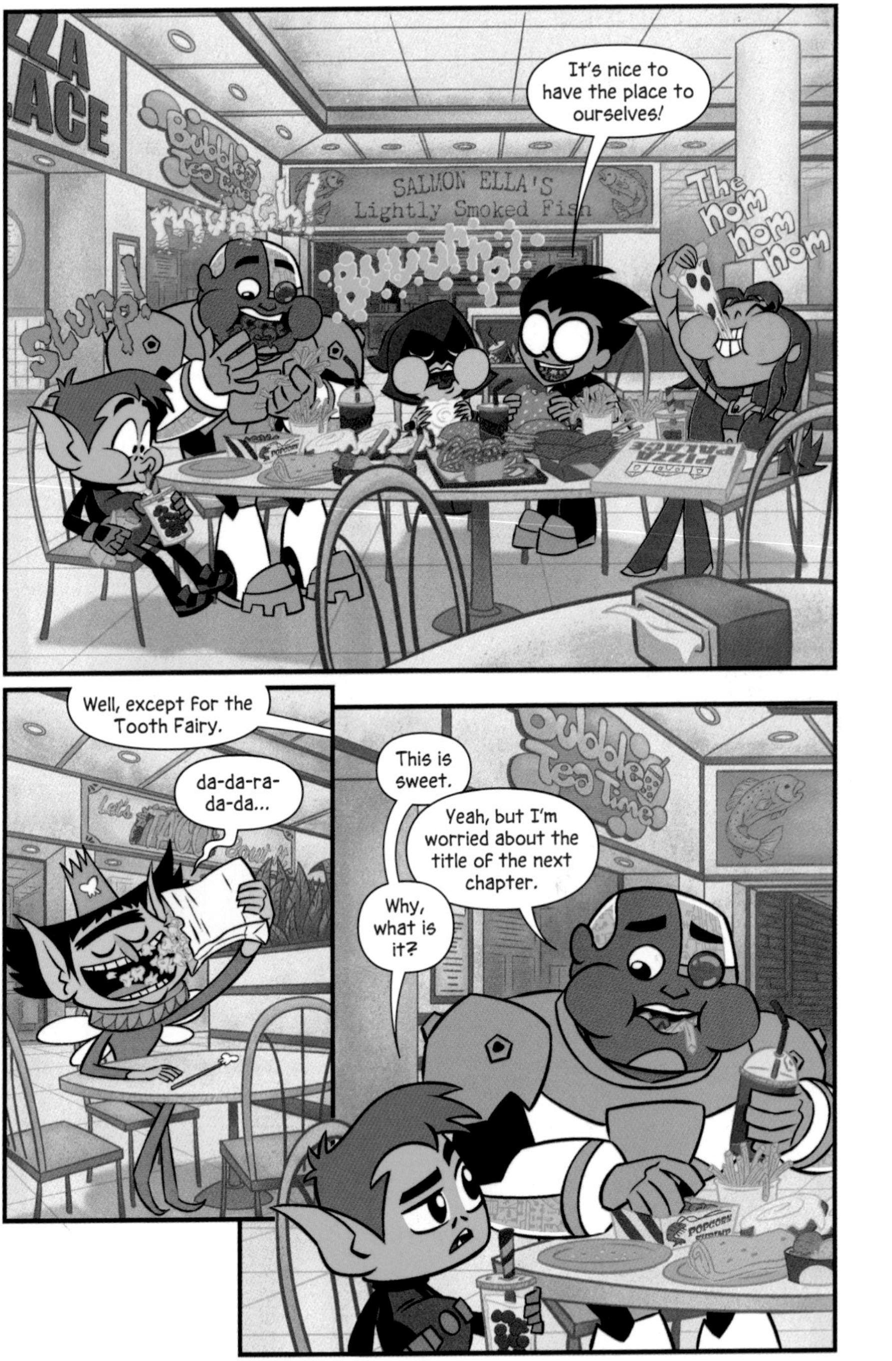

SALMON ELLA'S
Lightly Smoked Fish
munch!
Slurp!
Buuurrp!
It's nice to have the place to ourselves!
The nom nom nom
PIZZA PALACE
Well, except for the Tooth Fairy.
da-da-ra-da-da...
This is sweet.
Yeah, but I'm worried about the title of the next chapter.
Why, what is it?

Chapter Three

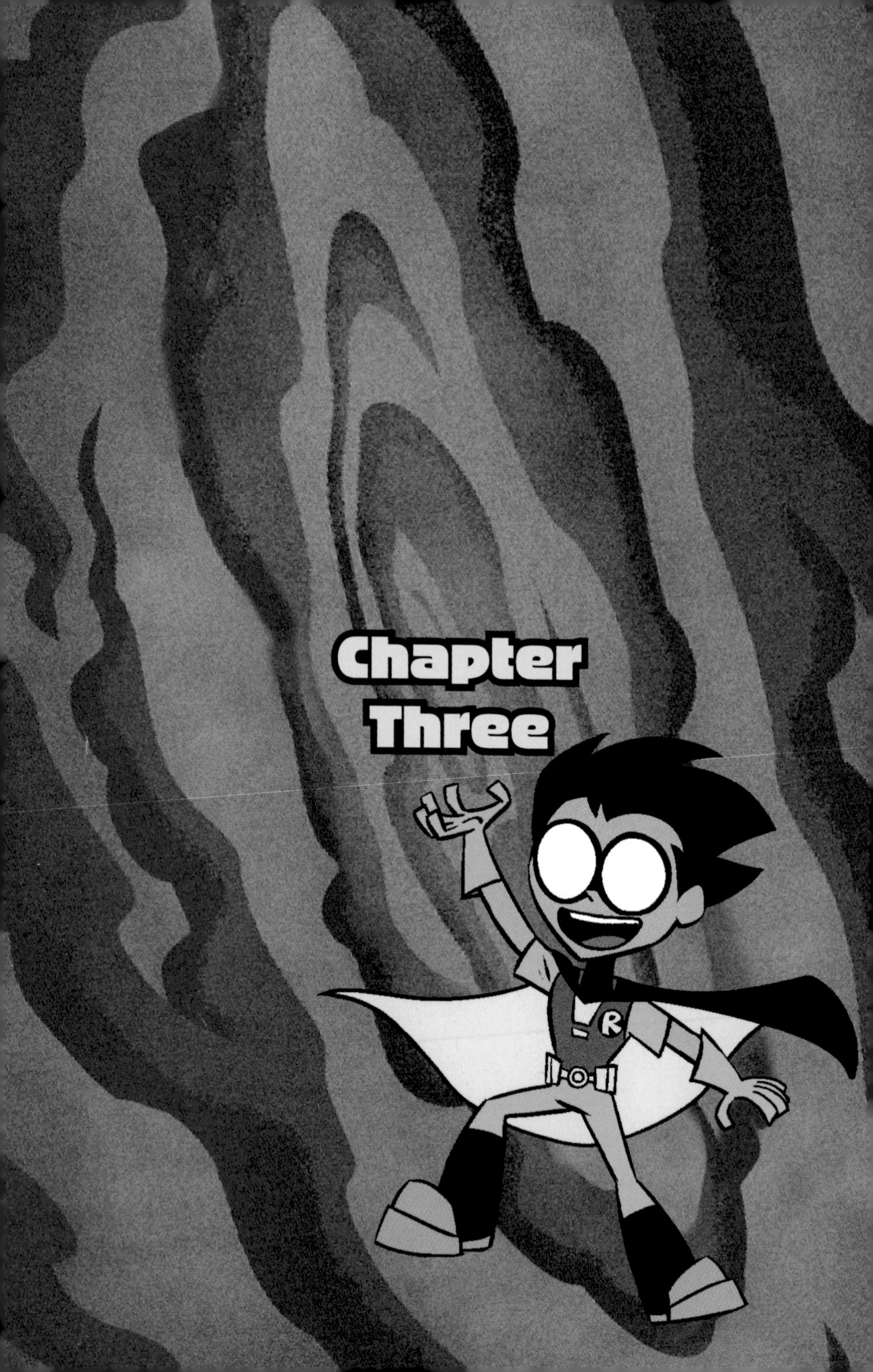

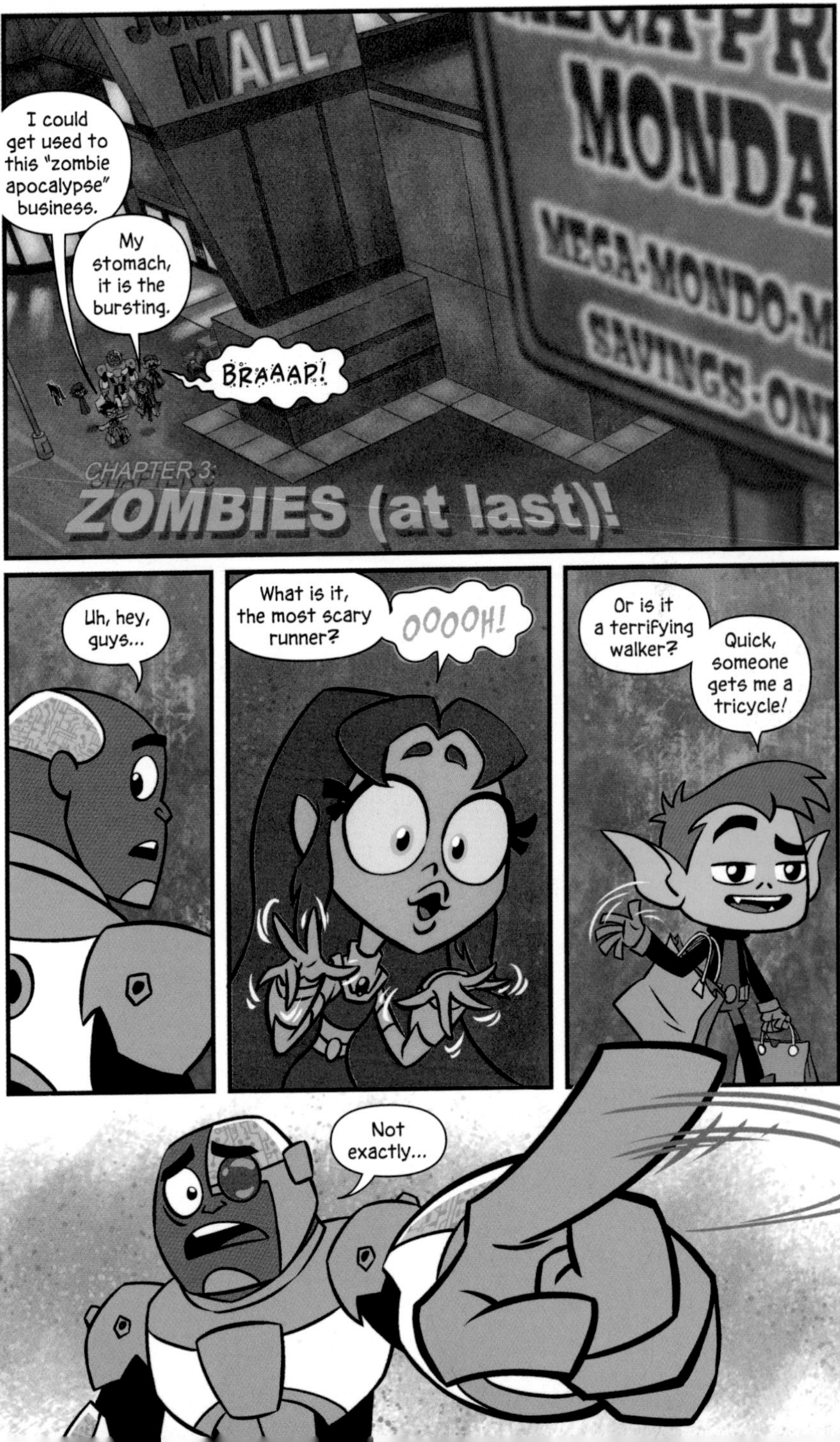
MALL
MONDA
MEGA-MONDO-M
SAVINGS-ON
I could get used to this "zombie apocalypse" business.
My stomach, it is the bursting.
BRAAAP!
CHAPTER 3:
ZOMBIES (at last)!
Uh, hey, guys...
What is it, the most scary runner?
OOOOH!
Or is it a terrifying walker?
Quick, someone gets me a tricycle!
Not exactly...

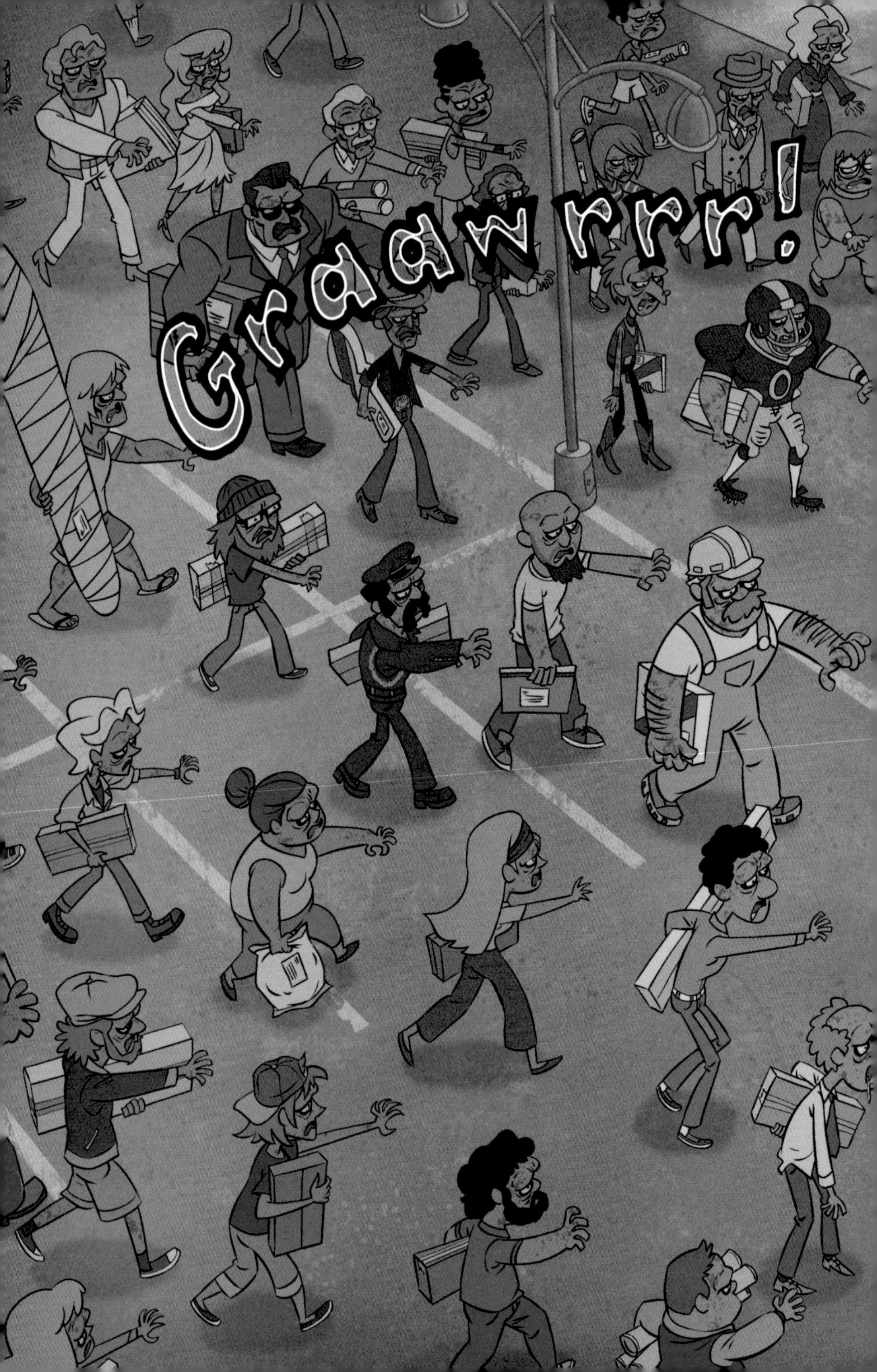
Graawrrr!

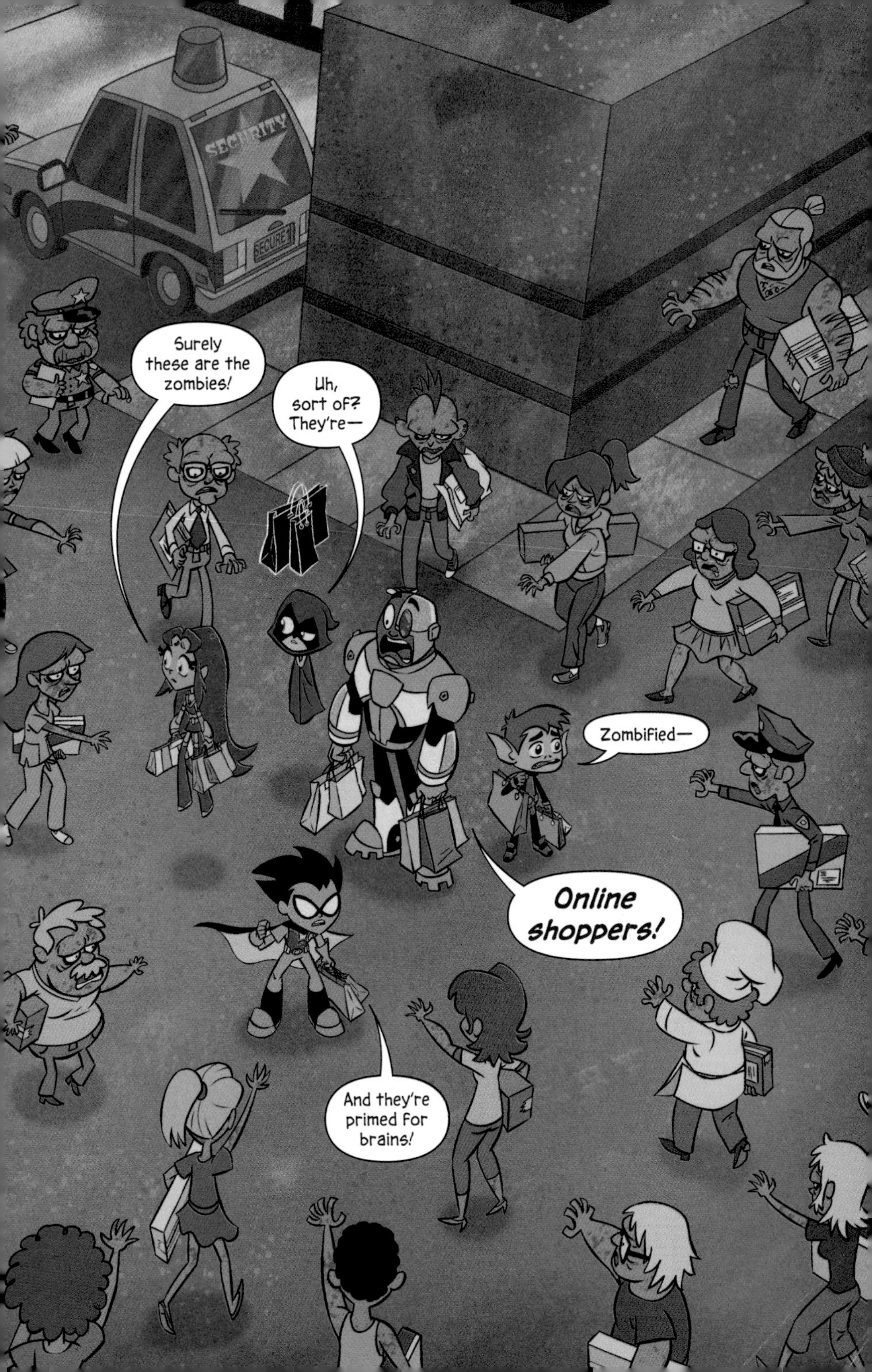
Surely these are the zombies!
Uh, sort of? They're—
Zombified—
Online shoppers!
And they're primed for brains!
SECURITY
SECURE1

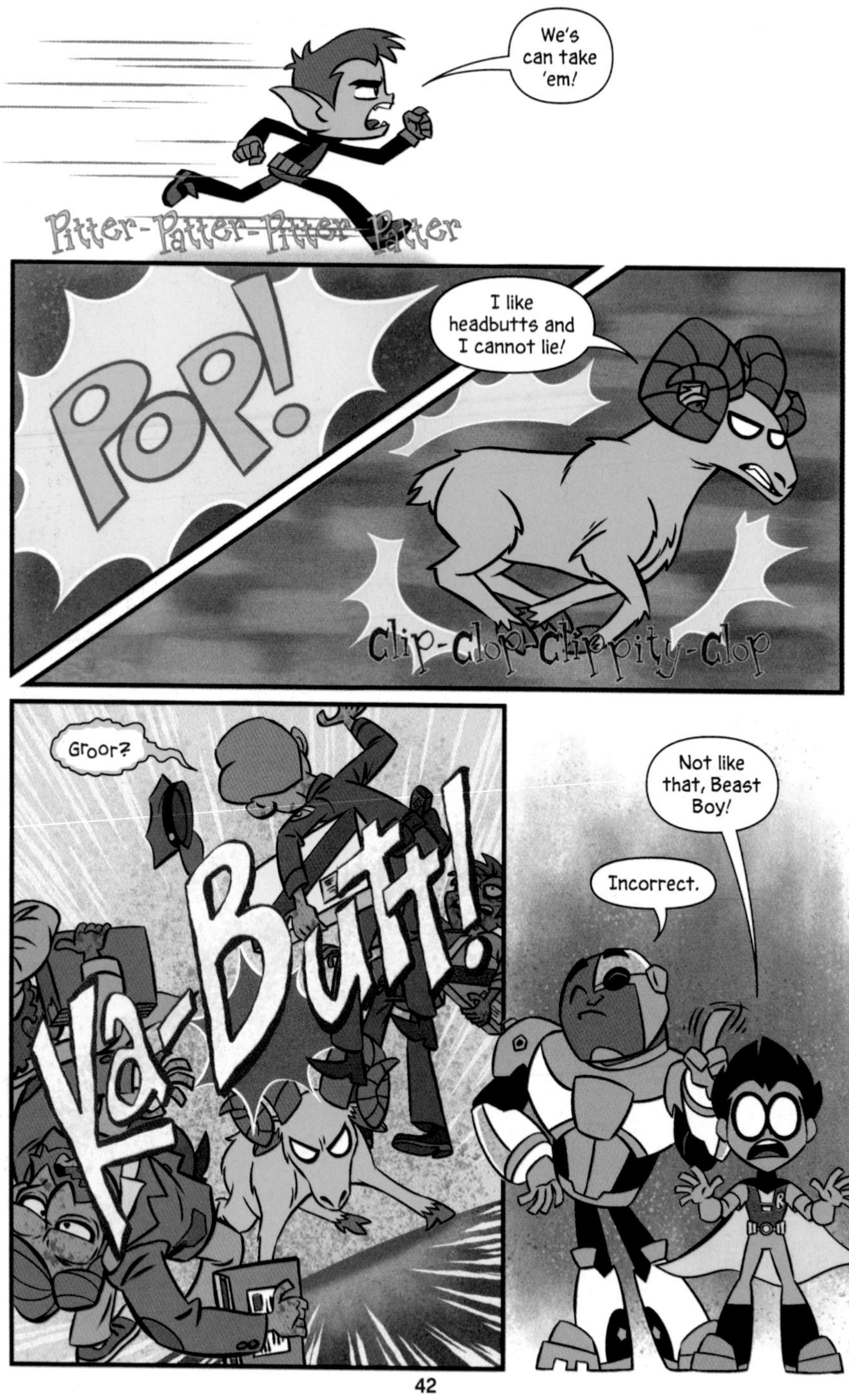
We's can take 'em!
Pitter-Patter-Pitter-Patter
POP!
I like headbutts and I cannot lie!
Clip-Clop-Clippity-Clop
Groor?
Ka-Butt!
Not like that, Beast Boy!
Incorrect.

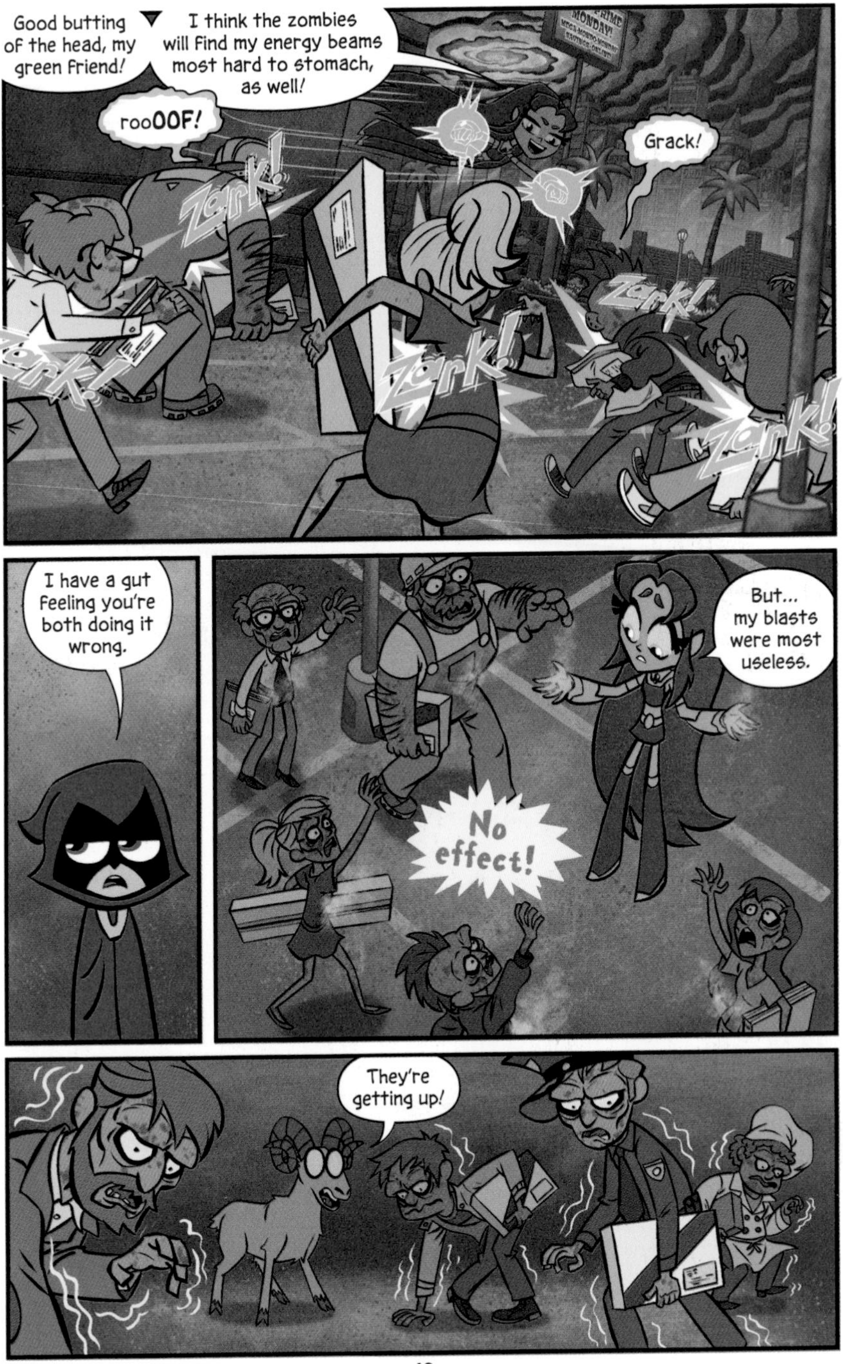
Good butting of the head, my green friend!
I think the zombies will find my energy beams most hard to stomach, as well!
rooOOF!
Grack!
Zark!
Zark!
Zark!
Zark!
Zark!
I have a gut feeling you're both doing it wrong.
But... my blasts were most useless.
No effect!
They're getting up!

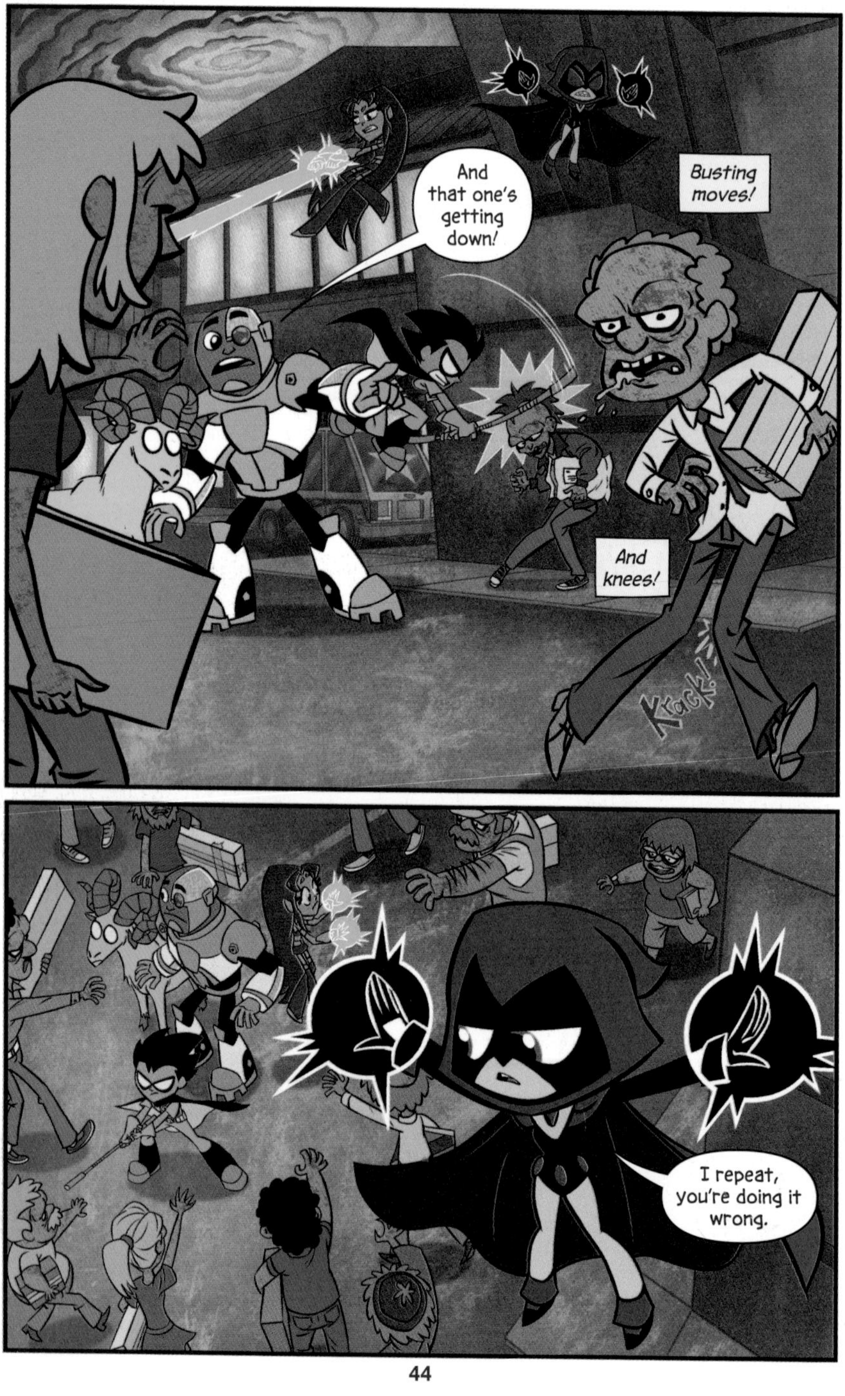
And that one's getting down!
Busting moves!
And knees!
Krack!
I repeat, you're doing it wrong.

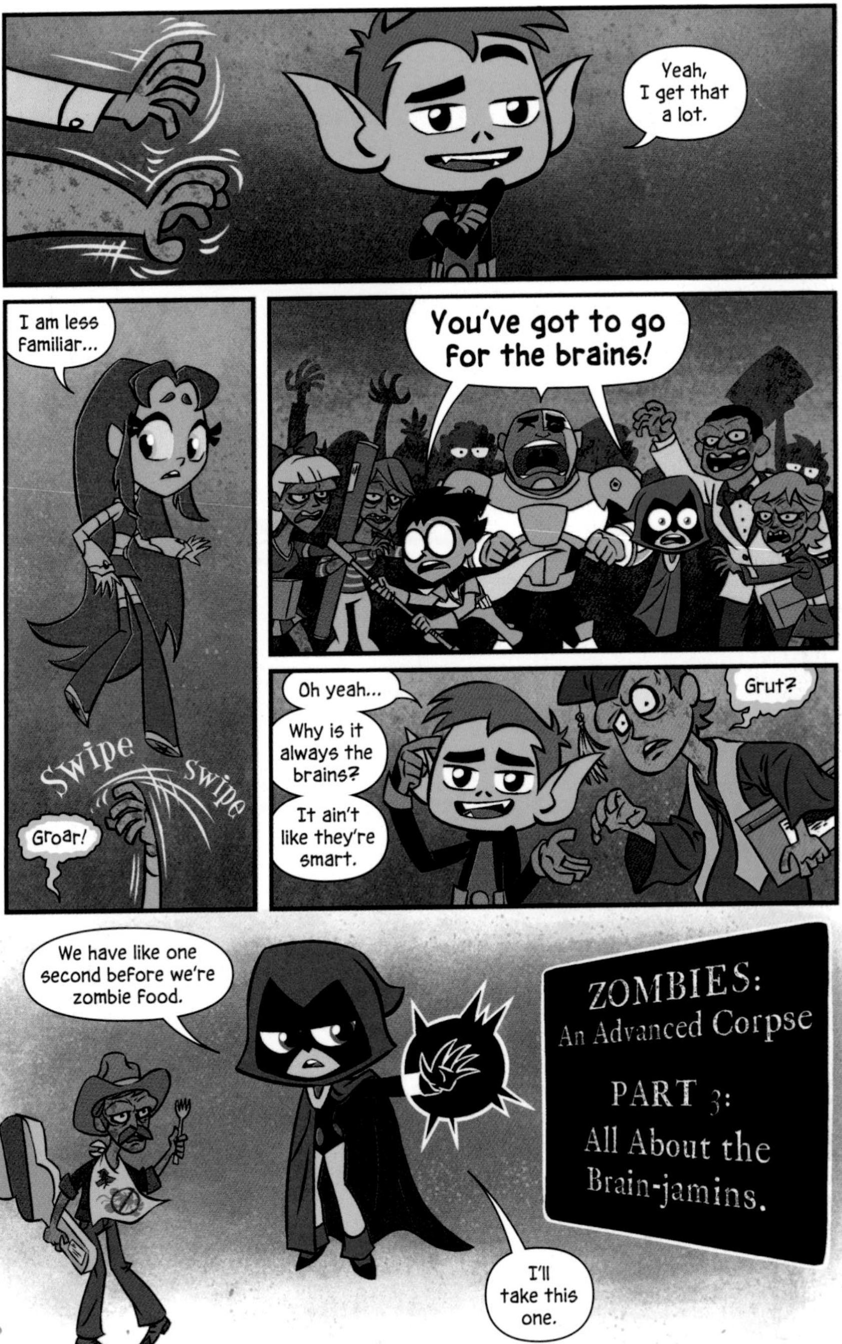

Yeah, I get that a lot.
I am less familiar...
Swipe
Swipe
Groar!
You've got to go for the brains!
Oh yeah...
Why is it always the brains?
It ain't like they're smart.
Grut?
We have like one second before we're zombie food.
ZOMBIES: An Advanced Corpse
PART 3: All About the Brain-jamins.
I'll take this one.

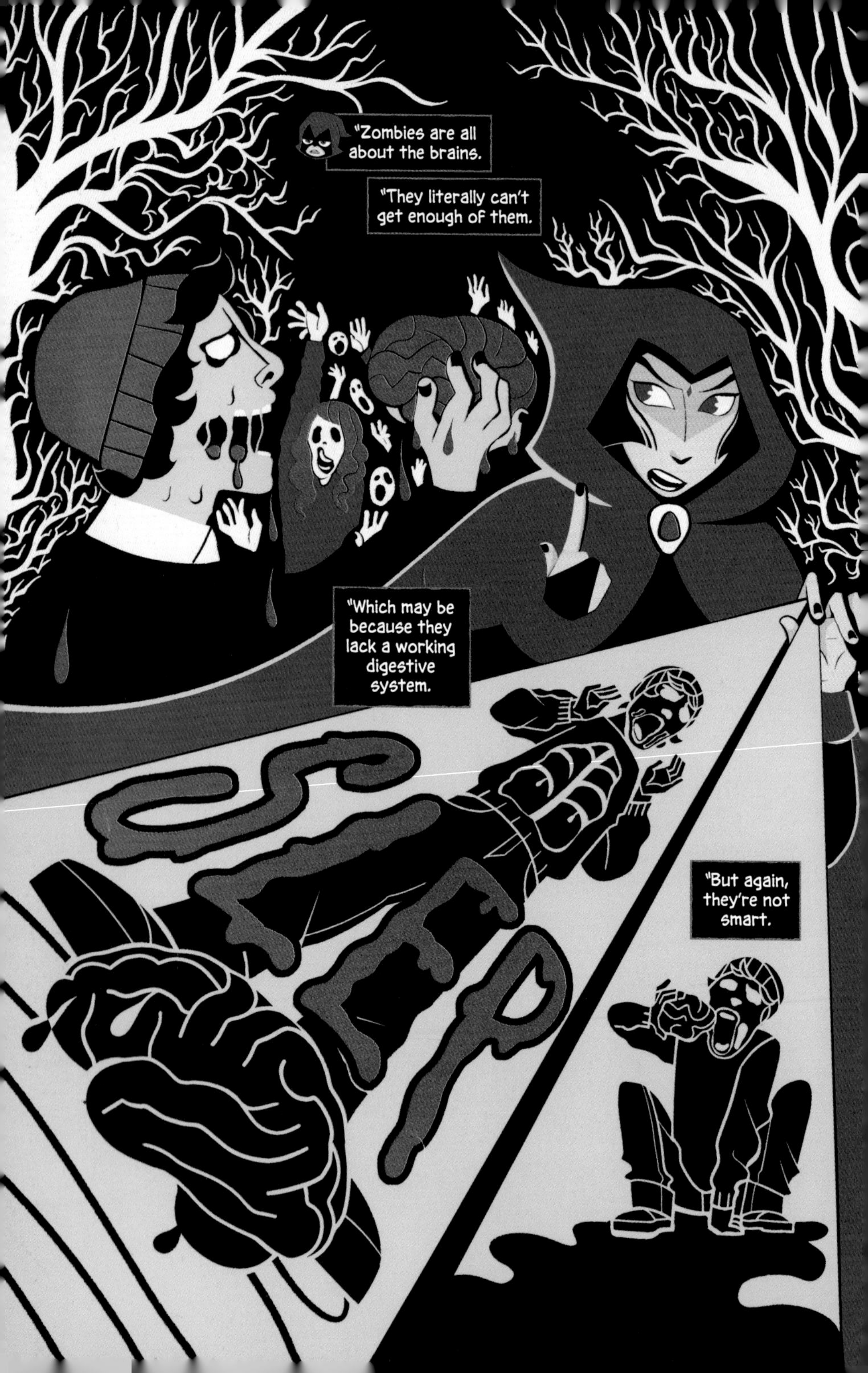
"Zombies are all about the brains.
"They literally can't get enough of them.
"Which may be because they lack a working digestive system.
"But again, they're not smart.

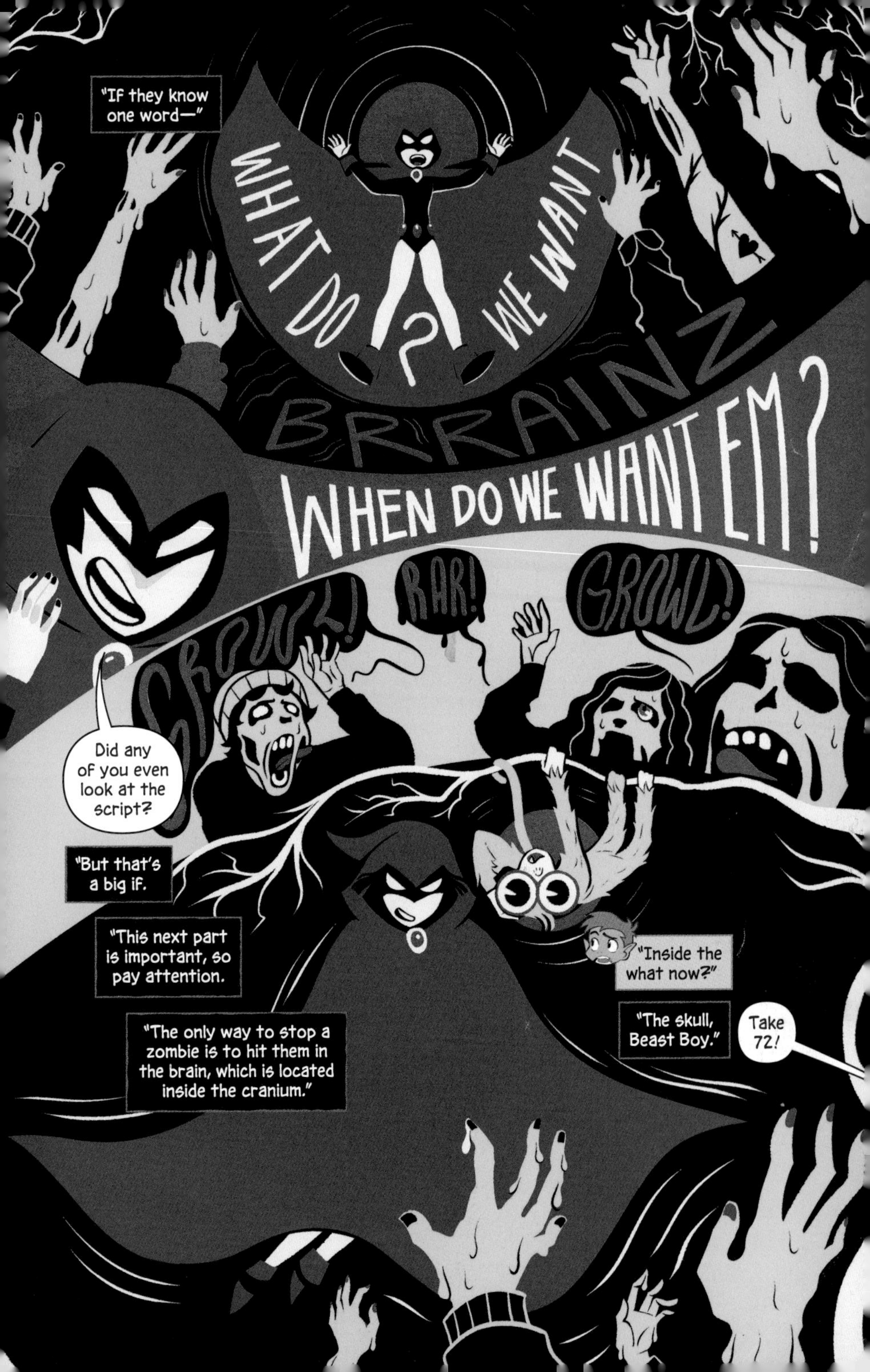
"If they know one word—"
WHAT DO WE WANT?
BRRAINZ
WHEN DO WE WANT EM?
GROWL!
RAR!
GROWL!
Did any of you even look at the script?
"But that's a big if.
"This next part is important, so pay attention.
"The only way to stop a zombie is to hit them in the brain, which is located inside the cranium."
"Inside the what now?"
"The skull, Beast Boy."
Take 72!

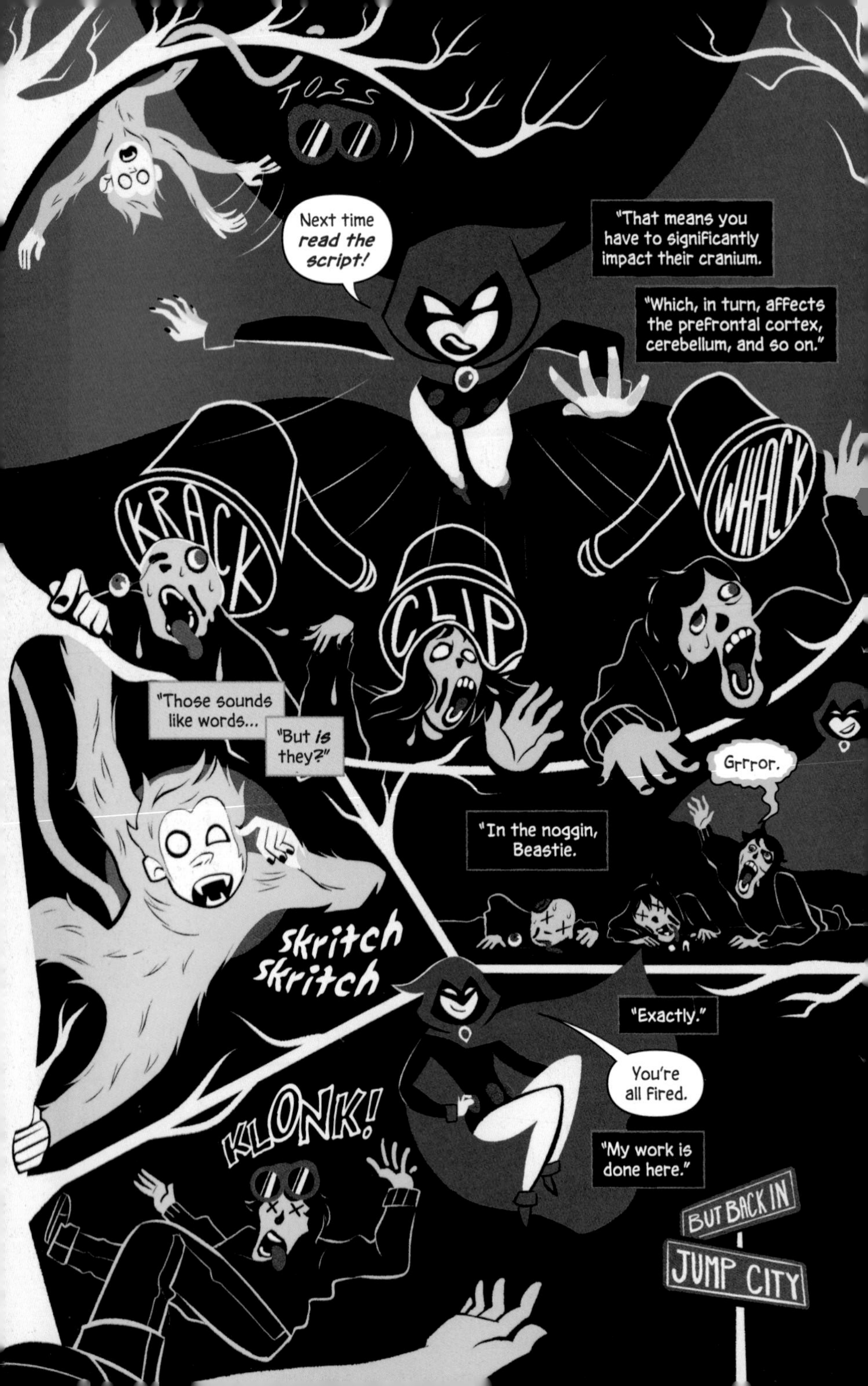
TOSS
Next time *read the script!*
"That means you have to significantly impact their cranium.
"Which, in turn, affects the prefrontal cortex, cerebellum, and so on."
KRACK
CLIP
WHACK
"Those sounds like words...
"But *is* they?"
Grrror.
"In the noggin, Beastie.
skritch skritch
"Exactly."
You're all fired.
KLONK!
"My work is done here."
BUT BACK IN
JUMP CITY

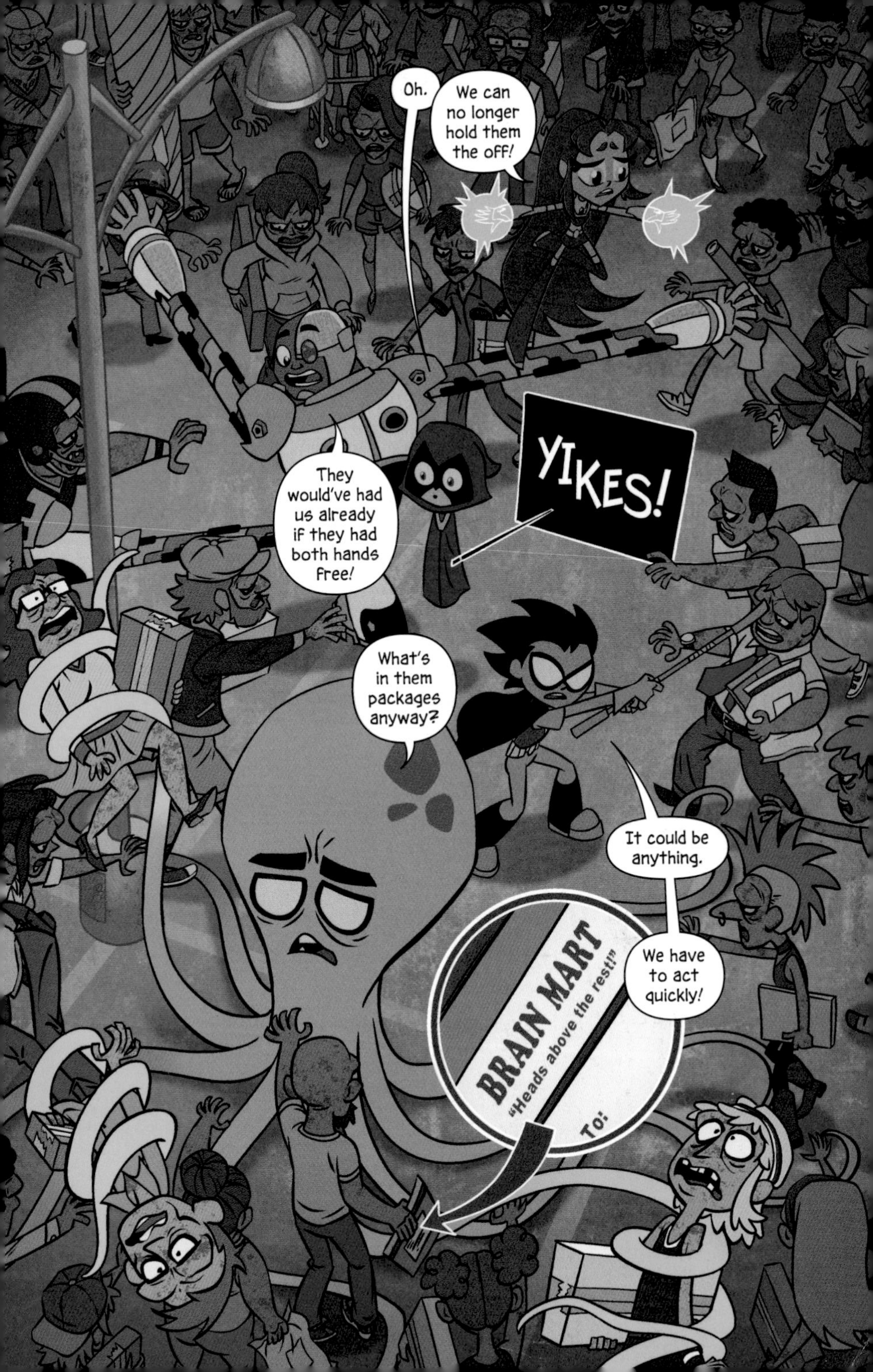
Oh.
We can no longer hold them the off!
They would've had us already if they had both hands free!
YIKES!
What's in them packages anyway?
It could be anything.
We have to act quickly!
BRAIN MART
"Heads above the rest!"
To:

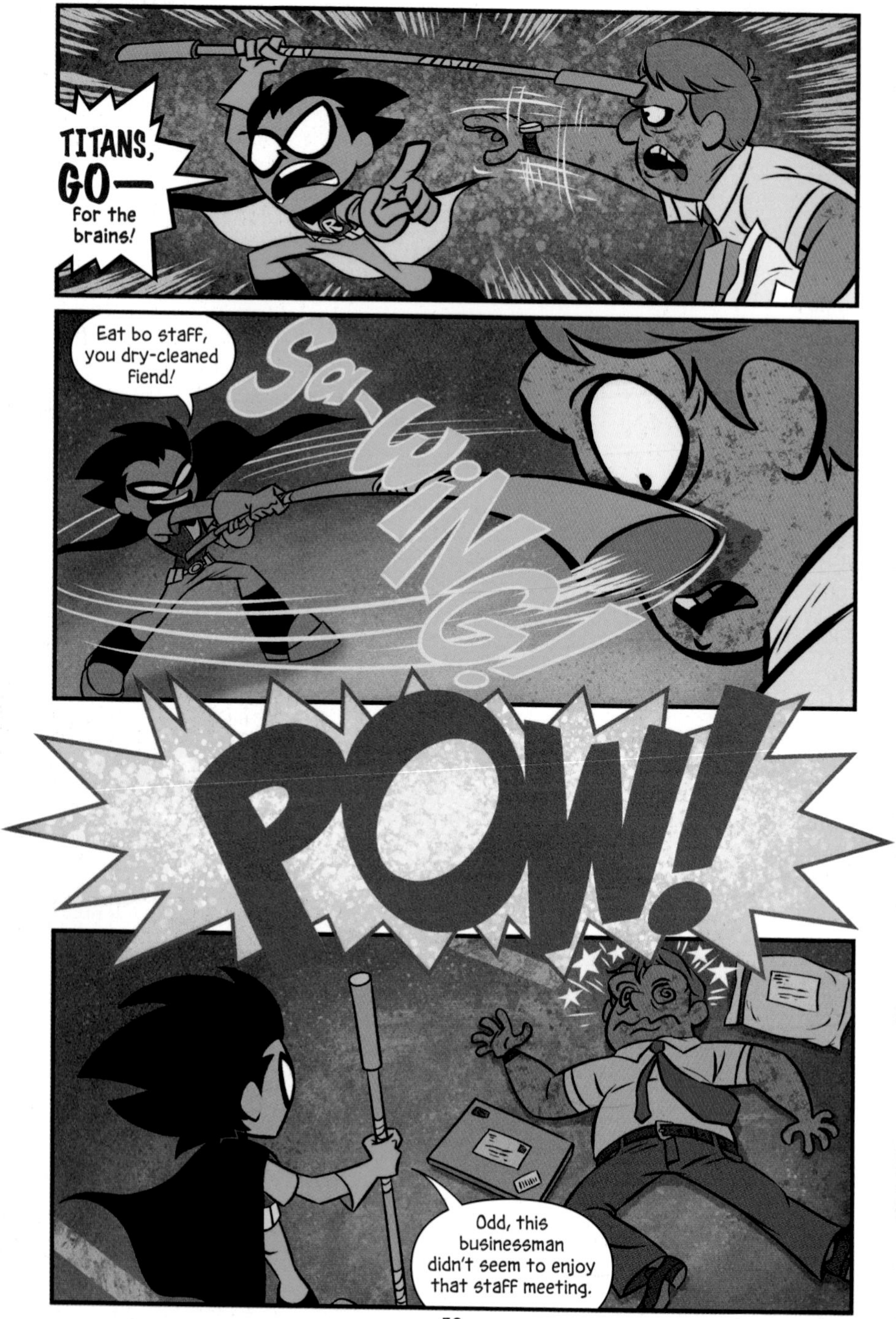
TITANS, GO— for the brains!
Eat bo staff, you dry-cleaned fiend!
Sa-WiNG!
POW!
Odd, this businessman didn't seem to enjoy that staff meeting.

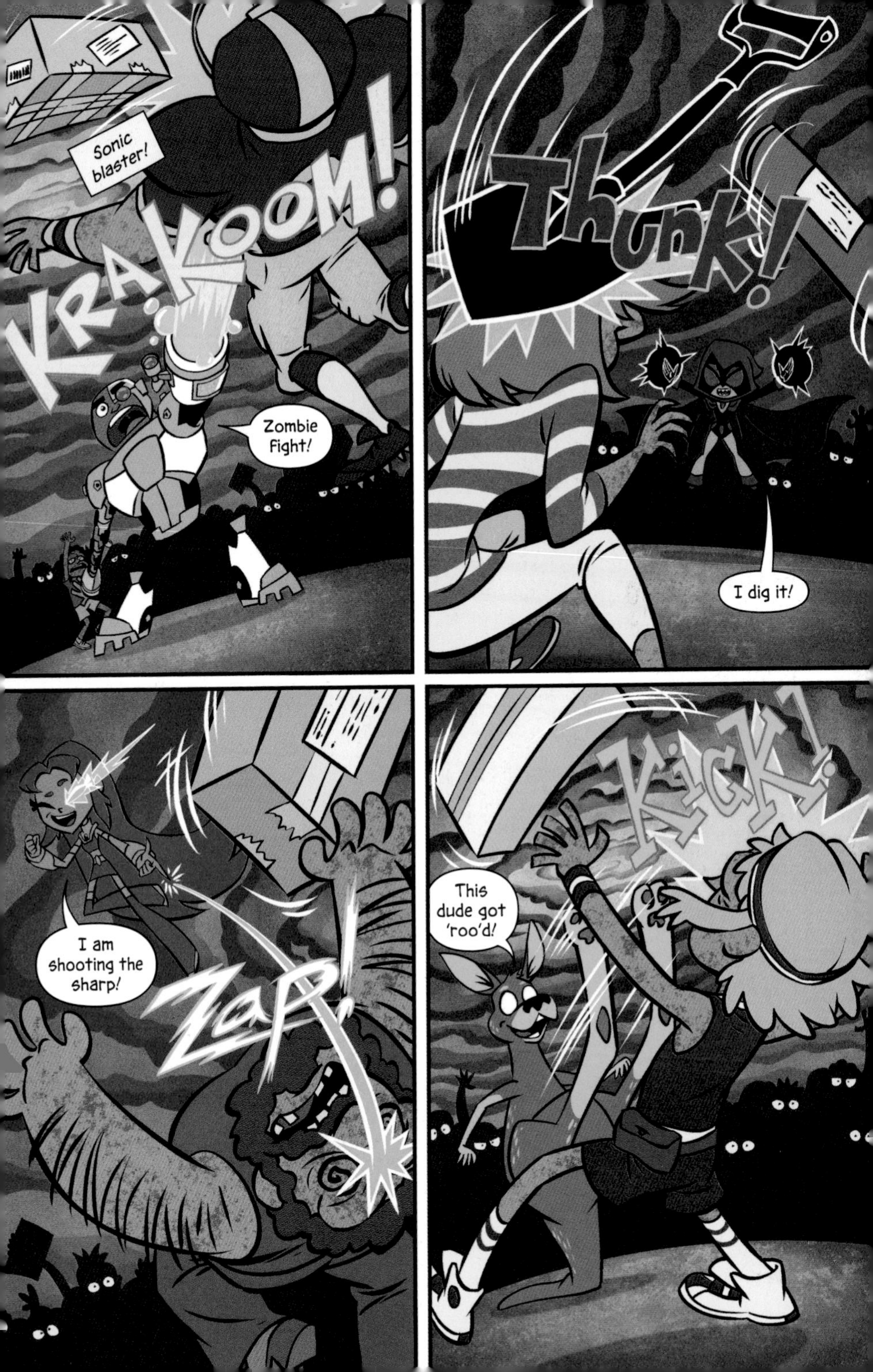
Sonic blaster!
KRAKOOM!
Zombie fight!
THUNK!
I dig it!
I am shooting the sharp!
ZAP!
KICK!
This dude got 'roo'd!

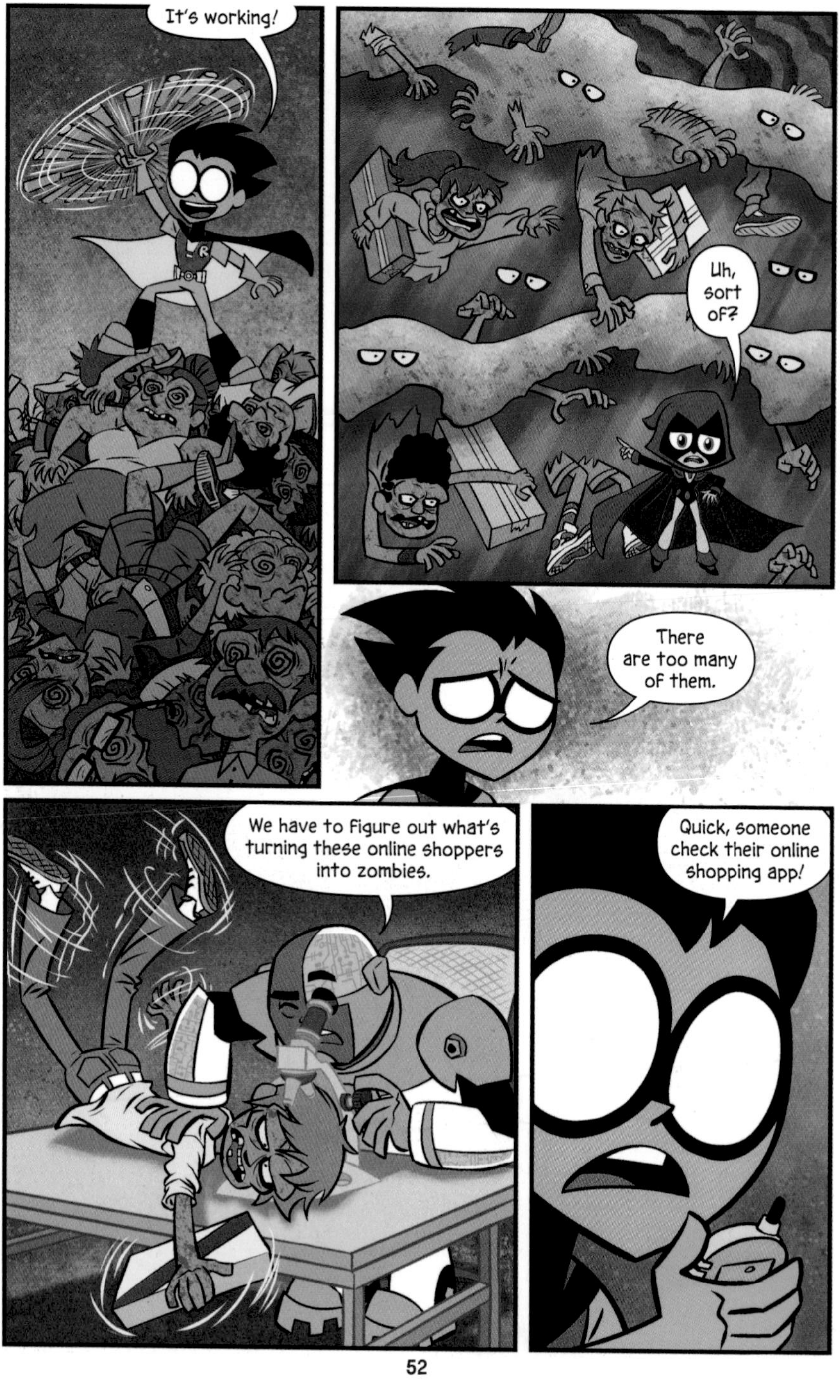
It's working!
Uh, sort of?
There are too many of them.
We have to figure out what's turning these online shoppers into zombies.
Quick, someone check their online shopping app!

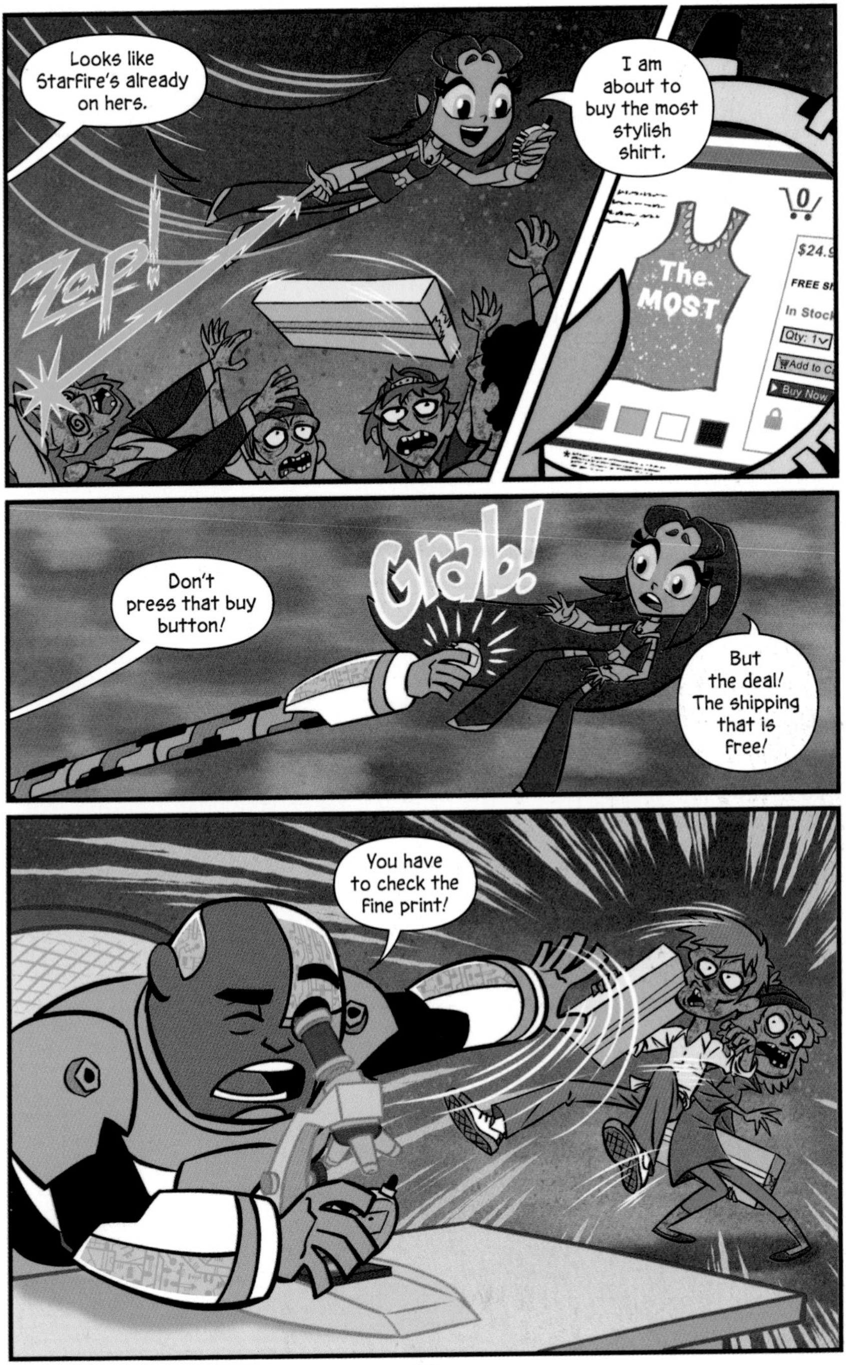
Looks like Starfire's already on hers.
I am about to buy the most stylish shirt.
Zap!
The MOST
$24.9
FREE SI
In Stock
Qty: 1
Add to C
Buy Now
Don't press that buy button!
Grab!
But the deal! The shipping that is free!
You have to check the fine print!

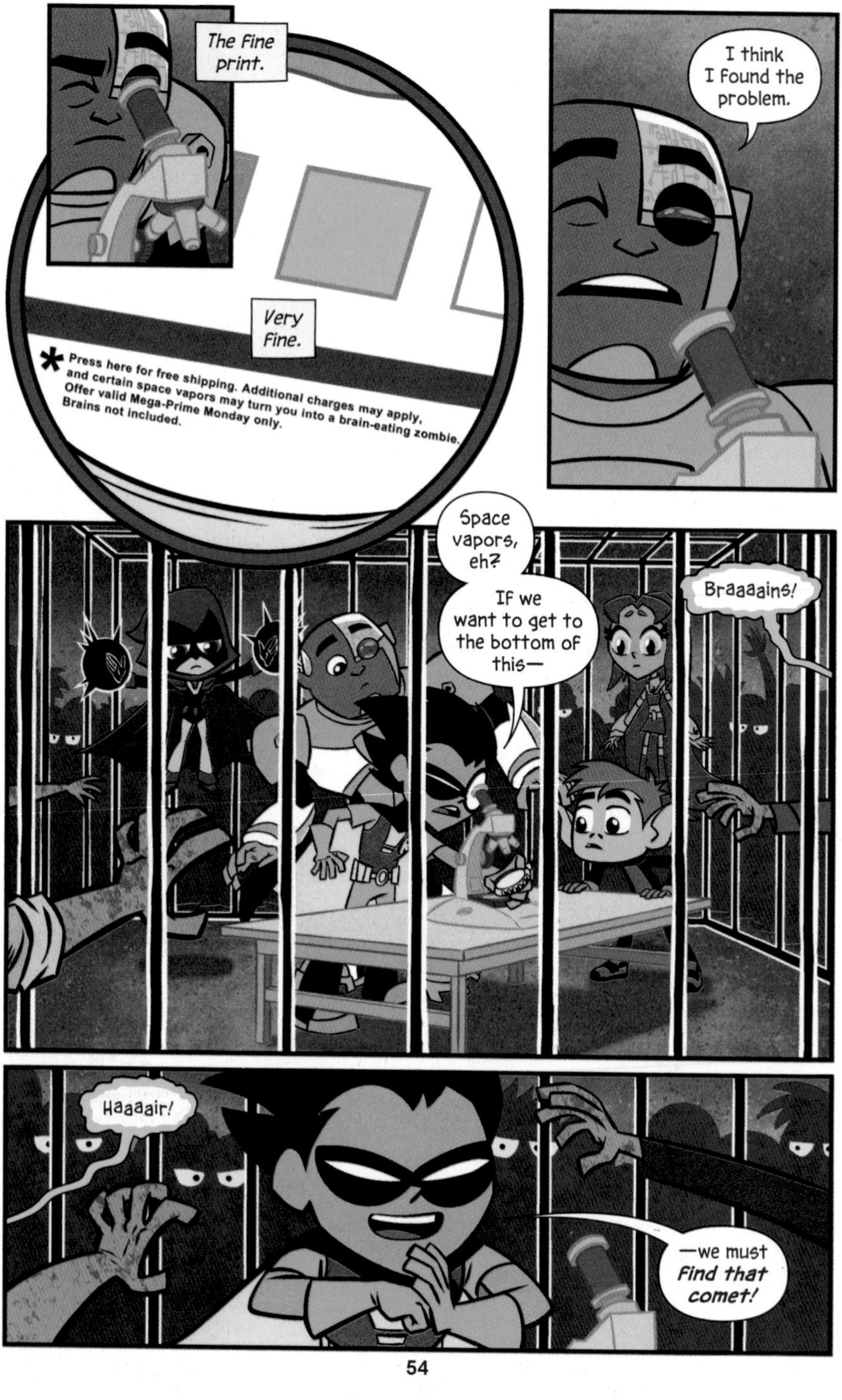
The fine print.
Very fine.
* Press here for free shipping. Additional charges may apply, and certain space vapors may turn you into a brain-eating zombie. Offer valid Mega-Prime Monday only. Brains not included.
I think I found the problem.
Space vapors, eh?
If we want to get to the bottom of this—
Braaaains!
Haaaair!
—we must find that comet!

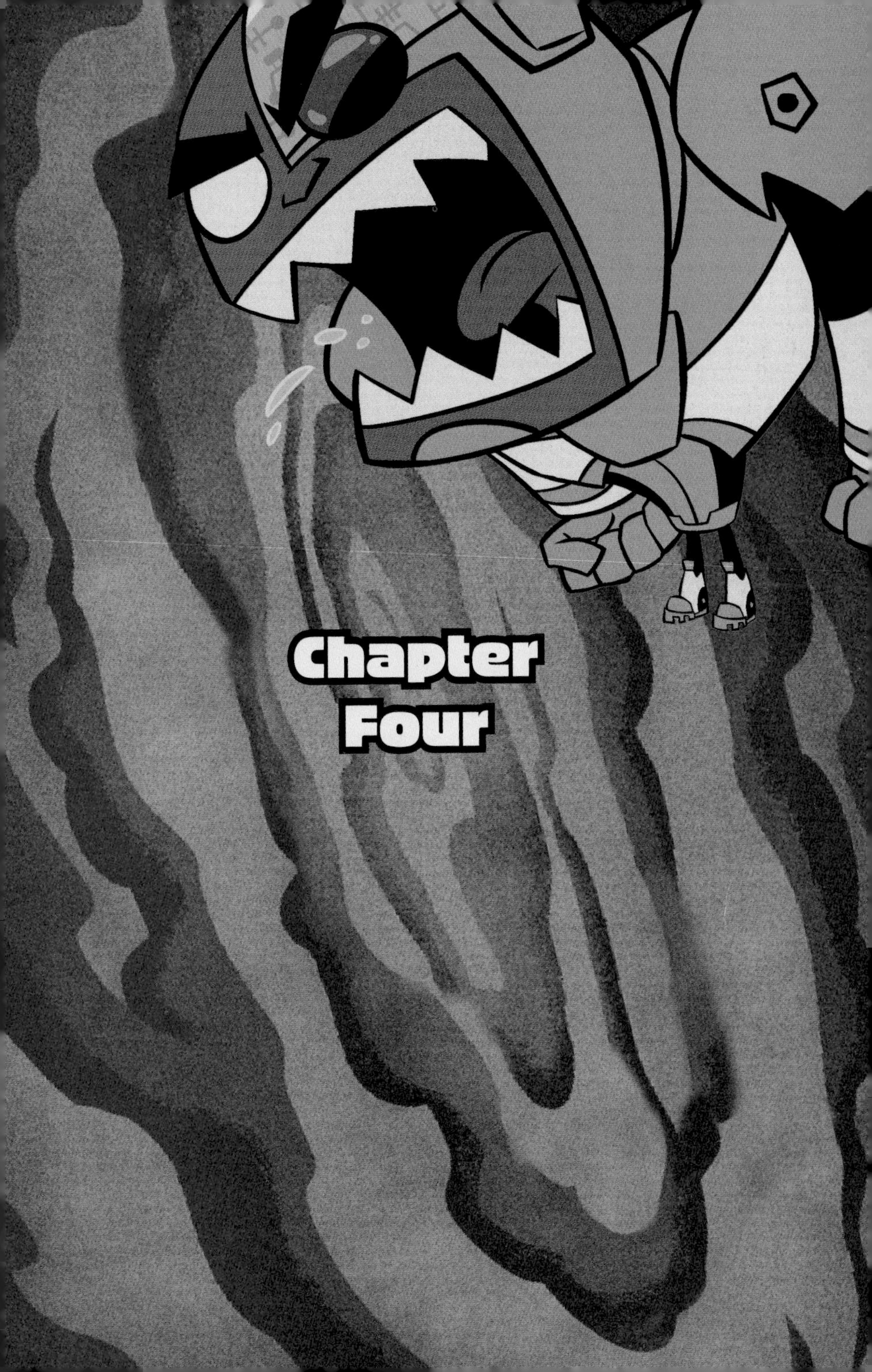

Chapter Four

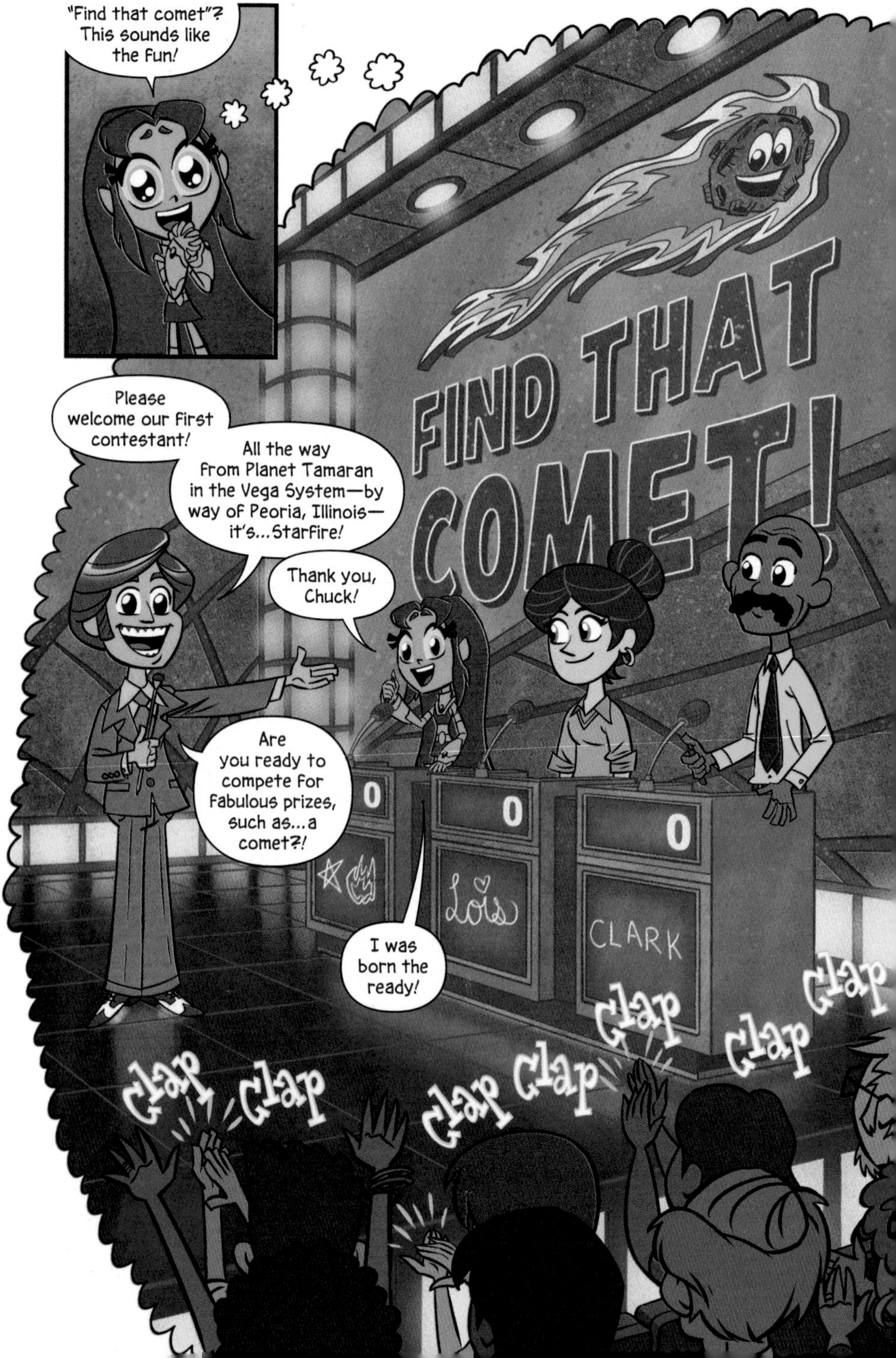
"Find that comet"? This sounds like the fun!
FIND THAT COMET!
Please welcome our first contestant!
All the way from Planet Tamaran in the Vega System—by way of Peoria, Illinois—it's...Starfire!
Thank you, Chuck!
Are you ready to compete for fabulous prizes, such as...a comet?!
I was born the ready!
0
0
0
Lois
CLARK
Clap Clap Clap Clap Clap Clap Clap

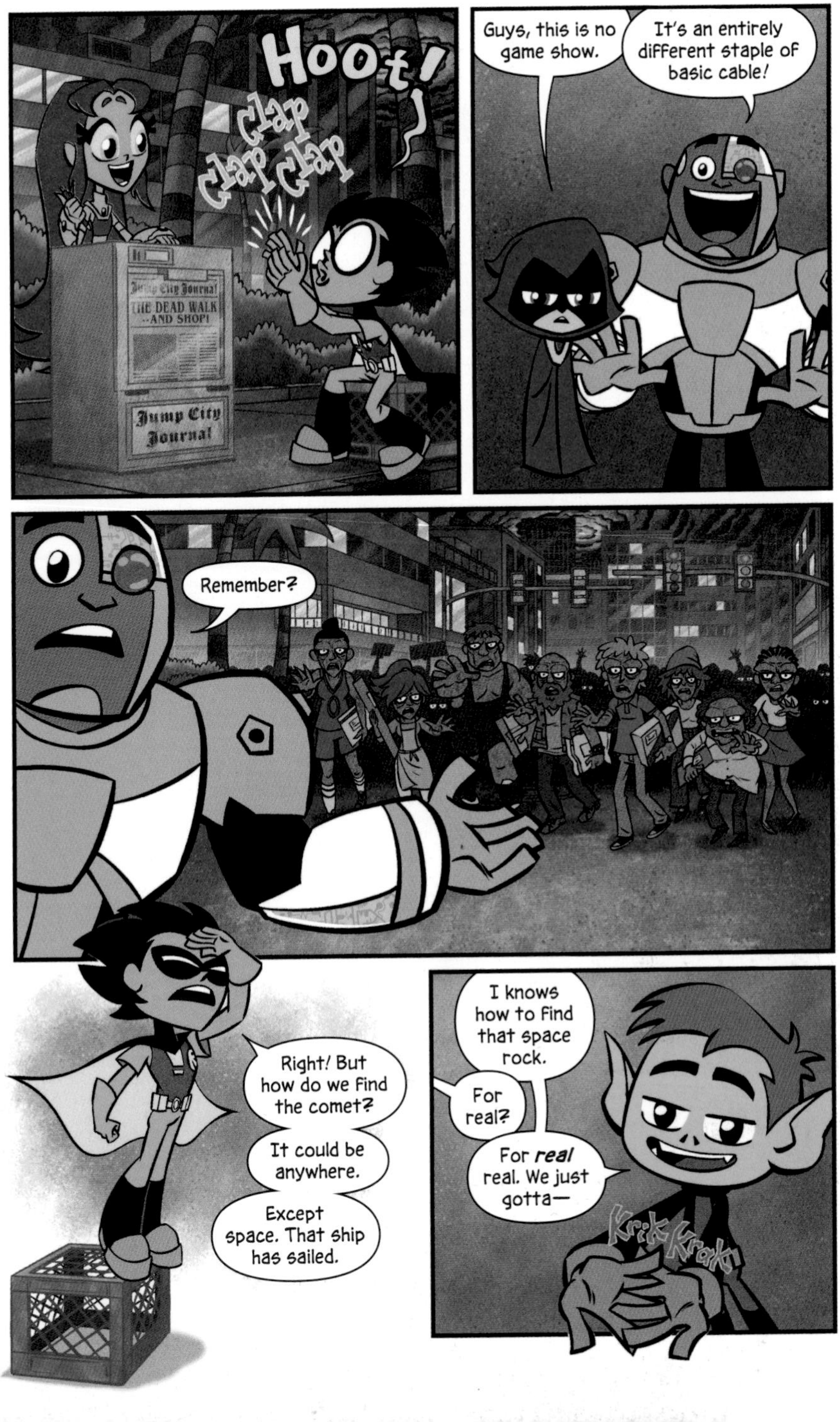
Hoot!
Clap Clap Clap Clap
Jump City Journal
THE DEAD WALK --AND SHOP!
Jump City Journal
Guys, this is no game show.
It's an entirely different staple of basic cable!
Remember?
Right! But how do we find the comet?
It could be anywhere.
Except space. That ship has sailed.
I knows how to find that space rock.
For real?
For *real* real. We just gotta—
Krik Krak!

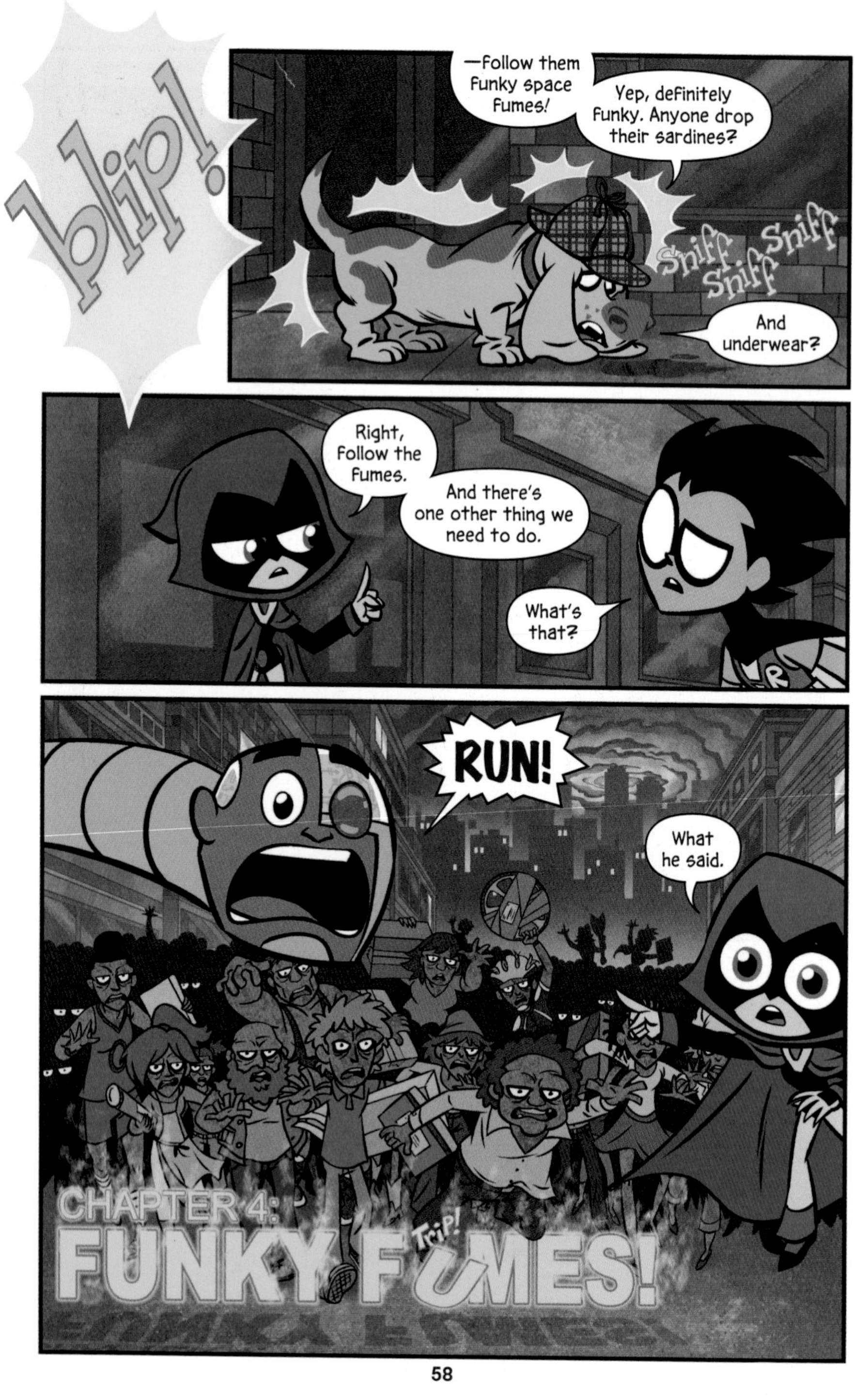
blip!
—Follow them funky space fumes!
Yep, definitely funky. Anyone drop their sardines?
Sniff Sniff Sniff
And underwear?
Right, follow the fumes.
And there's one other thing we need to do.
What's that?
RUN!
What he said.
CHAPTER 4:
FUNKY FUMES!
Trip!

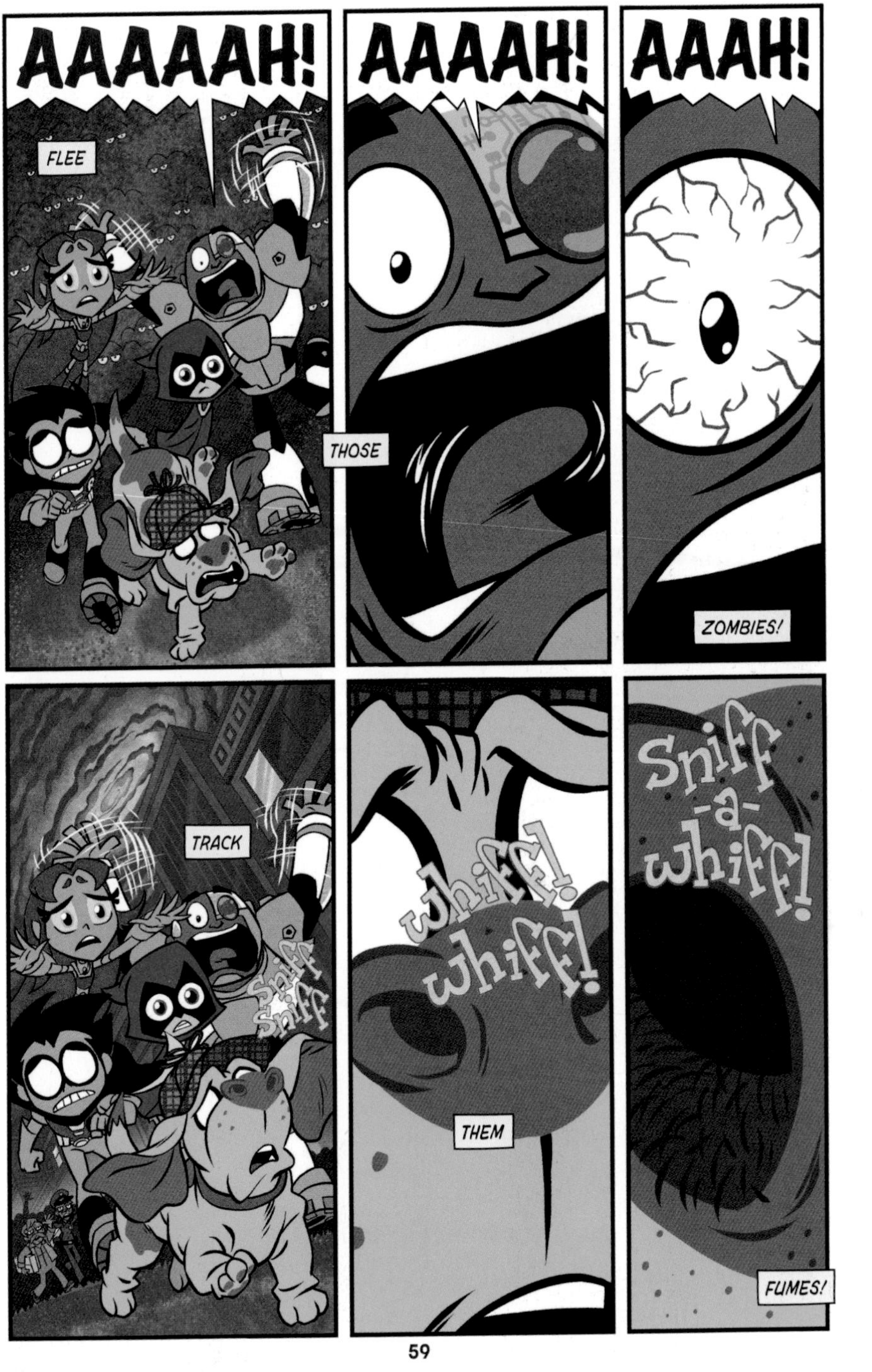
AAAAAH!
FLEE
AAAAH!
THOSE
AAAH!
ZOMBIES!
TRACK
Sniff
Sniff
whiff!
whiff!
THEM
Sniff
-a-
whiff!
FUMES!

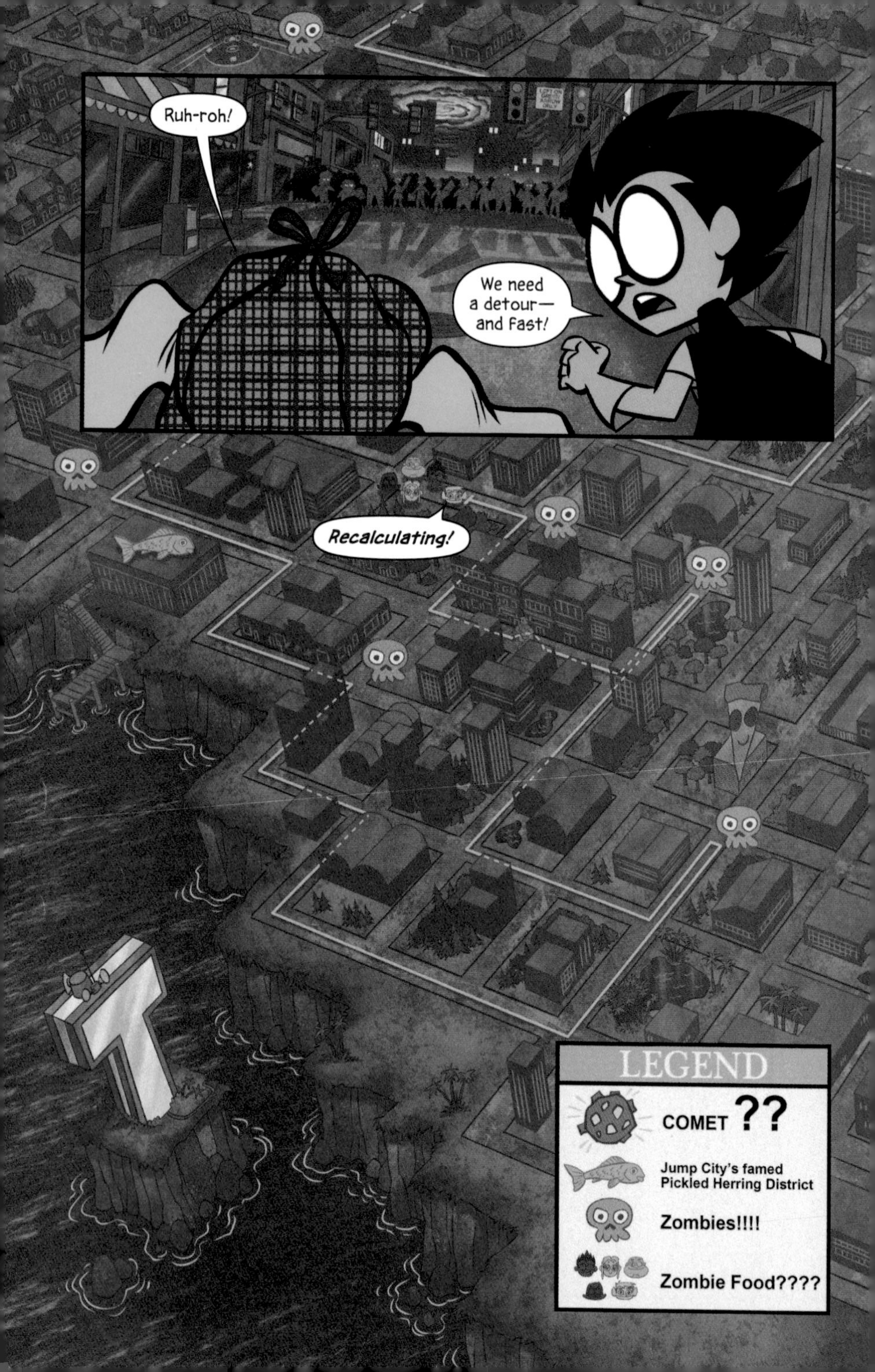

Ruh-roh!
We need a detour—and fast!
Recalculating!
LEGEND
COMET ??
Jump City's famed Pickled Herring District
Zombies!!!!
Zombie Food????

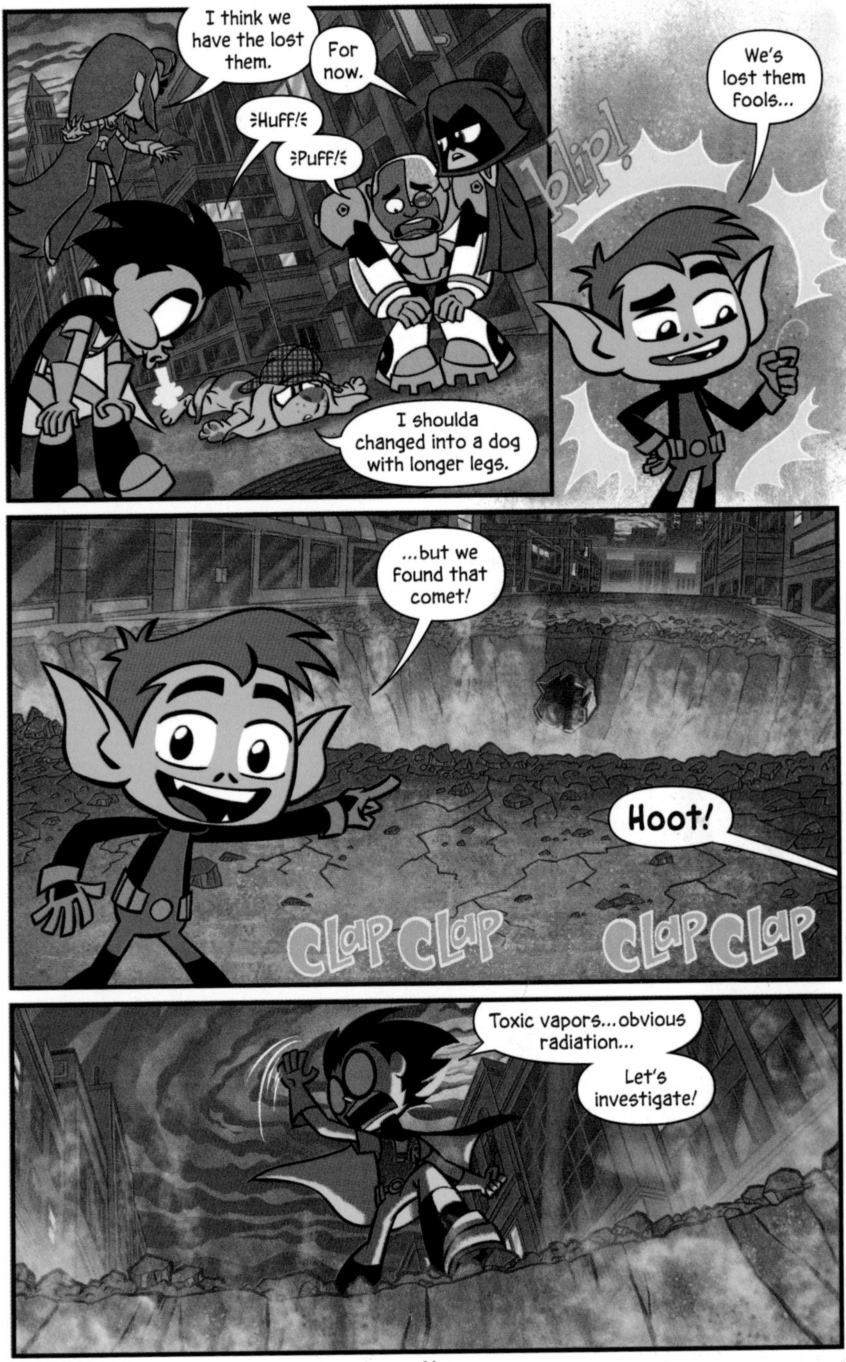
I think we have the lost them.
For now.
Huff!
Puff!
I shoulda changed into a dog with longer legs.
blip!
We's lost them fools...
...but we found that comet!
Hoot!
CLAP CLAP
CLAP CLAP
Toxic vapors...obvious radiation...
Let's investigate!

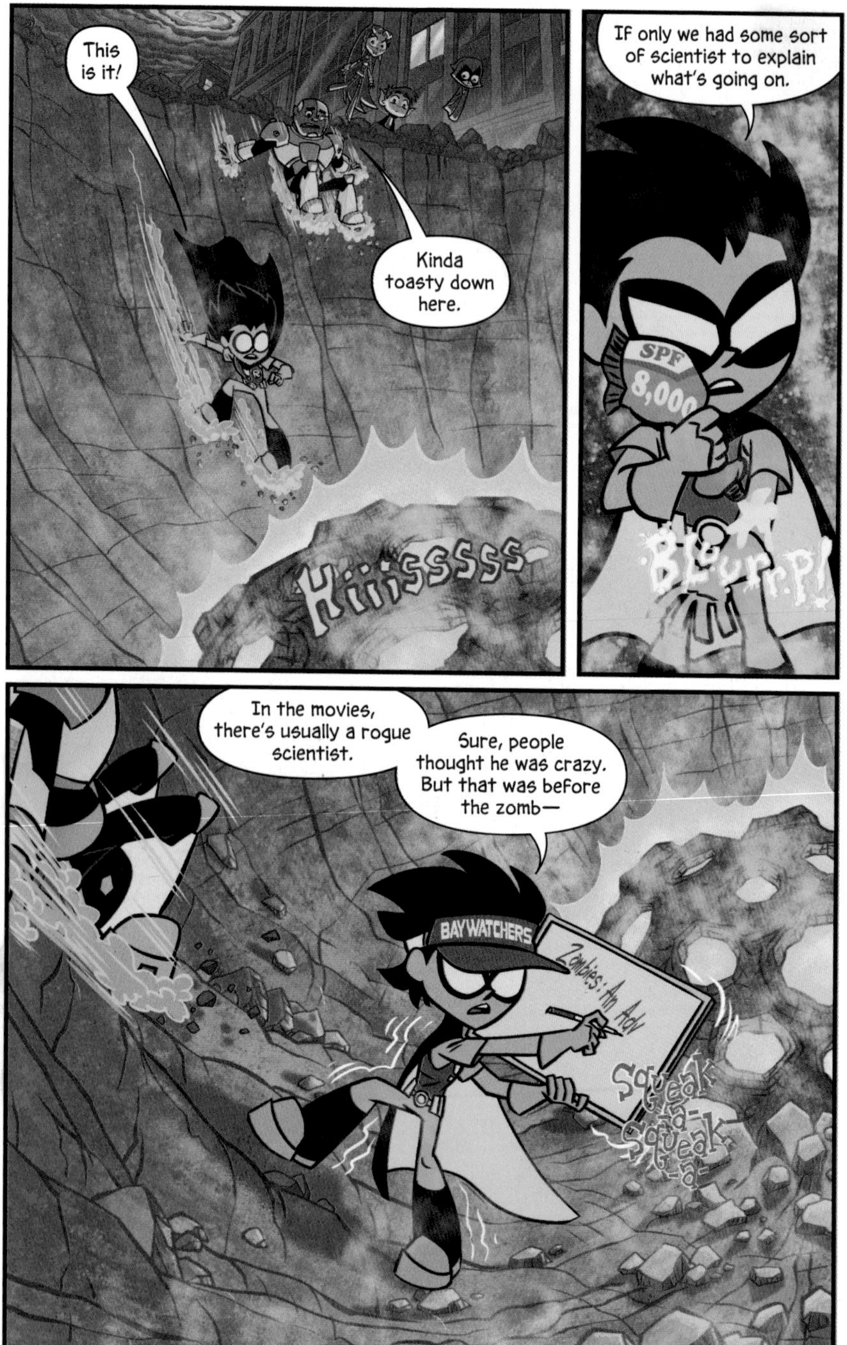
This is it!
Kinda toasty down here.
Hiiisssss
If only we had some sort of scientist to explain what's going on.
SPF 8,000
Blourrp!
In the movies, there's usually a rogue scientist.
Sure, people thought he was crazy. But that was before the zomb—
BAYWATCHERS
Zombies: An Adv
Squeak-a-squeak-a-

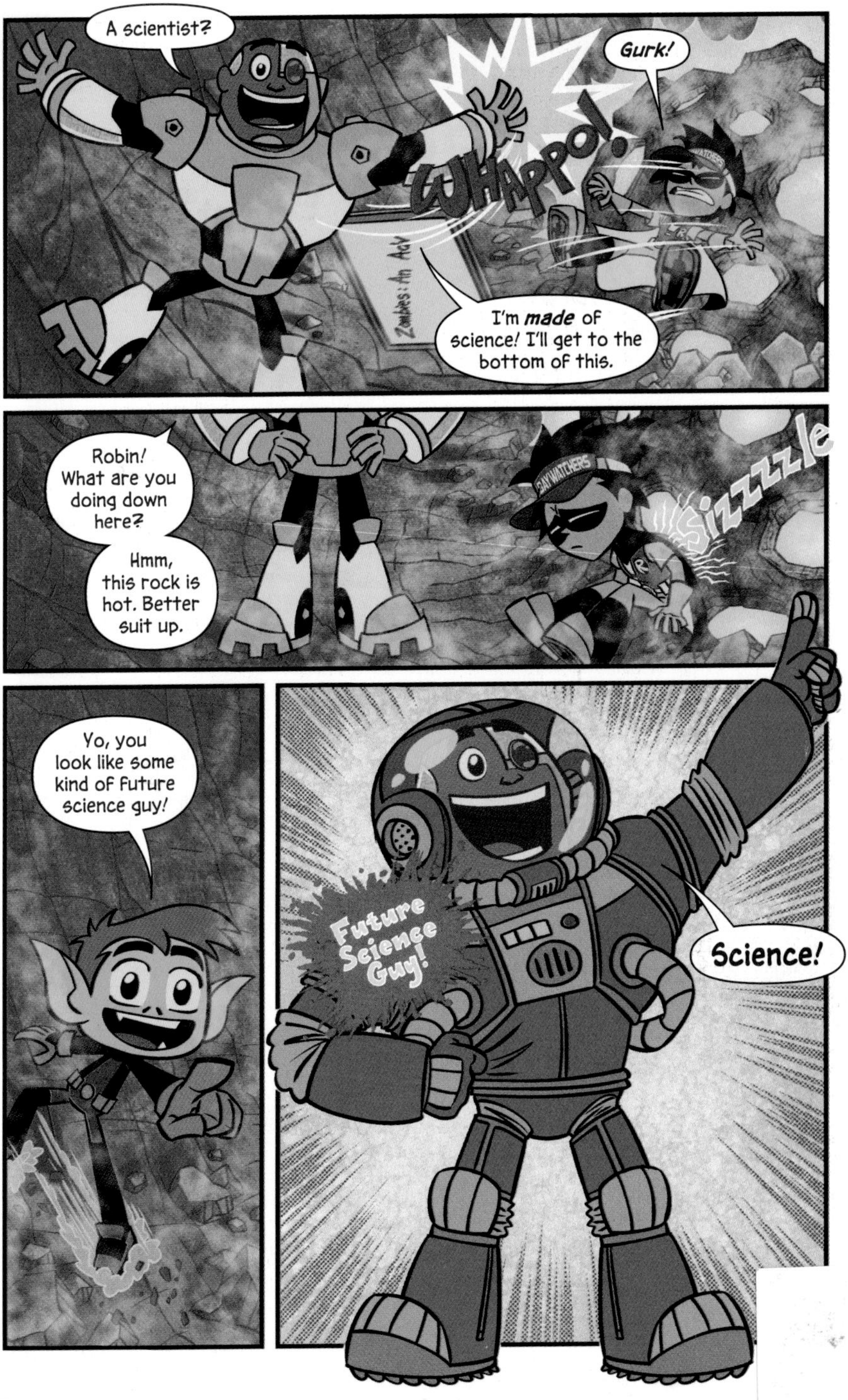

A scientist?
WHAPPO!
Gurk!
Zombies: An Acv
I'm *made* of science! I'll get to the bottom of this.
Robin! What are you doing down here?
Hmm, this rock is hot. Better suit up.
SAY WATCHERS
Sizzzzzle
Yo, you look like some kind of future science guy!
Future Science Guy!
Science!

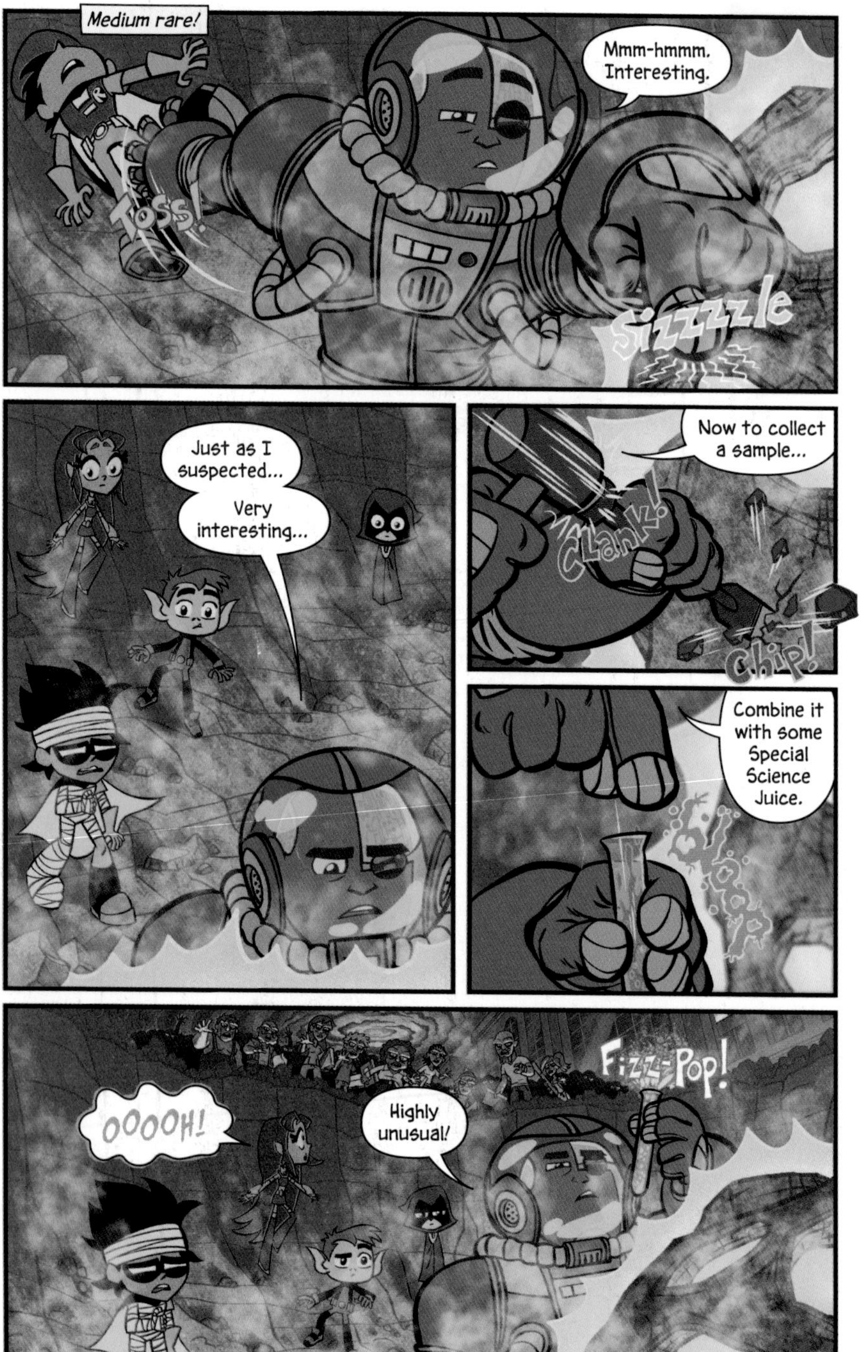
Medium rare!
Mmm-hmmm. Interesting.
TOSS!
Sizzzzzle
Just as I suspected...
Very interesting...
Now to collect a sample...
CLANK!
Chip!
Combine it with some Special Science Juice.
OOOOH!
Highly unusual!
Fizz-Pop!

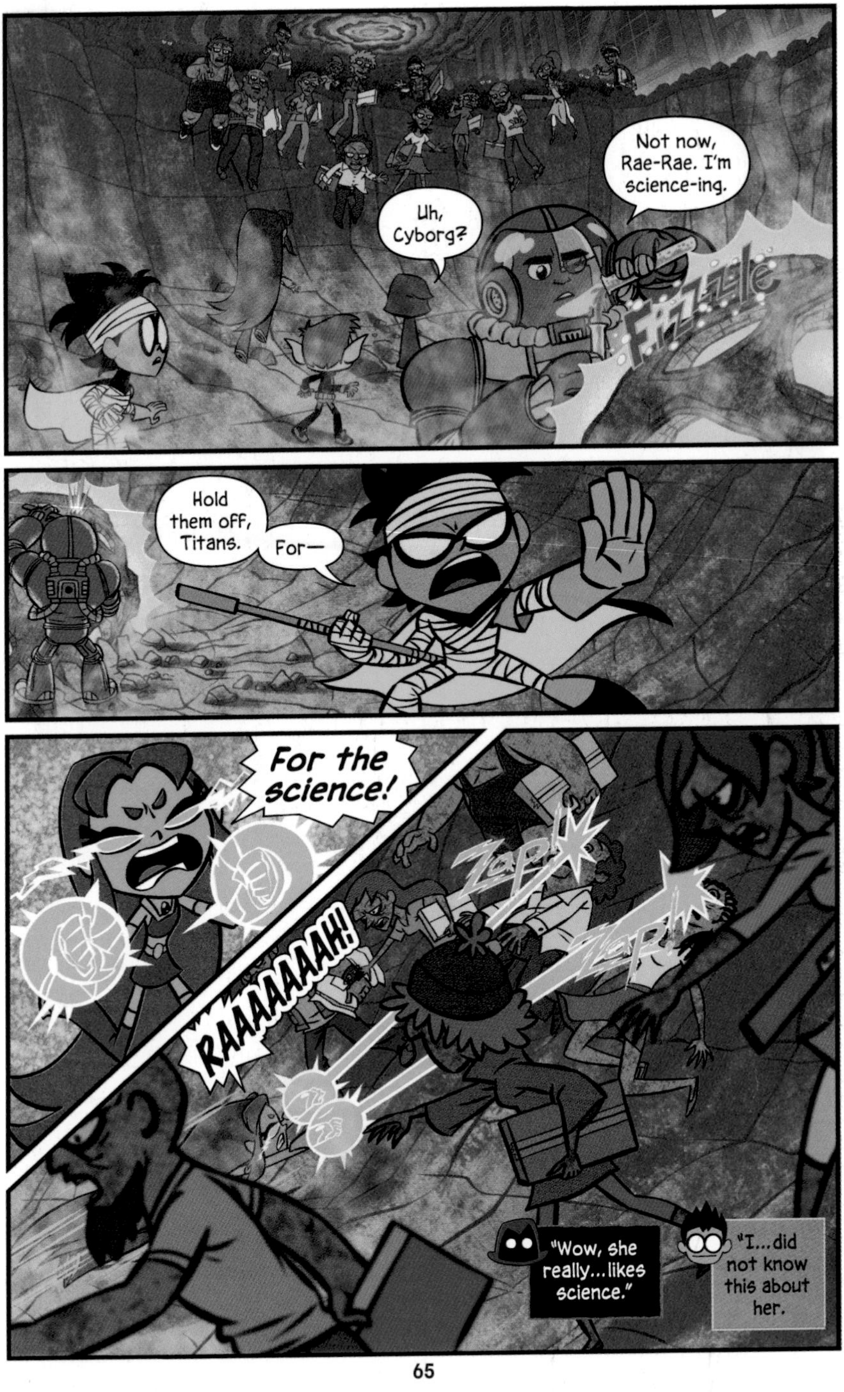

Not now, Rae-Rae. I'm science-ing.
Uh, Cyborg?
Fizzzzle
Hold them off, Titans.
For—
For the science!
Zap!
Zap!
RAAAAAAAH!
"Wow, she really...likes science."
"I...did not know this about her.

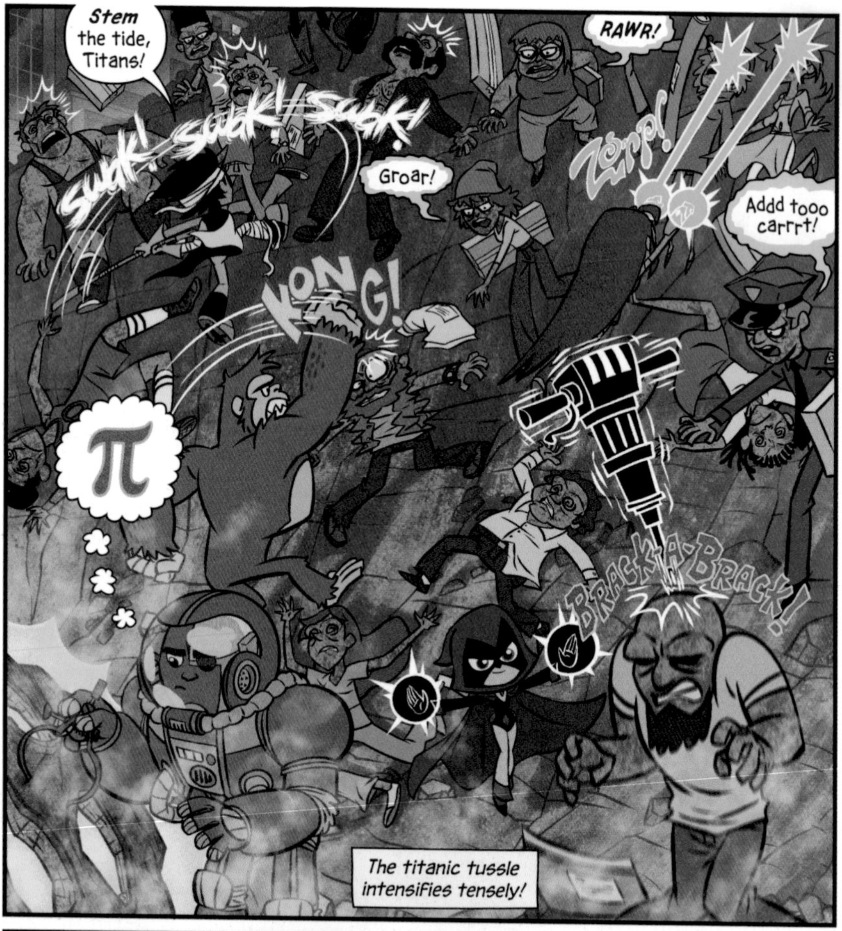
Stem the tide, Titans!
SWAK! SWAK! SWAK!
RAWR!
Groar!
ZORP!
Addd tooo carrrt!
KONG!
π
BRACK-A-BRACK!
The titanic tussle intensifies tensely!

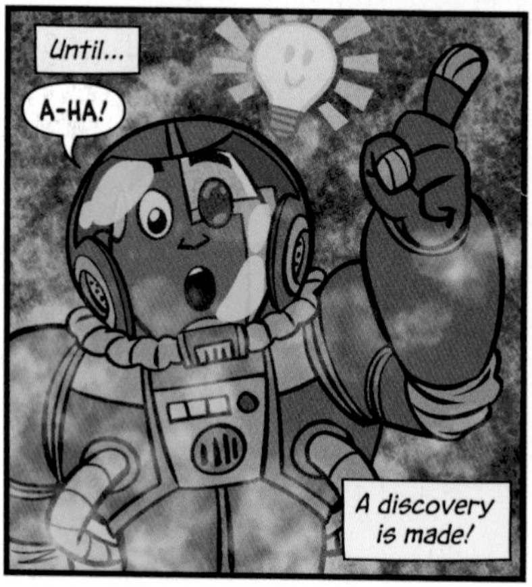
Until...
A-HA!
A discovery is made!

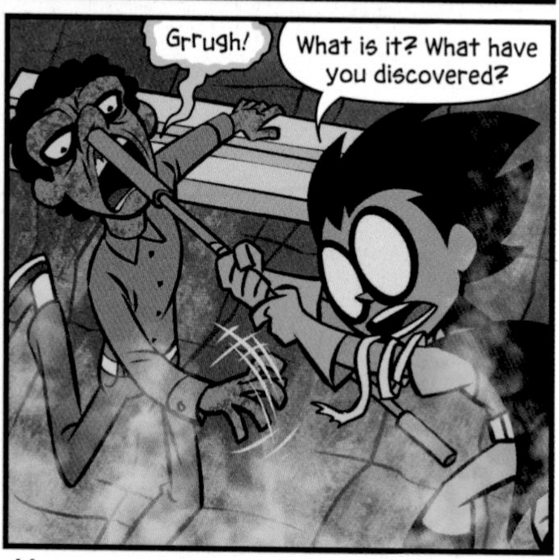
Grrugh!
What is it? What have you discovered?

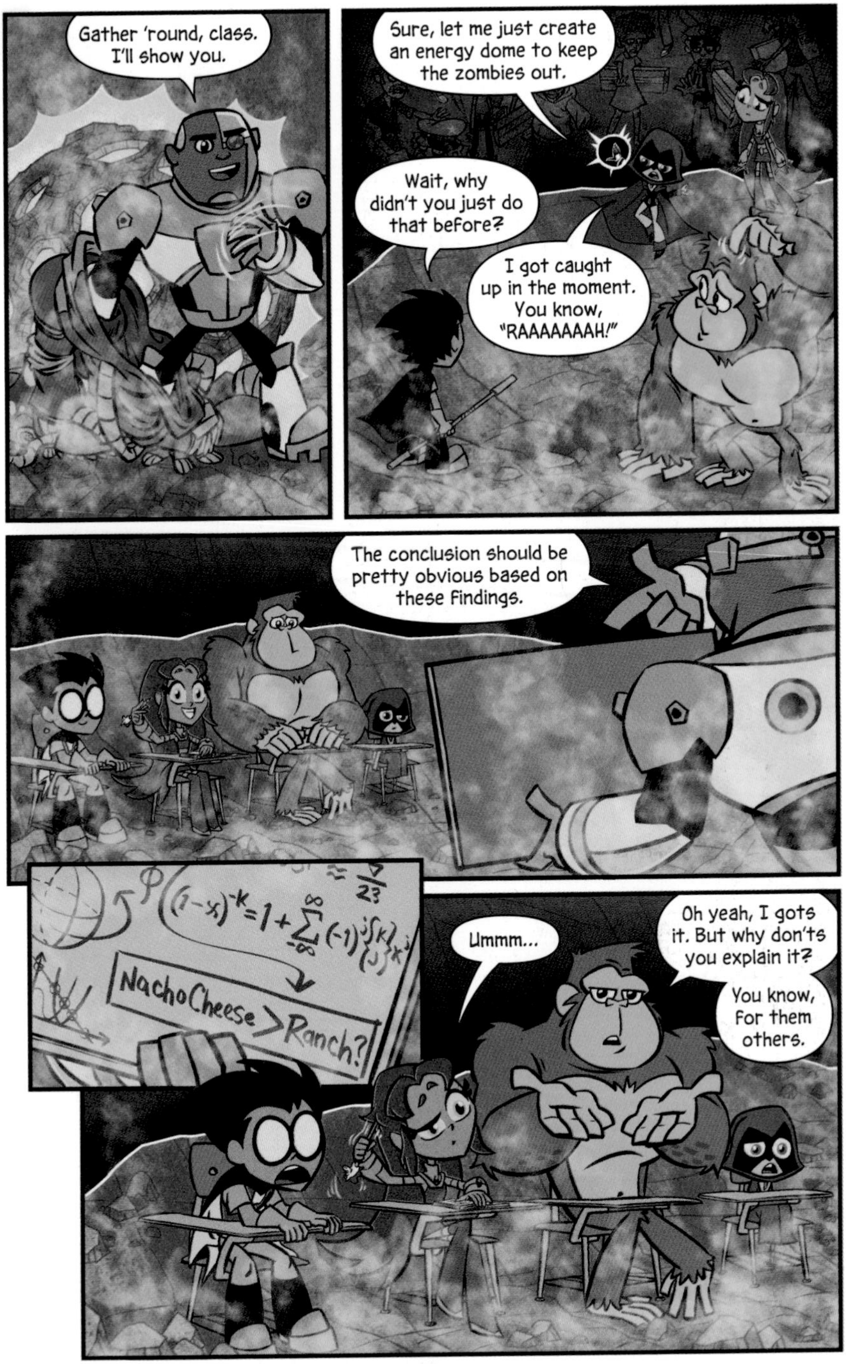
Gather 'round, class. I'll show you.
Sure, let me just create an energy dome to keep the zombies out.
Wait, why didn't you just do that before?
I got caught up in the moment. You know, "RAAAAAAAH!"
The conclusion should be pretty obvious based on these findings.
NachoCheese > Ranch?
Ummm...
Oh yeah, I gots it. But why don'ts you explain it?
You know, for them others.

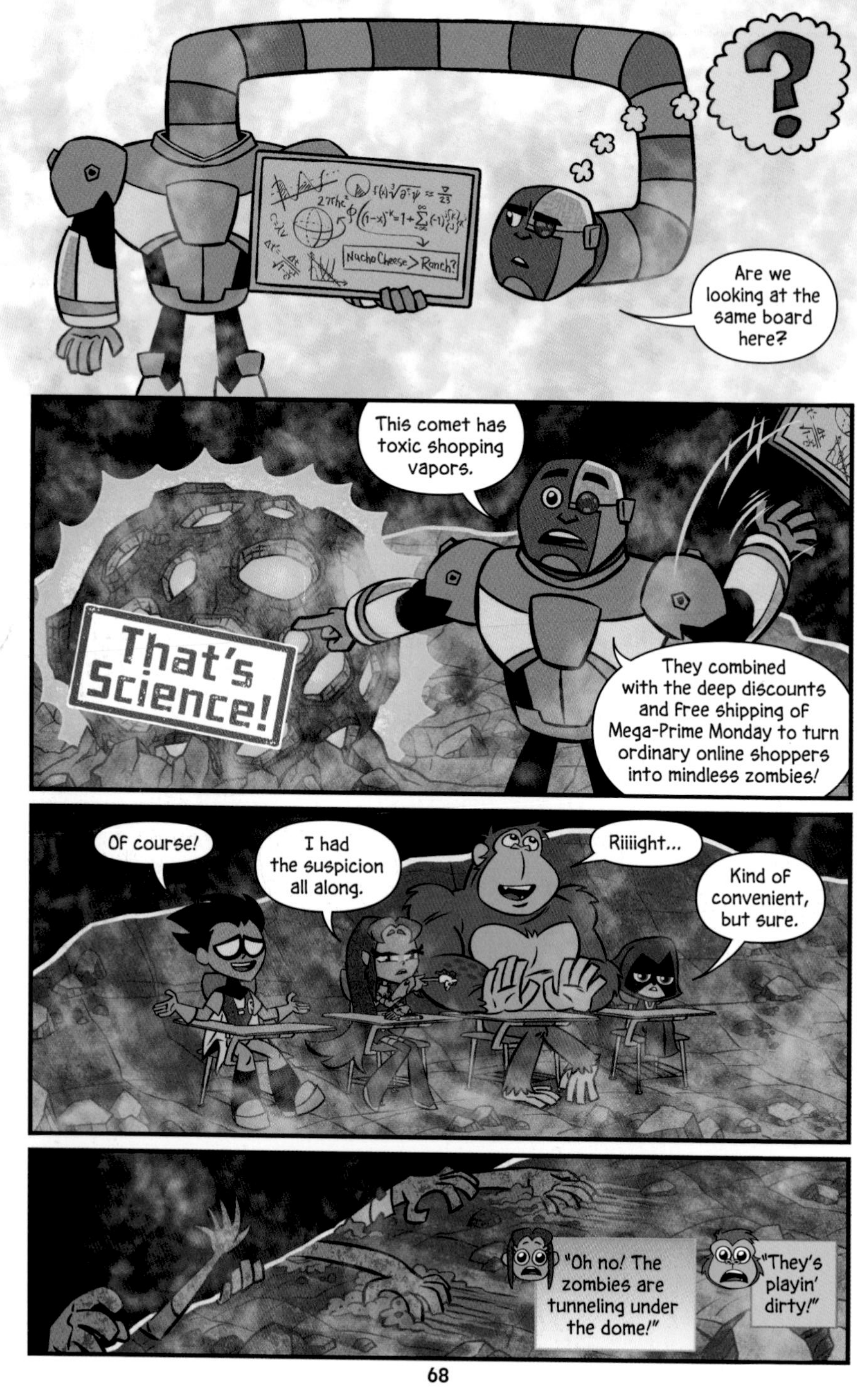

?
Nacho Cheese > Ranch?
Are we looking at the same board here?
This comet has toxic shopping vapors.
That's Science!
They combined with the deep discounts and free shipping of Mega-Prime Monday to turn ordinary online shoppers into mindless zombies!
Of course!
I had the suspicion all along.
Riiiight...
Kind of convenient, but sure.
"Oh no! The zombies are tunneling under the dome!"
"They's playin' dirty!"

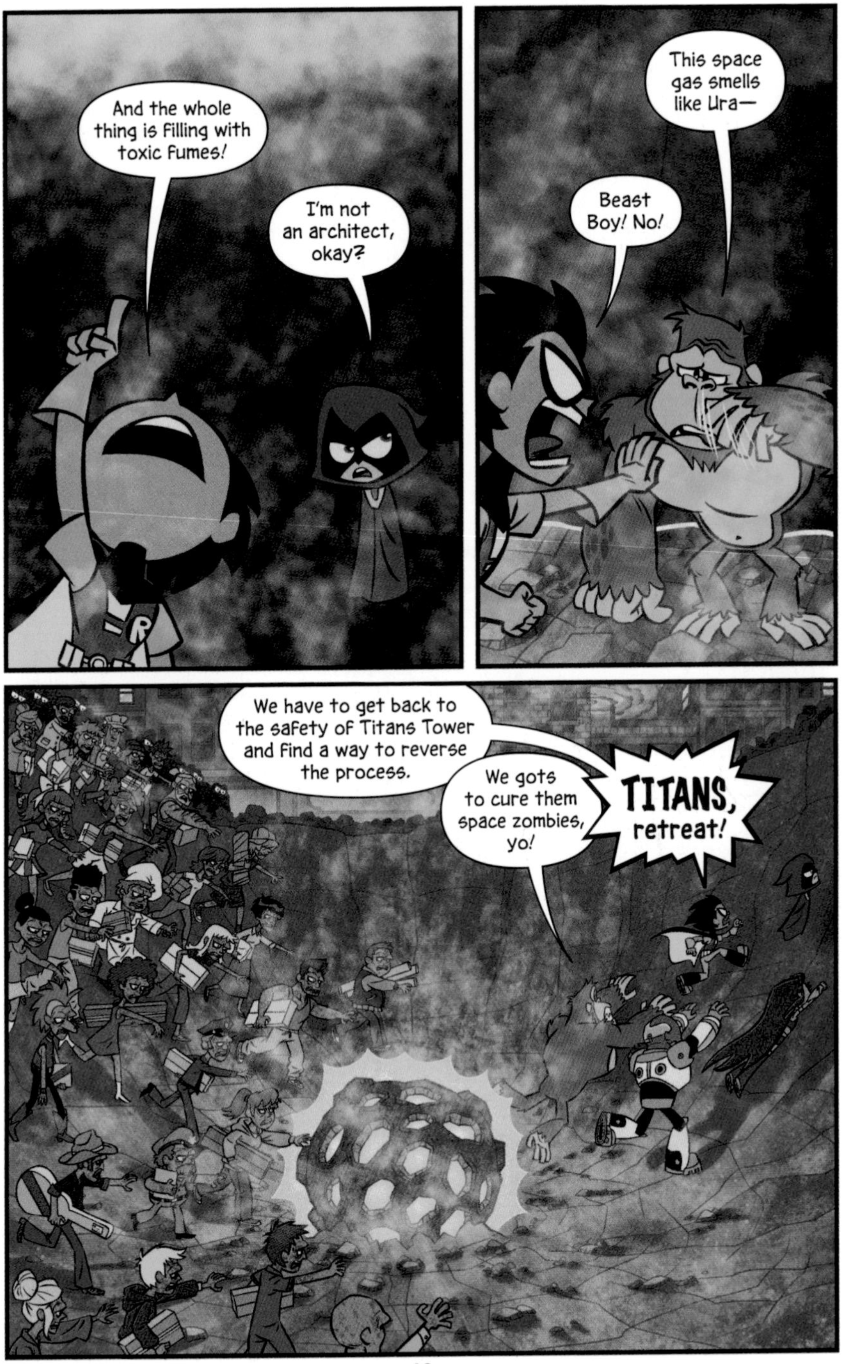
And the whole thing is filling with toxic fumes!
I'm not an architect, okay?
This space gas smells like Ura—
Beast Boy! No!
We have to get back to the safety of Titans Tower and find a way to reverse the process.
TITANS, retreat!
We gots to cure them space zombies, yo!

Chapter Five

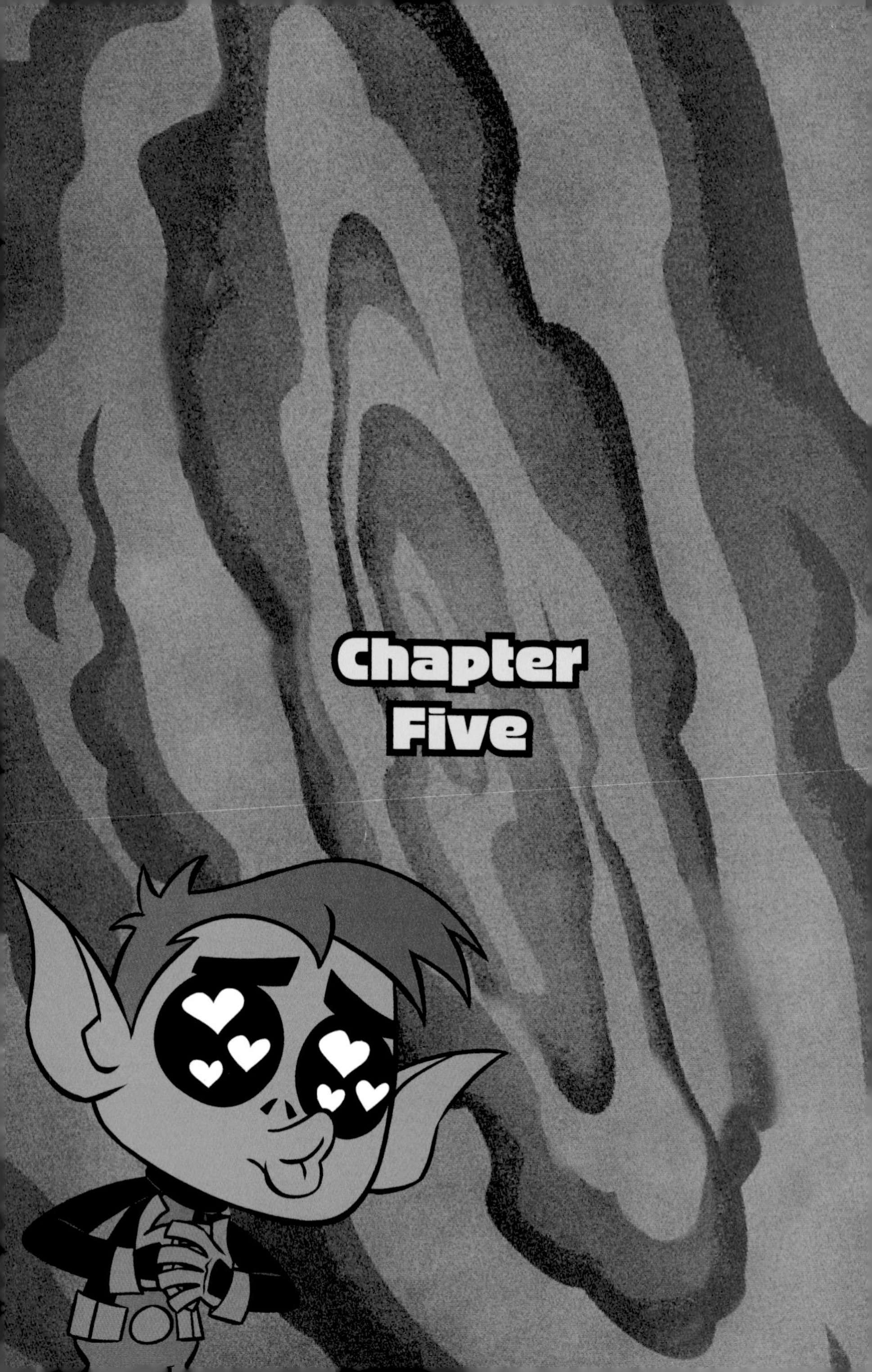

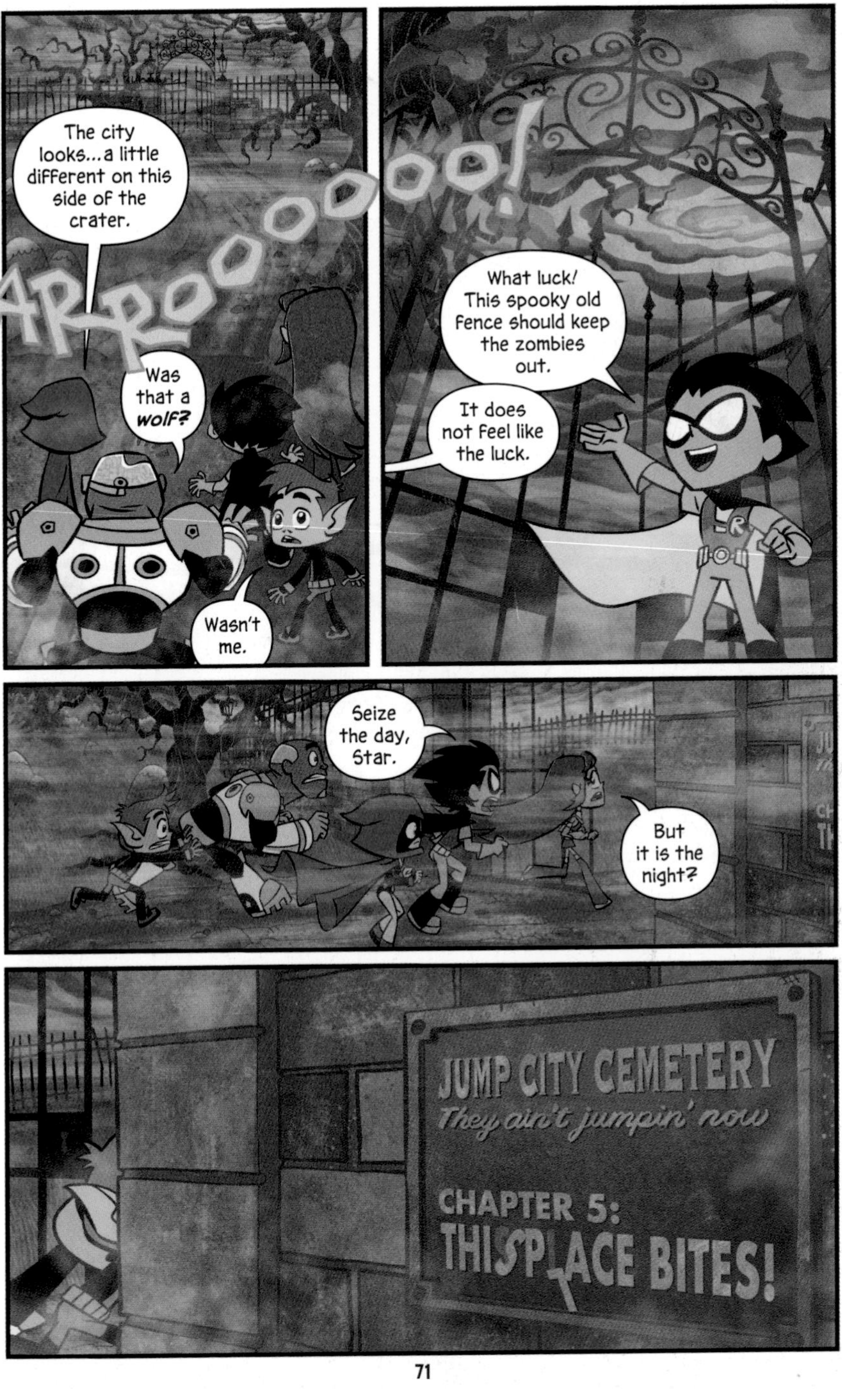
The city looks...a little different on this side of the crater.
AR-ROOOOOOO!
Was that a *wolf?*
Wasn't me.
What luck! This spooky old fence should keep the zombies out.
It does not feel like the luck.
Seize the day, Star.
But it is the night?
JUMP CITY CEMETERY
They ain't jumpin' now
CHAPTER 5:
THIS PLACE BITES!

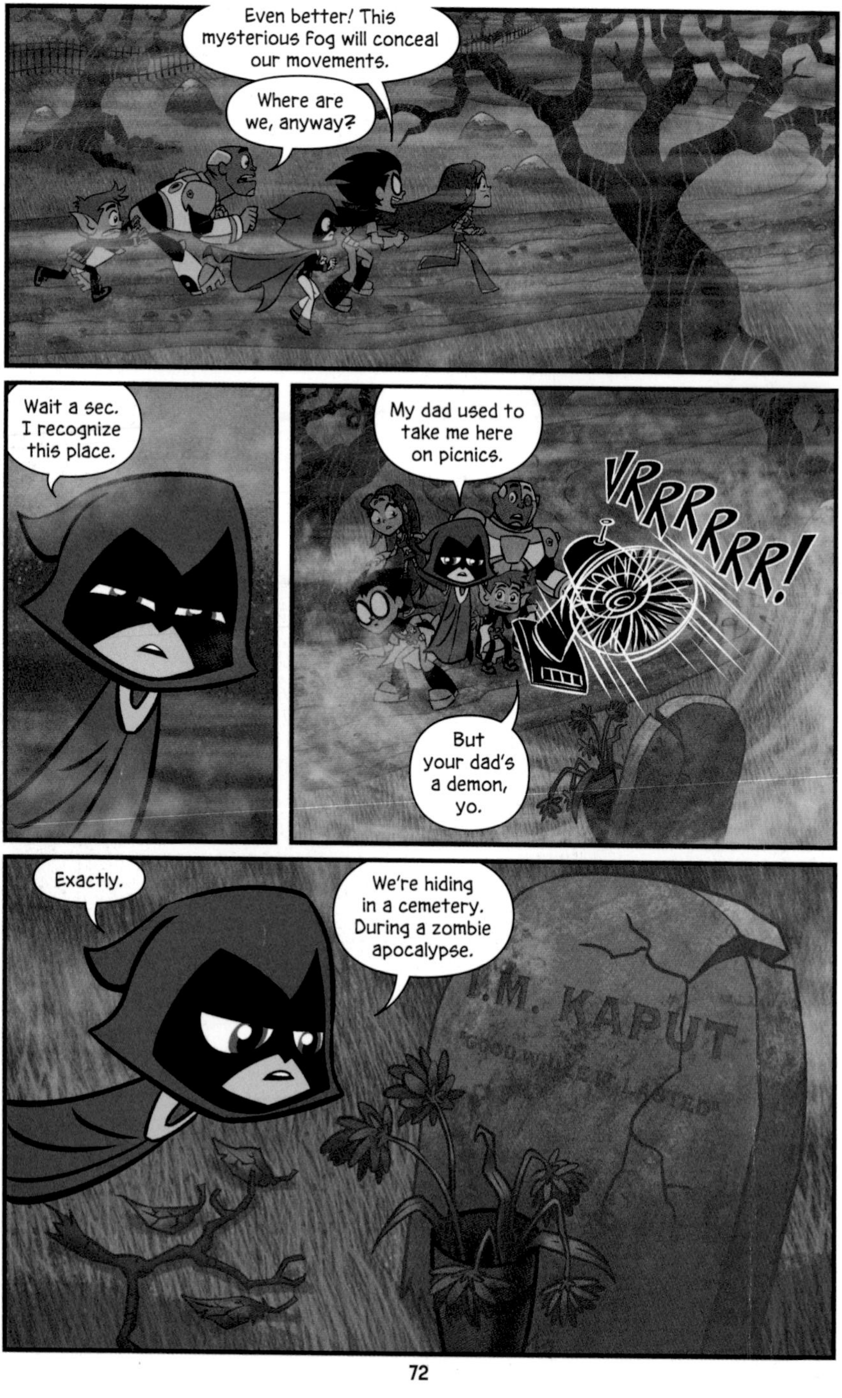
Even better! This mysterious fog will conceal our movements.
Where are we, anyway?
Wait a sec. I recognize this place.
My dad used to take me here on picnics.
VRRRRRR!
But your dad's a demon, yo.
Exactly.
We're hiding in a cemetery. During a zombie apocalypse.
I.M. KAPUT

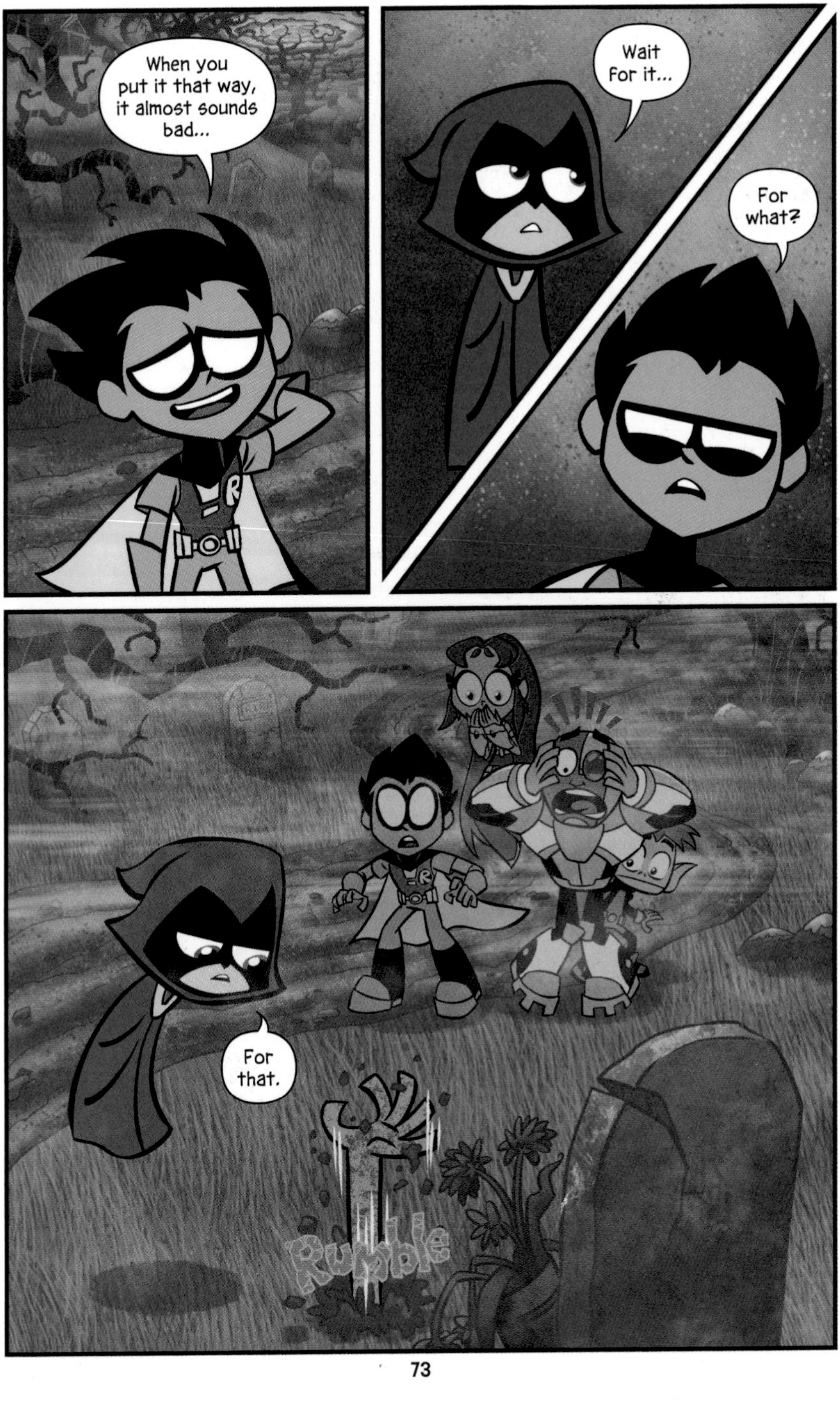
When you put it that way, it almost sounds bad...
Wait for it...
For what?
For that.
Rumble

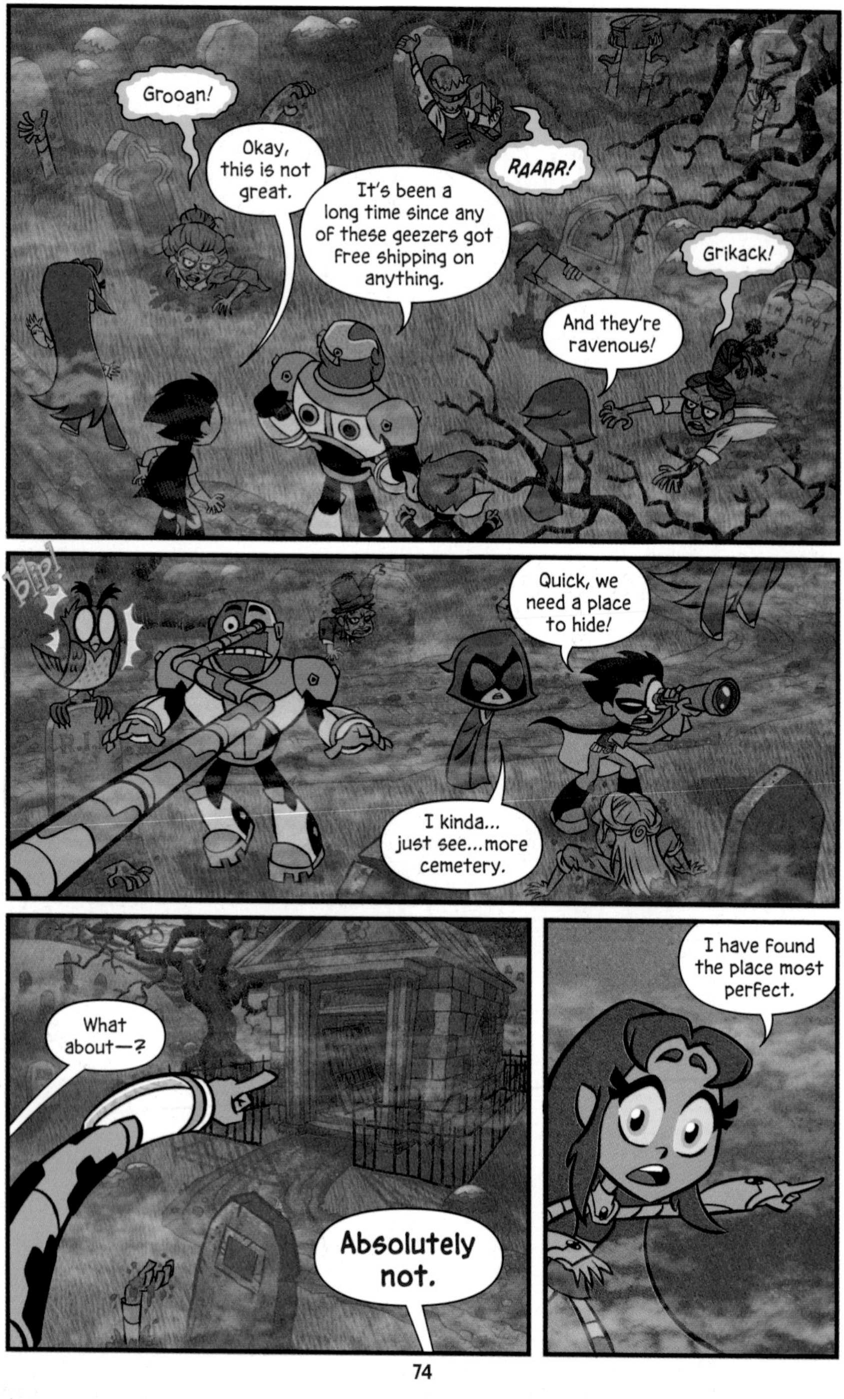
Grooan!
Okay, this is not great.
RAARR!
It's been a long time since any of these geezers got free shipping on anything.
Grikack!
And they're ravenous!
Quick, we need a place to hide!
I kinda... just see...more cemetery.
What about—?
Absolutely not.
I have found the place most perfect.

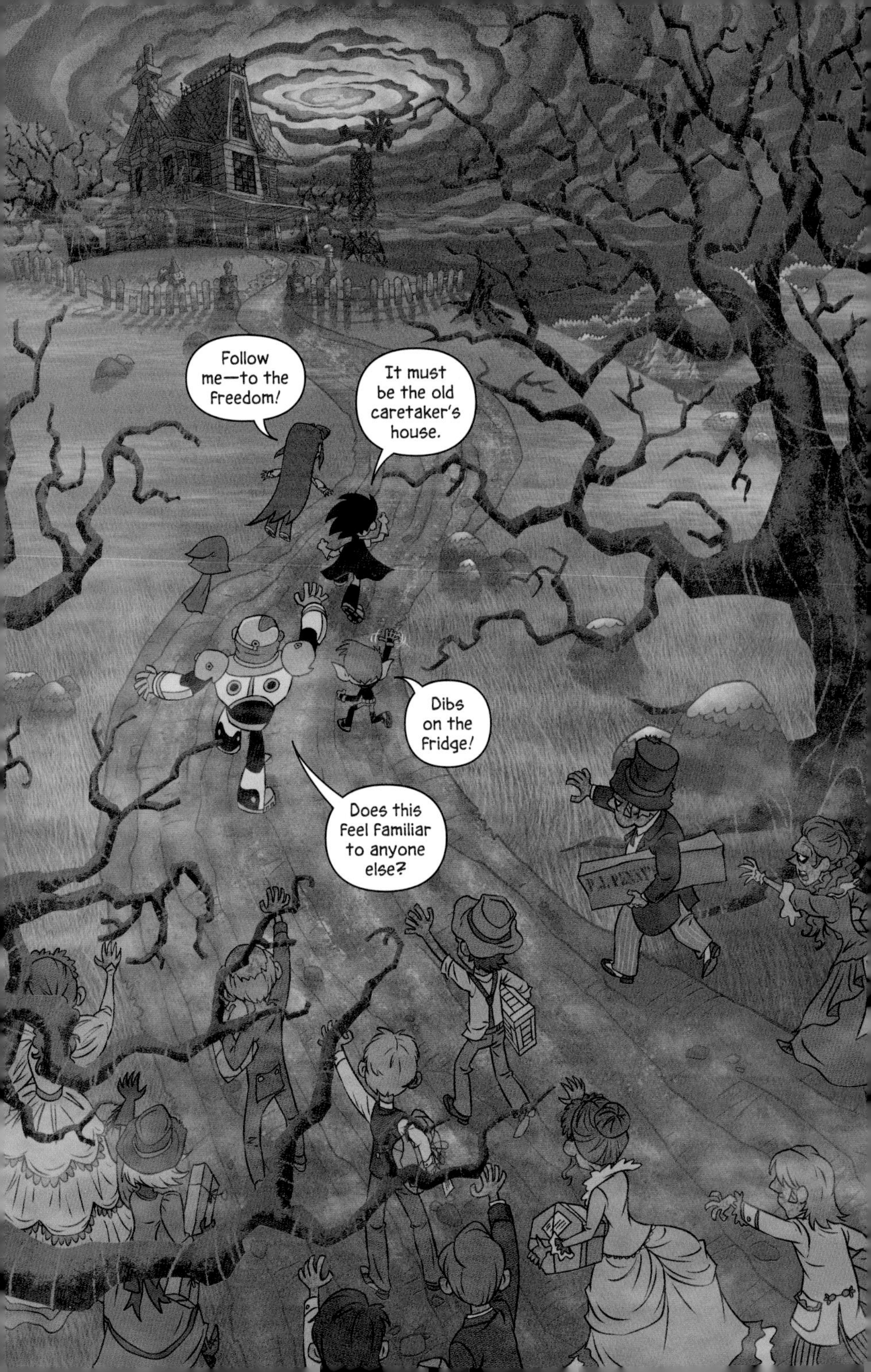
Follow me—to the freedom!
It must be the old caretaker's house.
Dibs on the fridge!
Does this feel familiar to anyone else?

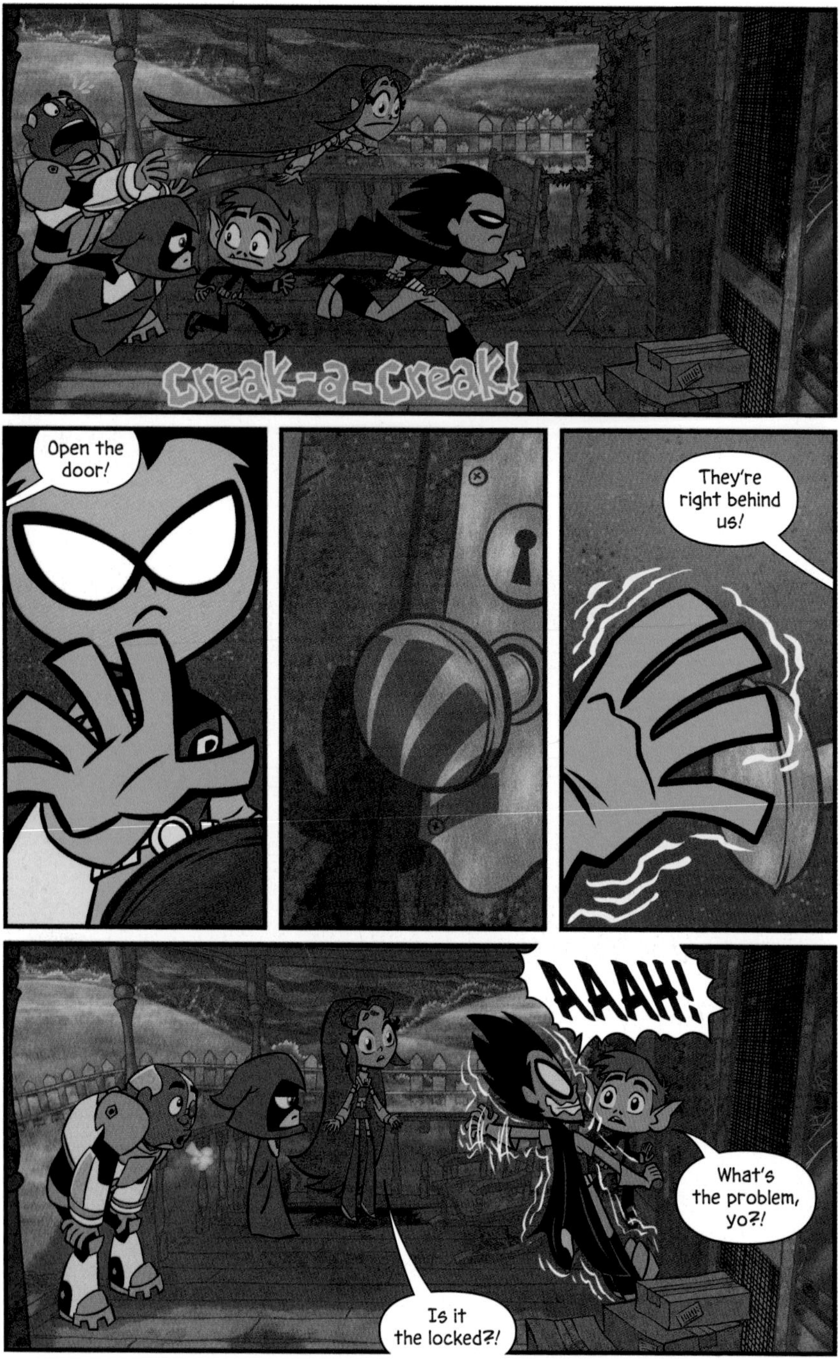
Creak-a-Creak!
Open the door!
They're right behind us!
AAAH!
What's the problem, yo?!
Is it the locked?!

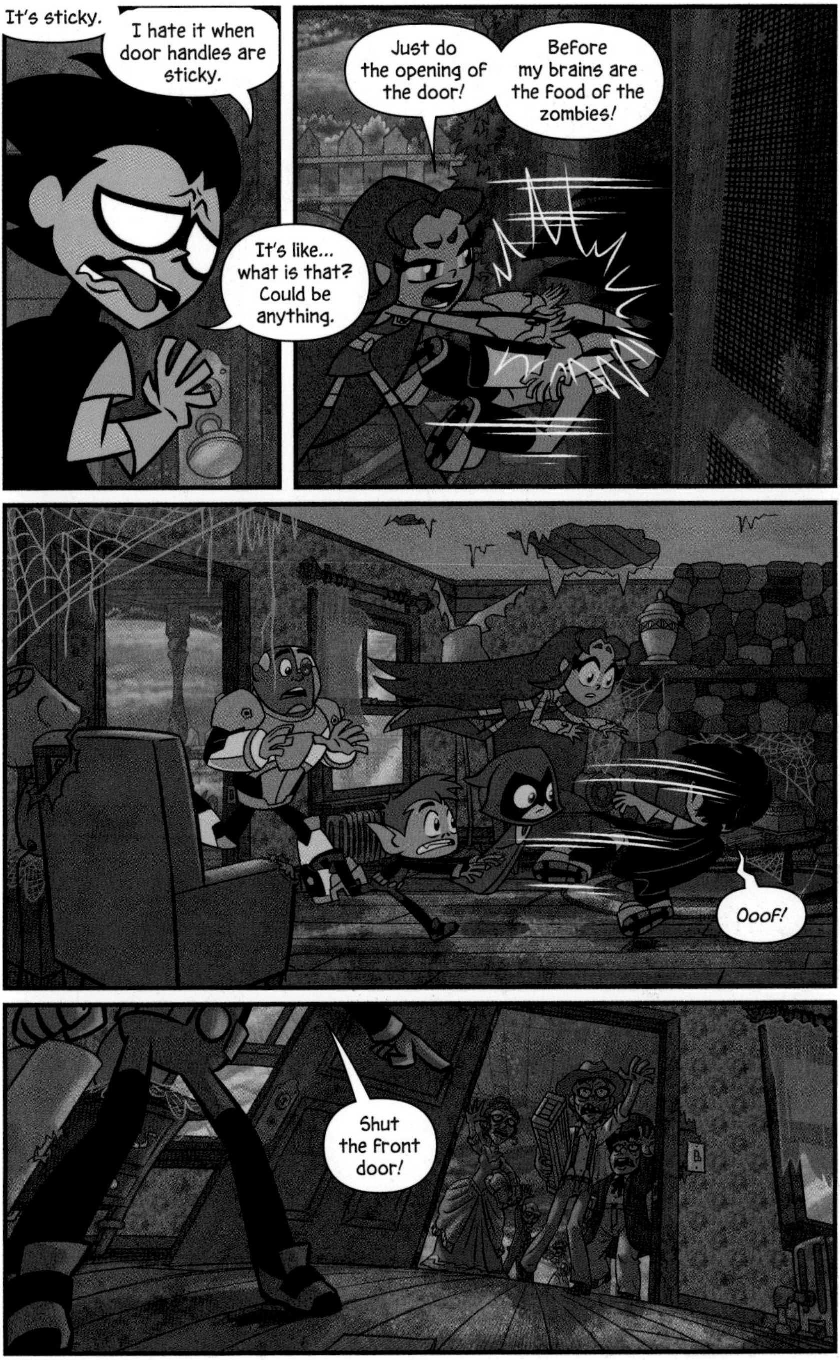
It's sticky.
I hate it when door handles are sticky.
Just do the opening of the door!
Before my brains are the food of the zombies!
It's like... what is that? Could be anything.
Ooof!
Shut the front door!

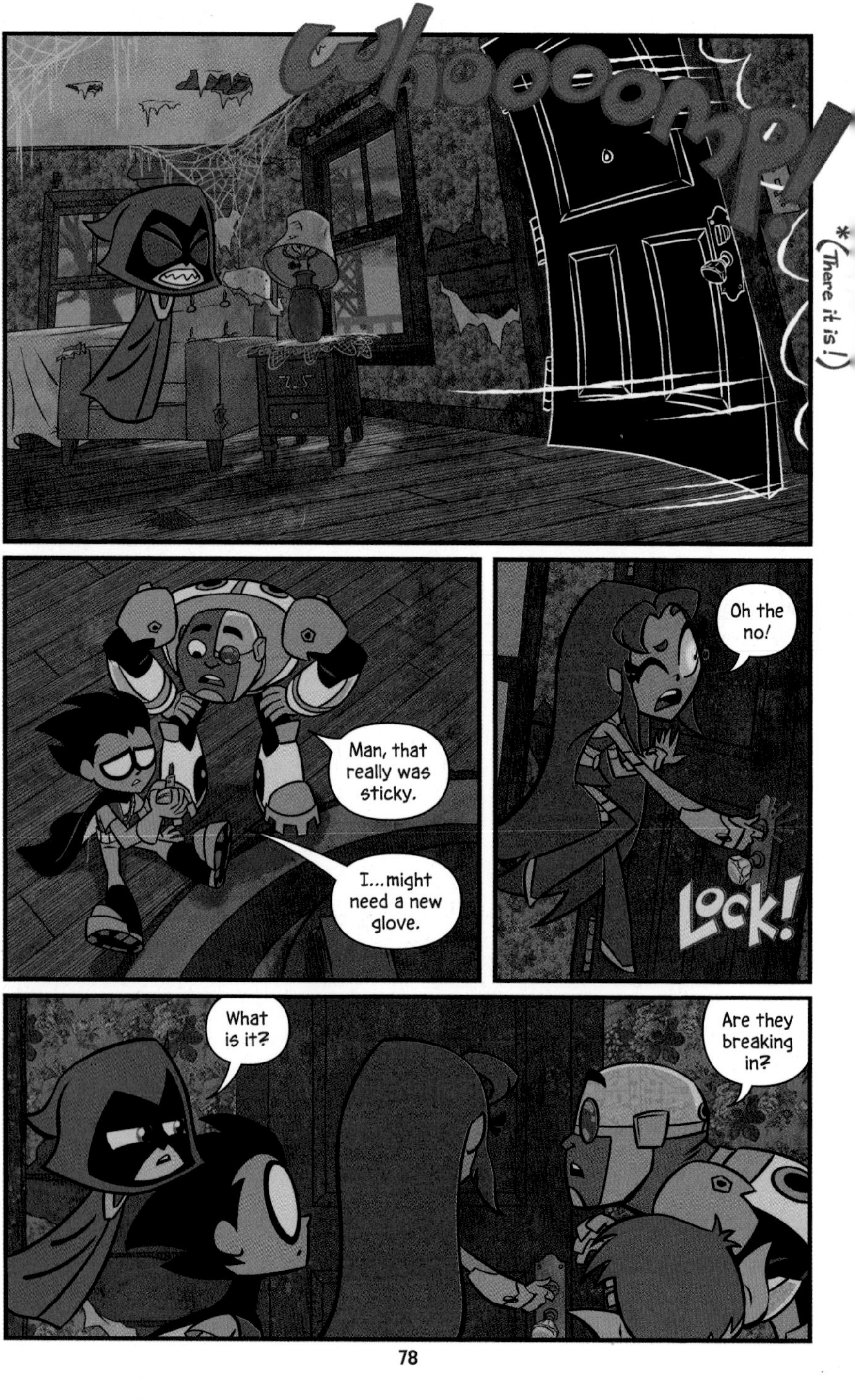
WHOOOOMP!*
*(There it is!)
Man, that really was sticky.
I...might need a new glove.
Oh the no!
LOCK!
What is it?
Are they breaking in?

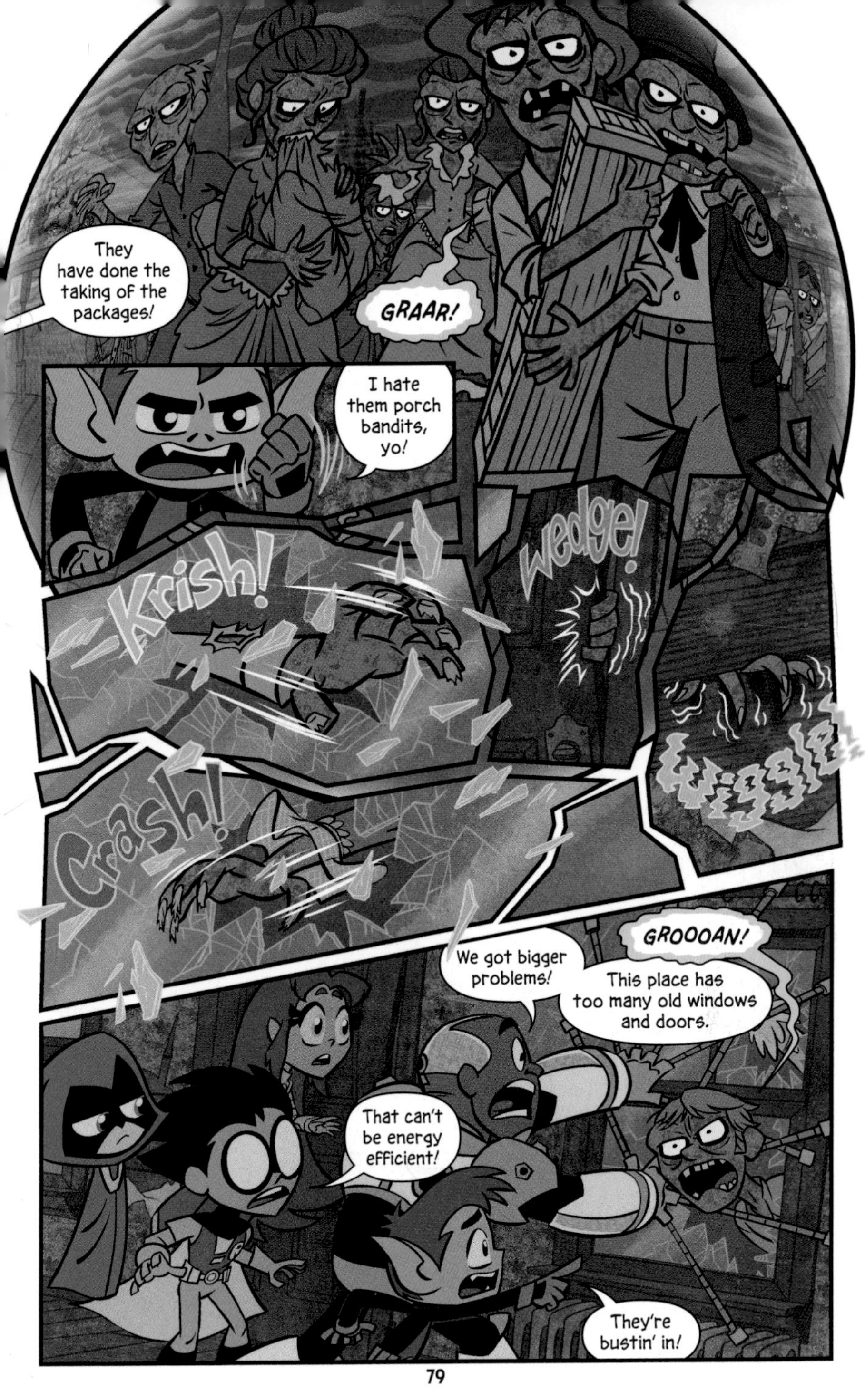

They have done the taking of the packages!
GRAAR!
I hate them porch bandits, yo!
Krish!
wedge!
Crash!
Wiggle!
We got bigger problems!
GROOOAN!
This place has too many old windows and doors.
That can't be energy efficient!
They're bustin' in!

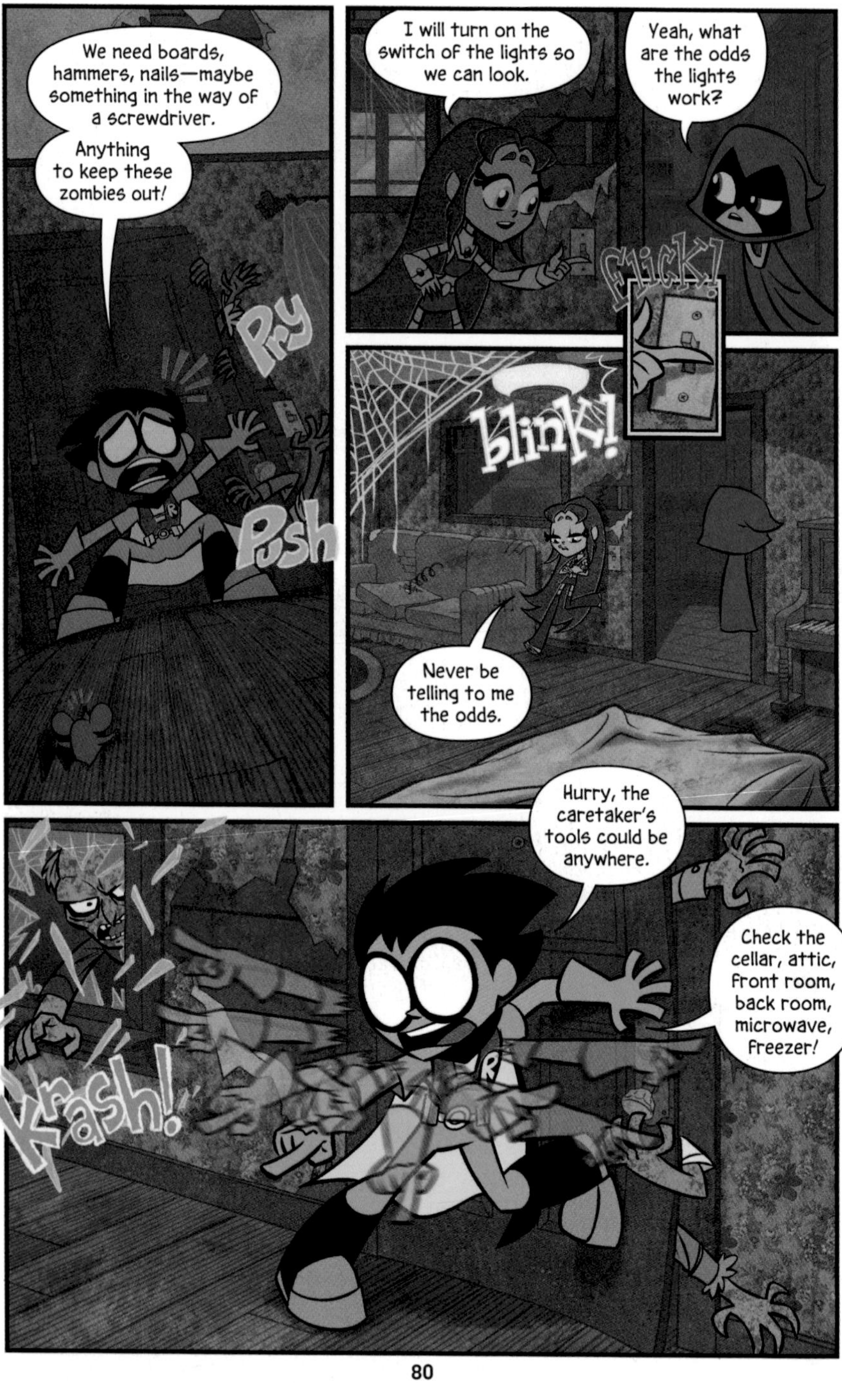
We need boards, hammers, nails—maybe something in the way of a screwdriver.
Anything to keep these zombies out!
Pry
Push
I will turn on the switch of the lights so we can look.
Yeah, what are the odds the lights work?
FLICK!
blink!
Never be telling to me the odds.
Hurry, the caretaker's tools could be anywhere.
Check the cellar, attic, front room, back room, microwave, freezer!
Krash!

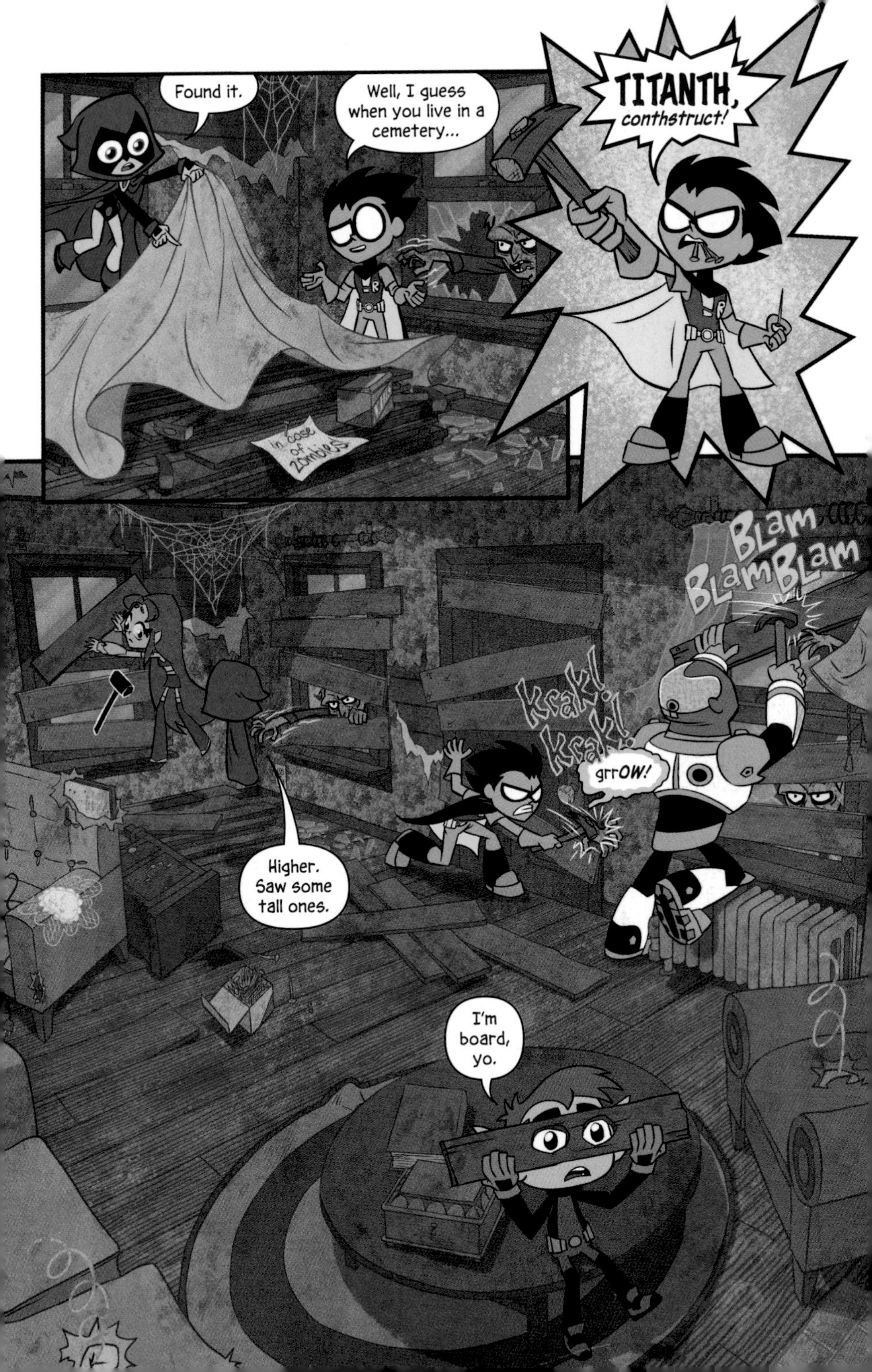
Found it.
Well, I guess when you live in a cemetery...
In case of zombies
TITANTH, conthstruct!
BLAM BLAM BLAM
KRAK! KRAK!
grrOW!
Higher. Saw some tall ones.
I'm board, yo.

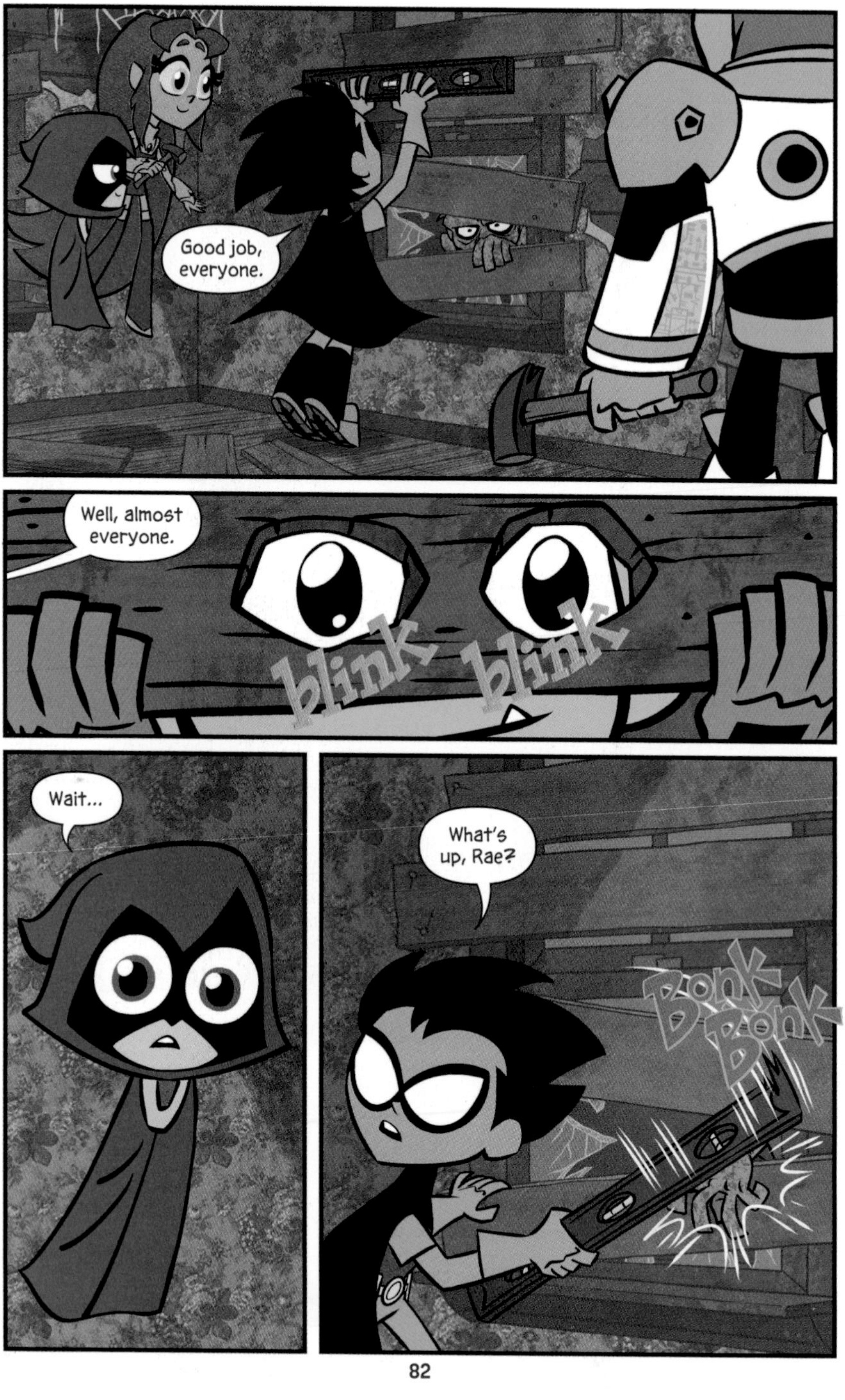
Good job, everyone.
Well, almost everyone.
blink blink
Wait...
What's up, Rae?
Bonk Bonk Bonk

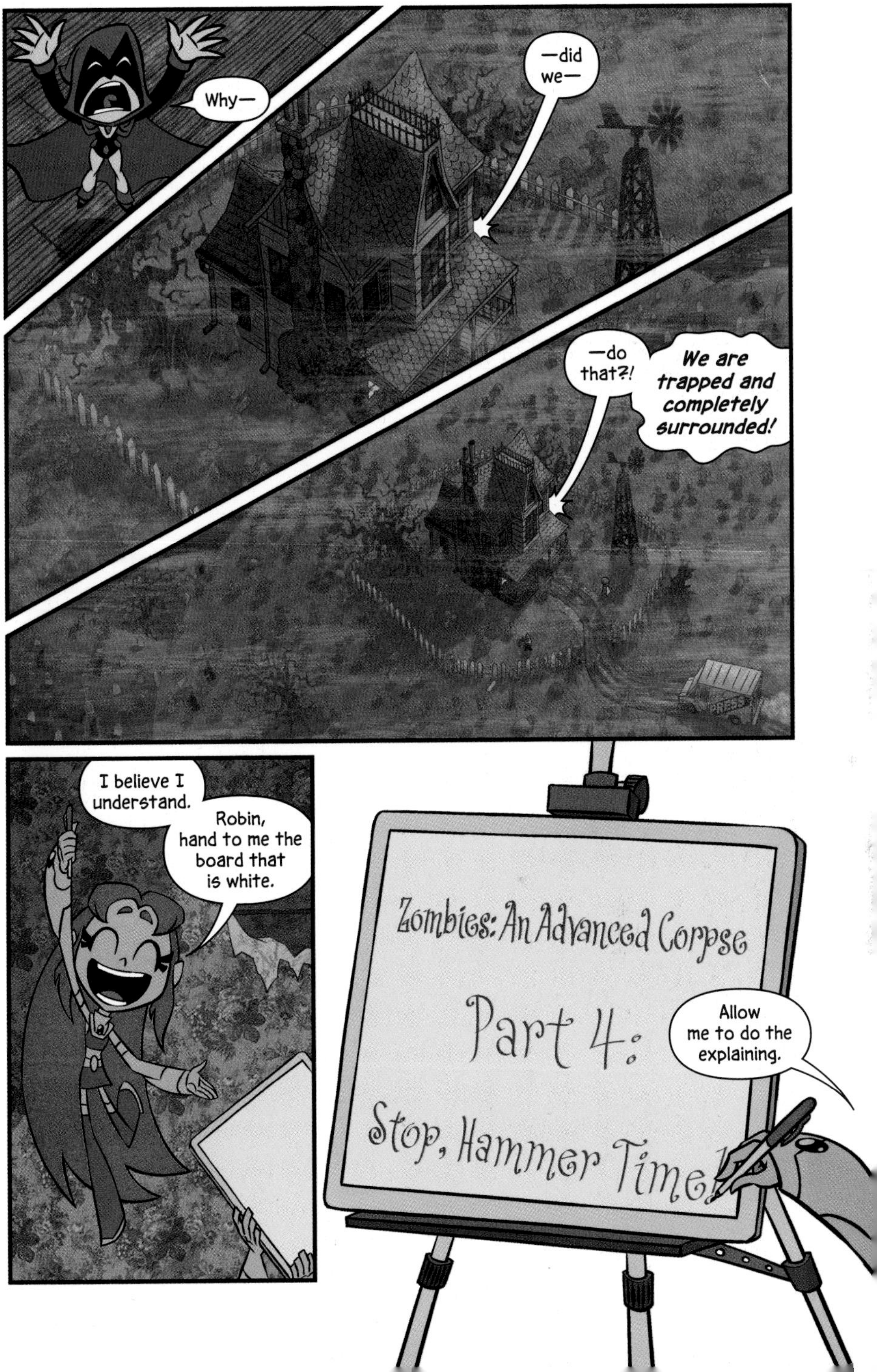
Why—
—did we—
—do that?!
We are trapped and completely surrounded!
PRESS
I believe I understand.
Robin, hand to me the board that is white.
Zombies: An Advanced Corpse
Part 4:
Stop, Hammer Time!
Allow me to do the explaining.

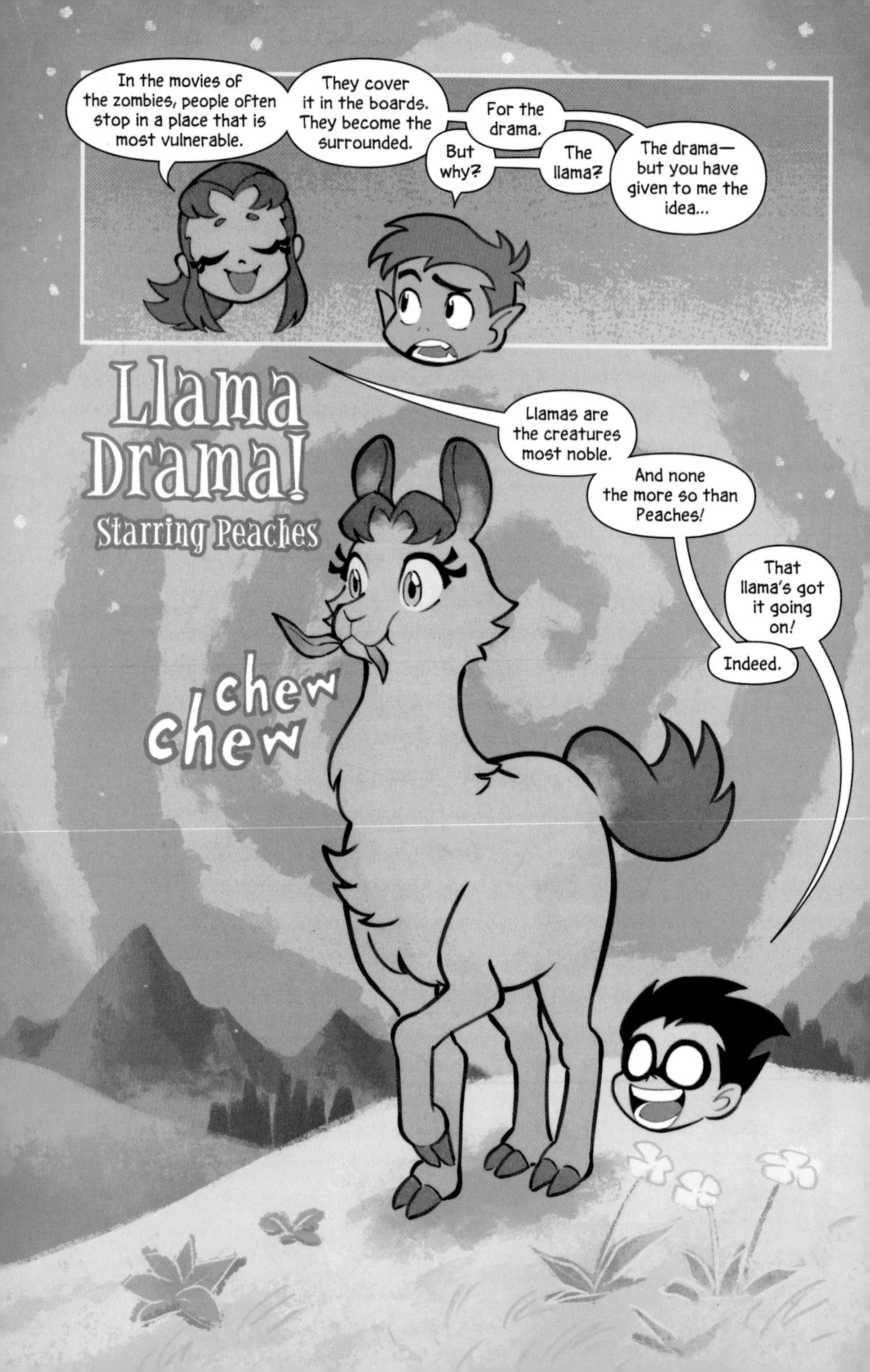
In the movies of the zombies, people often stop in a place that is most vulnerable.
They cover it in the boards. They become the surrounded.
For the drama.
But why?
The llama?
The drama— but you have given to me the idea...
Llama Drama!
Starring Peaches
Llamas are the creatures most noble.
And none the more so than Peaches!
That llama's got it going on!
Indeed.
chew chew

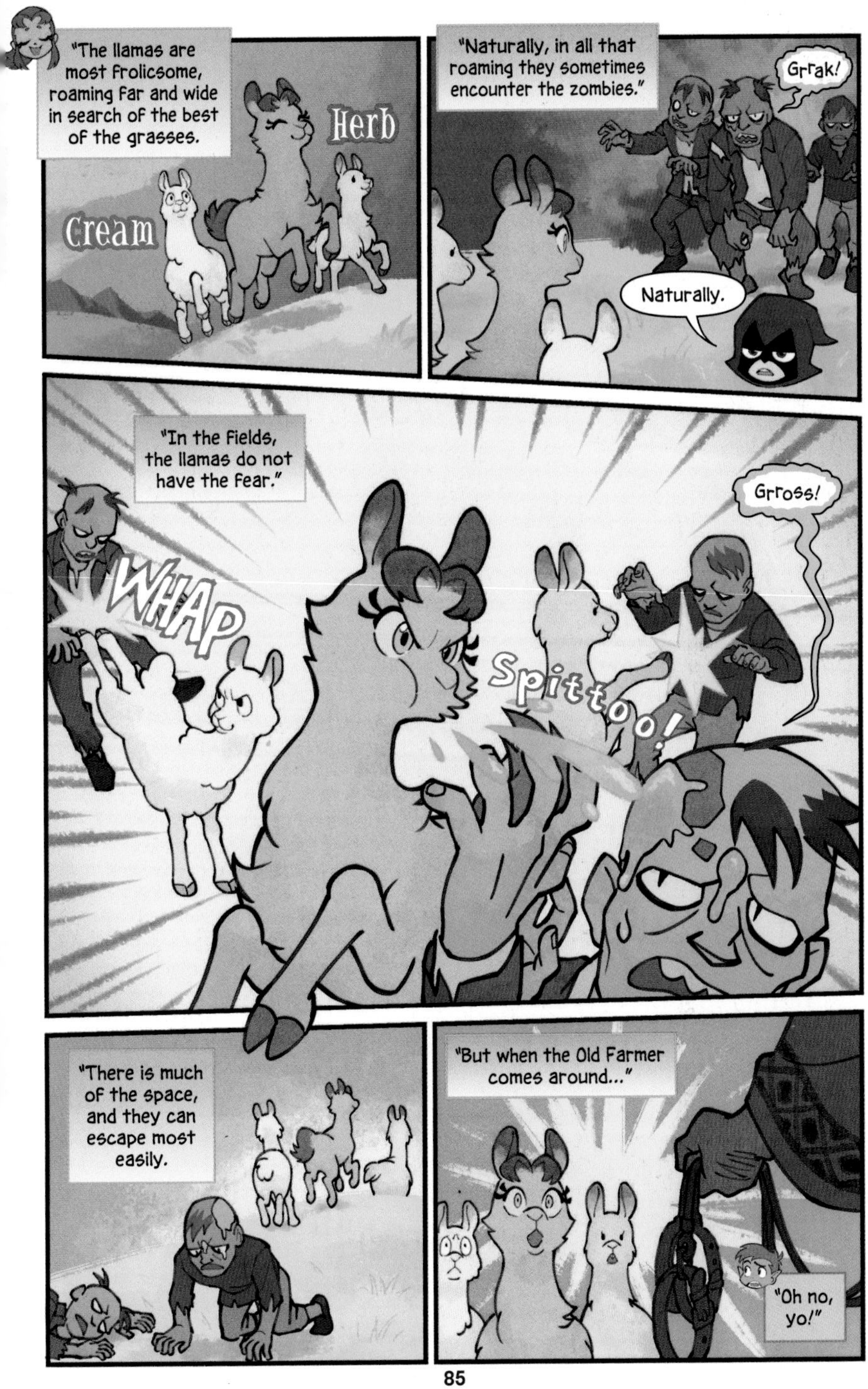
"The llamas are most frolicsome, roaming far and wide in search of the best of the grasses.
Herb
Cream
"Naturally, in all that roaming they sometimes encounter the zombies."
Grrak!
Naturally.
"In the Fields, the llamas do not have the fear."
Grross!
WHAP
Spittoo!
"There is much of the space, and they can escape most easily.
"But when the Old Farmer comes around..."
"Oh no, yo!"

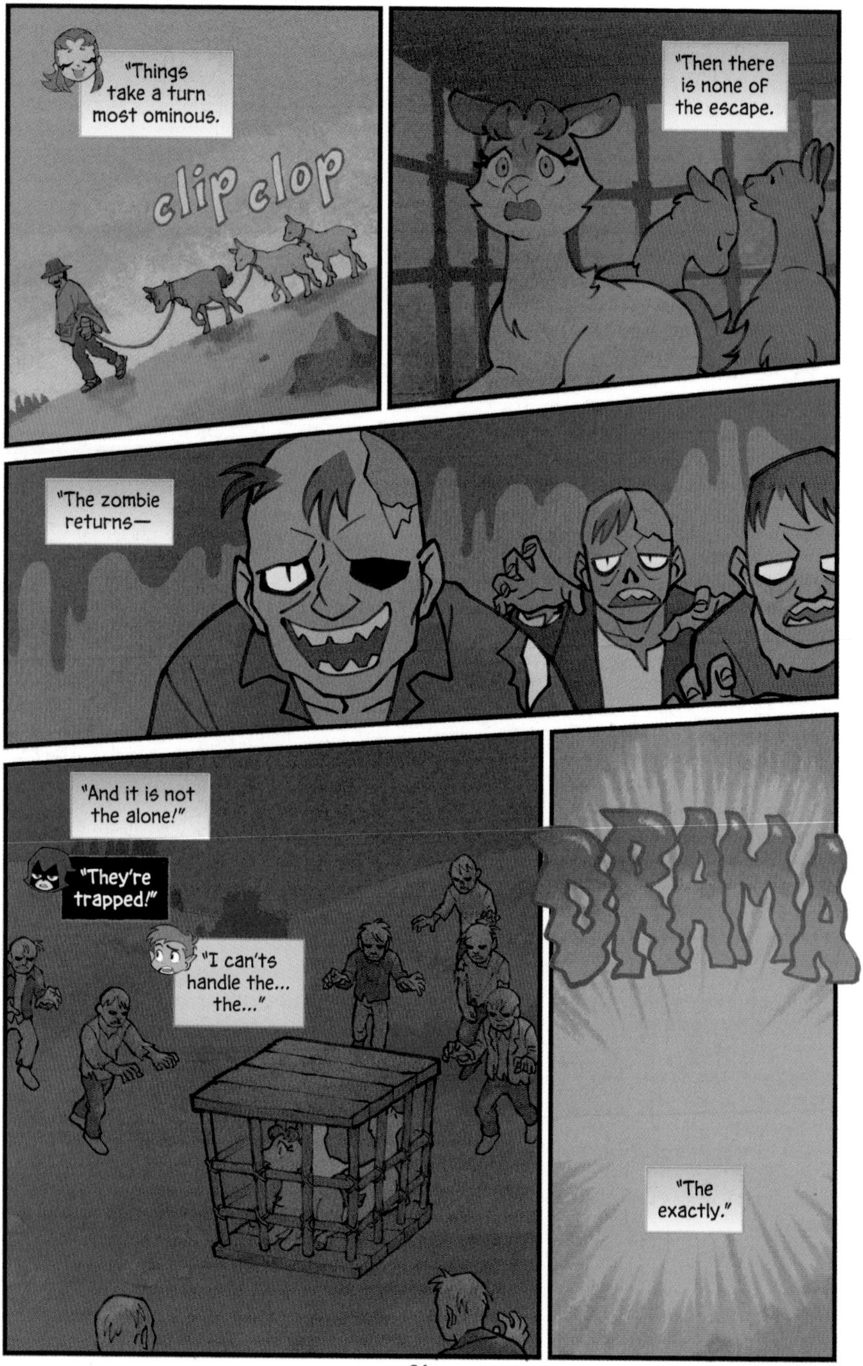
"Things take a turn most ominous.
clip clop
"Then there is none of the escape.
"The zombie returns—
"And it is not the alone!"
"They're trapped!"
"I can'ts handle the... the..."
DRAMA
"The exactly."

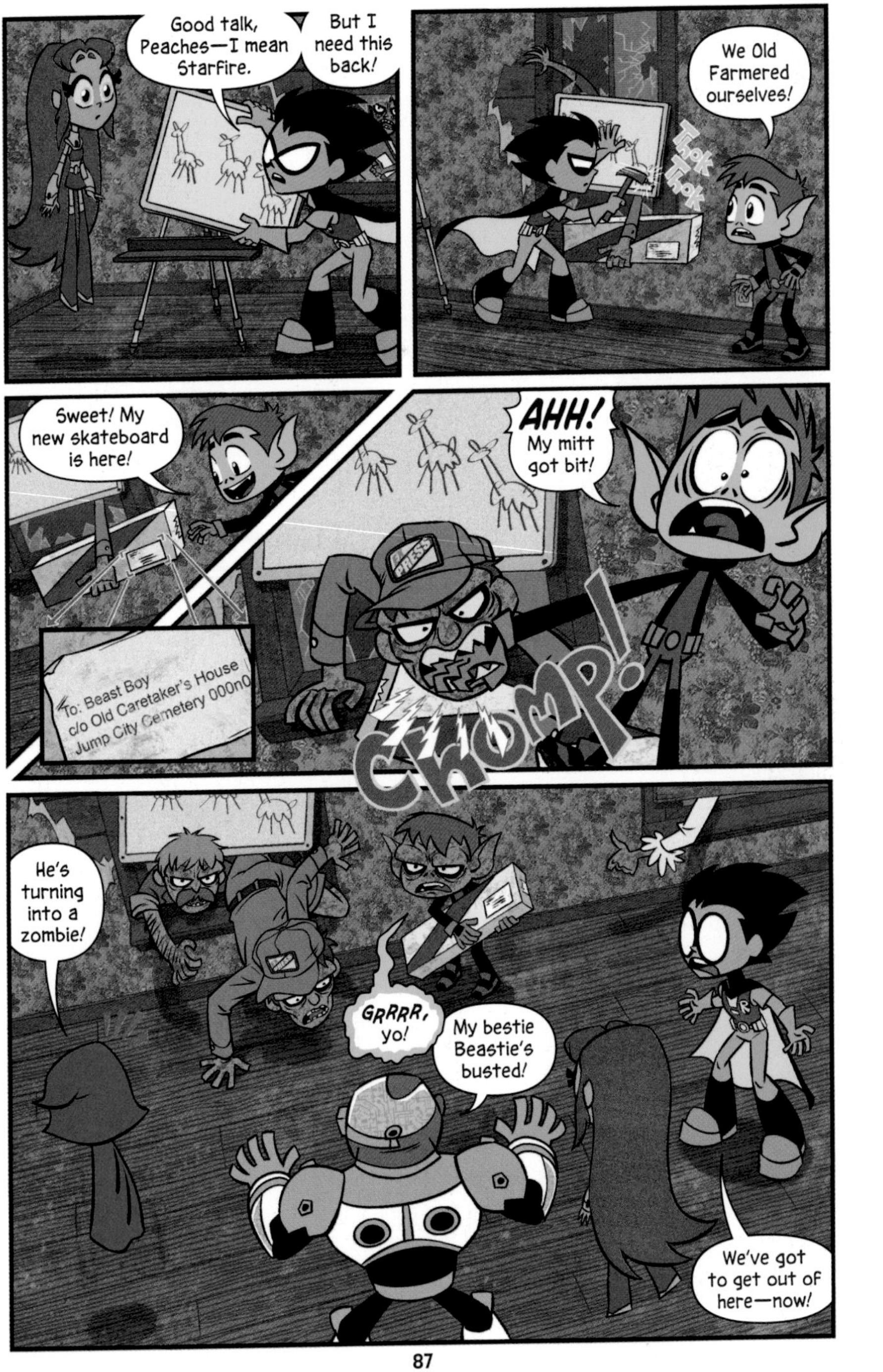

Good talk, Peaches—I mean Starfire.
But I need this back!
THOK THOK
We Old Farmered ourselves!
Sweet! My new skateboard is here!
To: Beast Boy
c/o Old Caretaker's House
Jump City Cemetery 000n0
AHH! My mitt got bit!
PRESS
CHOMP!
He's turning into a zombie!
GRRRR, yo!
My bestie Beastie's busted!
We've got to get out of here—now!

Chapter Six

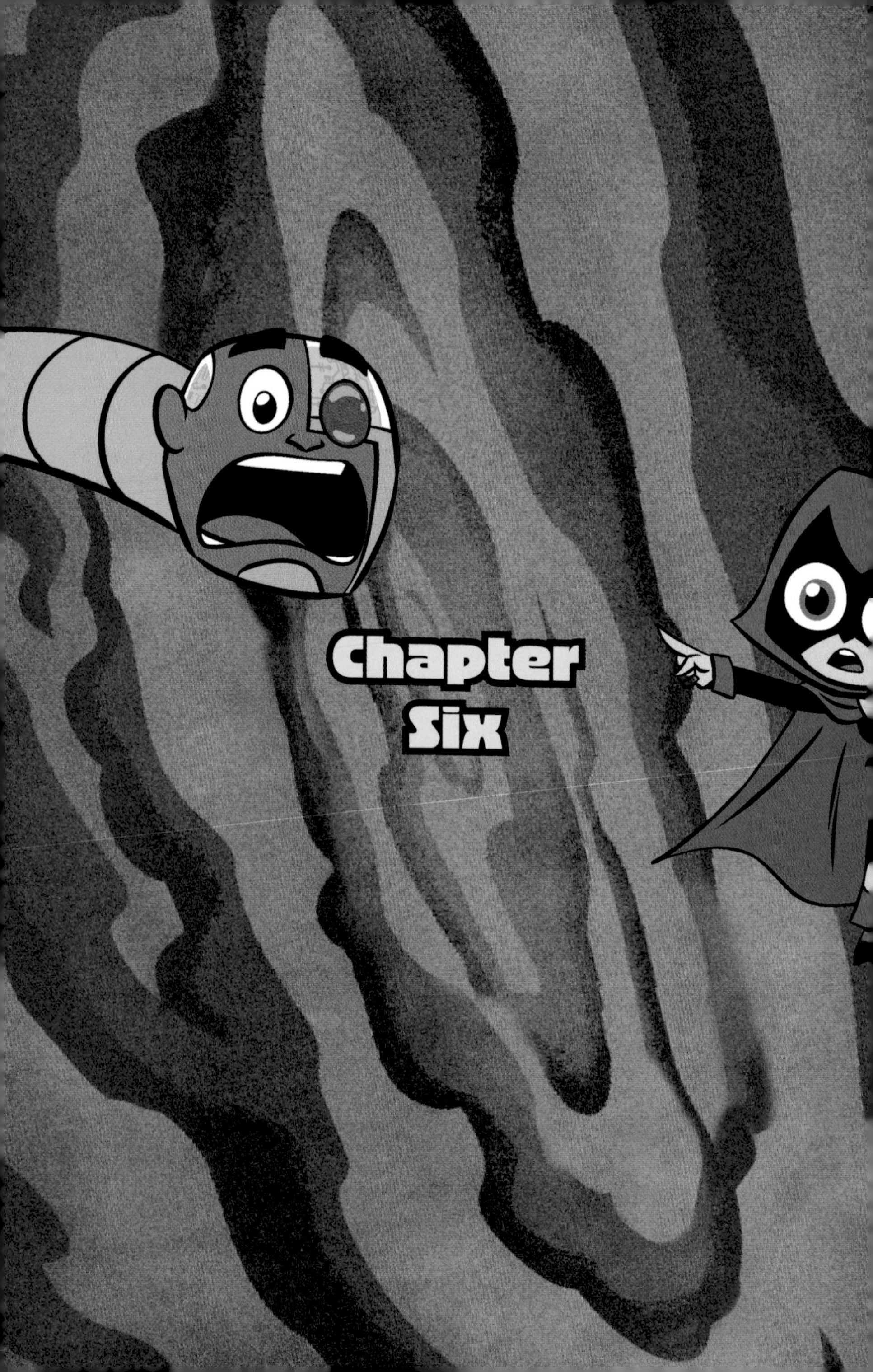

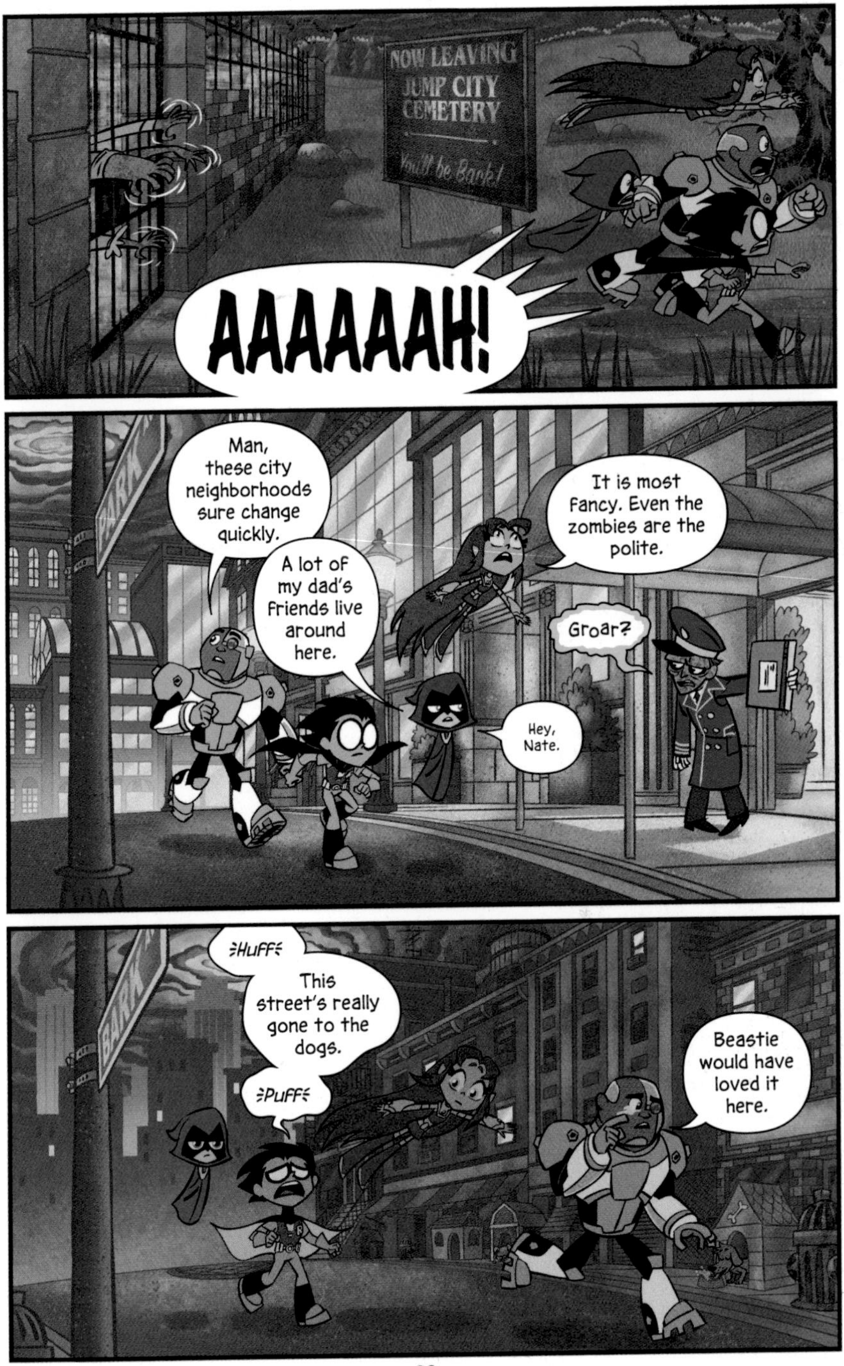
NOW LEAVING
JUMP CITY
CEMETERY
You'll be Back!
AAAAAAH!
PARK
Man, these city neighborhoods sure change quickly.
A lot of my dad's friends live around here.
It is most fancy. Even the zombies are the polite.
Groar?
Hey, Nate.
BARK
⚡Huff⚡
This street's really gone to the dogs.
⚡Puff⚡
Beastie would have loved it here.

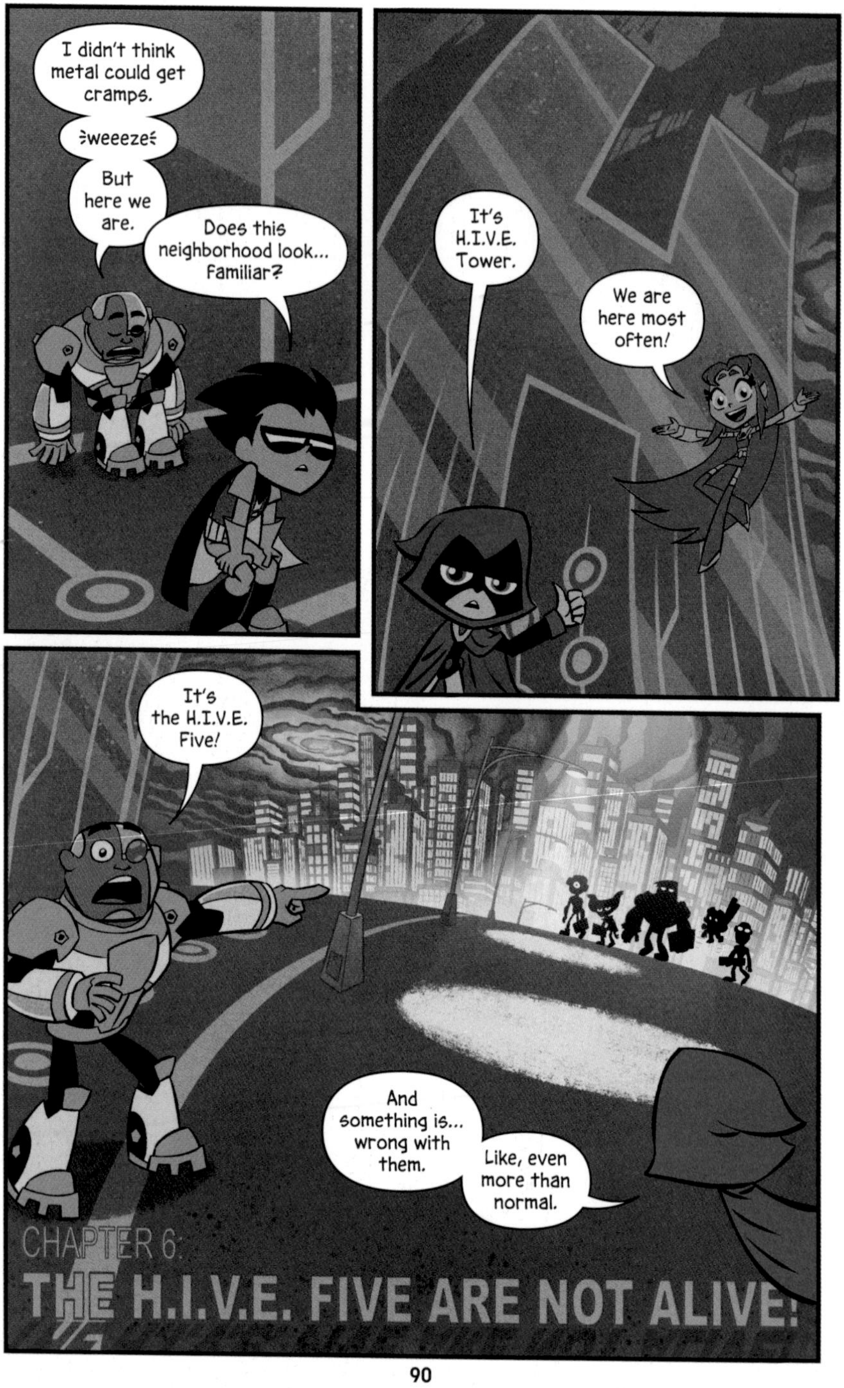
I didn't think metal could get cramps.
⋛weeeze⋚
But here we are.
Does this neighborhood look... familiar?
It's H.I.V.E. Tower.
We are here most often!
It's the H.I.V.E. Five!
And something is... wrong with them.
Like, even more than normal.
CHAPTER 6:
THE H.I.V.E. FIVE ARE NOT ALIVE!

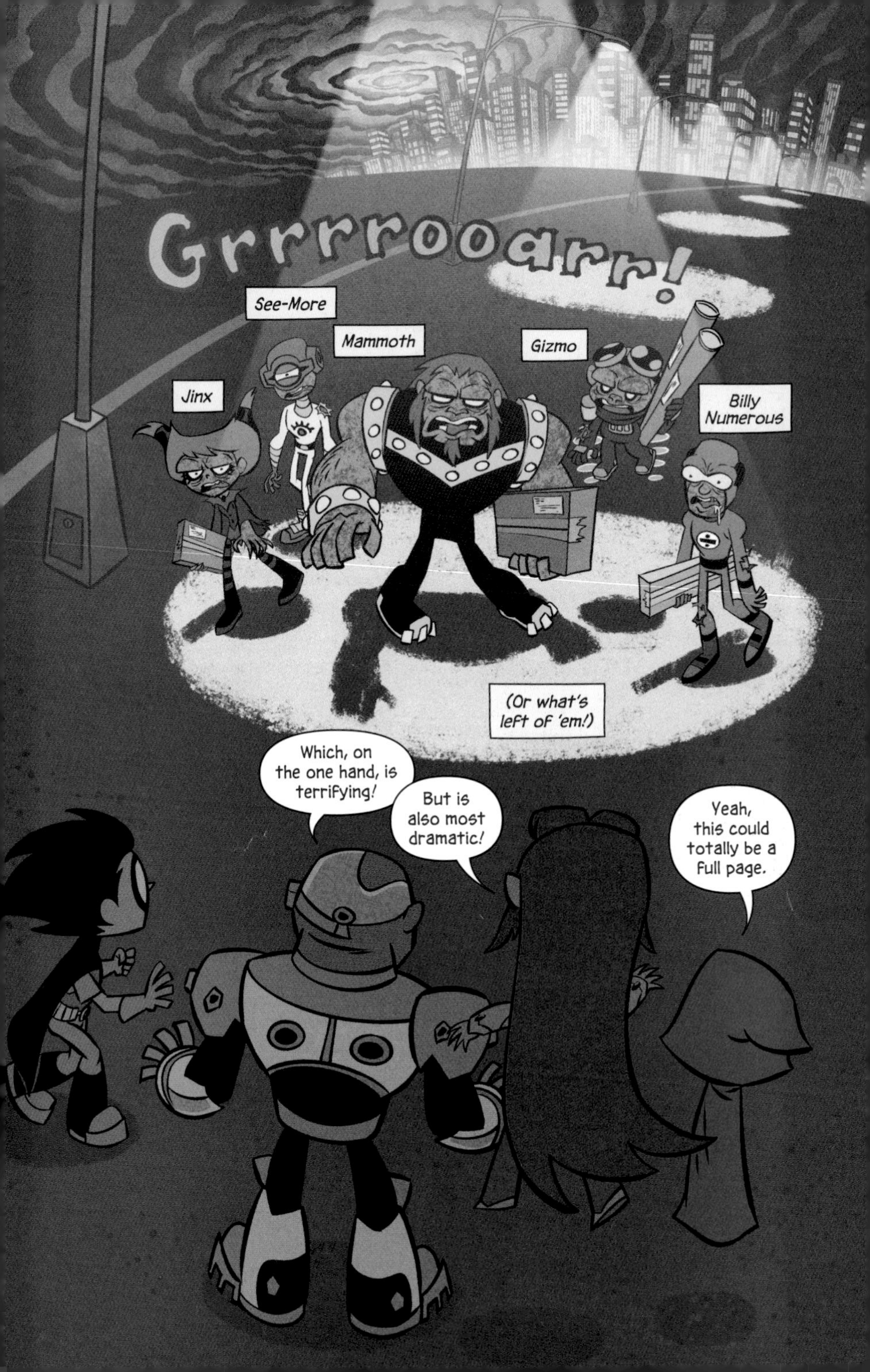
Grrrrooarrr!
See-More
Mammoth
Gizmo
Jinx
Billy Numerous
(Or what's left of 'em!)
Which, on the one hand, is terrifying!
But is also most dramatic!
Yeah, this could totally be a full page.

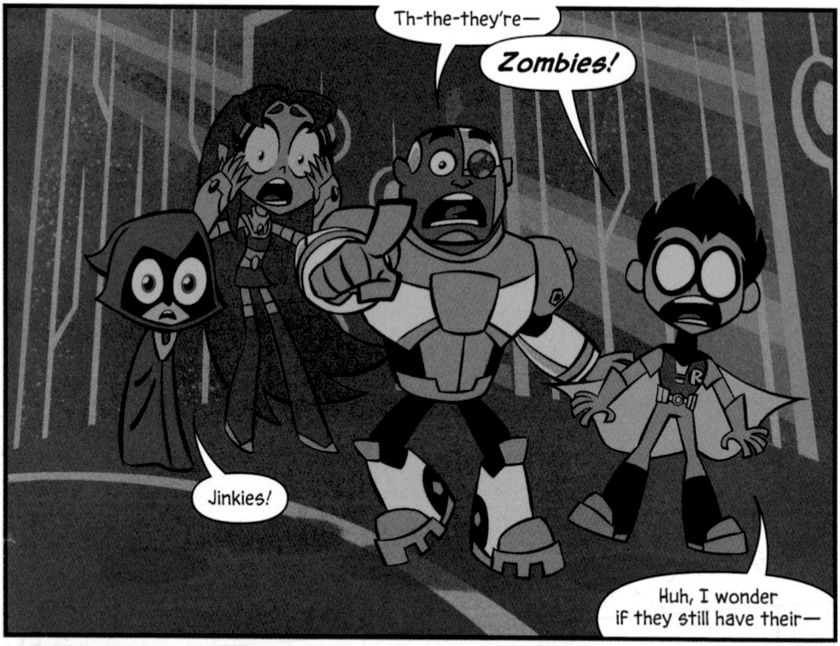
Th-the-they're—
Zombies!
Jinkies!
Huh, I wonder if they still have their—

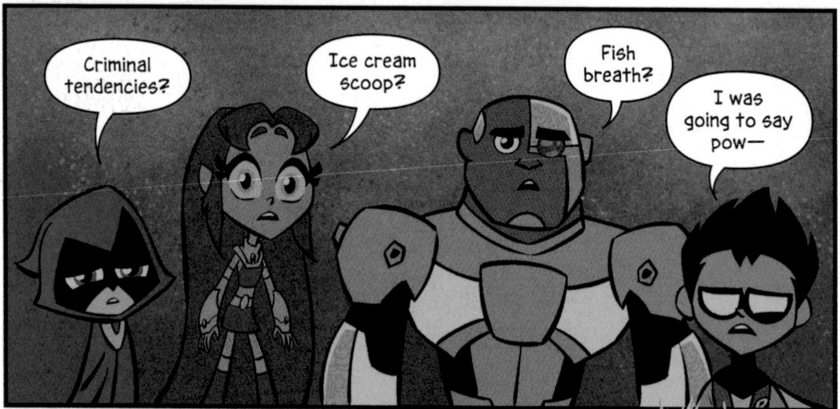
Criminal tendencies?
Ice cream scoop?
Fish breath?
I was going to say pow—

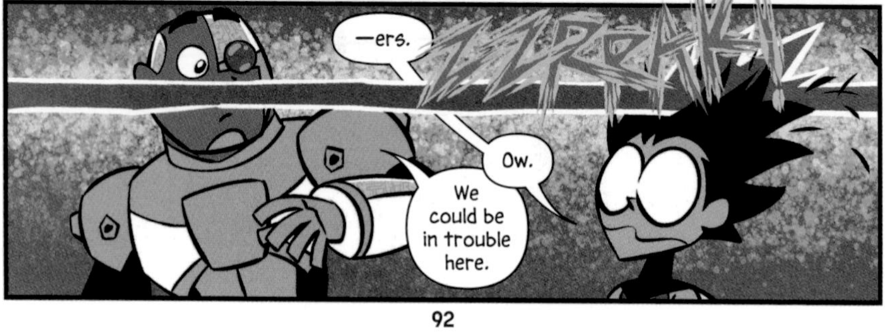
—ers.
Ow.
We could be in trouble here.

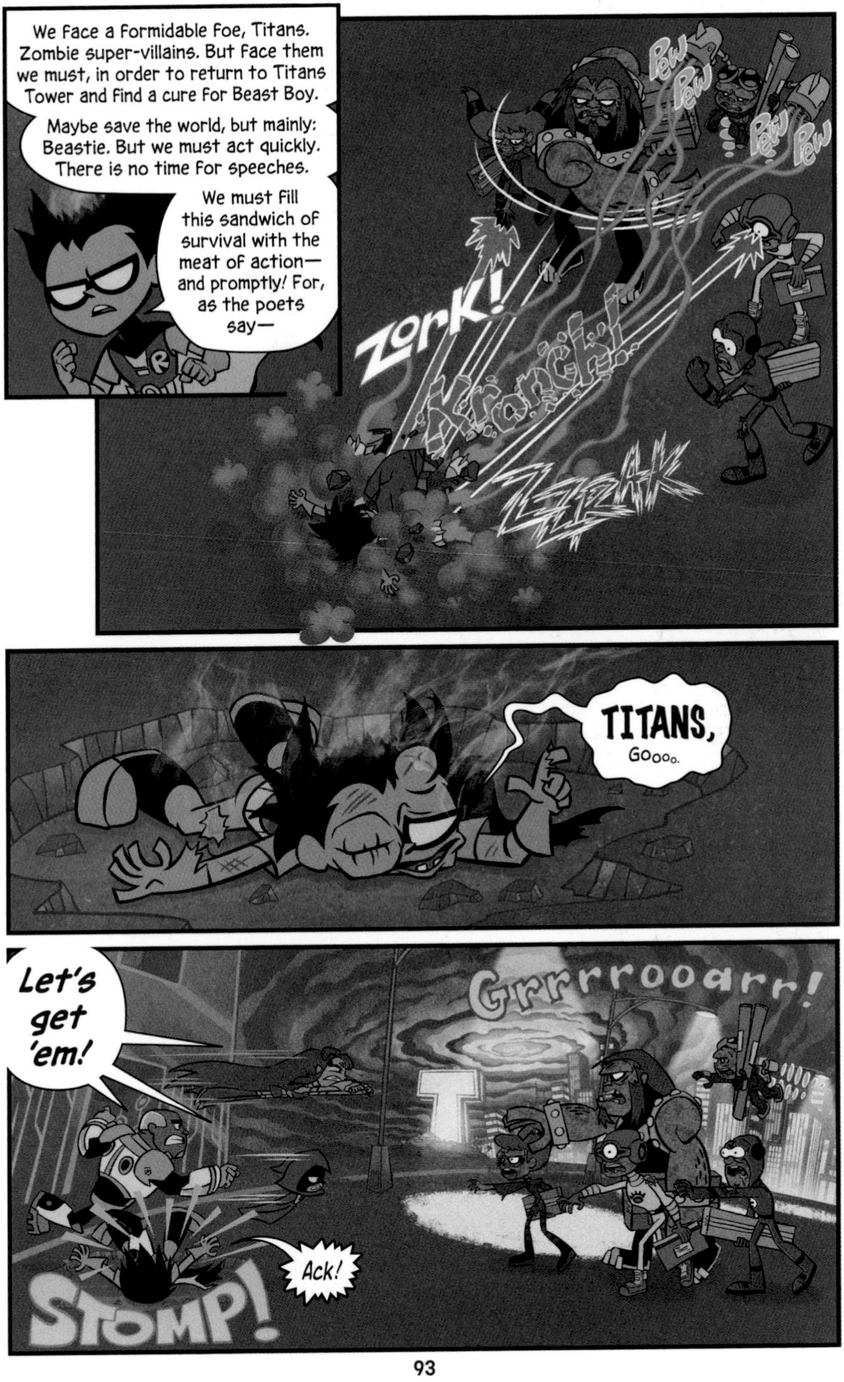
We face a formidable foe, Titans. Zombie super-villains. But face them we must, in order to return to Titans Tower and find a cure for Beast Boy.
Maybe save the world, but mainly: Beastie. But we must act quickly. There is no time for speeches.
We must fill this sandwich of survival with the meat of action—and promptly! For, as the poets say—
Pew
Pew
Pew
Pew
ZORK!
KRANCH!
ZZRAK
TITANS, Goooo.
Let's get 'em!
Grrrrooarr!
Ack!
STOMP!

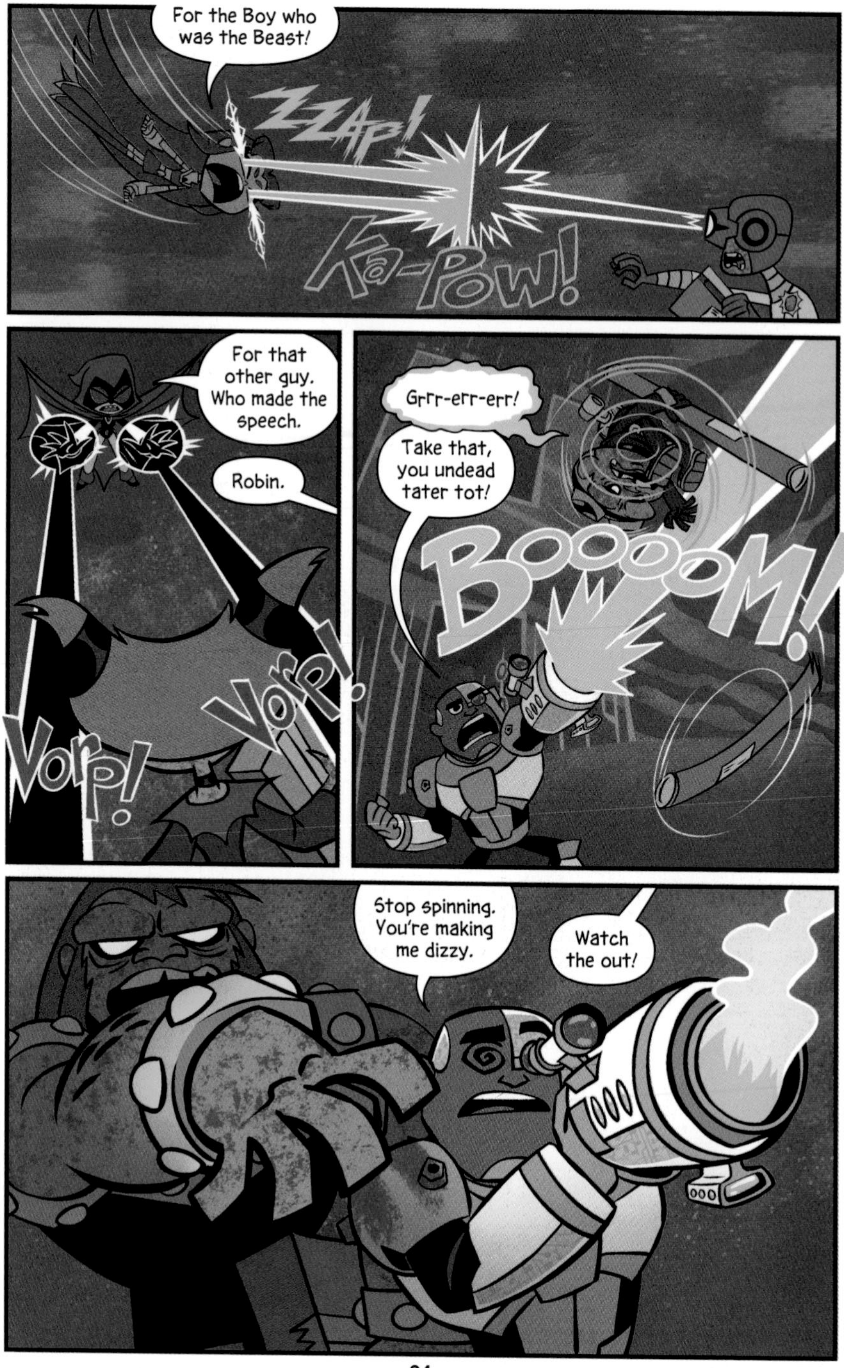
For the Boy who was the Beast!
ZZAP!
Ka-POW!
For that other guy. Who made the speech.
Robin.
Vorp!
Vorp!
Grrr-err-err!
Take that, you undead tater tot!
BOOOOOM!
Stop spinning. You're making me dizzy.
Watch the out!

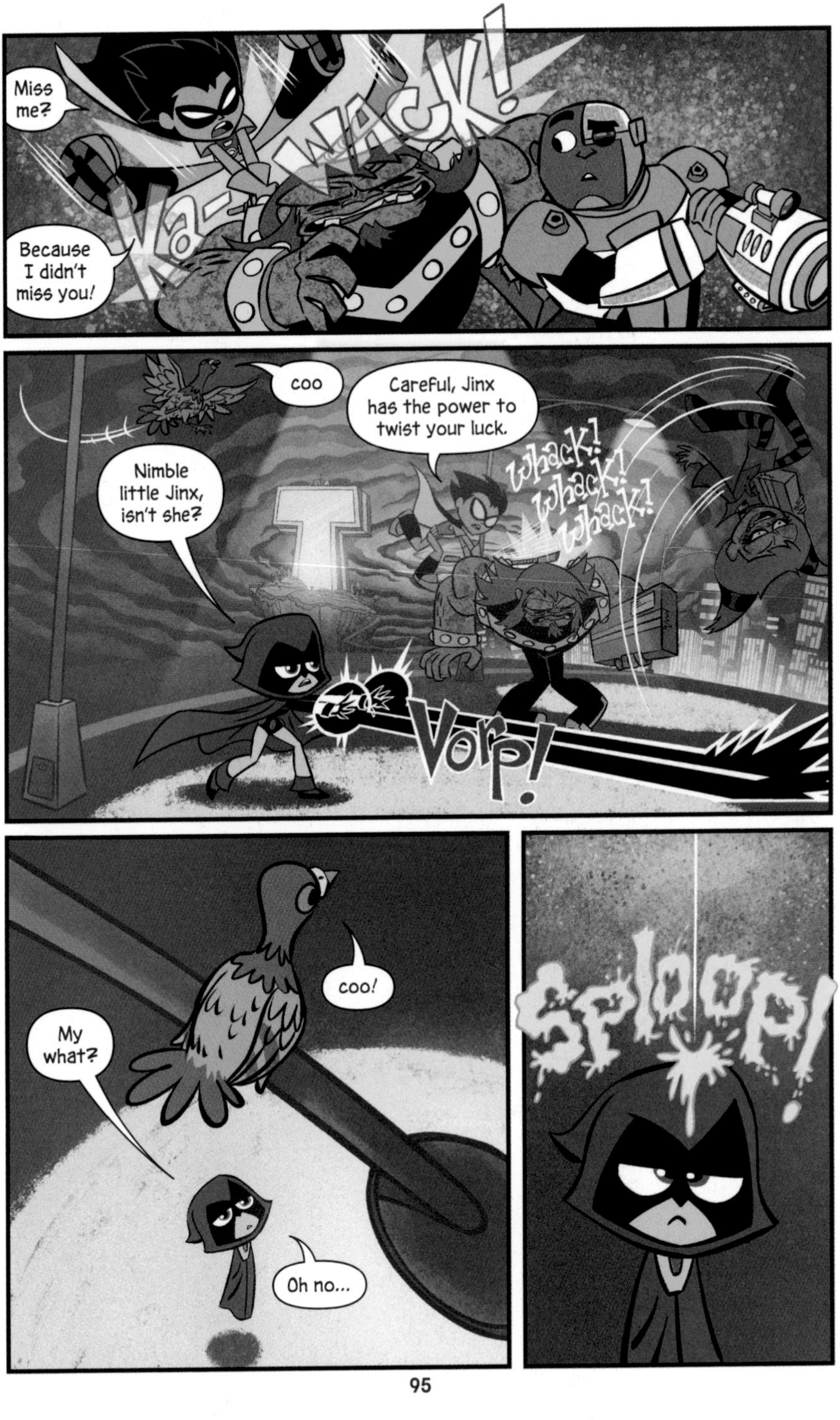
Miss me?
KA-WACK!
Because I didn't miss you!
coo
Careful, Jinx has the power to twist your luck.
Nimble little Jinx, isn't she?
WHACK! WHACK! WHACK!
VORP!
coo!
My what?
Oh no...
SPLOOP!

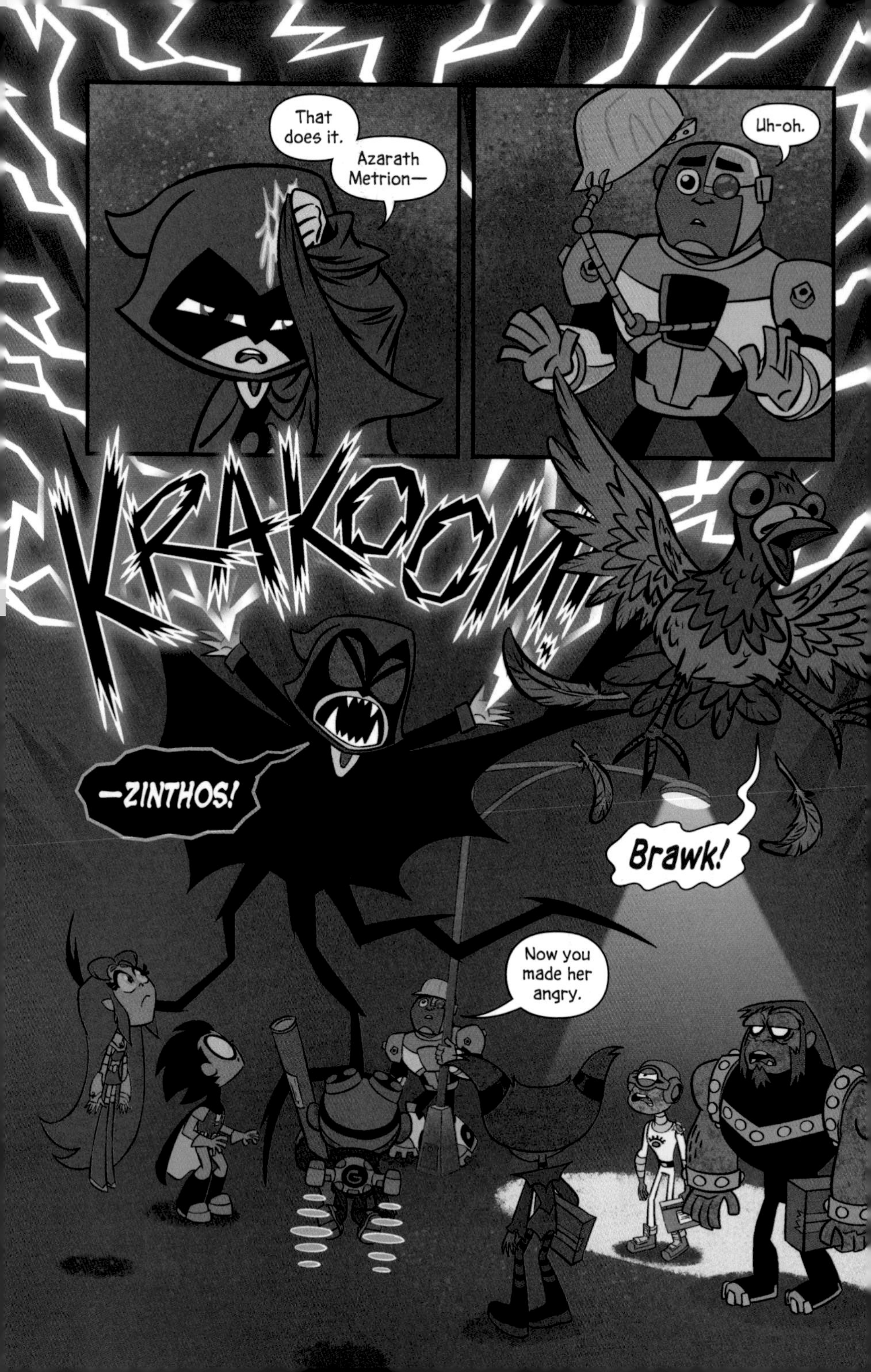
That does it.
Azarath Metrion—
Uh-oh.
KRAKOOM!
—ZINTHOS!
Brawk!
Now you made her angry.

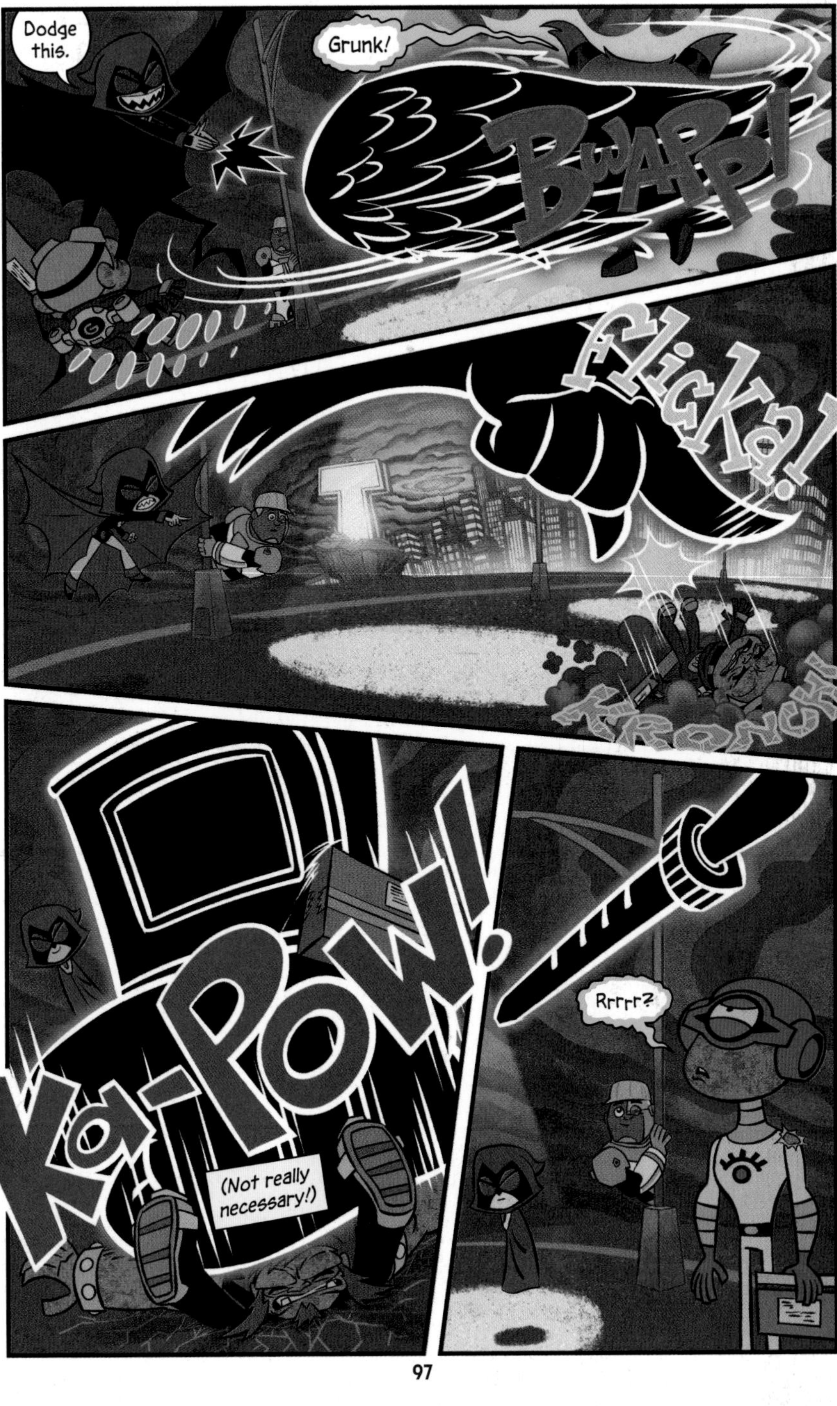
Dodge this.
Grunk!
BWAPP!
Flicka!
KRONCH!
Ka-POW!
(Not really necessary!)
Rrrrr?

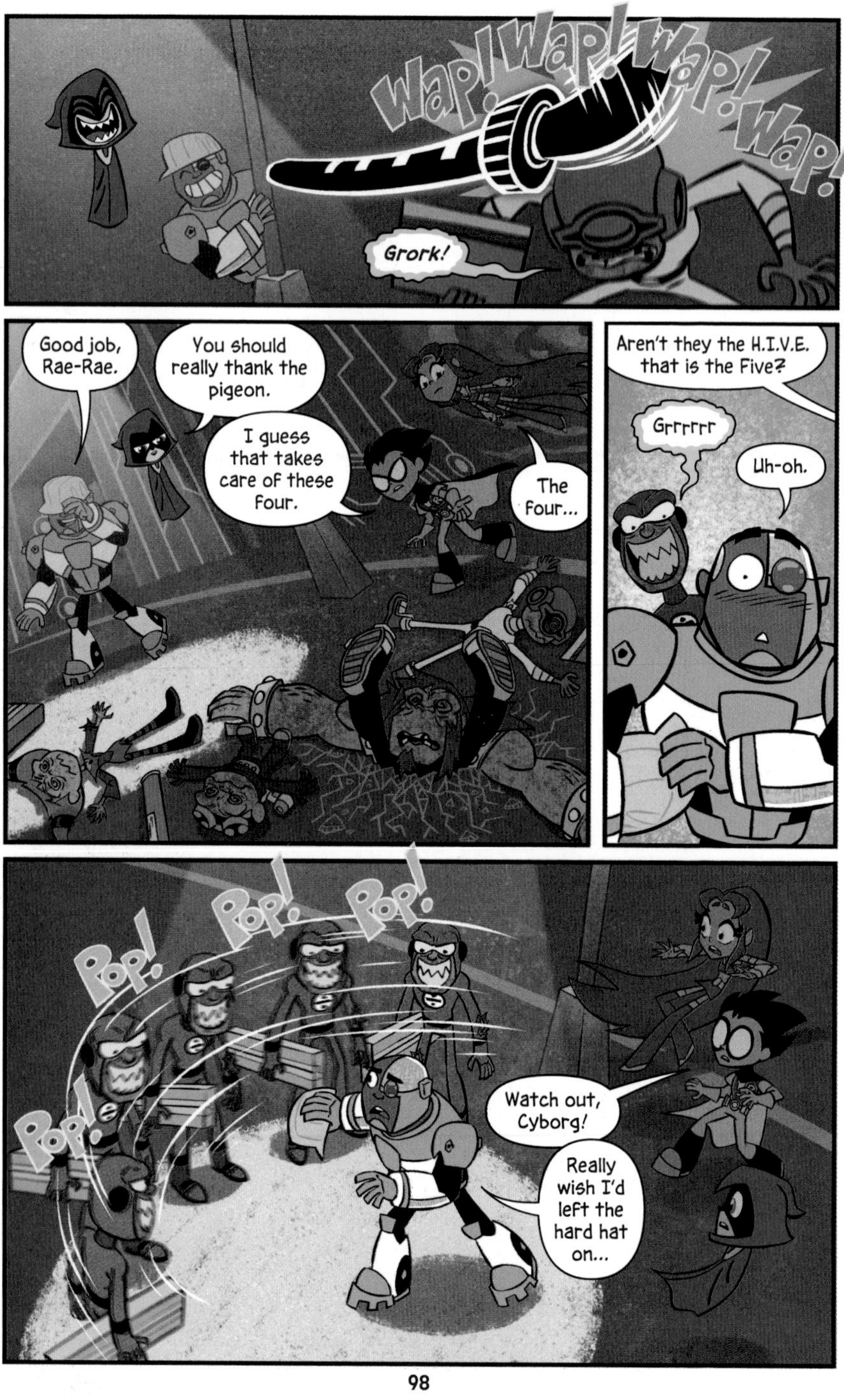
Wap! Wap! Wap! Wap!
Grork!
Good job, Rae-Rae.
You should really thank the pigeon.
I guess that takes care of these four.
The four...
Aren't they the H.I.V.E. that is the Five?
Grrrrrr
Uh-oh.
Pop! Pop! Pop! Pop!
Watch out, Cyborg!
Really wish I'd left the hard hat on...

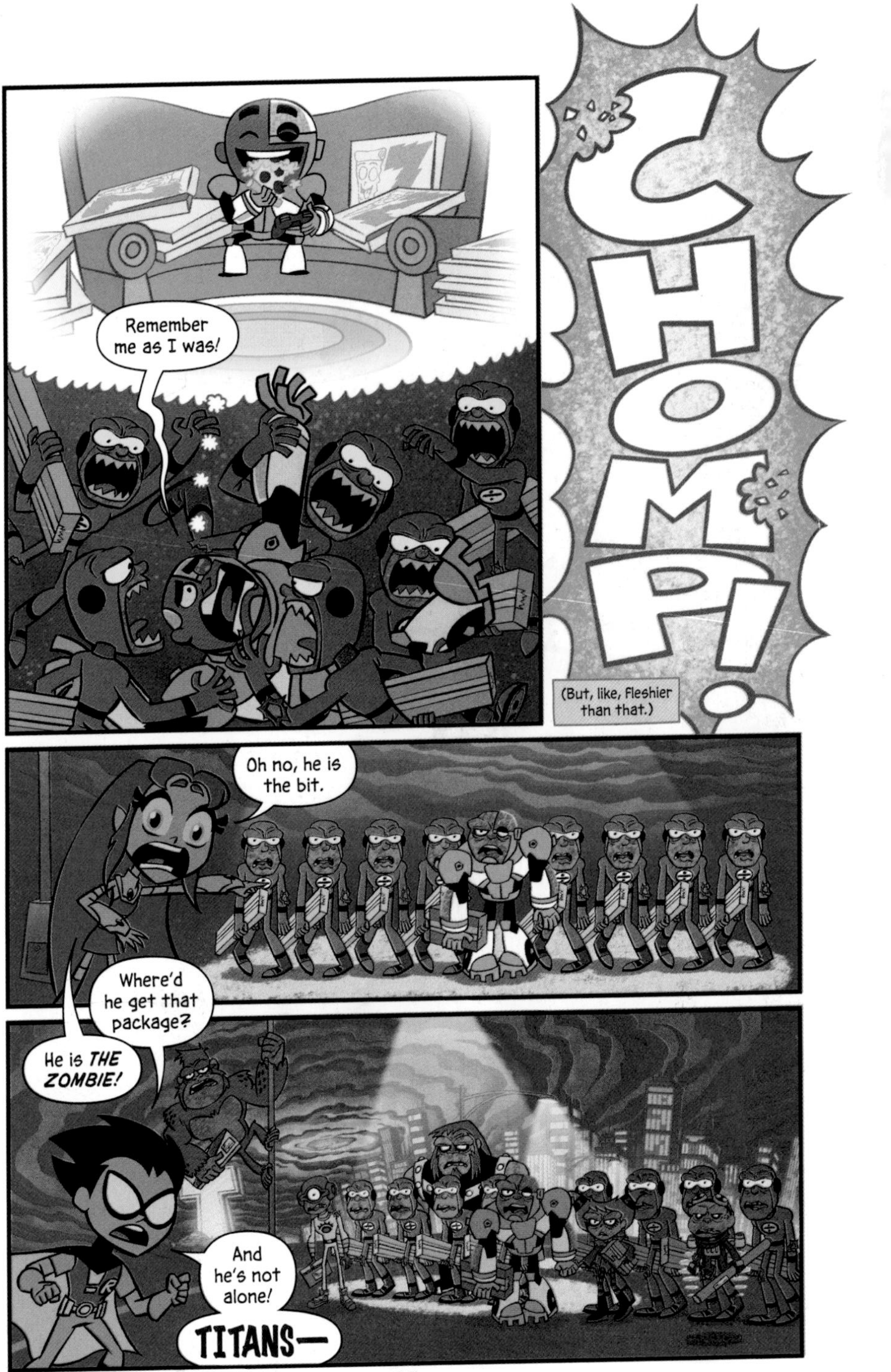
Remember me as I was!
CHOMP!
(But, like, Fleshier than that.)
Oh no, he is the bit.
Where'd he get that package?
He is THE ZOMBIE!
And he's not alone!
TITANS—

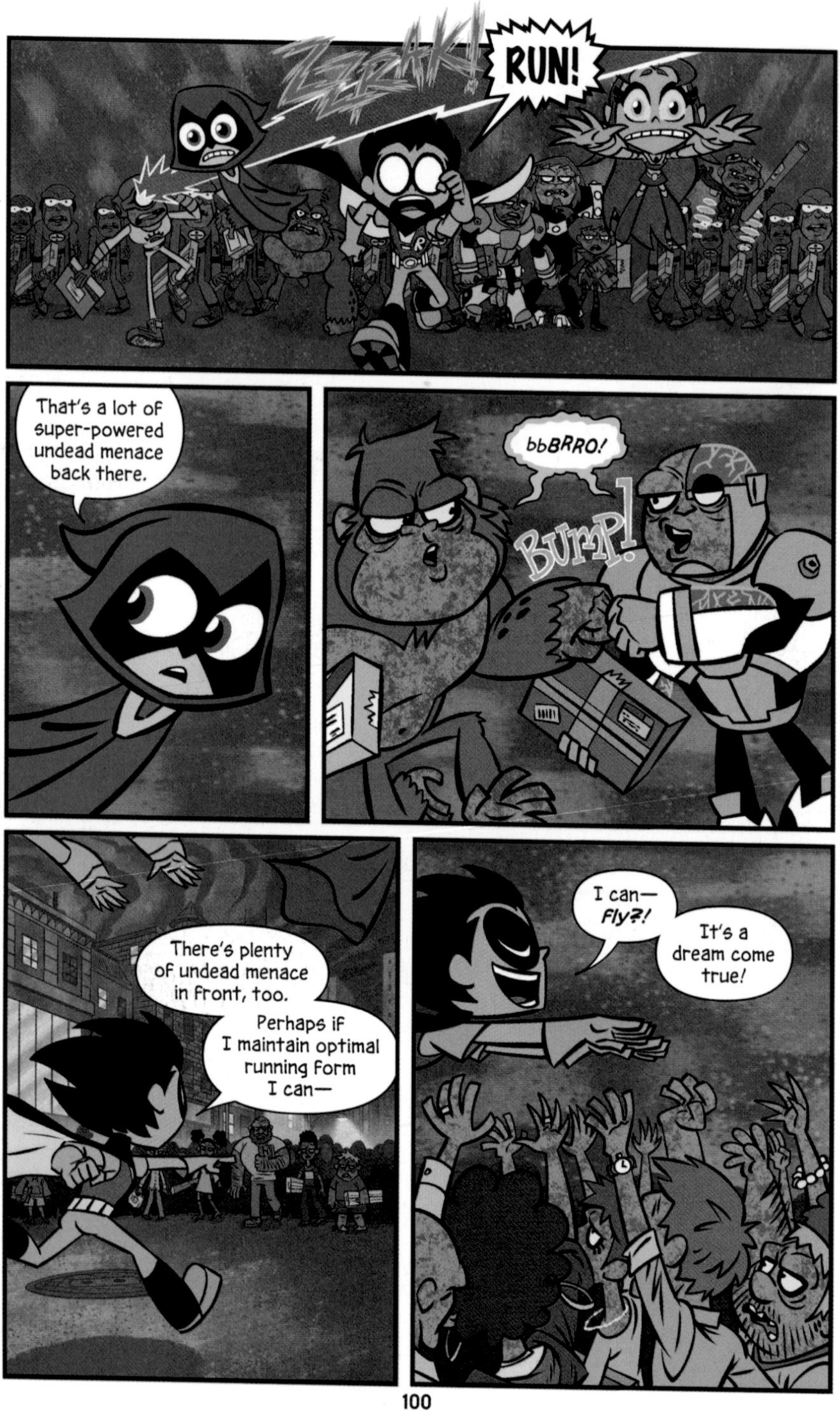
ZZZRAK!
RUN!
That's a lot of super-powered undead menace back there.
bbBRRO!
BUMP!
There's plenty of undead menace in front, too.
Perhaps if I maintain optimal running form I can—
I can— *Fly?!*
It's a dream come true!

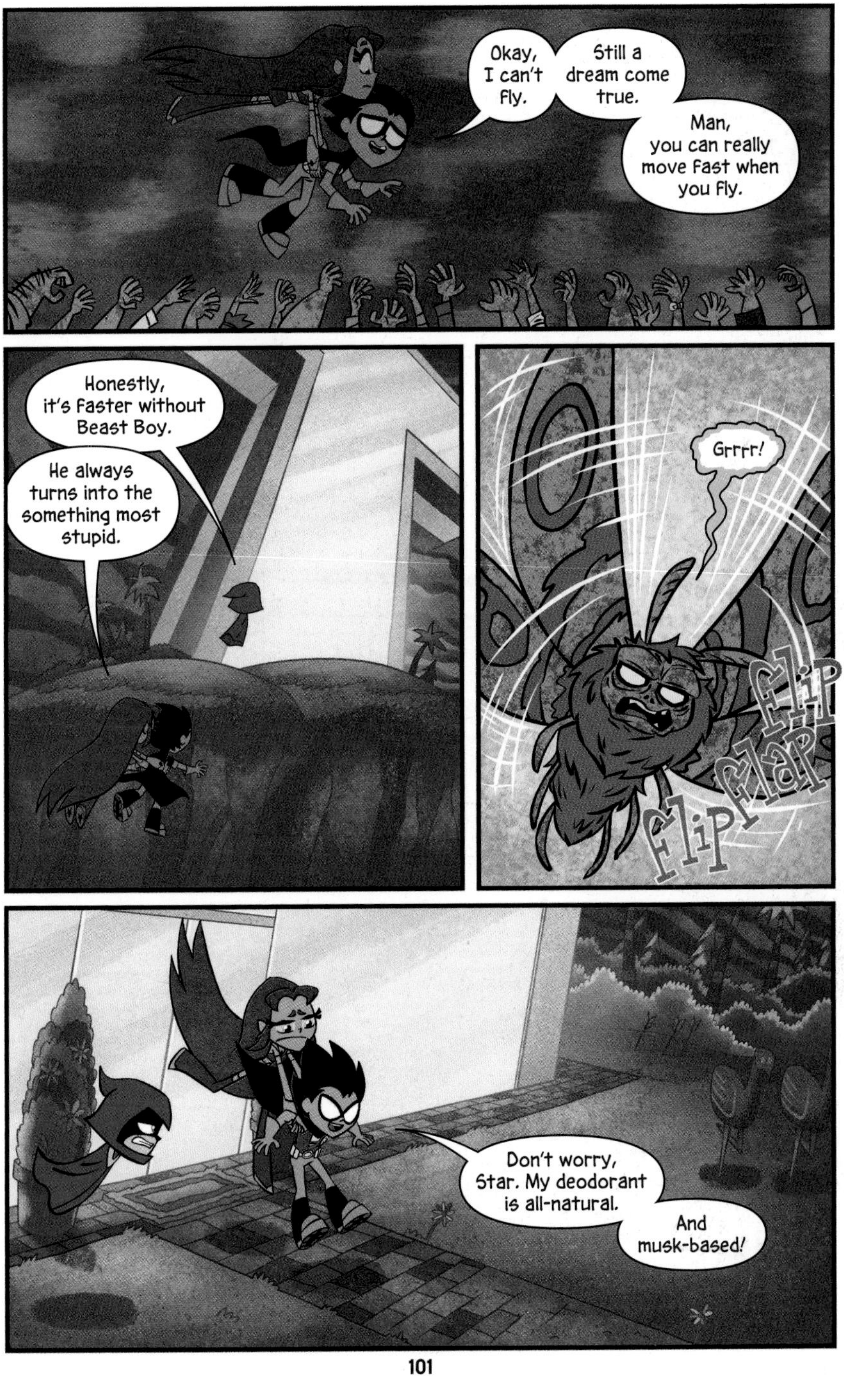

Okay, I can't fly.
Still a dream come true.
Man, you can really move fast when you fly.
Honestly, it's faster without Beast Boy.
He always turns into the something most stupid.
Grrrr!
flip flap flip
Don't worry, Star. My deodorant is all-natural.
And musk-based!

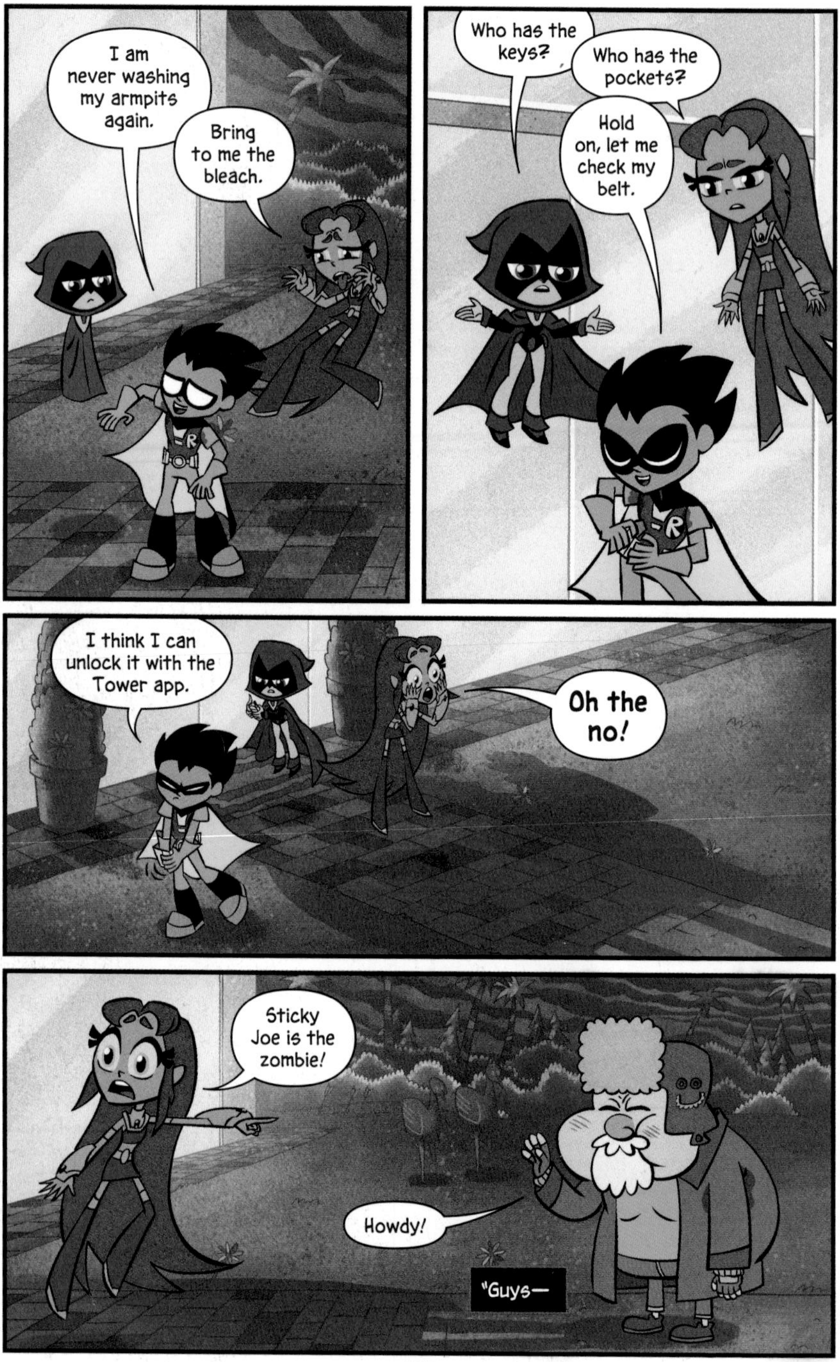

I am never washing my armpits again.
Bring to me the bleach.
Who has the keys?
Who has the pockets?
Hold on, let me check my belt.
I think I can unlock it with the Tower app.
Oh the no!
Sticky Joe is the zombie!
Howdy!
"Guys—

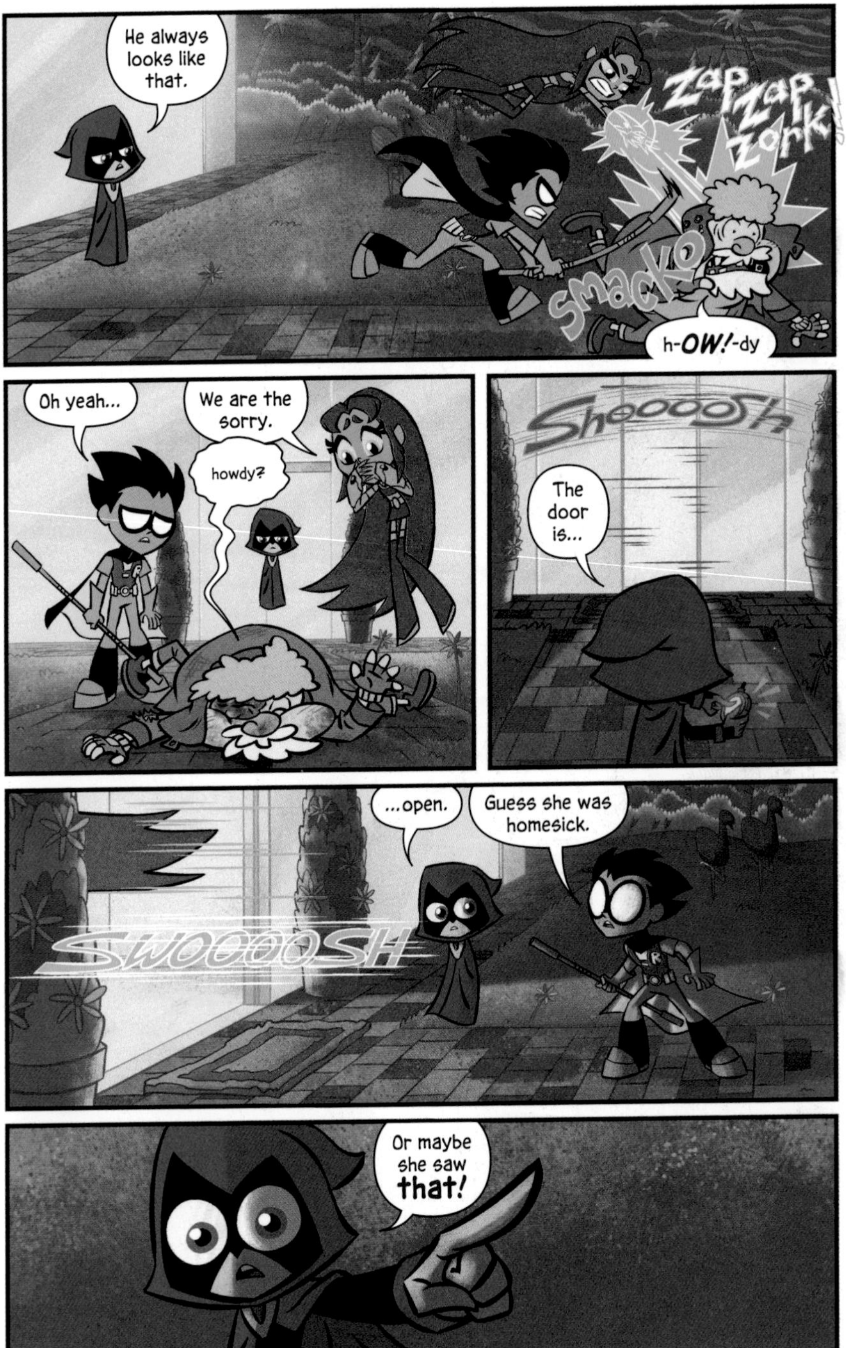
He always looks like that.
Zap Zap Zork!
SMACKO
h-OW!-dy
Oh yeah...
We are the sorry.
howdy?
Shooooosh
The door is...
SWOOOOOSH
...open.
Guess she was homesick.
Or maybe she saw that!

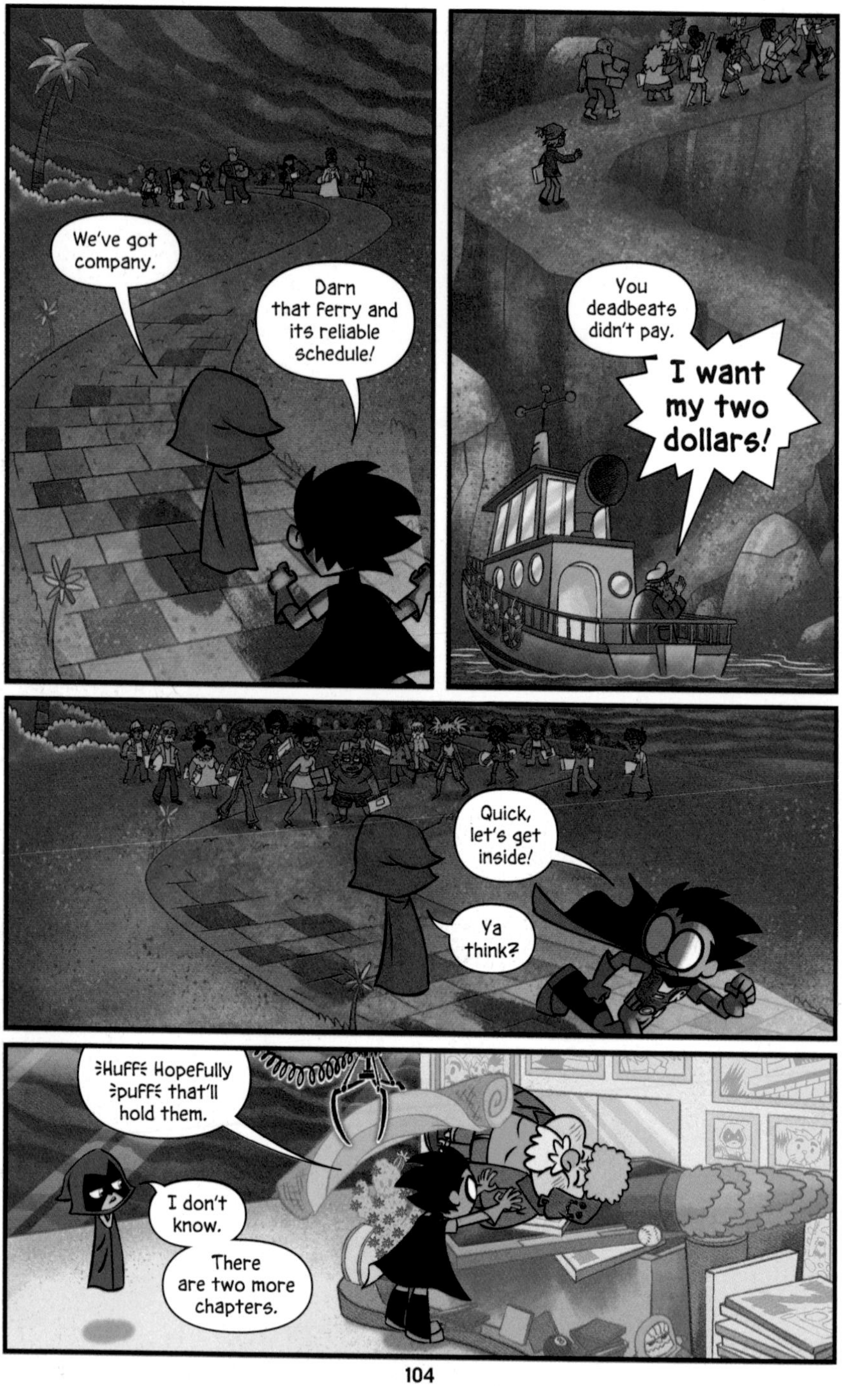

We've got company.
Darn that ferry and its reliable schedule!
You deadbeats didn't pay.
I want my two dollars!
Quick, let's get inside!
Ya think?
≷Huff≶ Hopefully ≷puff≶ that'll hold them.
I don't know.
There are two more chapters.

Chapter Seven

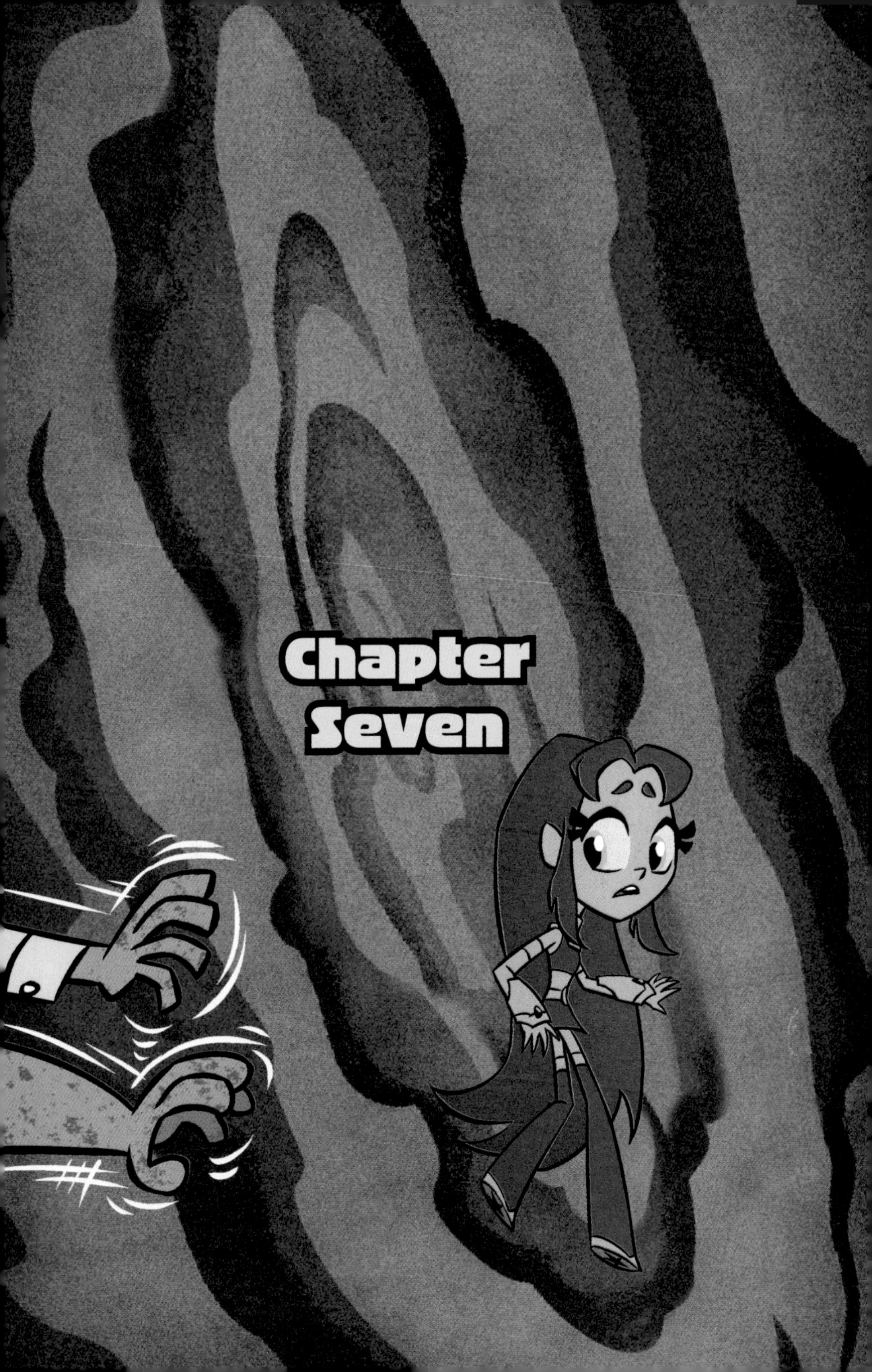

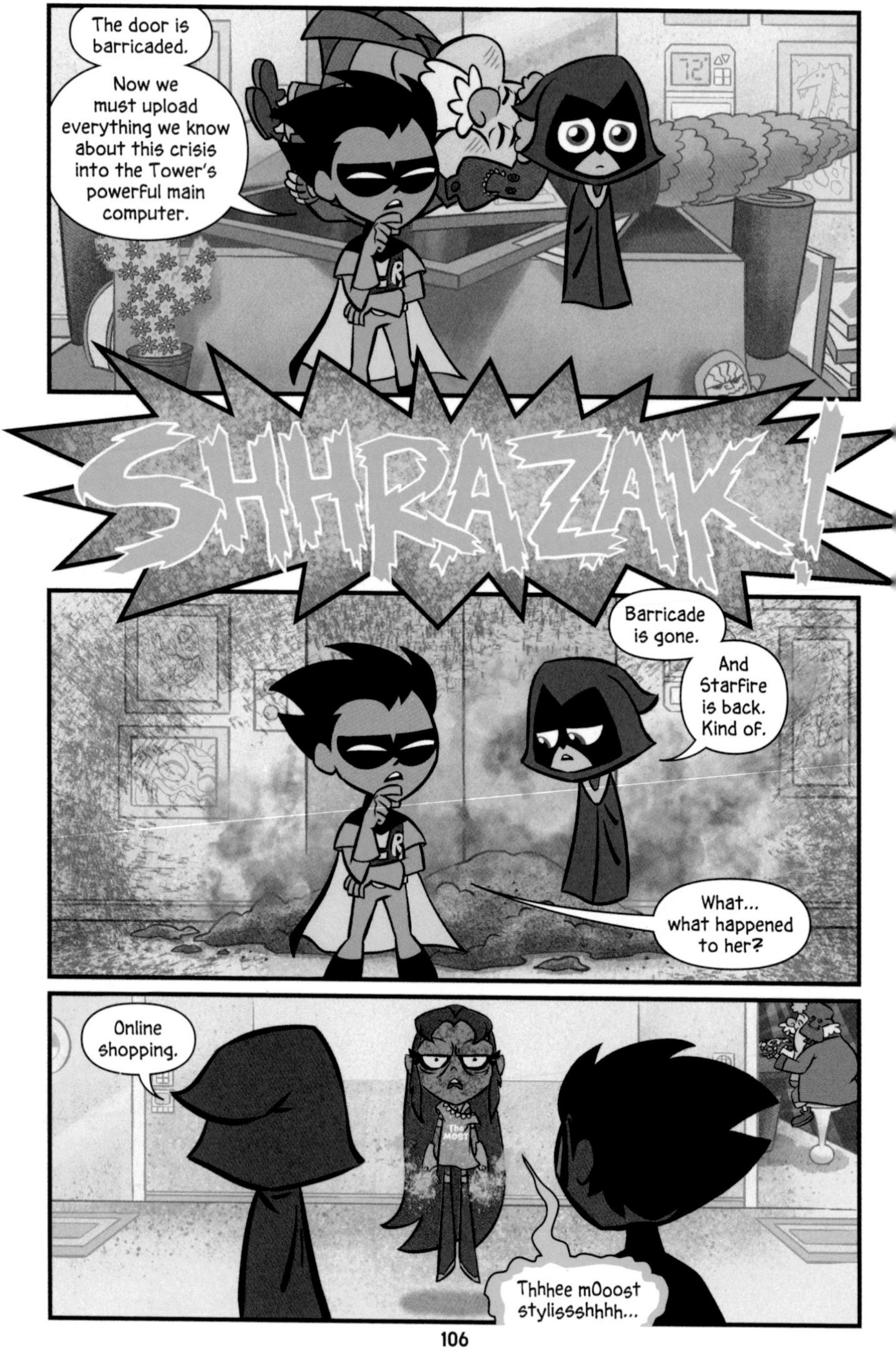
The door is barricaded.
Now we must upload everything we know about this crisis into the Tower's powerful main computer.
72°
SHHRAZAK!
Barricade is gone.
And Starfire is back. Kind of.
What... what happened to her?
Online shopping.
The MOST
Thhhee mOoost stylissshhhh...

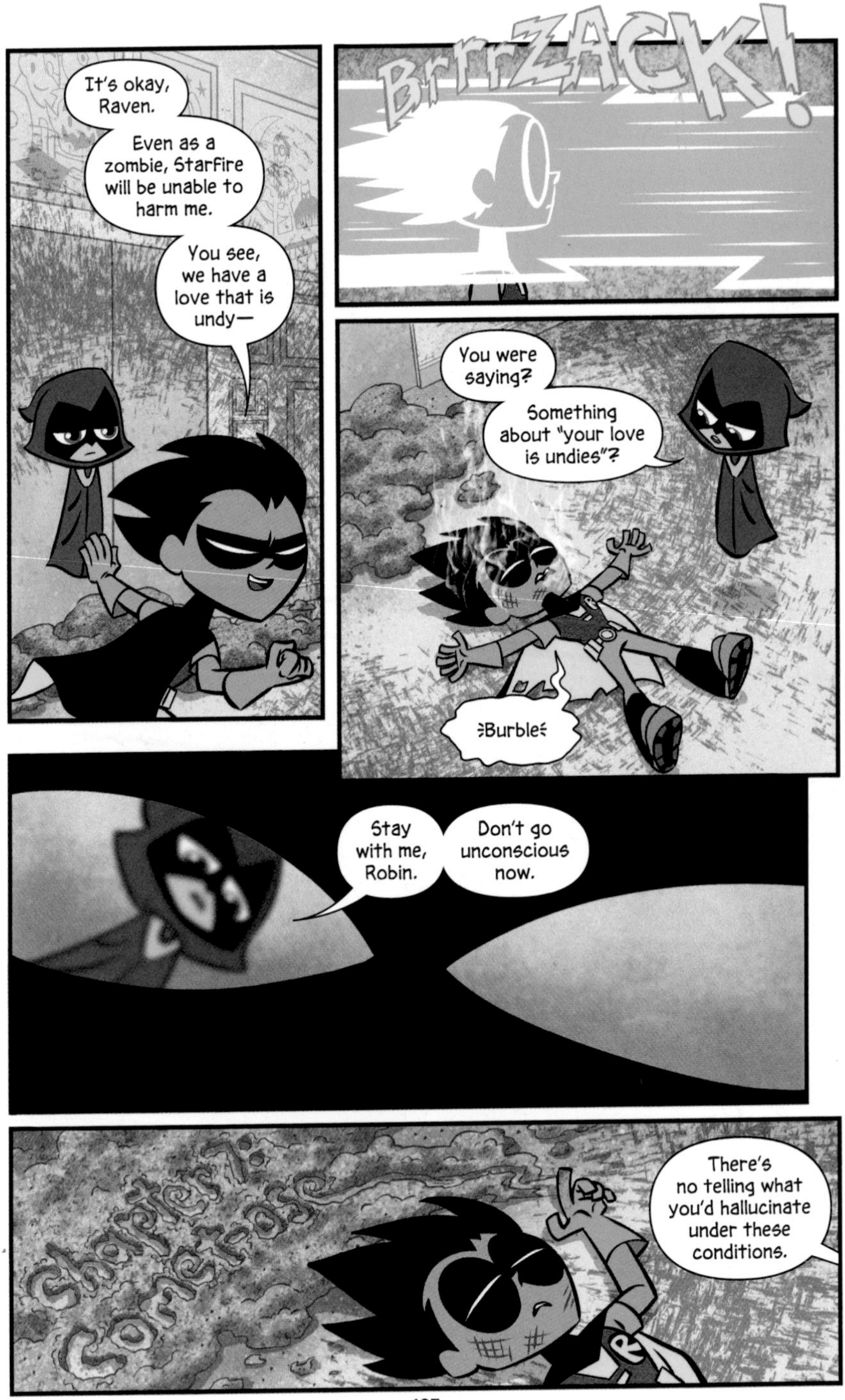
It's okay, Raven.
Even as a zombie, Starfire will be unable to harm me.
You see, we have a love that is undy—
BrrrZACK!
You were saying?
Something about "your love is undies"?
Burble
Stay with me, Robin.
Don't go unconscious now.
There's no telling what you'd hallucinate under these conditions.

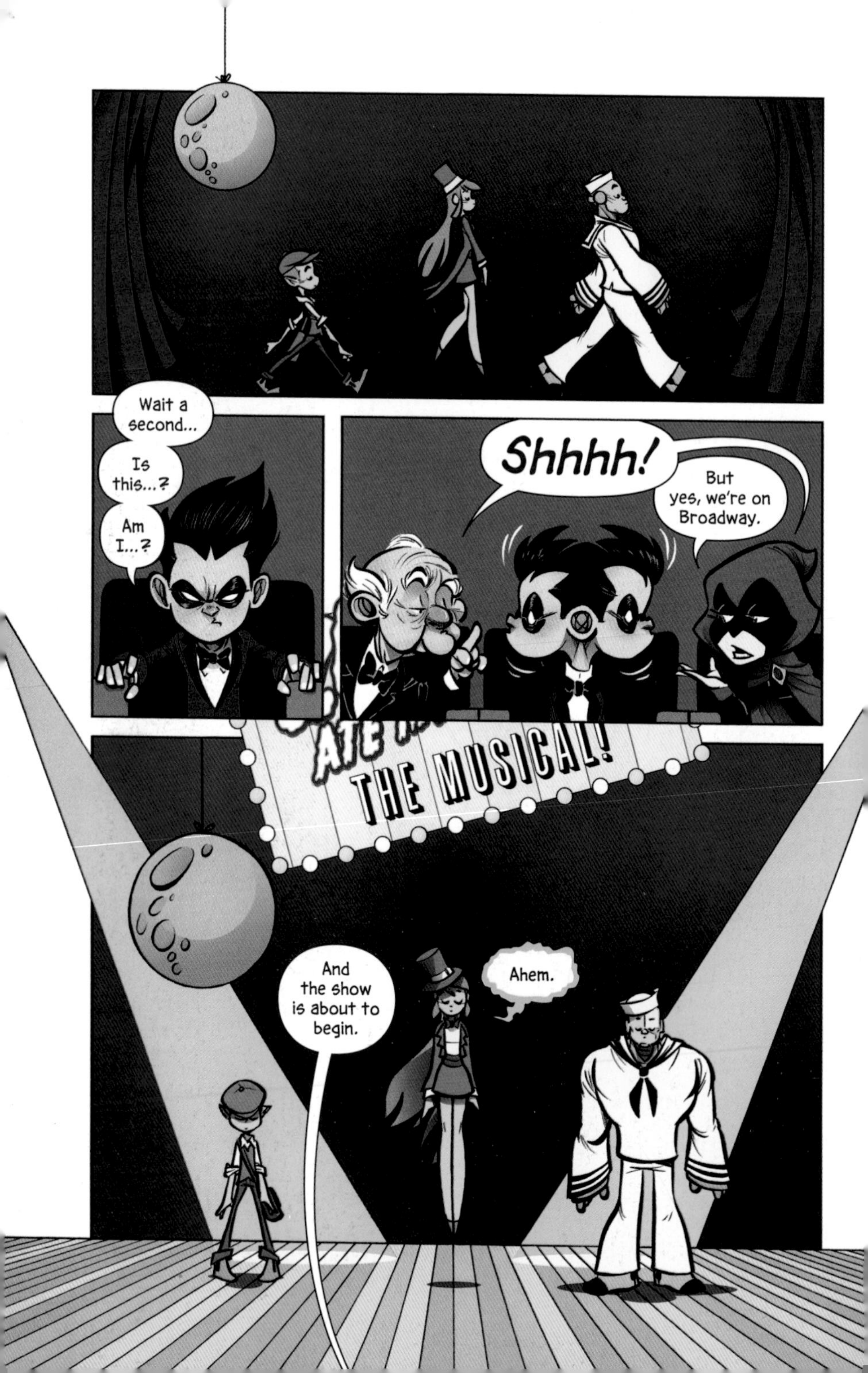

Wait a second...
Is this...?
Am I...?
Shhhh!
But yes, we're on Broadway.
THE MUSICAL!
And the show is about to begin.
Ahem.

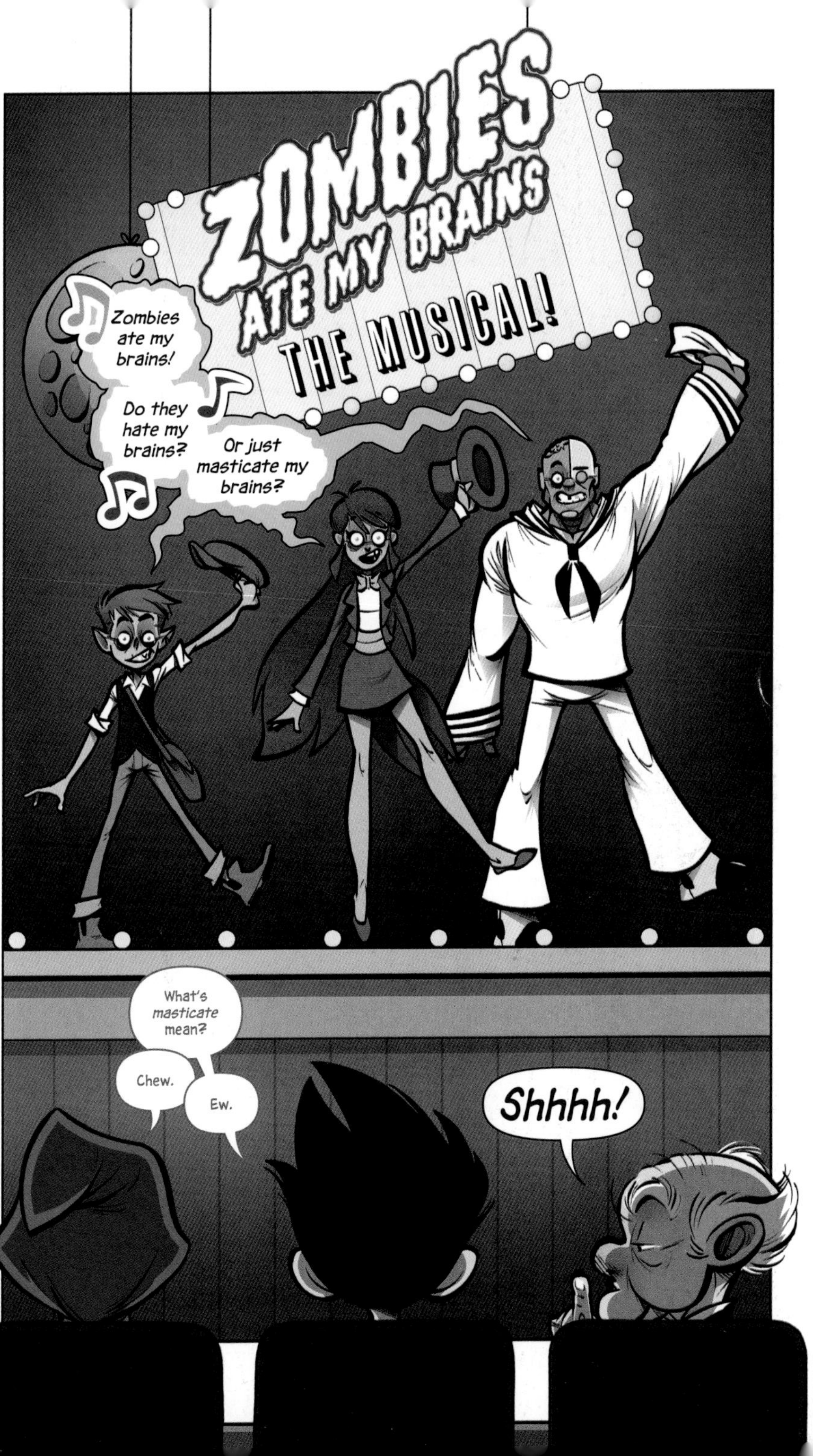
ZOMBIES ATE MY BRAINS
THE MUSICAL!
Zombies ate my brains!
Do they hate my brains?
Or just masticate my brains?
What's masticate mean?
Chew.
Ew.
Shhhh!

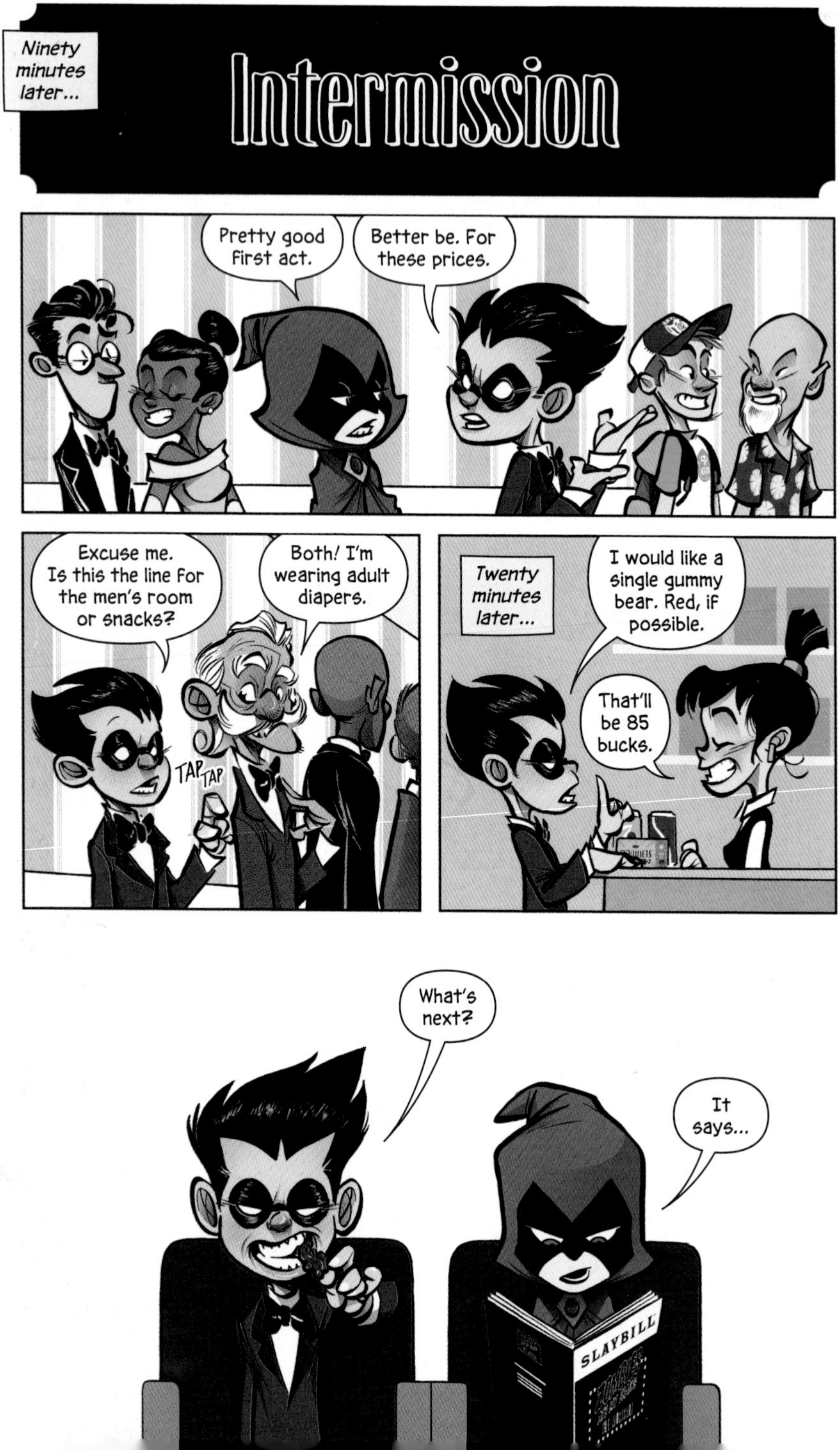
Ninety minutes later...
Intermission
Pretty good first act.
Better be. For these prices.
Excuse me. Is this the line for the men's room or snacks?
Both! I'm wearing adult diapers.
TAP TAP
Twenty minutes later...
I would like a single gummy bear. Red, if possible.
That'll be 85 bucks.
What's next?
It says...
SLAYBILL

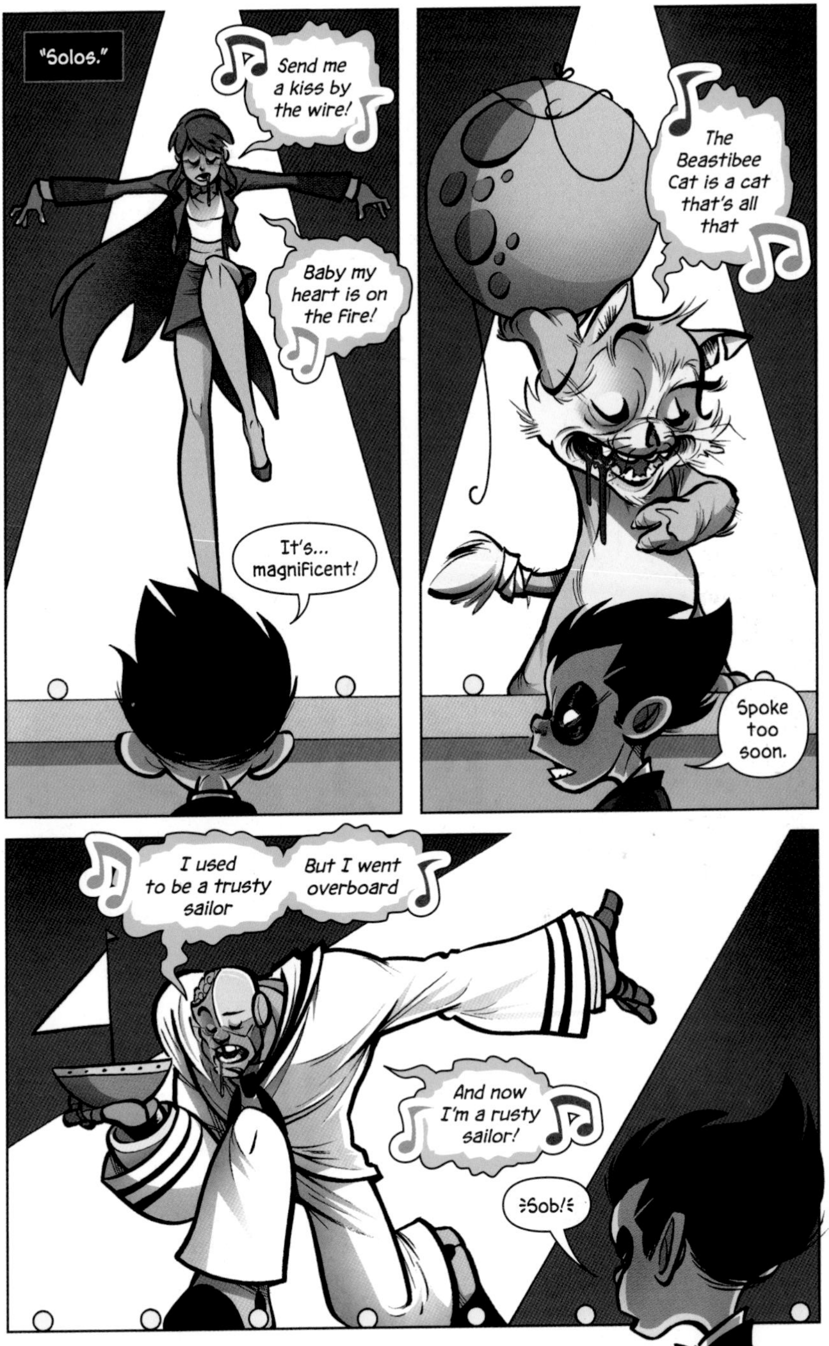
"Solos."
Send me a kiss by the wire!
Baby my heart is on the fire!
It's... magnificent!
The Beastibee Cat is a cat that's all that
Spoke too soon.
I used to be a trusty sailor
But I went overboard
And now I'm a rusty sailor!
Sob!

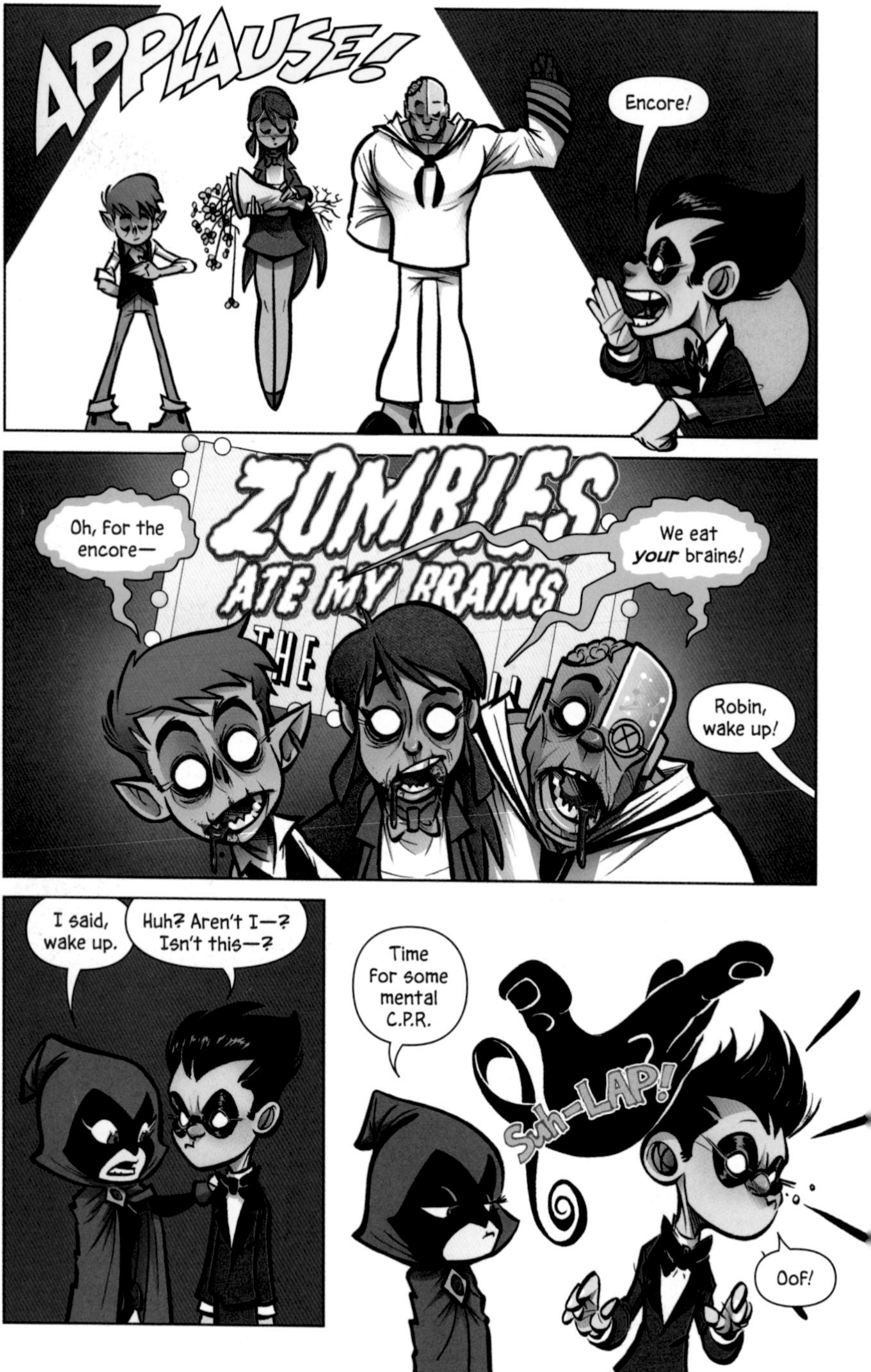
APPLAUSE!
Encore!
ZOMBIES ATE MY BRAINS
Oh, for the encore—
We eat *your* brains!
Robin, wake up!
I said, wake up.
Huh? Aren't I—? Isn't this—?
Time for some mental C.P.R.
SUH-LAP!
Oof!

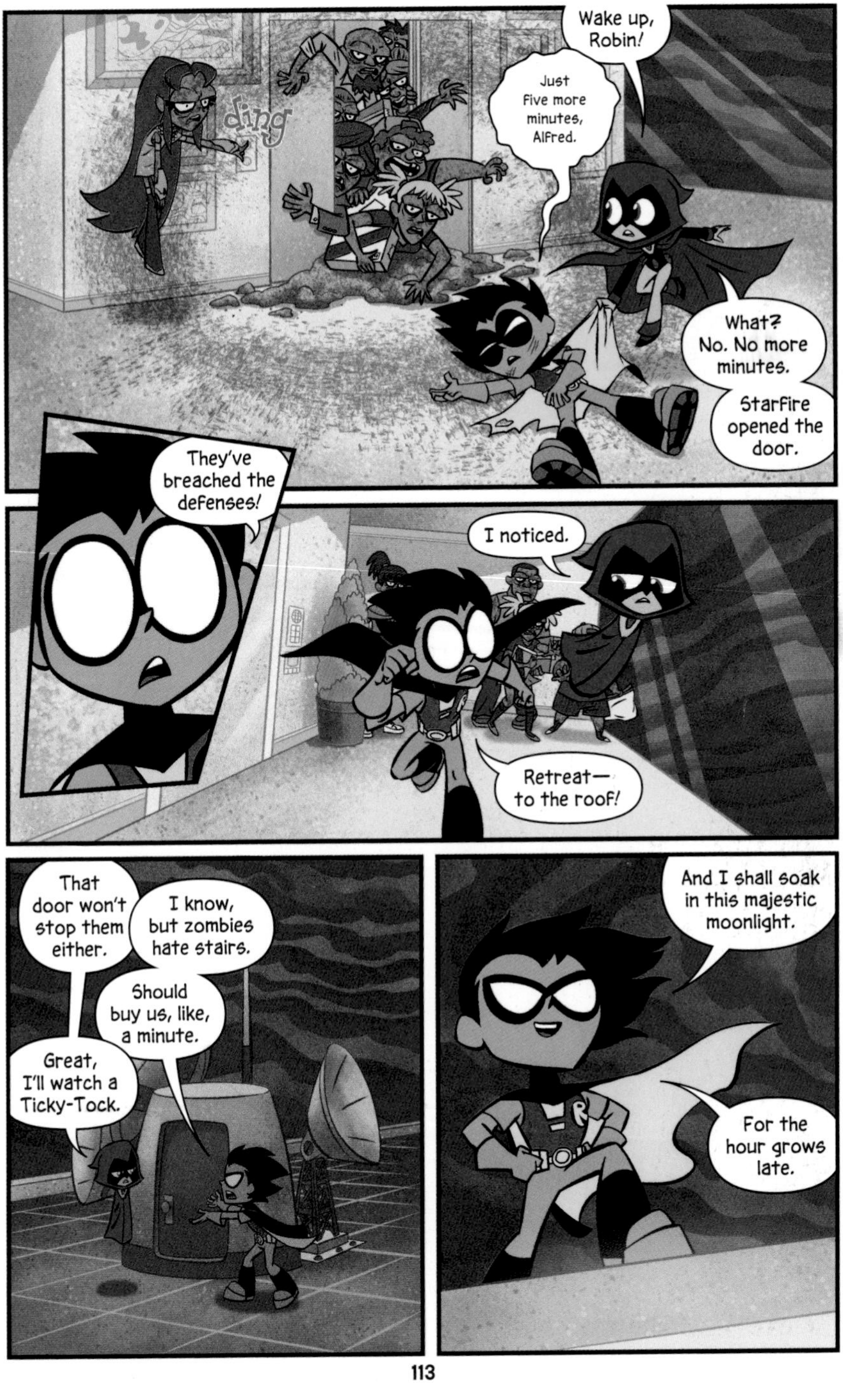
ding
Wake up, Robin!
Just five more minutes, Alfred.
What? No. No more minutes.
Starfire opened the door.
They've breached the defenses!
I noticed.
Retreat— to the roof!
That door won't stop them either.
I know, but zombies hate stairs.
Should buy us, like, a minute.
Great, I'll watch a Ticky-Tock.
And I shall soak in this majestic moonlight.
For the hour grows late.

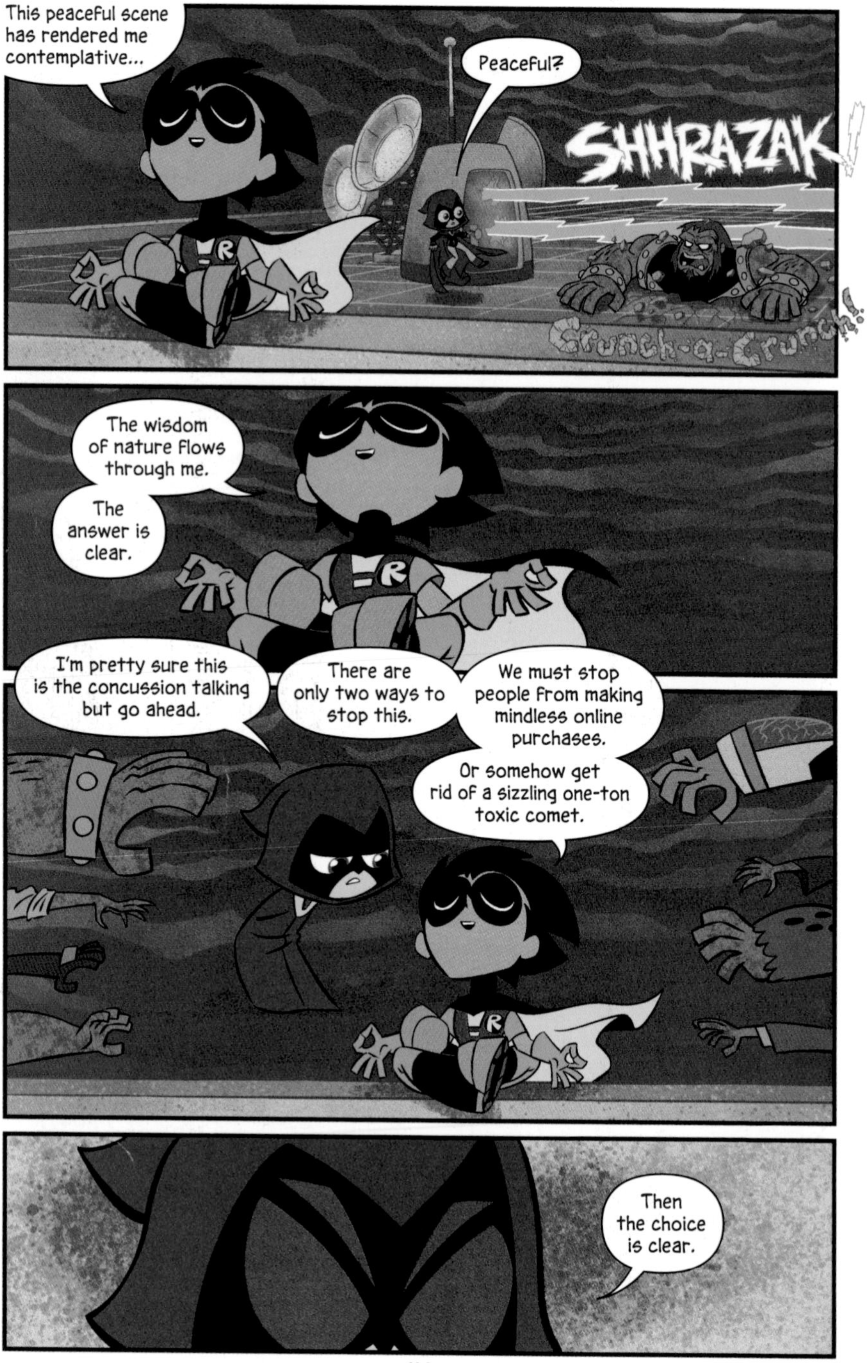
This peaceful scene has rendered me contemplative...
Peaceful?
SHHRAZAK!
Crunch-a-Crunch!
The wisdom of nature flows through me.
The answer is clear.
I'm pretty sure this is the concussion talking but go ahead.
There are only two ways to stop this.
We must stop people from making mindless online purchases.
Or somehow get rid of a sizzling one-ton toxic comet.
Then the choice is clear.

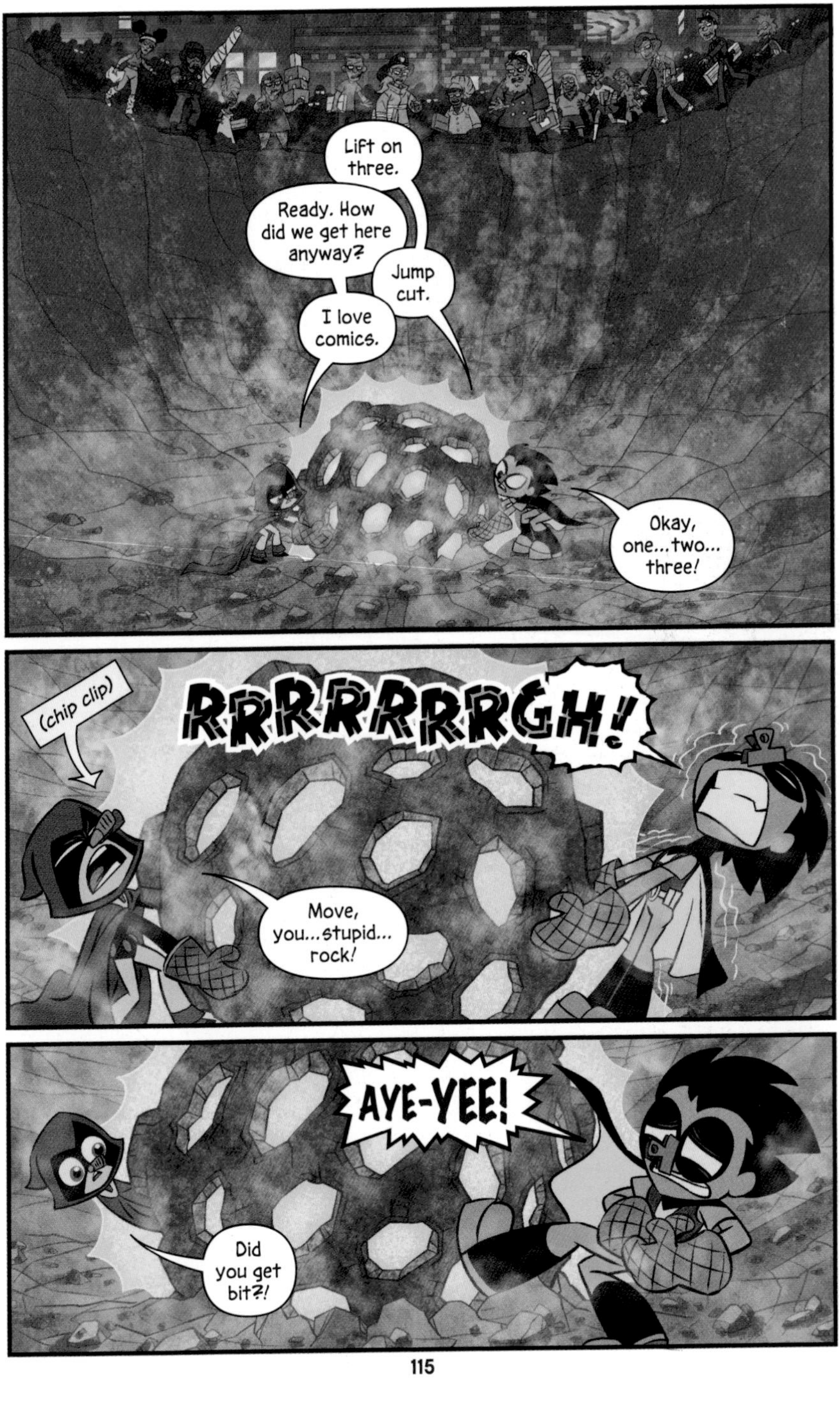
Lift on three.
Ready. How did we get here anyway?
Jump cut.
I love comics.
Okay, one...two... three!
(chip clip)
RRRRRRRGH!
Move, you...stupid... rock!
AYE-YEE!
Did you get bit?!

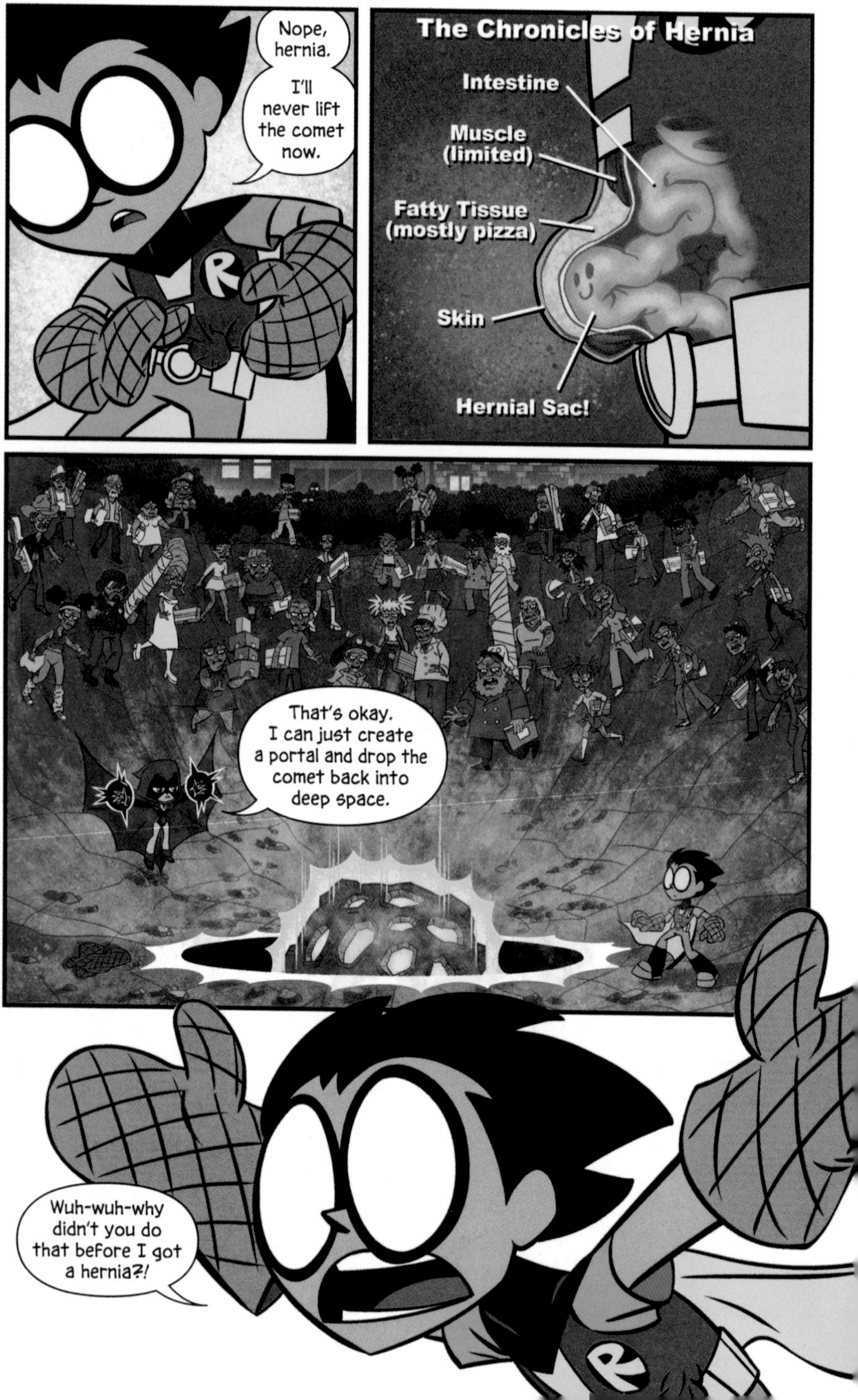
Nope, hernia.
I'll never lift the comet now.
The Chronicles of Hernia
Intestine
Muscle (limited)
Fatty Tissue (mostly pizza)
Skin
Hernial Sac!
That's okay. I can just create a portal and drop the comet back into deep space.
Wuh-wuh-why didn't you do that before I got a hernia?!

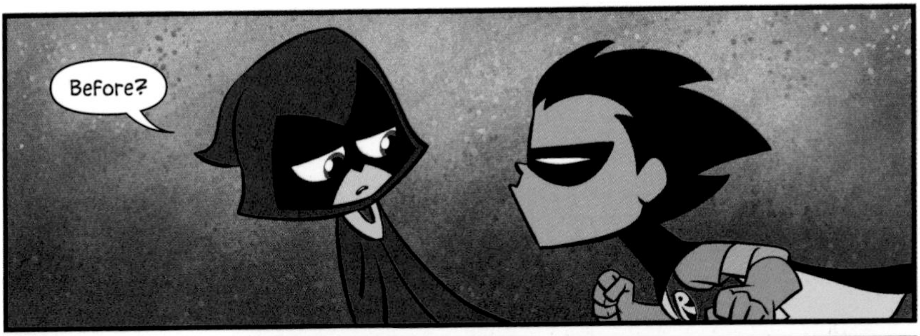
Before?

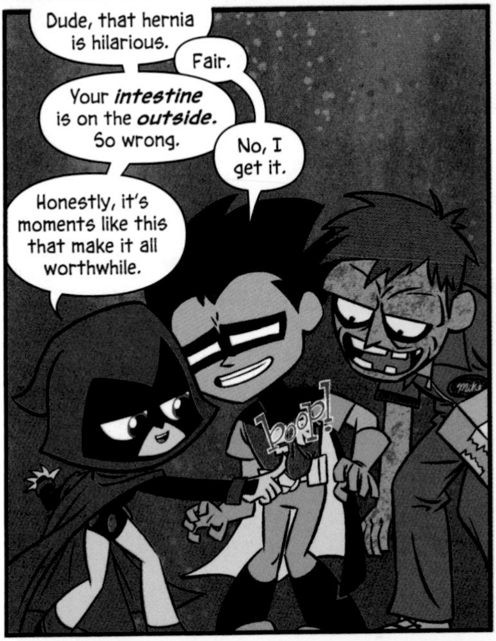
Dude, that hernia is hilarious.
Fair.
Your *intestine* is on the *outside.* So wrong.
No, I get it.
Honestly, it's moments like this that make it all worthwhile.
boop!

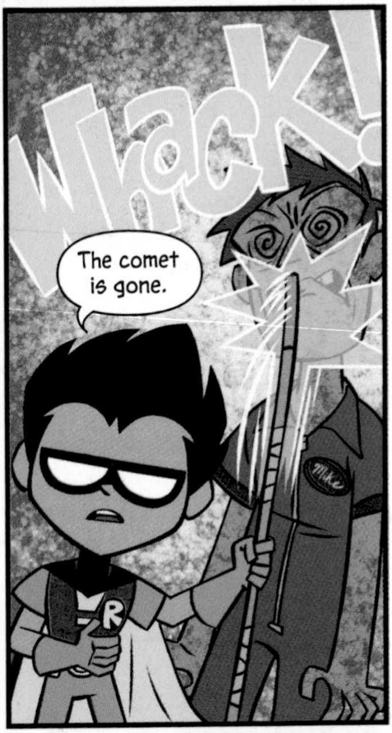
WHACK!
The comet is gone.

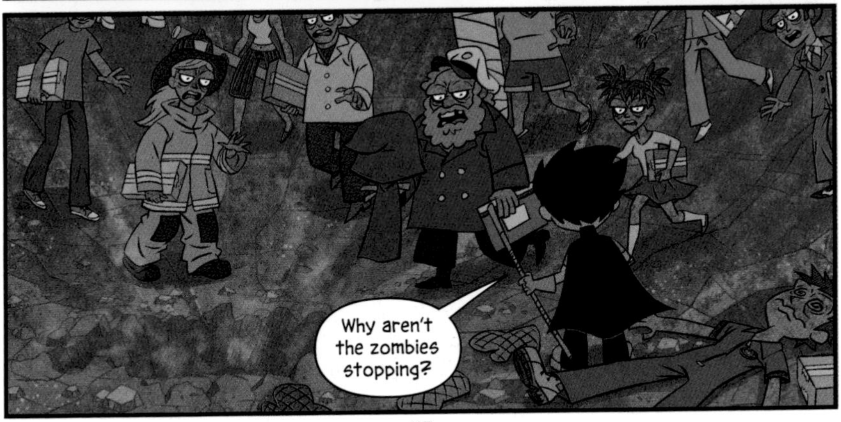
Why aren't the zombies stopping?

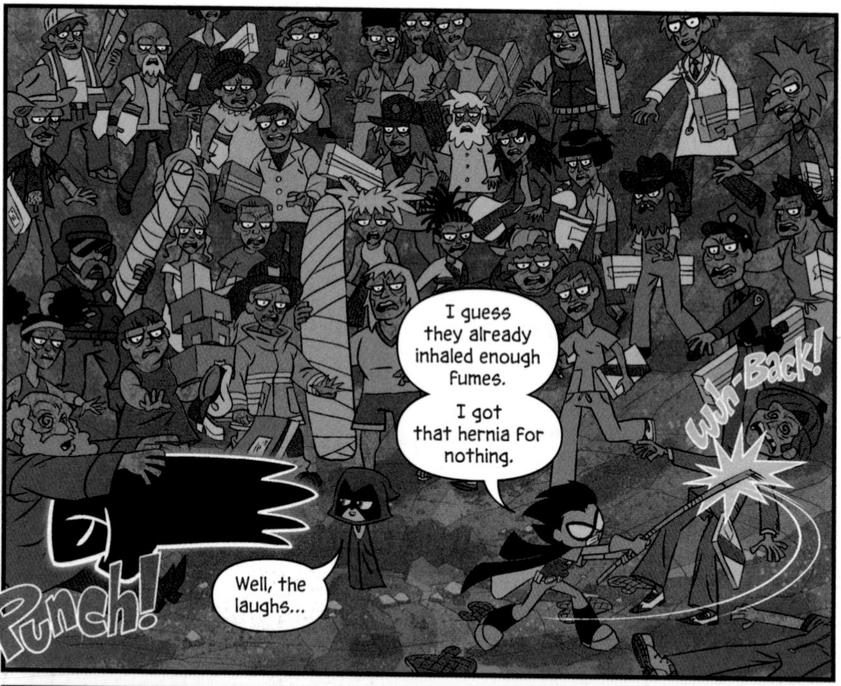
I guess they already inhaled enough fumes.
I got that hernia for nothing.
Wuh-Back!
Well, the laughs...
Punch!

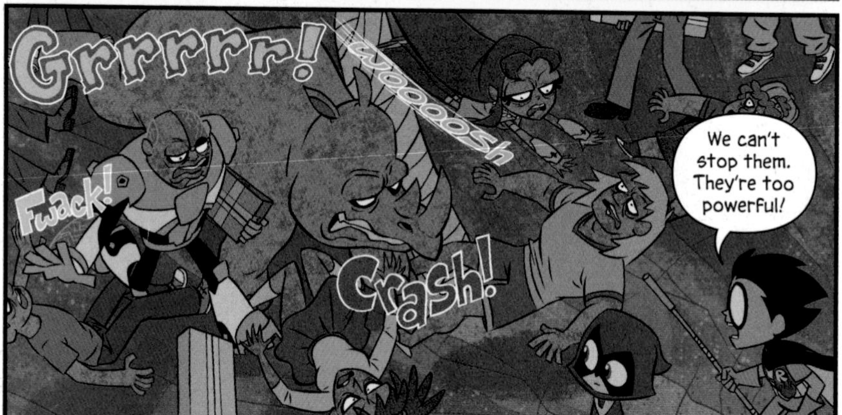
Grrrrrr!
Wooooosh
Fwack!
Crash!
We can't stop them. They're too powerful!

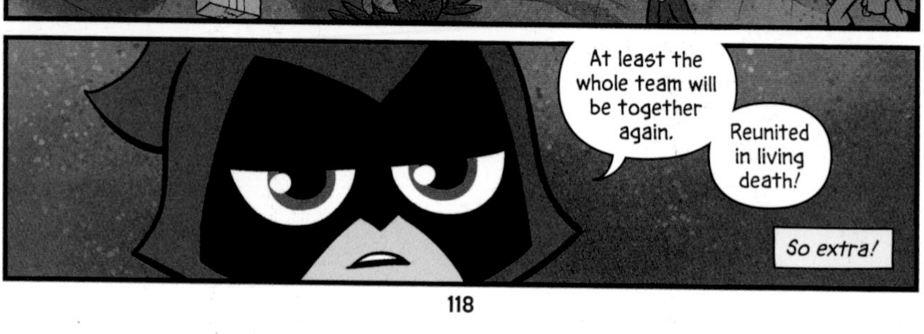
At least the whole team will be together again.
Reunited in living death!
So extra!

Chapter Eight

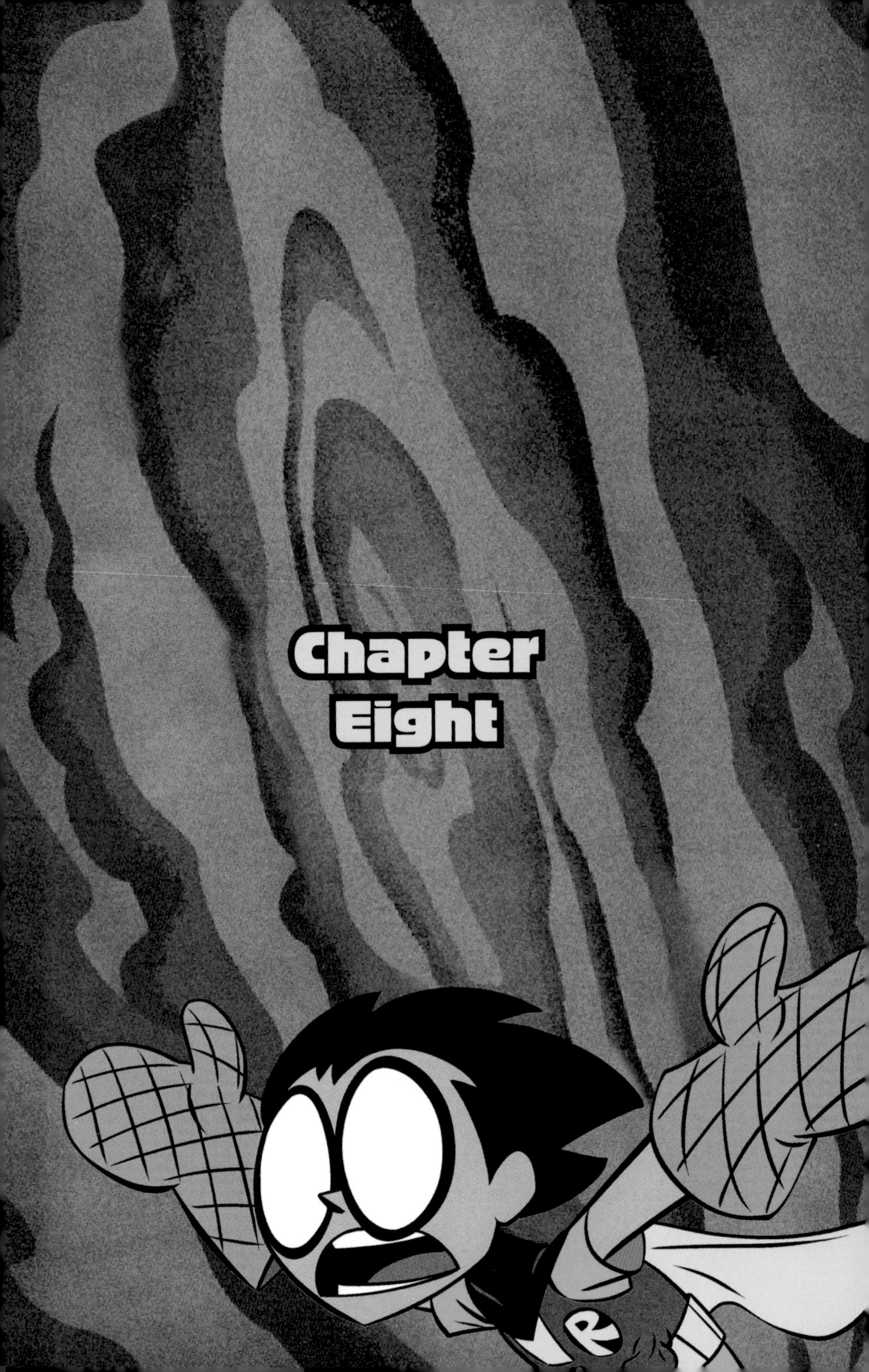

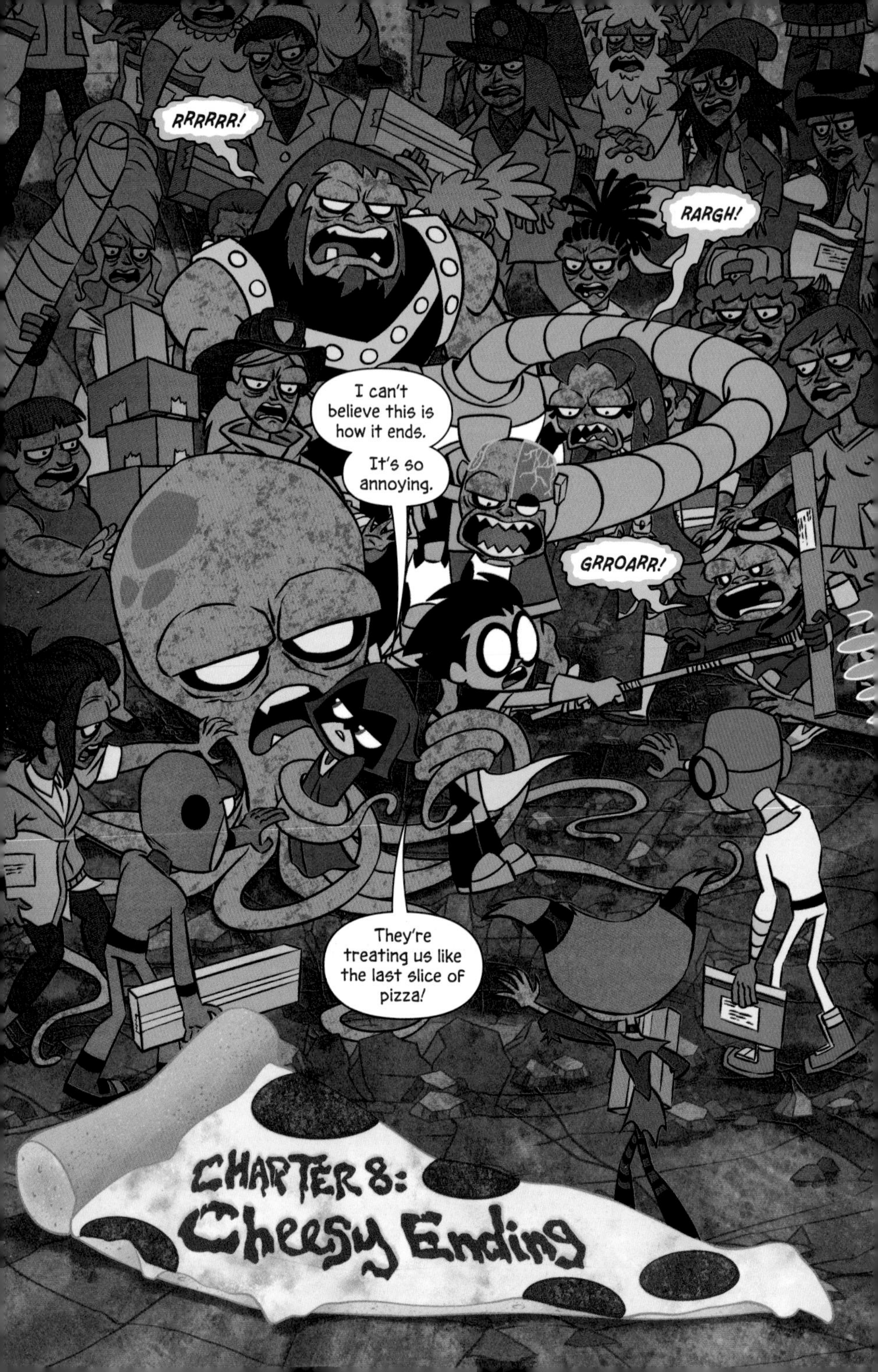
RRRRRR!
RARGH!
I can't believe this is how it ends.
It's so annoying.
GRROARR!
They're treating us like the last slice of pizza!
CHAPTER 8:
Cheesy Ending

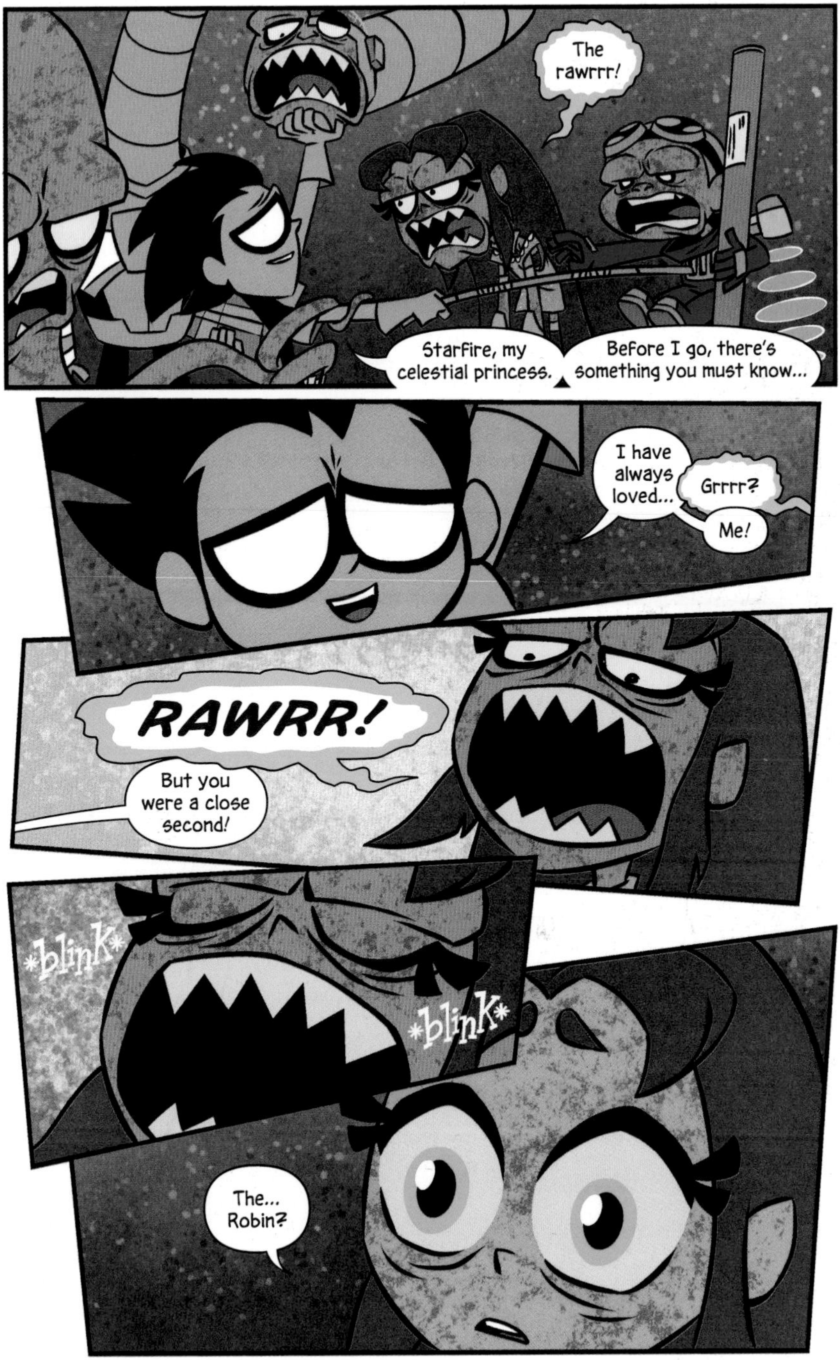
The rawrrr!
Starfire, my celestial princess.
Before I go, there's something you must know...
I have always loved...
Grrrr?
Me!
RAWRR!
But you were a close second!
blink
blink
The... Robin?

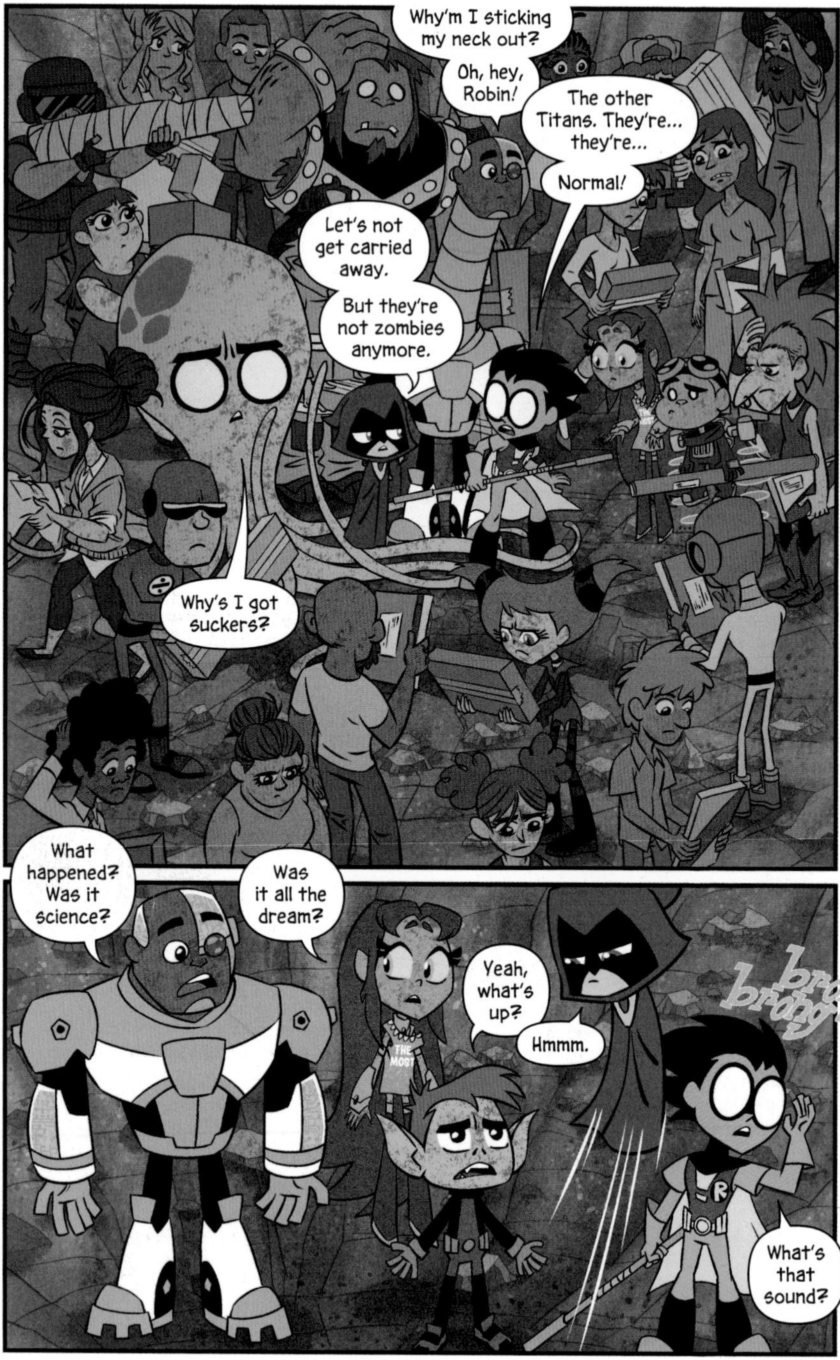
Why'm I sticking my neck out?
Oh, hey, Robin!
The other Titans. They're... they're...
Normal!
Let's not get carried away.
But they're not zombies anymore.
Why's I got suckers?
What happened? Was it science?
Was it all the dream?
Yeah, what's up?
Hmmm.
brong brong
What's that sound?

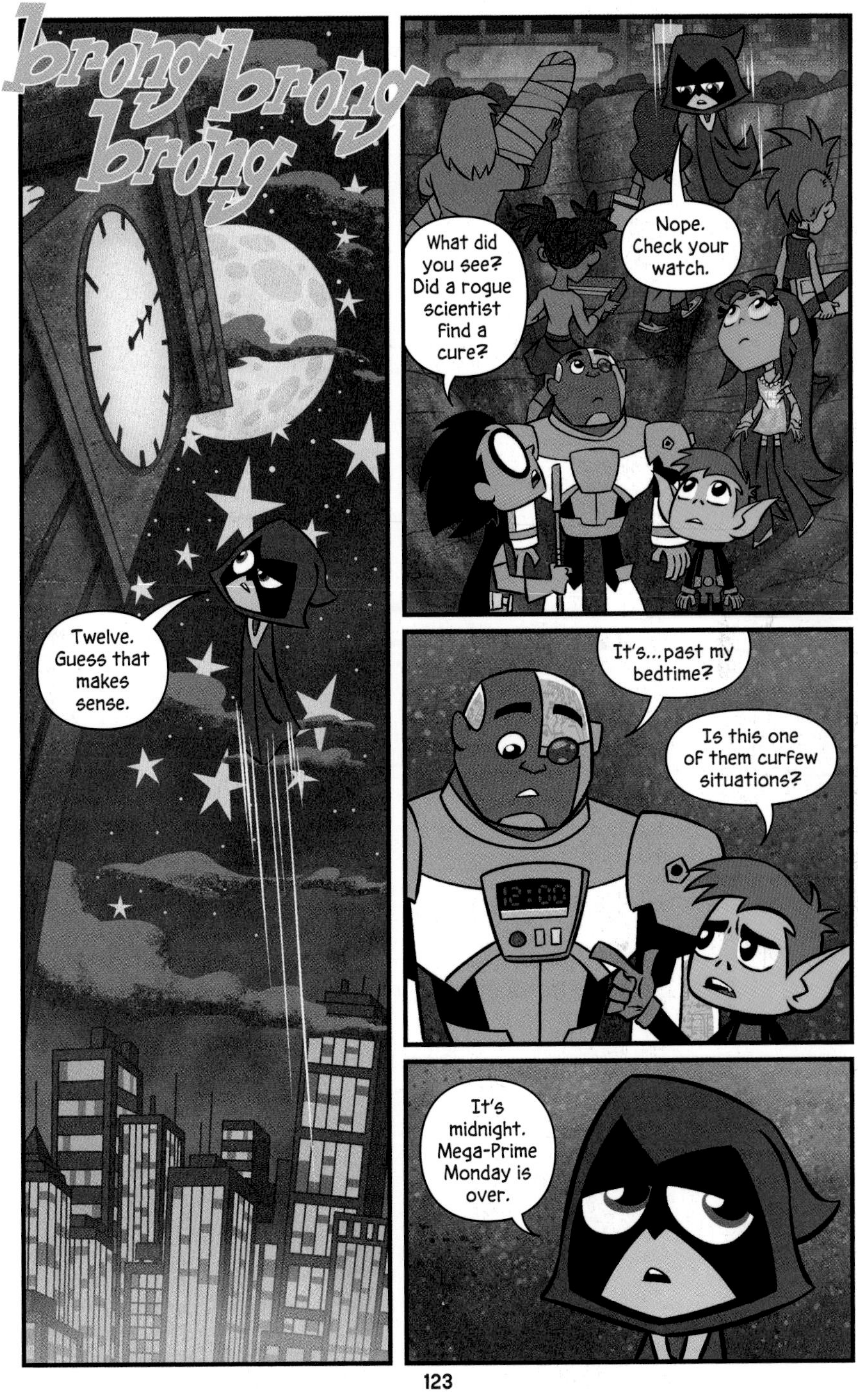
brong brong brong
Twelve. Guess that makes sense.
What did you see? Did a rogue scientist find a cure?
Nope. Check your watch.
It's...past my bedtime?
Is this one of them curfew situations?
12:00
It's midnight. Mega-Prime Monday is over.

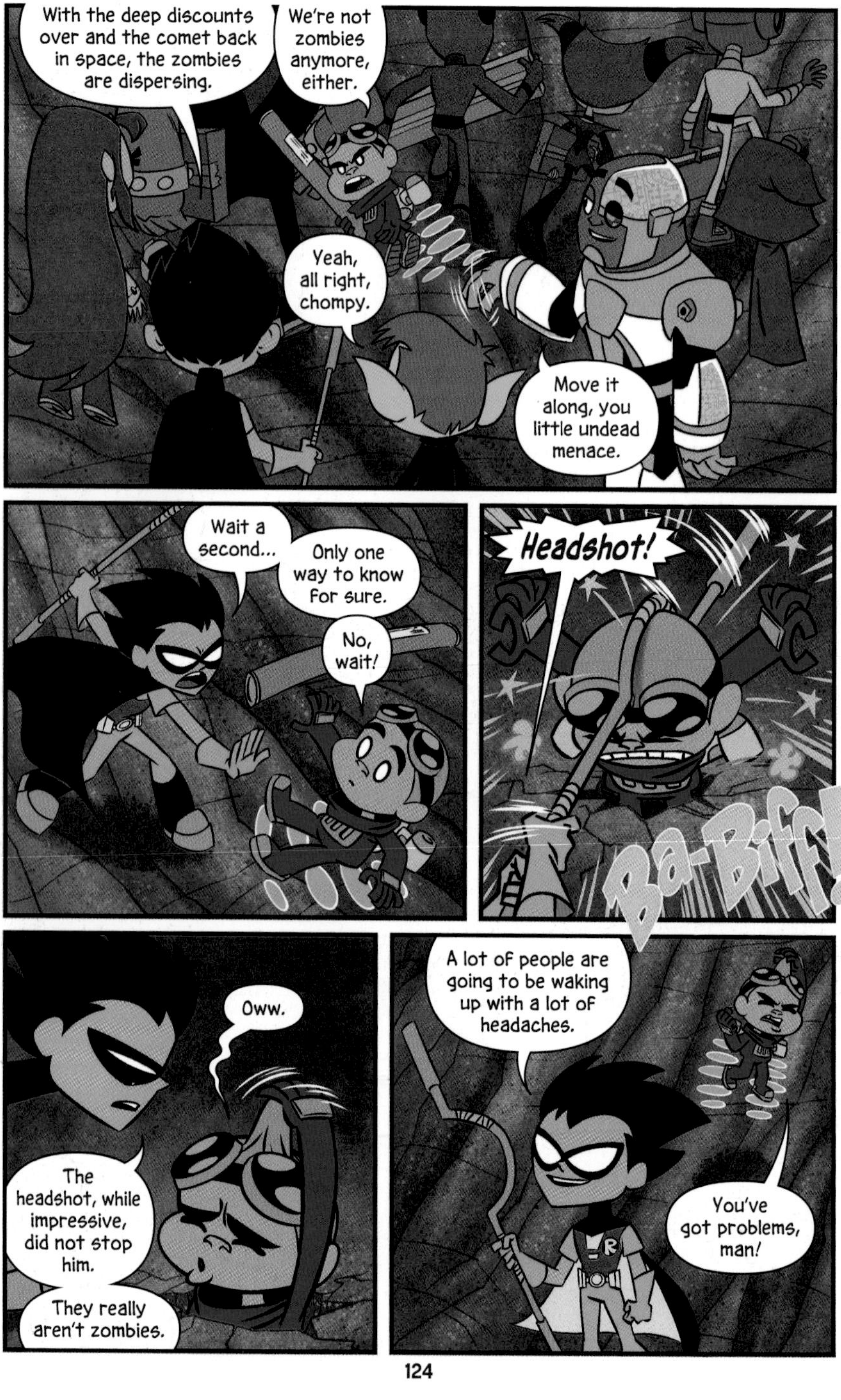
With the deep discounts over and the comet back in space, the zombies are dispersing.
We're not zombies anymore, either.
Yeah, all right, chompy.
Move it along, you little undead menace.
Wait a second...
Only one way to know for sure.
No, wait!
Headshot!
Ba-Biff!
Oww.
The headshot, while impressive, did not stop him.
They really aren't zombies.
A lot of people are going to be waking up with a lot of headaches.
You've got problems, man!

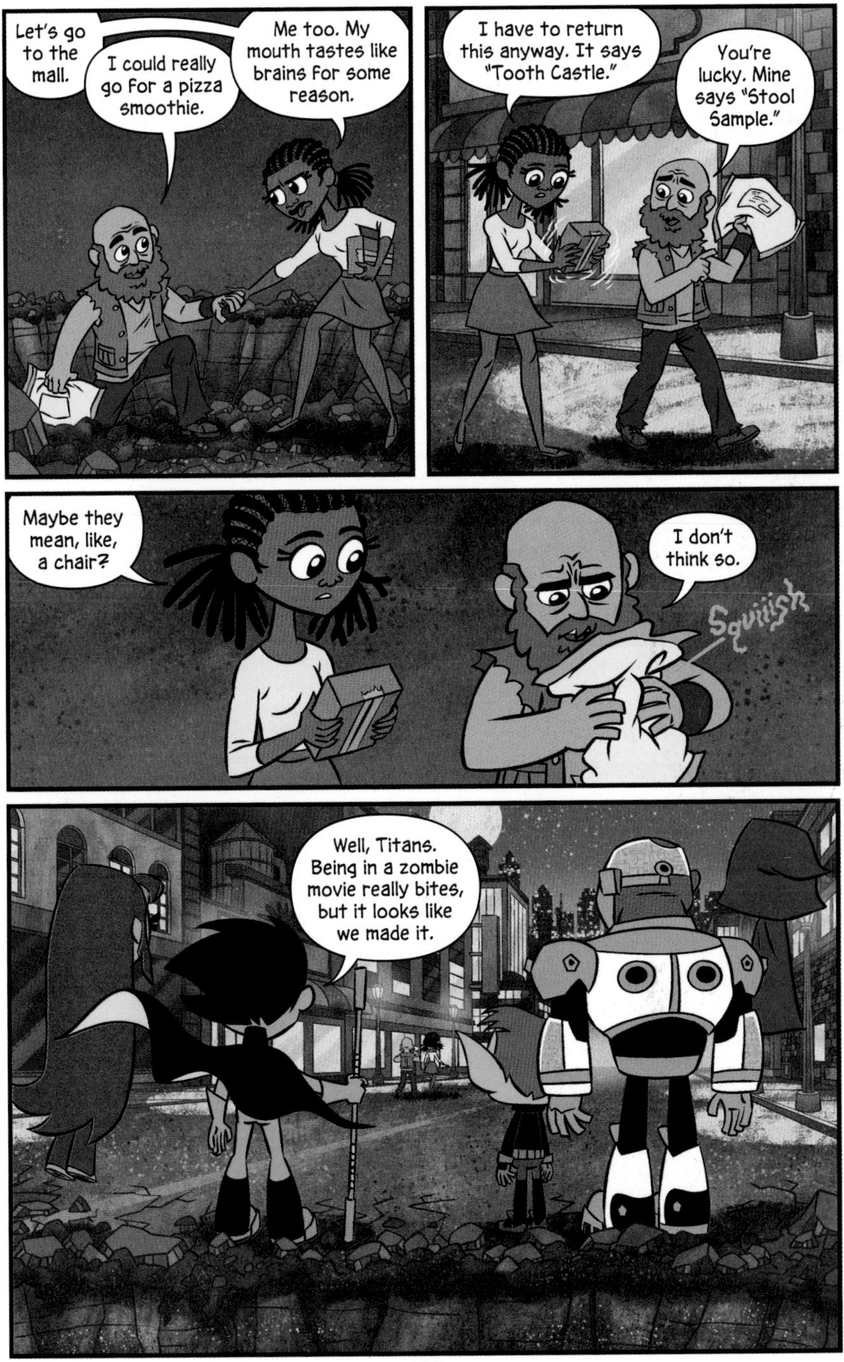
Let's go to the mall.
I could really go for a pizza smoothie.
Me too. My mouth tastes like brains for some reason.
I have to return this anyway. It says "Tooth Castle."
You're lucky. Mine says "Stool Sample."
Maybe they mean, like, a chair?
I don't think so.
Squiiish
Well, Titans. Being in a zombie movie really bites, but it looks like we made it.

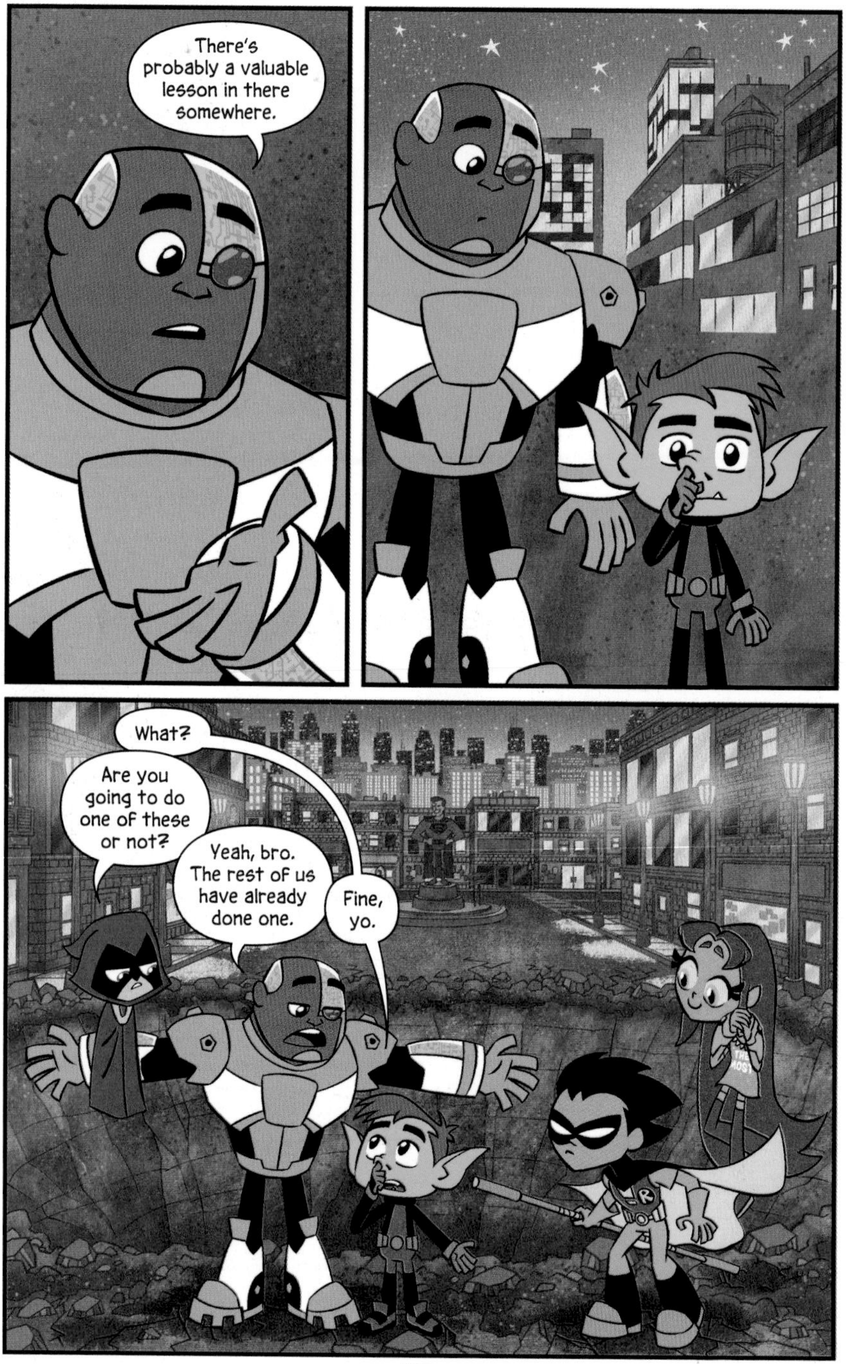
There's probably a valuable lesson in there somewhere.
What?
Are you going to do one of these or not?
Yeah, bro. The rest of us have already done one.
Fine, yo.

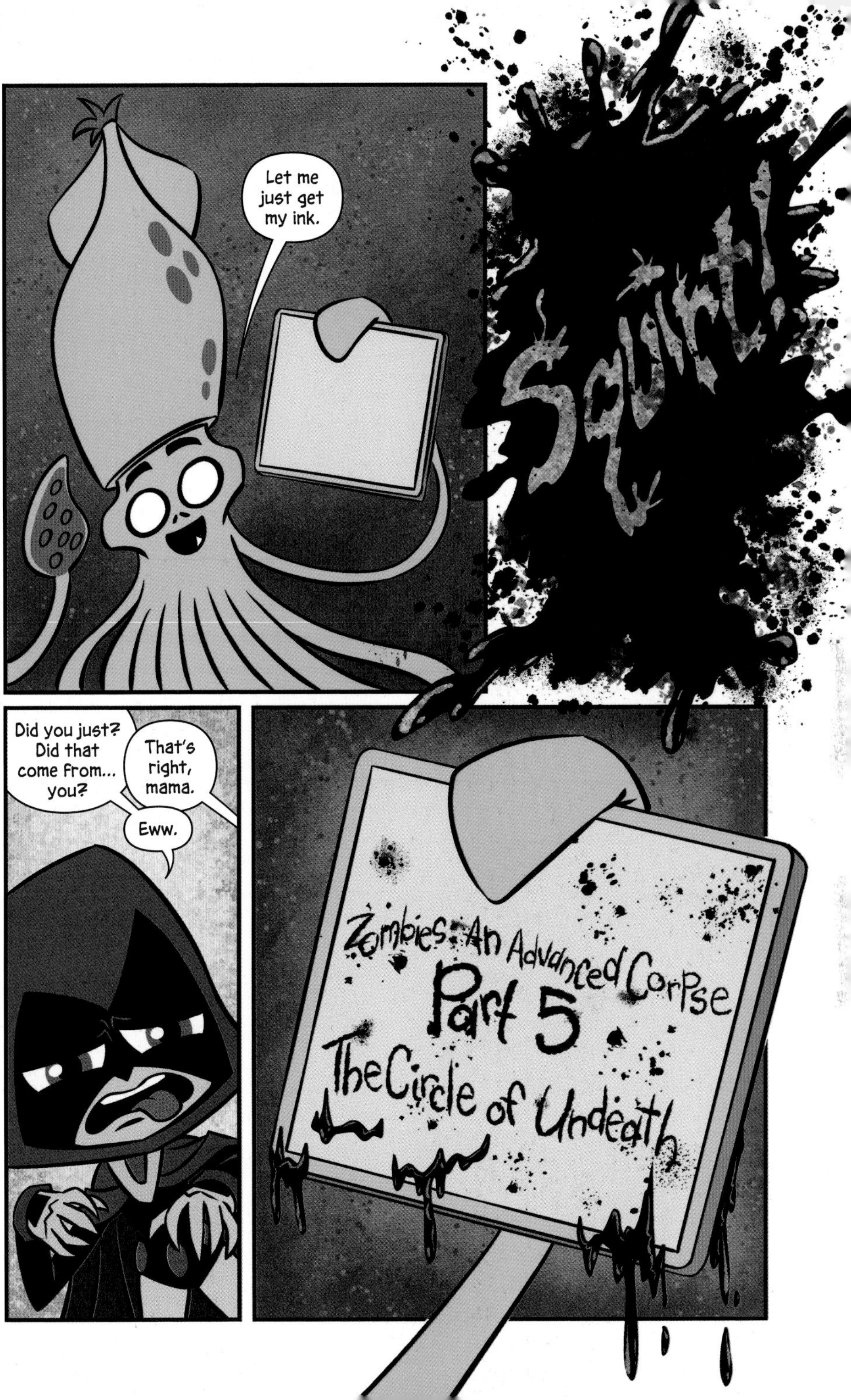
Let me just get my ink.
Squirt!
Did you just? Did that come from... you?
That's right, mama.
Eww.
Zombies: An Advanced Corpse
Part 5
The Circle of Undeath

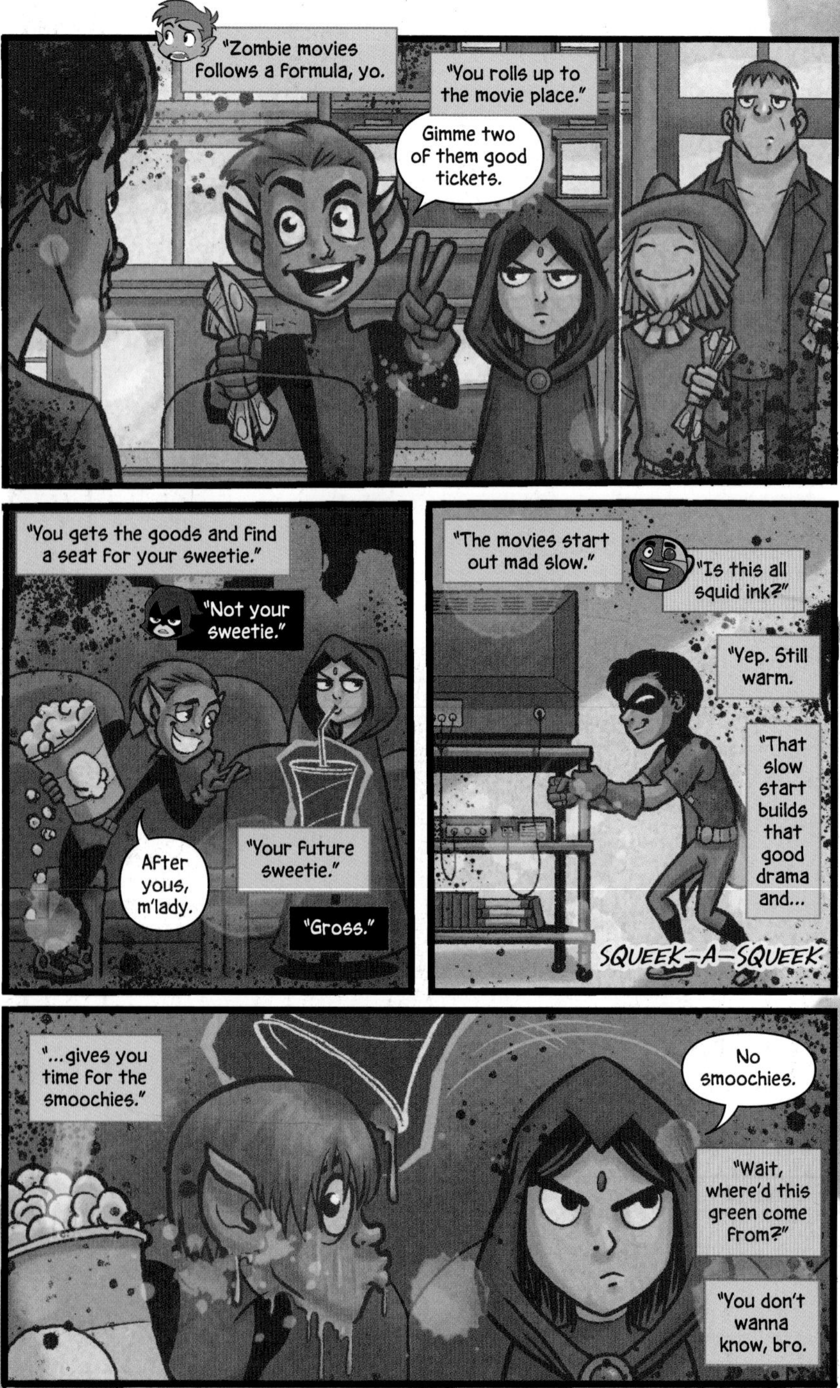
"Zombie movies follows a formula, yo.
"You rolls up to the movie place."
Gimme two of them good tickets.
"You gets the goods and find a seat for your sweetie."
"Not your sweetie."
After yous, m'lady.
"Your future sweetie."
"Gross."
"The movies start out mad slow."
"Is this all squid ink?"
"Yep. Still warm.
"That slow start builds that good drama and...
SQUEEK—A—SQUEEK
"...gives you time for the smoochies."
No smoochies.
"Wait, where'd this green come from?"
"You don't wanna know, bro.

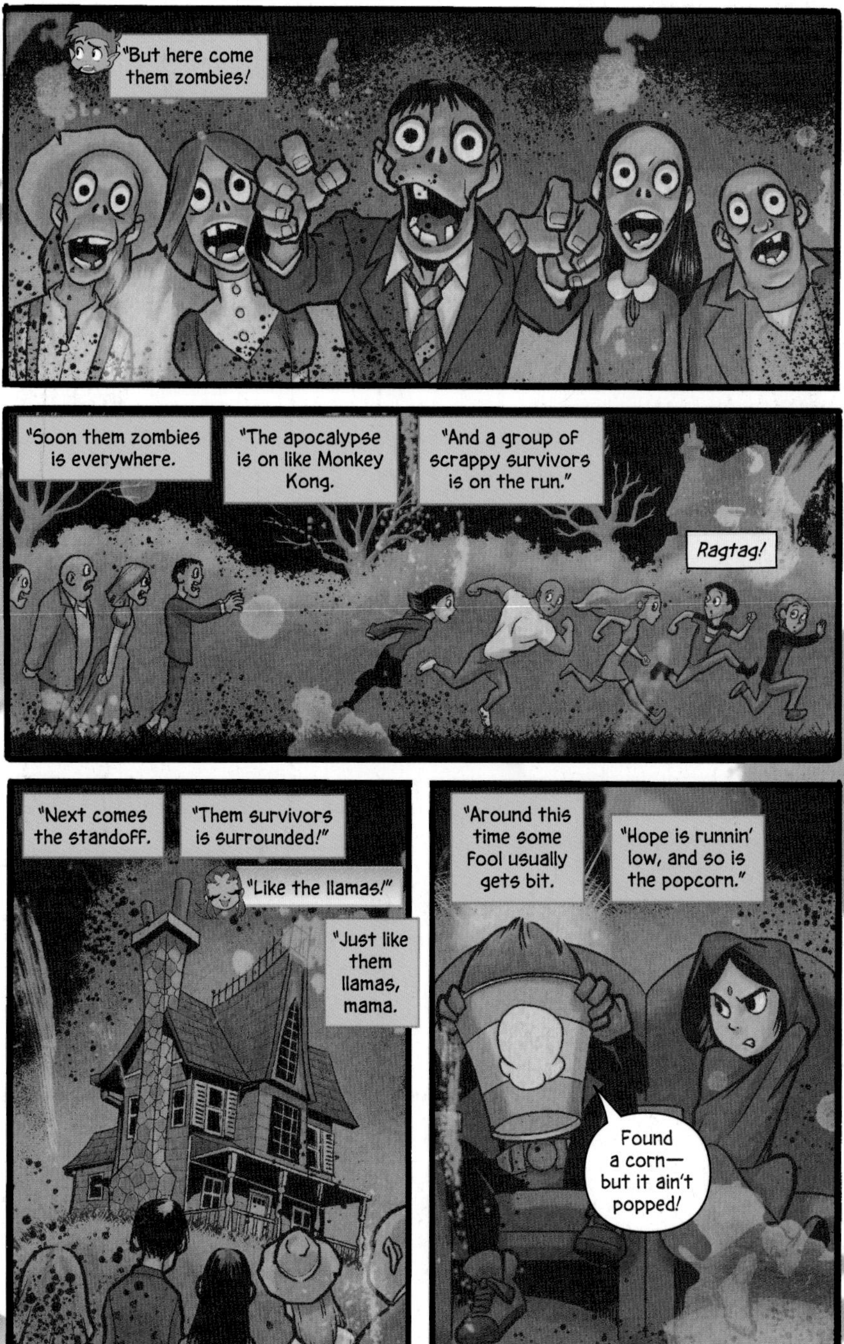
"But here come them zombies!
"Soon them zombies is everywhere.
"The apocalypse is on like Monkey Kong.
"And a group of scrappy survivors is on the run."
Ragtag!
"Next comes the standoff.
"Them survivors is surrounded!"
"Like the llamas!"
"Just like them llamas, mama.
"Around this time some fool usually gets bit.
"Hope is runnin' low, and so is the popcorn."
Found a corn— but it ain't popped!

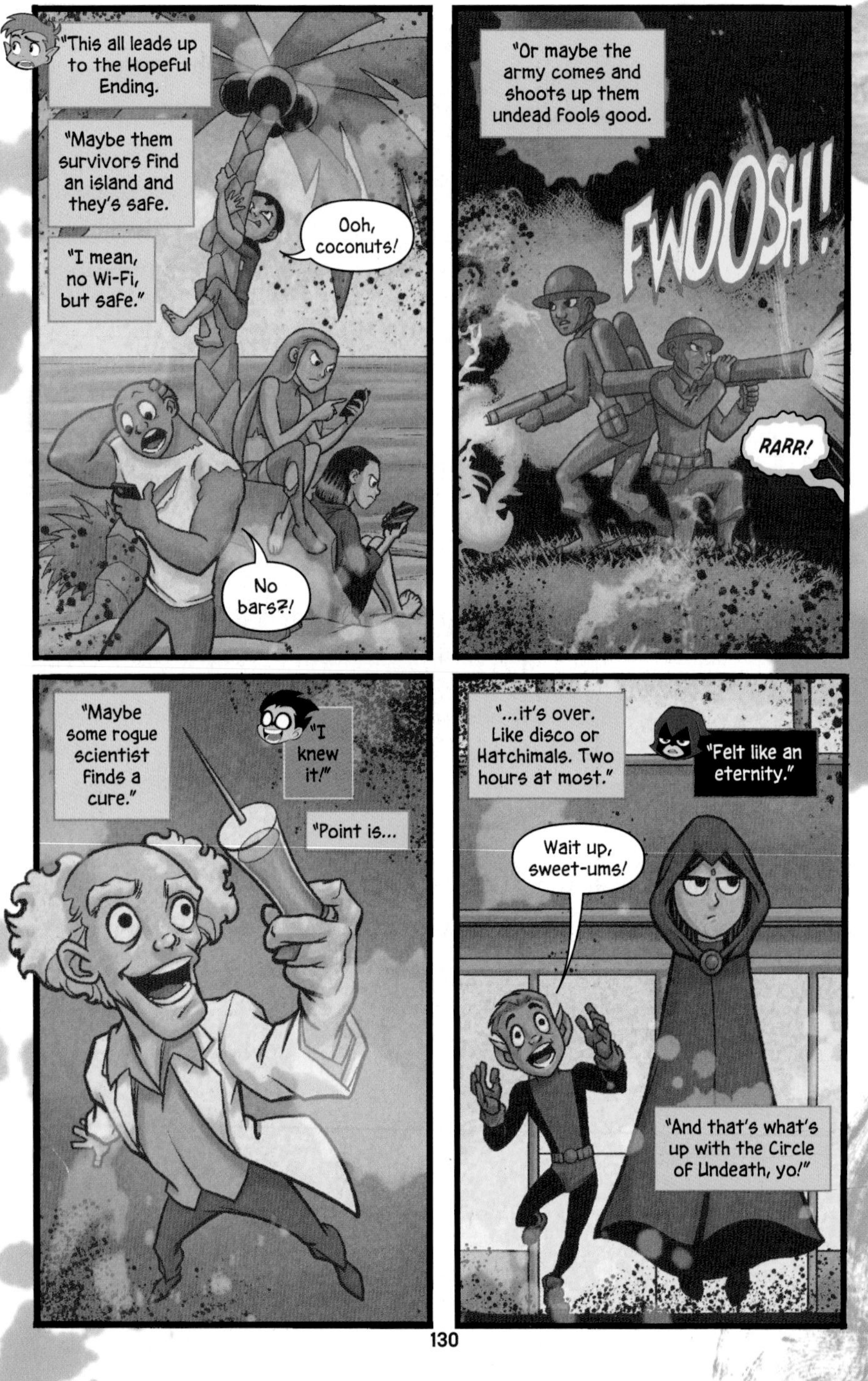
"This all leads up to the Hopeful Ending.
"Maybe them survivors find an island and they's safe.
"I mean, no Wi-Fi, but safe."
Ooh, coconuts!
No bars?!
"Or maybe the army comes and shoots up them undead fools good.
FWOOSH!
RARR!
"Maybe some rogue scientist finds a cure."
"I knew it!"
"Point is...
"...it's over. Like disco or Hatchimals. Two hours at most."
"Felt like an eternity."
Wait up, sweet-ums!
"And that's what's up with the Circle of Undeath, yo!"

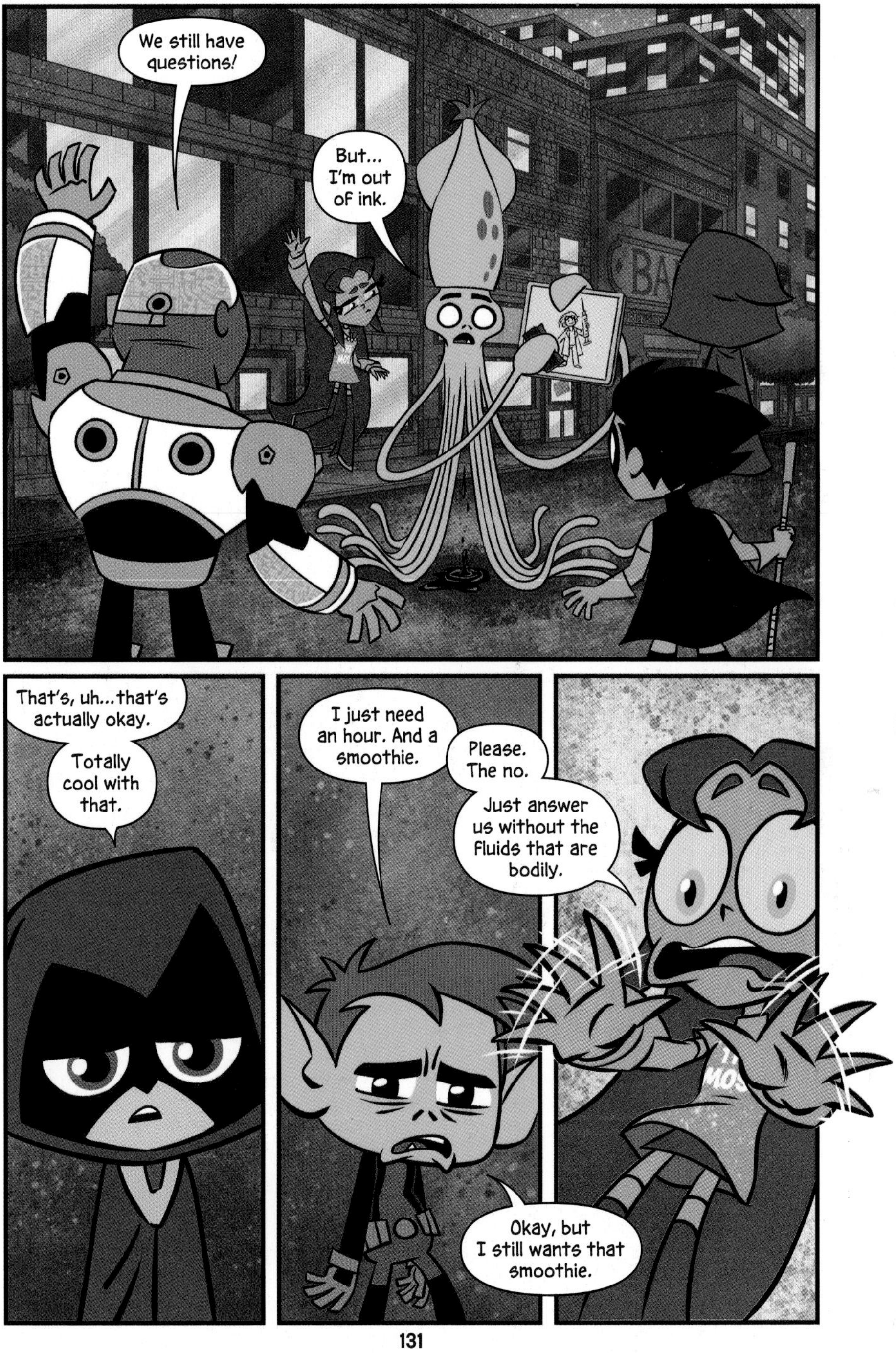
We still have questions!
But... I'm out of ink.
That's, uh...that's actually okay.
Totally cool with that.
I just need an hour. And a smoothie.
Please. The no.
Just answer us without the fluids that are bodily.
Okay, but I still wants that smoothie.

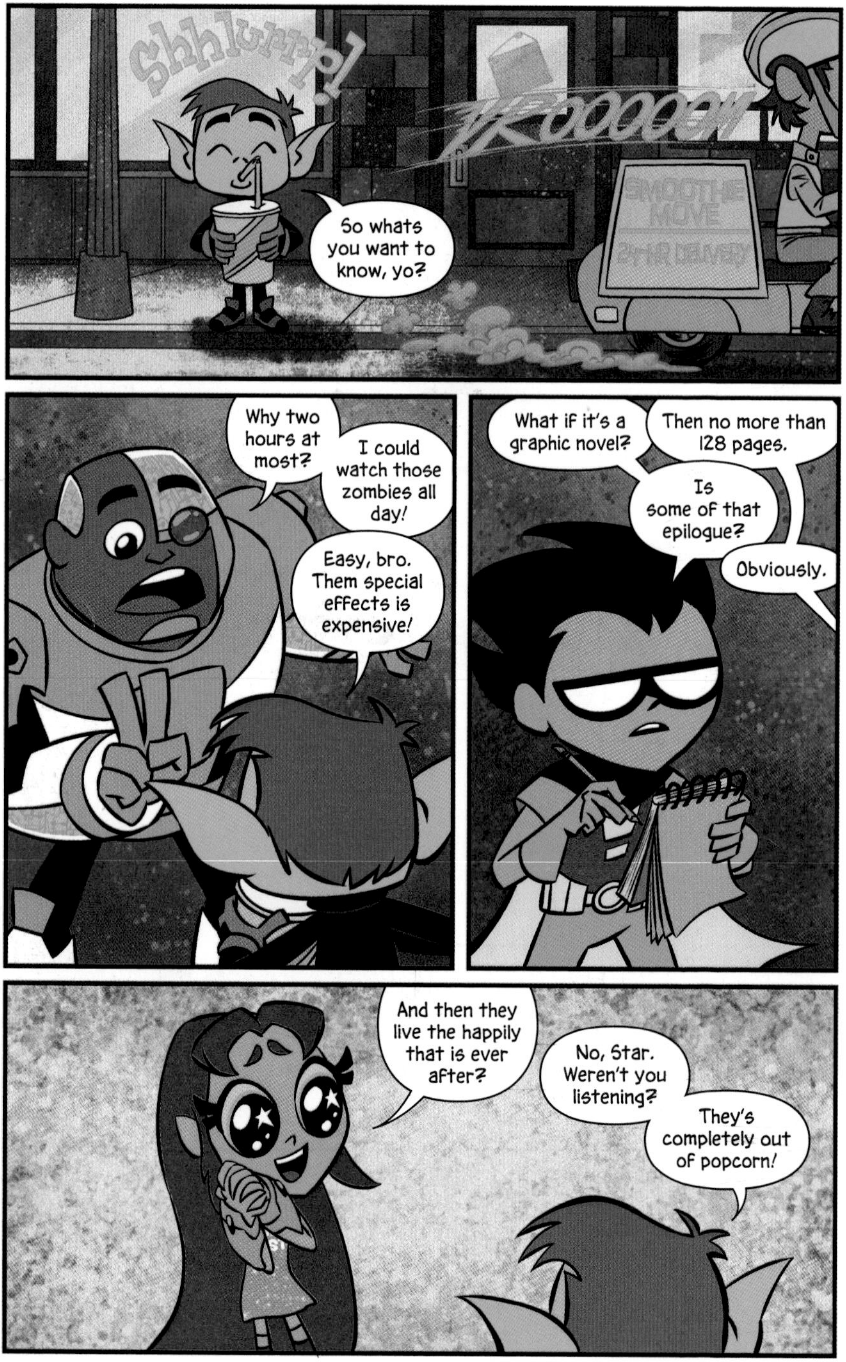
Shhlurrp!
KROOOOOM
SMOOTHIE MOVE
24-HR DELIVERY
So whats you want to know, yo?
Why two hours at most?
I could watch those zombies all day!
Easy, bro. Them special effects is expensive!
What if it's a graphic novel?
Then no more than 128 pages.
Is some of that epilogue?
Obviously.
And then they live the happily that is ever after?
No, Star. Weren't you listening?
They's completely out of popcorn!

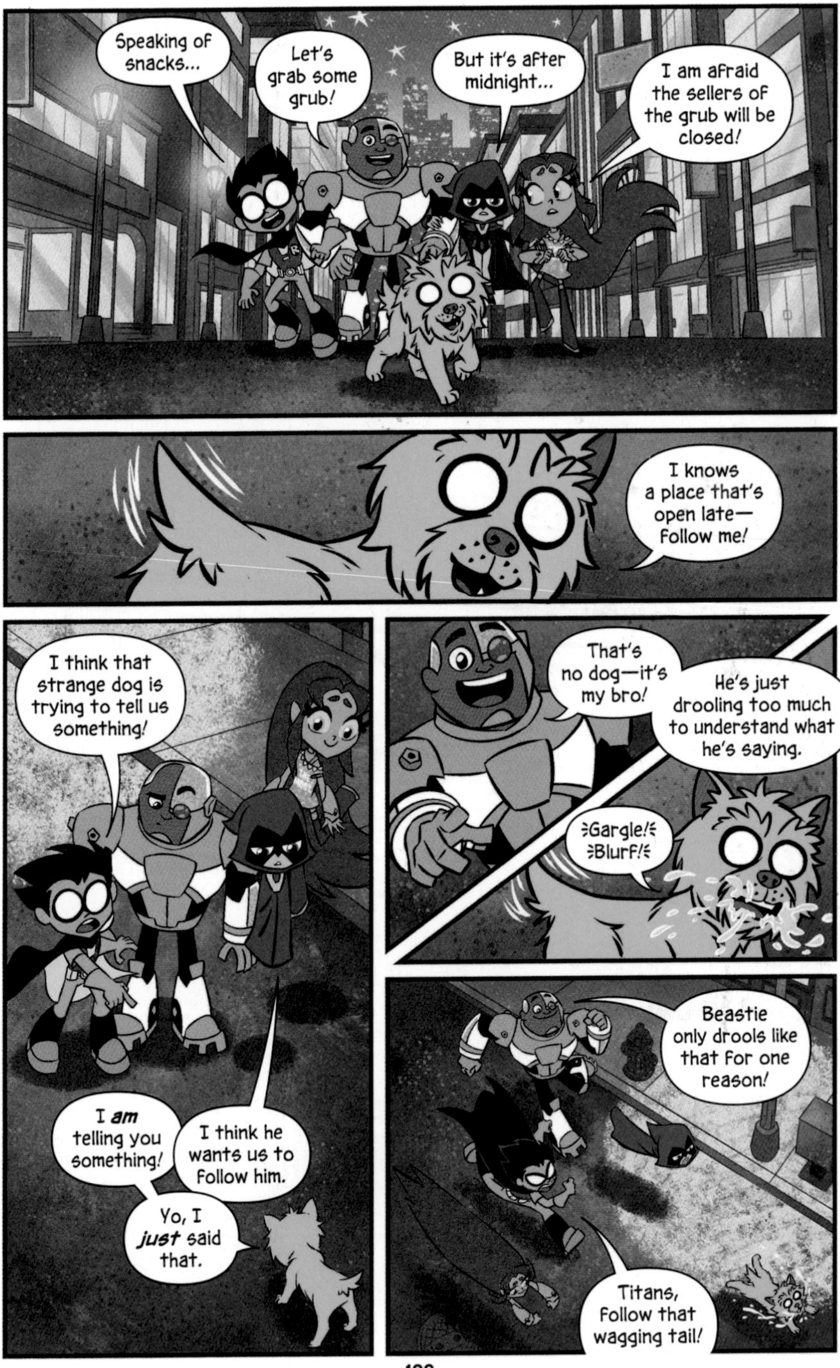
Speaking of snacks...
Let's grab some grub!
But it's after midnight...
I am afraid the sellers of the grub will be closed!
I knows a place that's open late—Follow me!
I think that strange dog is trying to tell us something!
I *am* telling you something!
I think he wants us to follow him.
Yo, I *just* said that.
That's no dog—it's my bro!
He's just drooling too much to understand what he's saying.
Gargle!
Blurf!
Beastie only drools like that for one reason!
Titans, follow that wagging tail!

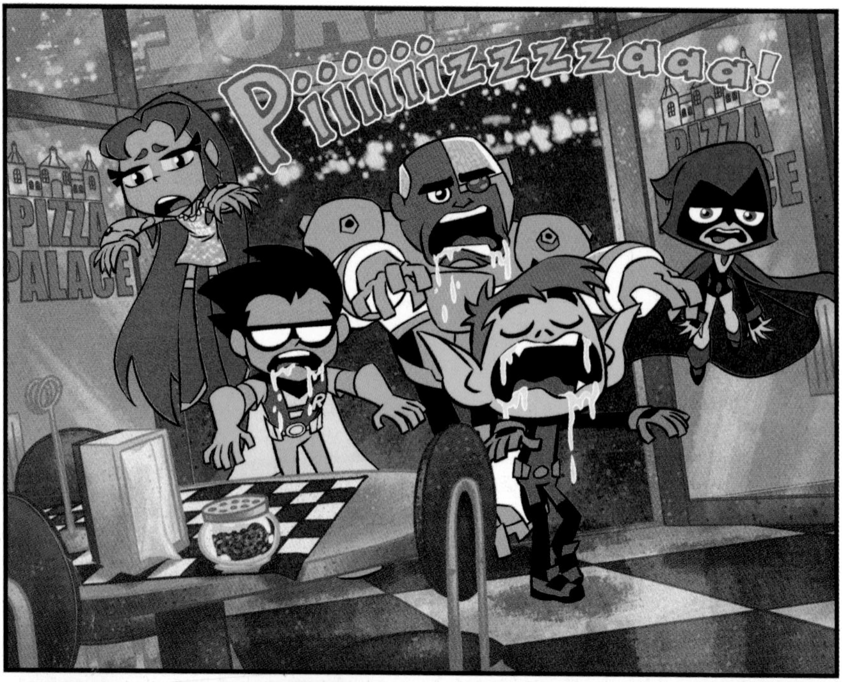
Piiiiiizzzzzaaaa!

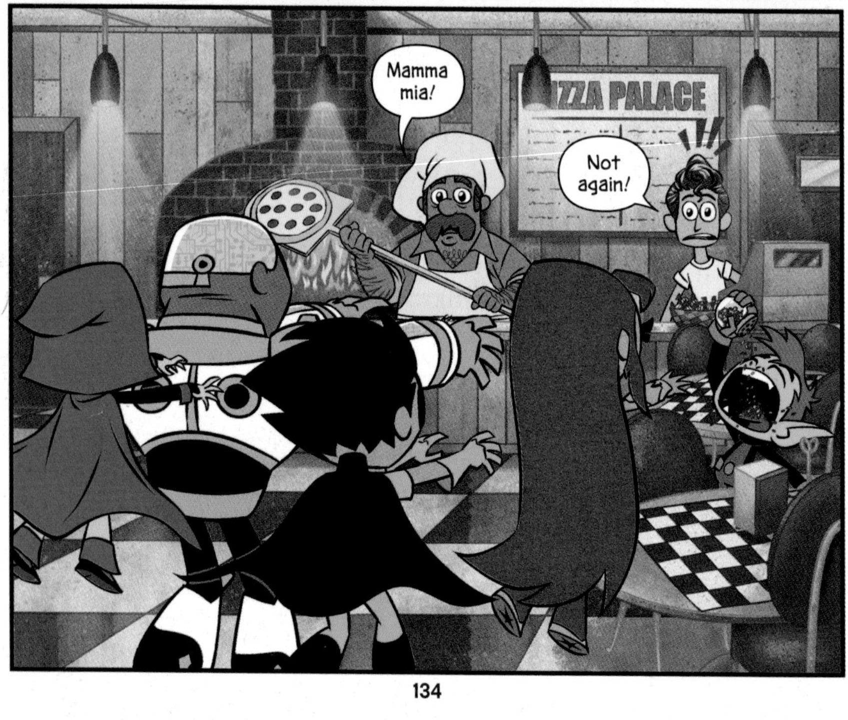
Mamma mia!
Not again!
PIZZA PALACE

Chapter Nine

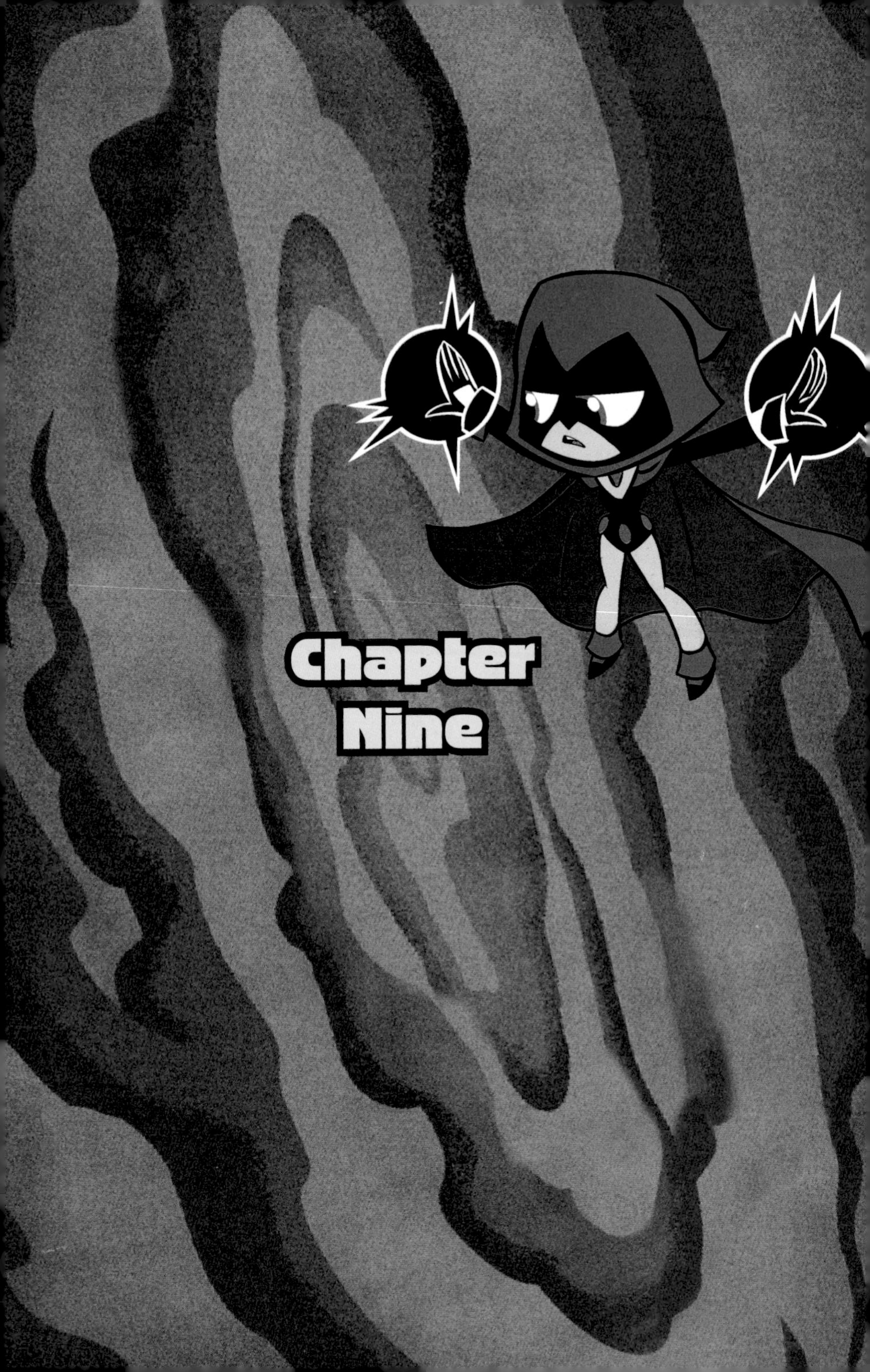

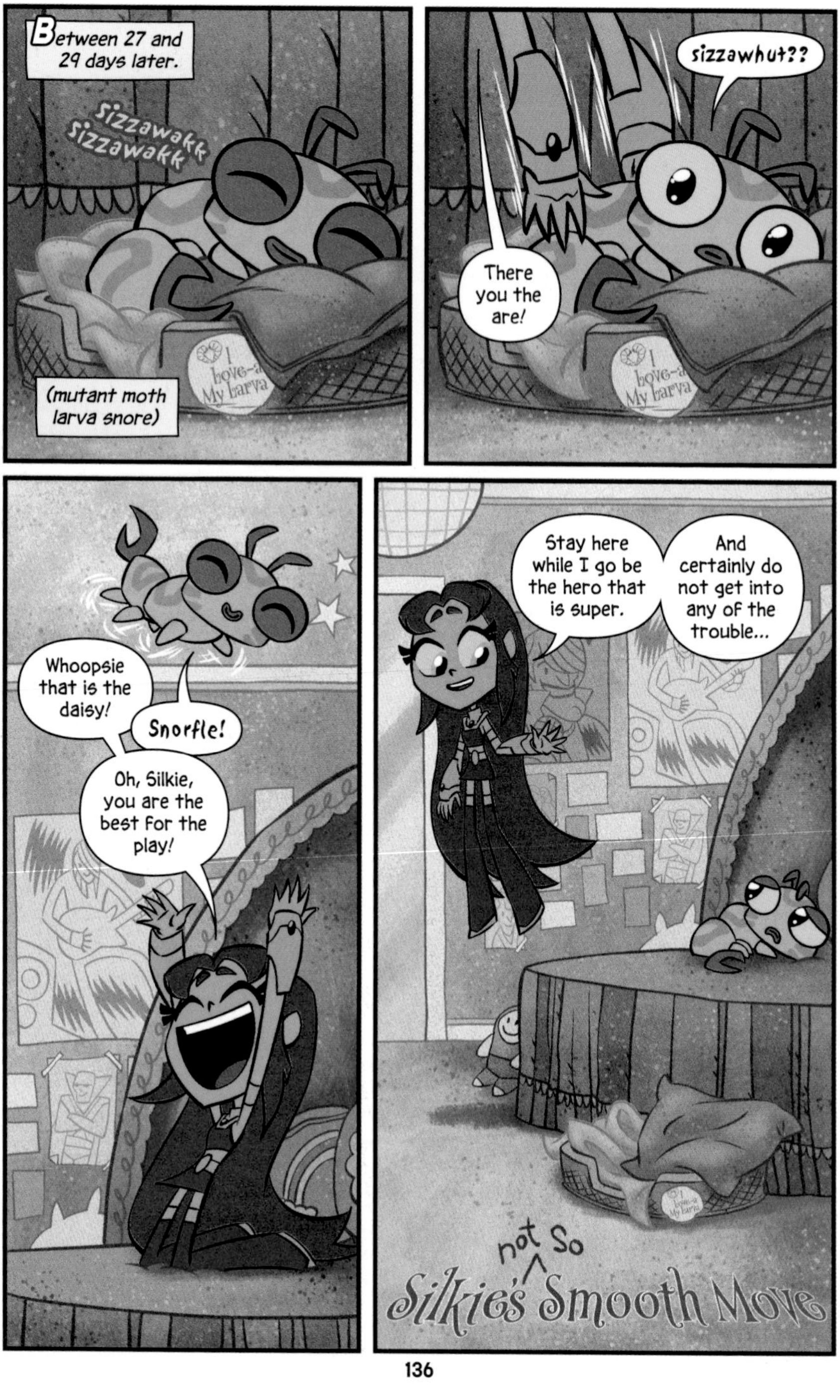
Between 27 and 29 days later.
Sizzawakk Sizzawakk
(mutant moth larva snore)
I love-a My larva
sizzawhut??
There you the are!
I love-a My larva
Whoopsie that is the daisy!
Snorfle!
Oh, Silkie, you are the best for the play!
Stay here while I go be the hero that is super.
And certainly do not get into any of the trouble...
Silkie's not So Smooth Move

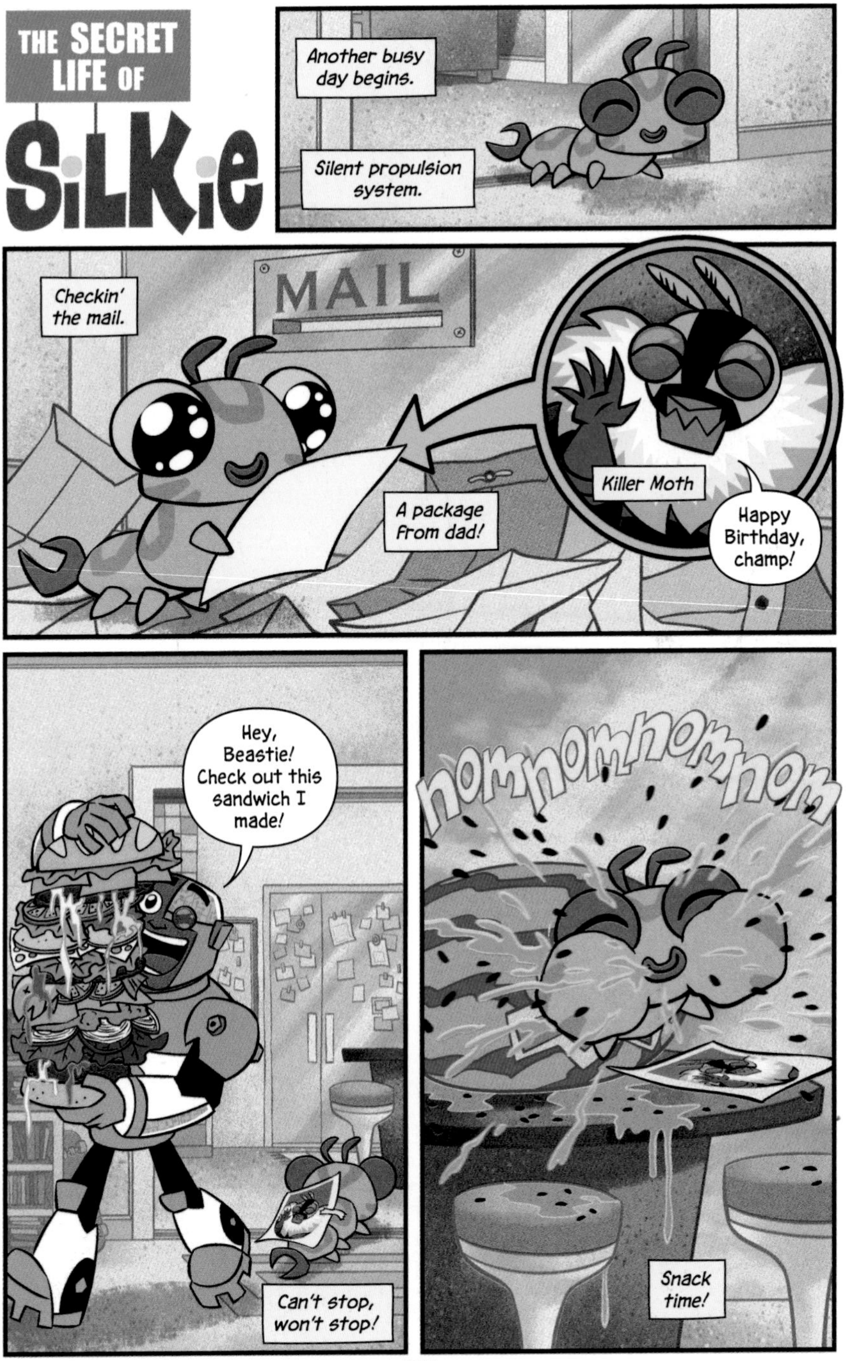
THE SECRET LIFE OF SILKIE
Another busy day begins.
Silent propulsion system.
MAIL
Checkin' the mail.
A package from dad!
Killer Moth
Happy Birthday, champ!
Hey, Beastie! Check out this sandwich I made!
Can't stop, won't stop!
nomnomnomnomnom
Snack time!

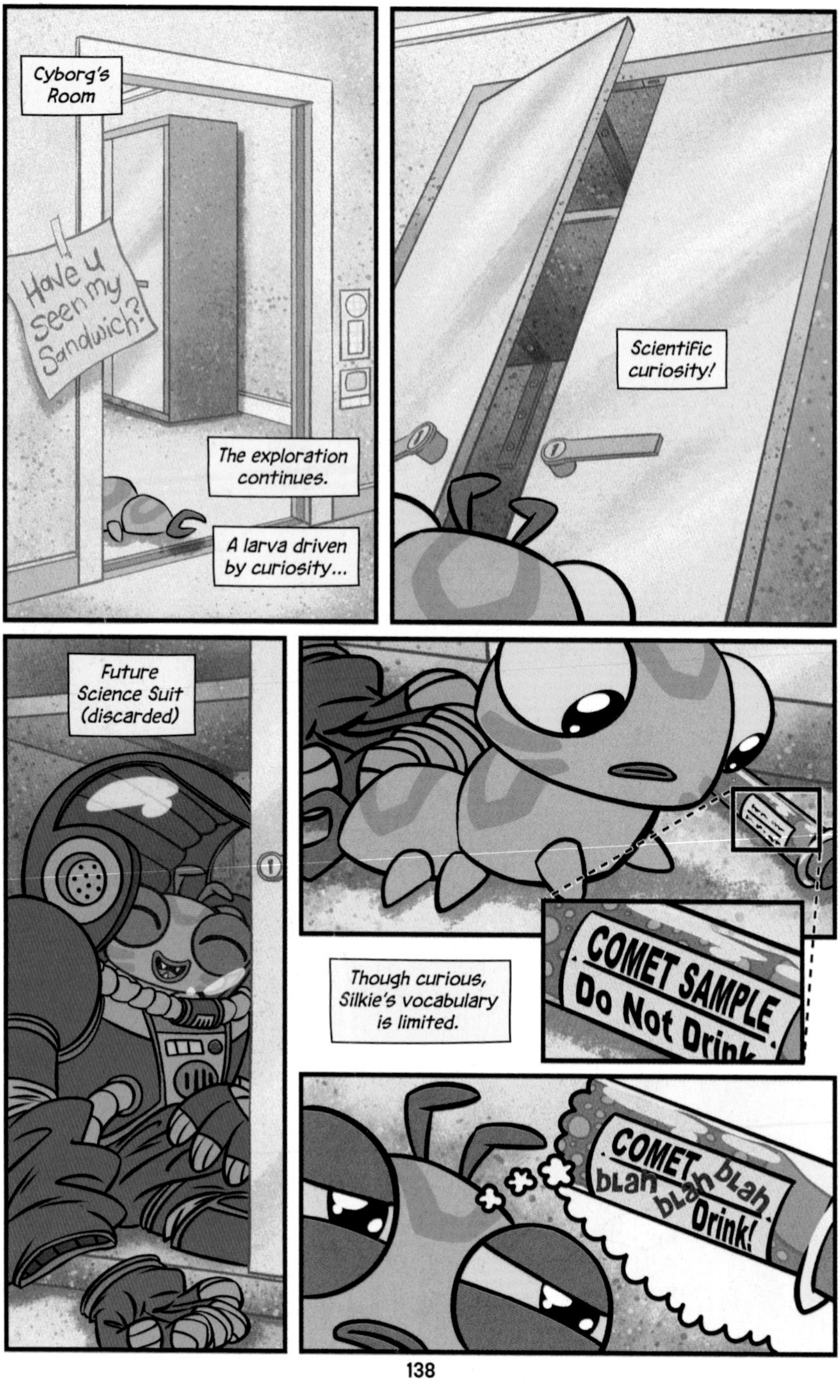
Cyborg's Room
Have u seen my Sandwich?
The exploration continues.
A larva driven by curiosity...
Scientific curiosity!
Future Science Suit (discarded)
COMET SAMPLE
Do Not Drink
Though curious, Silkie's vocabulary is limited.
COMET blah blah blah Drink!

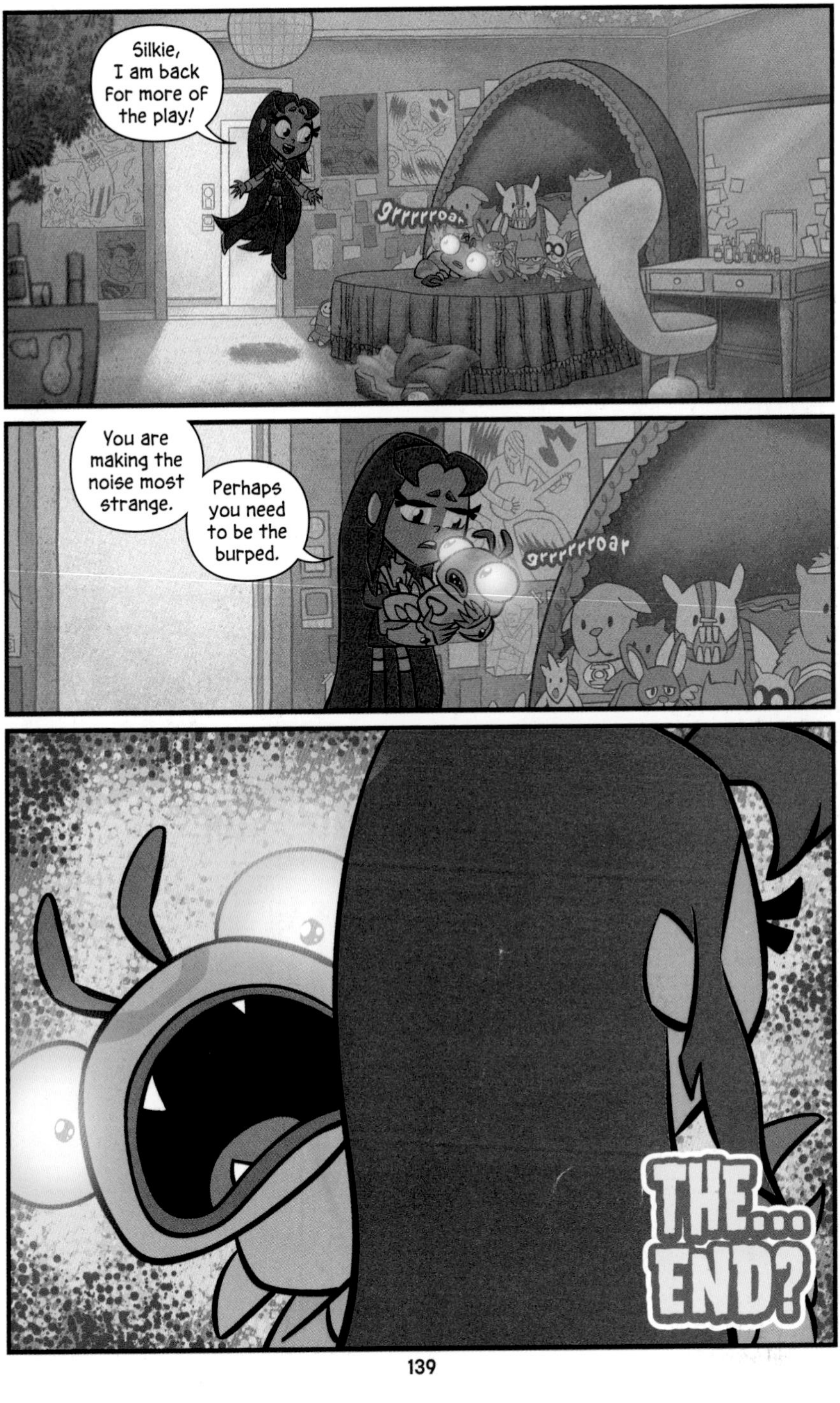
Silkie, I am back for more of the play!
grrrrroar
You are making the noise most strange.
Perhaps you need to be the burped.
grrrrrroar
THE... END?

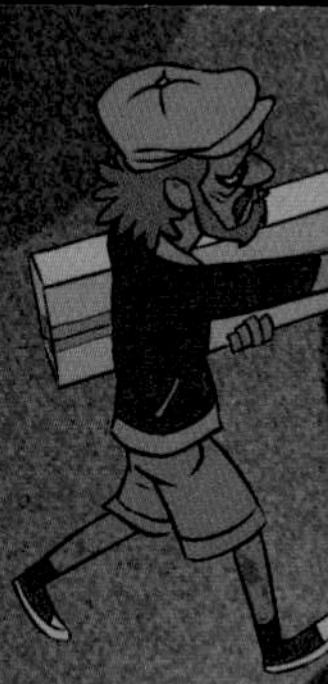

MICHAEL NORTHROP is the *New York Times* bestselling author of 14 books for young readers, including the bestselling TombQuest adventure series and the hit graphic novel *Dear Justice League*. He's been named a *Publishers Weekly* Flying Start, and his books have been selected for the Indie Next List, the Junior Library Guild, and numerous state lists. Collectively, they have sold more than a million copies. He is originally from Salisbury, Connecticut, a small town in the foothills of the Berkshire Mountains, where he mastered the arts of tree climbing, BB gun shooting, and field goal kicking with only moderate injuries. After graduating from NYU, he worked at *Sports Illustrated for Kids* magazine for 12 years, the last five of those as baseball editor.

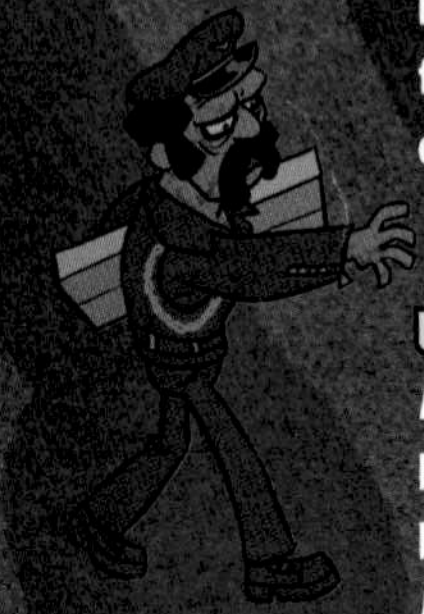

ERICH OWEN is a cartoonist living in San Diego. His first graphic novel, *Mail Order Ninja*, which he co-created and illustrated, was published in 2005 and became a multi-volume series. Since then, he's been drawing all kinds of comic book projects! Recently, he's drawn he draws *Teen Titans Go!* and *Batman: Knightwatch* for DC Comics.

WES ABBOTT has at one point or another lettered every major character at DC and Marvel, including lengthy runs on titles such as *Legion of Super-Heroes*, *Thor*, and *Teen Titans Go!* Also known as the creator and writer/artist of the Dogby Walks Alone books, Wes currently lives in Japan with his wife Chise and their two kids Takeru and Nene.

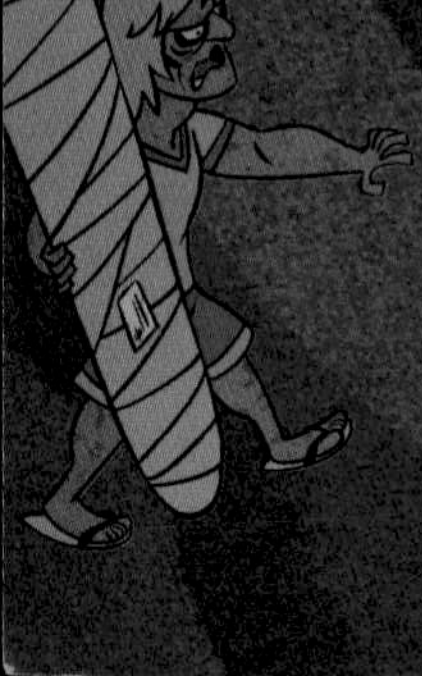

Gustavo Duarte is a comics artist and writer from São Paulo, Brazil. His books are published in Brazil, the USA, Germany, France, Belgium, Argentina, Uruguay, and other countries. His work has also appeared in *Dear Justice League*, *Dear DC Super-Villains*, *Bizarro*, *Moon Girl and Devil Dinosaur*, and *Lockjaw*. In his rare free time, he likes zapping his television between *Looney Tunes*, NBA, *Seinfeld*, the classic *Magnum, P.I.*, *Ancient Aliens*, and, sure, *Teen Titans Go!*

D.J. Kirkland is a comic book artist and writer based in the San Francisco Bay Area. His work has appeared in his debut graphic novel *The Black Mage* as well as *Young Men in Love*, *Aggretsuko*, and *Dream Daddy*. When he's not juggling his day job and comic book work, you can find D.J. powerlifting, playing lots of fighting games, watching anime, and making silly videos on TikTok.

Yancey Labat has been illustrating since elementary school when his friends would ask him to draw action heroes. He started his career in the art corrections department at Marvel Comics and has since illustrated many comic books, children's books, and graphic novels, including the *New York Times* bestselling DC Super Hero Girls series. He lives in California with his wife and two daughters.

Abigail Larson, a Hugo Award winner, has worked on DC titles such as *Sandman: The Dreaming* and *Teen Titans Go! To Camp!* She's also worked with Netflix Animation and Disney Publishing Worldwide, and loves all things strange and spooky, especially scary books and movies!

Mayo "SEN" Naito is an artist from Japan. Her work has appeared in *Shazam and the Seven Magic Lands*. She also did promotional art for DC's middle grade original graphic novel launch. Her most favorite superhero is Shazam, and she displays Shazam merchandise on her TV racks and calls it a Shazam shrine. Most of the time, SEN enjoys watching content on streaming services.

Safiya Zerrougui is a cartoonist based in Montreal, Canada. You can find her work in DC Comics' *Wonderful Women of the World* as well as *We Are Big Time* (Knopf 2023). She's been drawing ever since she could hold a pen and now, years later, you can still find her doodling her days away!

Carrie Strachan is an award-awaiting colorist from San Diego, California. Her work has appeared in such titles as *DC Super Hero Girls*, *Hellblazer*, *MAD*, and *Suicide Squad Most Wanted: Deadshot & Katana*. When she's not trying to meet her deadlines, Carrie enjoys reading, playing video games, and watching old movies.

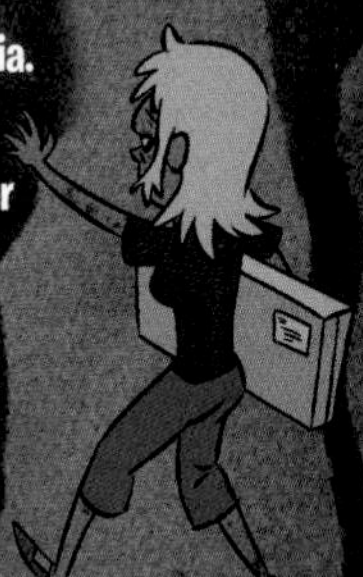

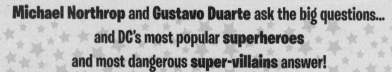

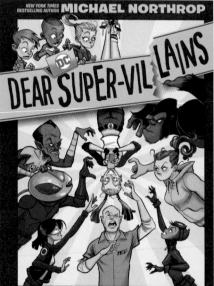

WANT TO READ MORE BOOKS BY THESE CREATORS? ERICH DREW STORIES IN:

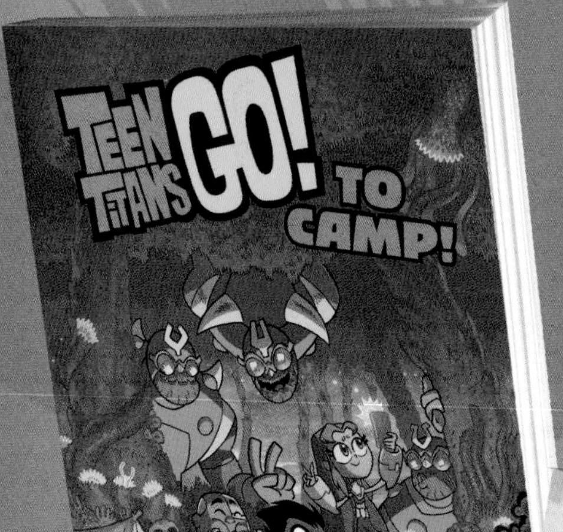
TEEN TITANS GO! TO CAMP!
Written by Sholly Fisch
Illustrated by Marcelo DiChiara and more!

Teen Titans Go! To Camp!
Sholly Fisch, Marcelo diChiara, and more!
ISBN-13: 978-1-77950-317-6

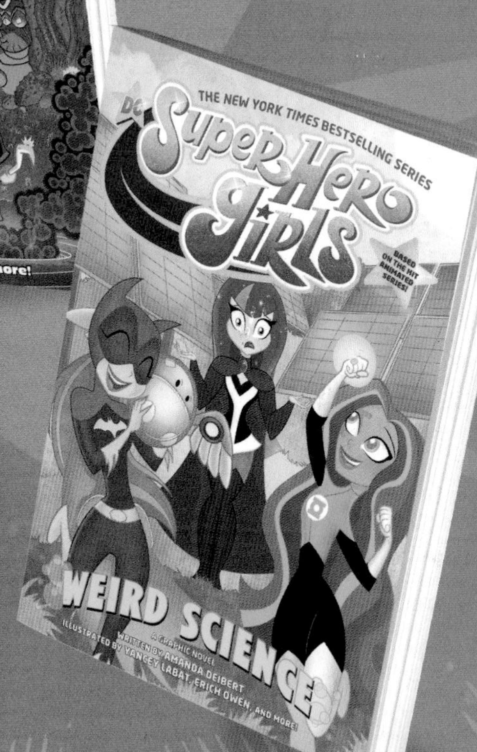
THE NEW YORK TIMES BESTSELLING SERIES
DC SUPER HERO GIRLS
BASED ON THE HIT ANIMATED SERIES!
WEIRD SCIENCE
A GRAPHIC NOVEL
WRITTEN BY AMANDA DEIBERT
ILLUSTRATED BY YANCEY LABAT, ERICH OWEN, AND MORE!

DC Super Hero Girls: Weird Science
Amanda Deibert, Yancey Labat, Erich Owen, and more!
ISBN-13: 978-1-4012-9846-3

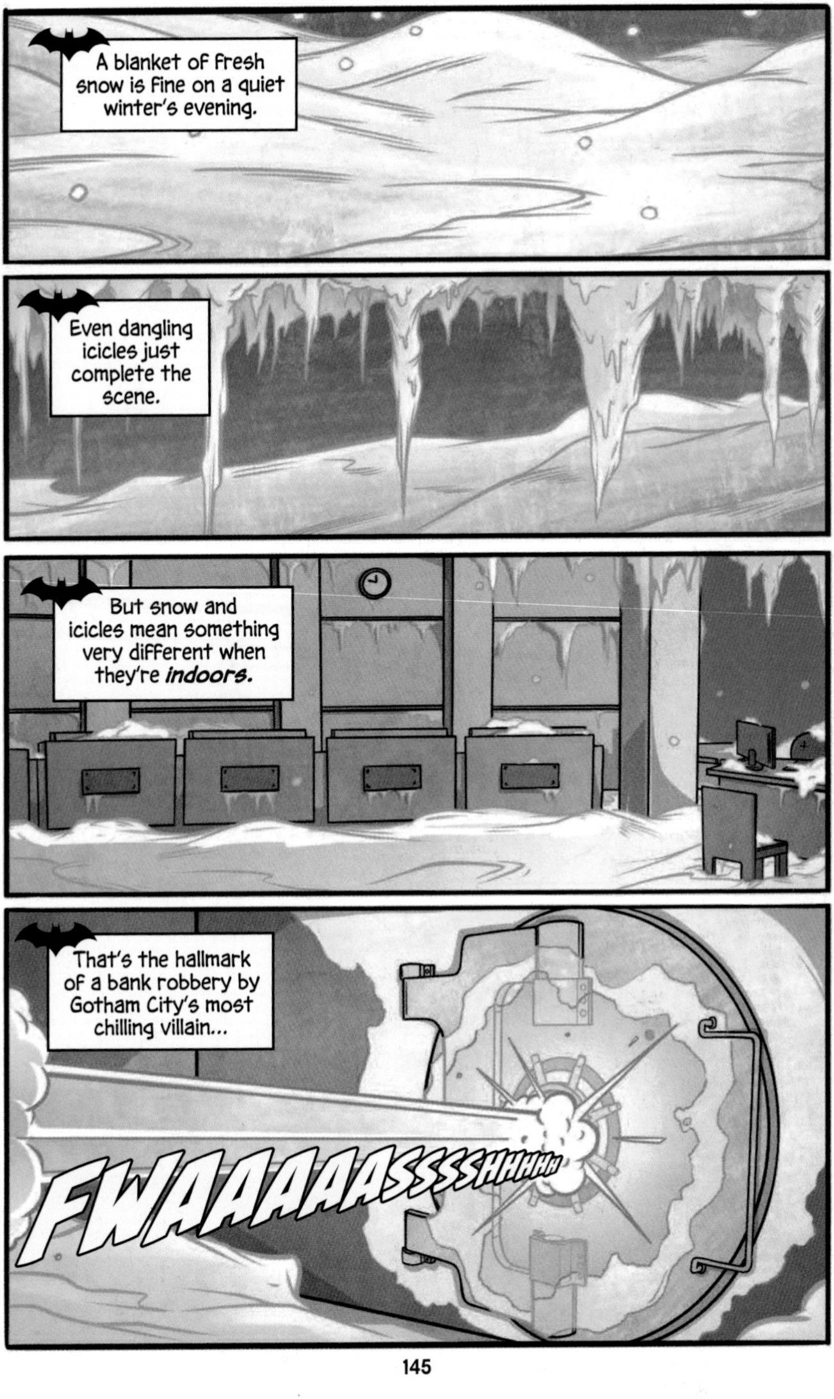
A blanket of fresh snow is fine on a quiet winter's evening.
Even dangling icicles just complete the scene.
But snow and icicles mean something very different when they're *indoors.*
That's the hallmark of a bank robbery by Gotham City's most chilling villain...
FWAAAAAASSSSHHHHH

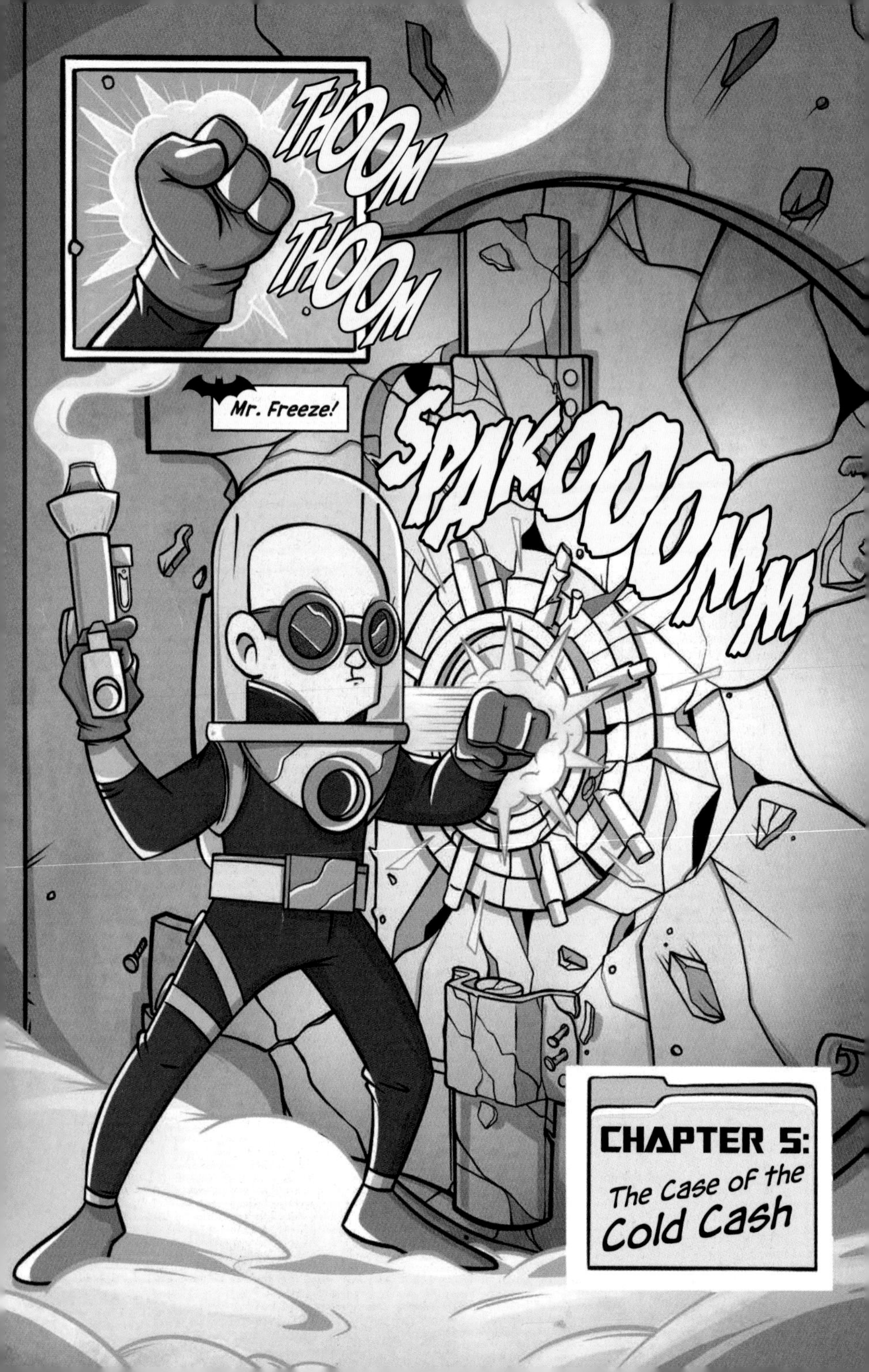

THOOM
THOOM
Mr. Freeze!
SPAKOOOOMM
CHAPTER 5:
The Case of the Cold Cash

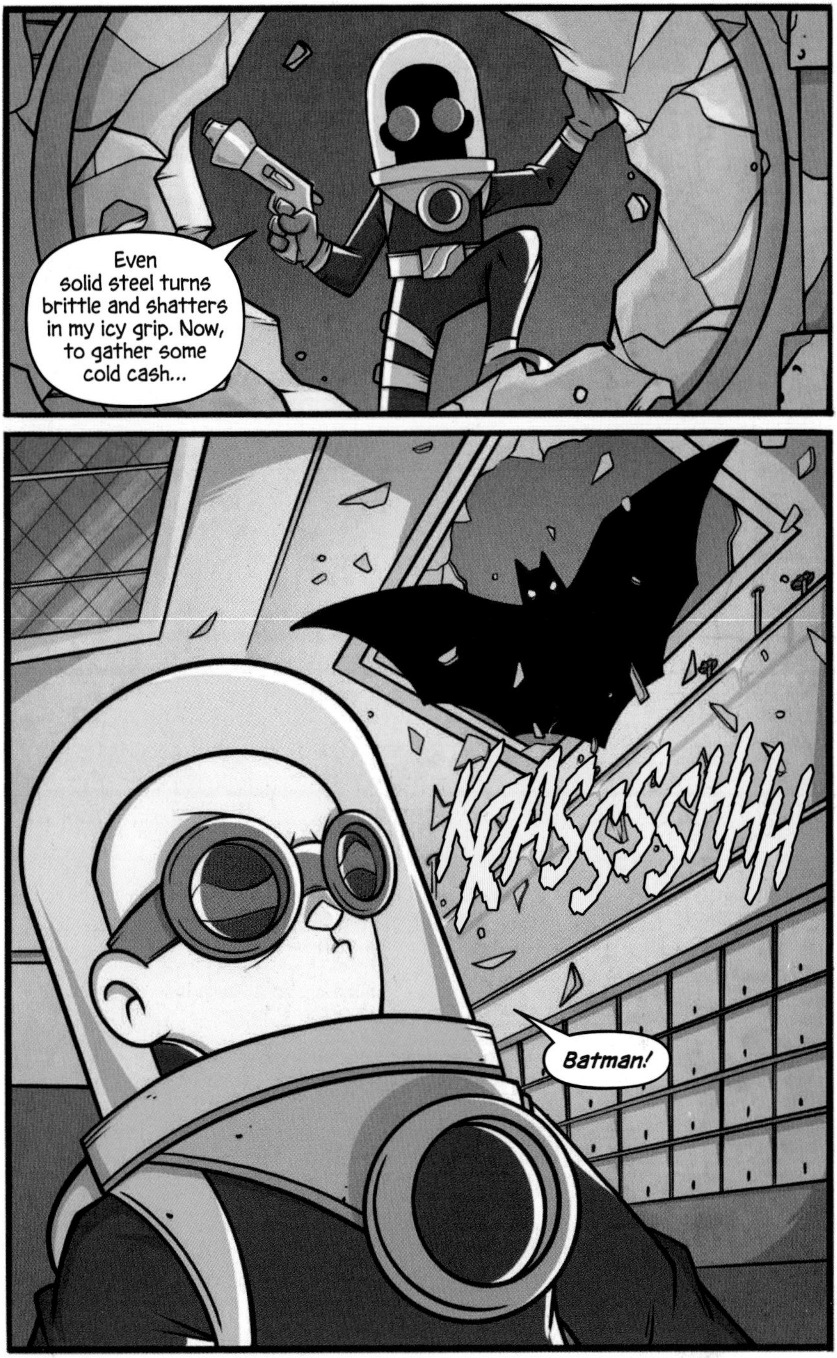
Even solid steel turns brittle and shatters in my icy grip. Now, to gather some cold cash...
KRASSSSHHH
Batman!

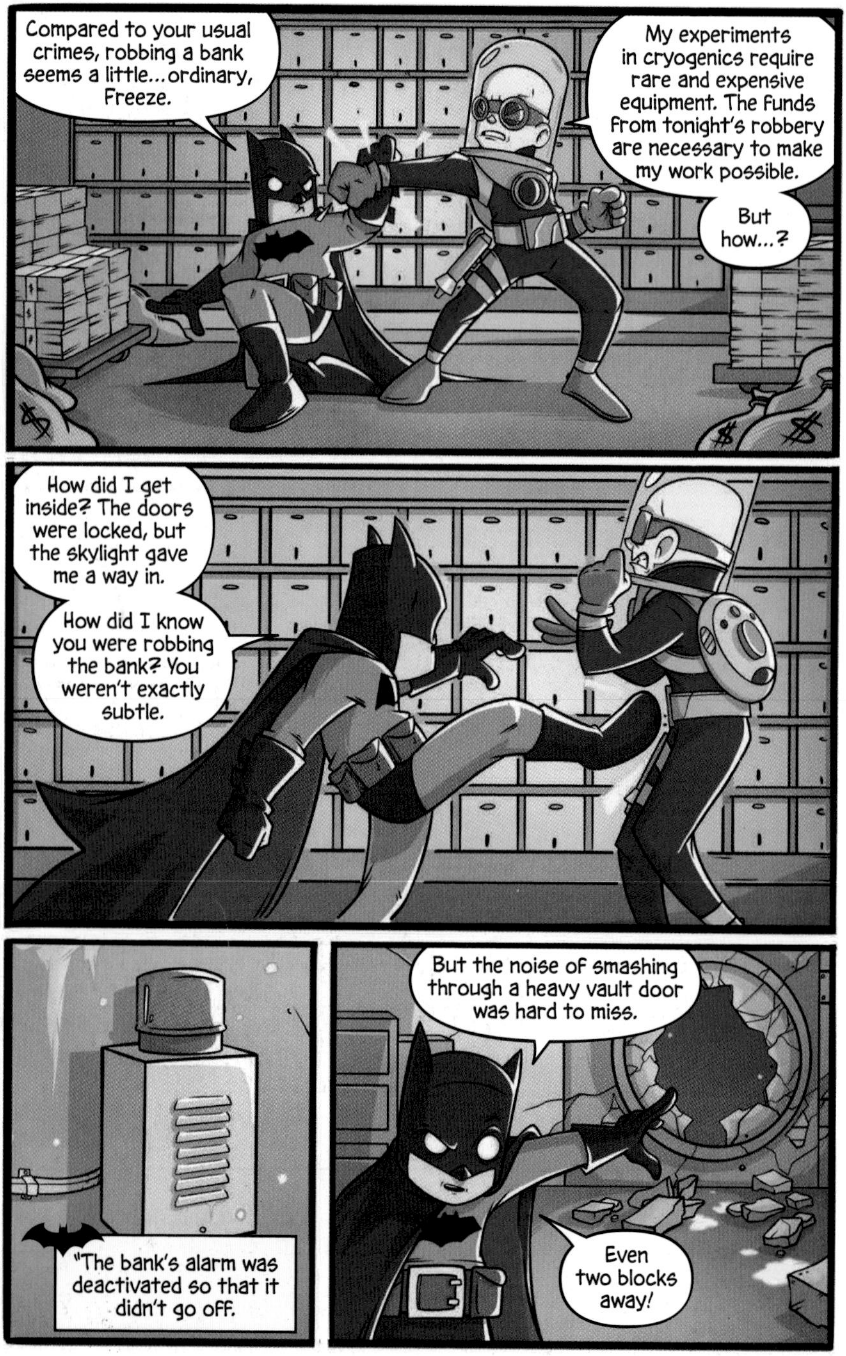

Compared to your usual crimes, robbing a bank seems a little...ordinary, Freeze.
My experiments in cryogenics require rare and expensive equipment. The funds from tonight's robbery are necessary to make my work possible.
But how...?
How did I get inside? The doors were locked, but the skylight gave me a way in.
How did I know you were robbing the bank? You weren't exactly subtle.
"The bank's alarm was deactivated so that it didn't go off.
But the noise of smashing through a heavy vault door was hard to miss.
Even two blocks away!

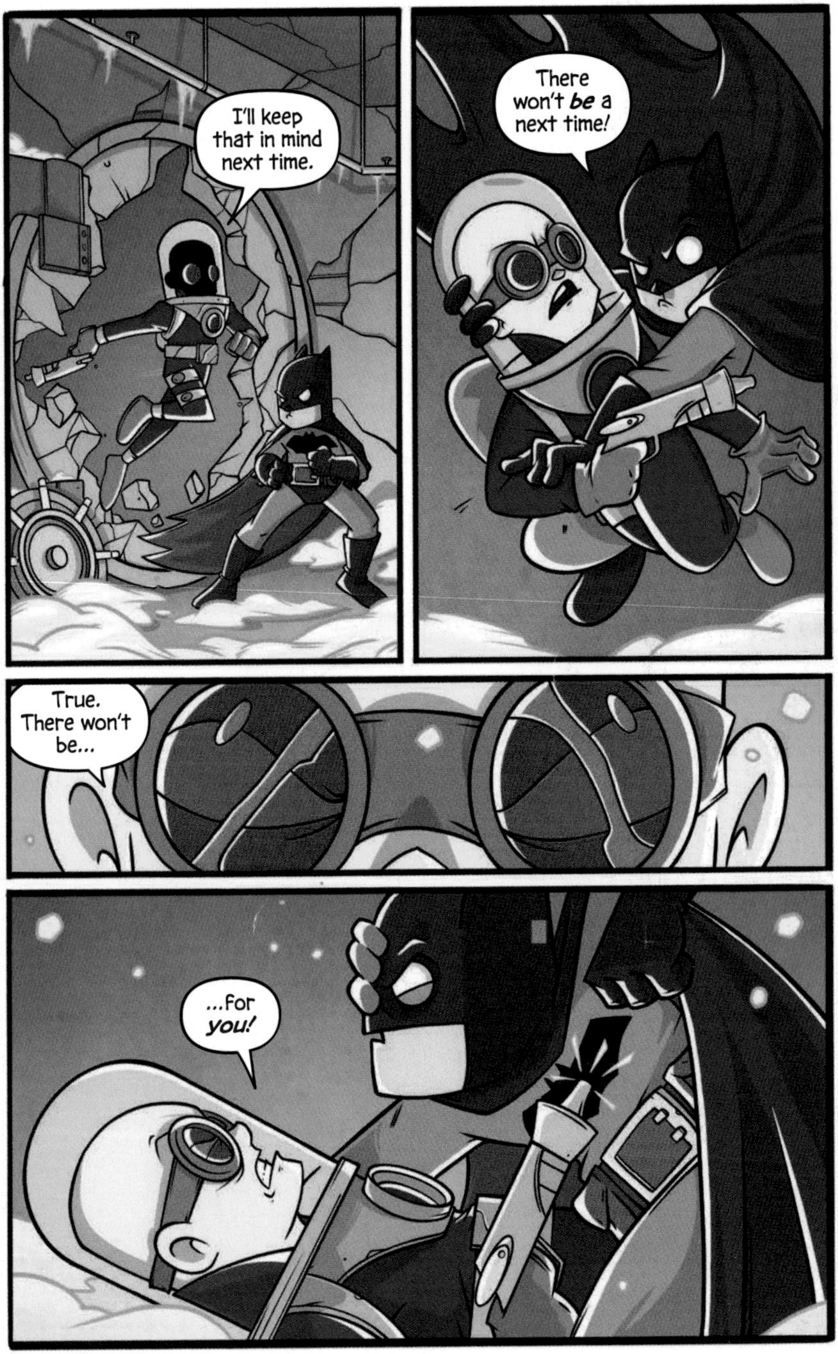
I'll keep that in mind next time.
There won't *be* a next time!
True. There won't be...
...for *you!*

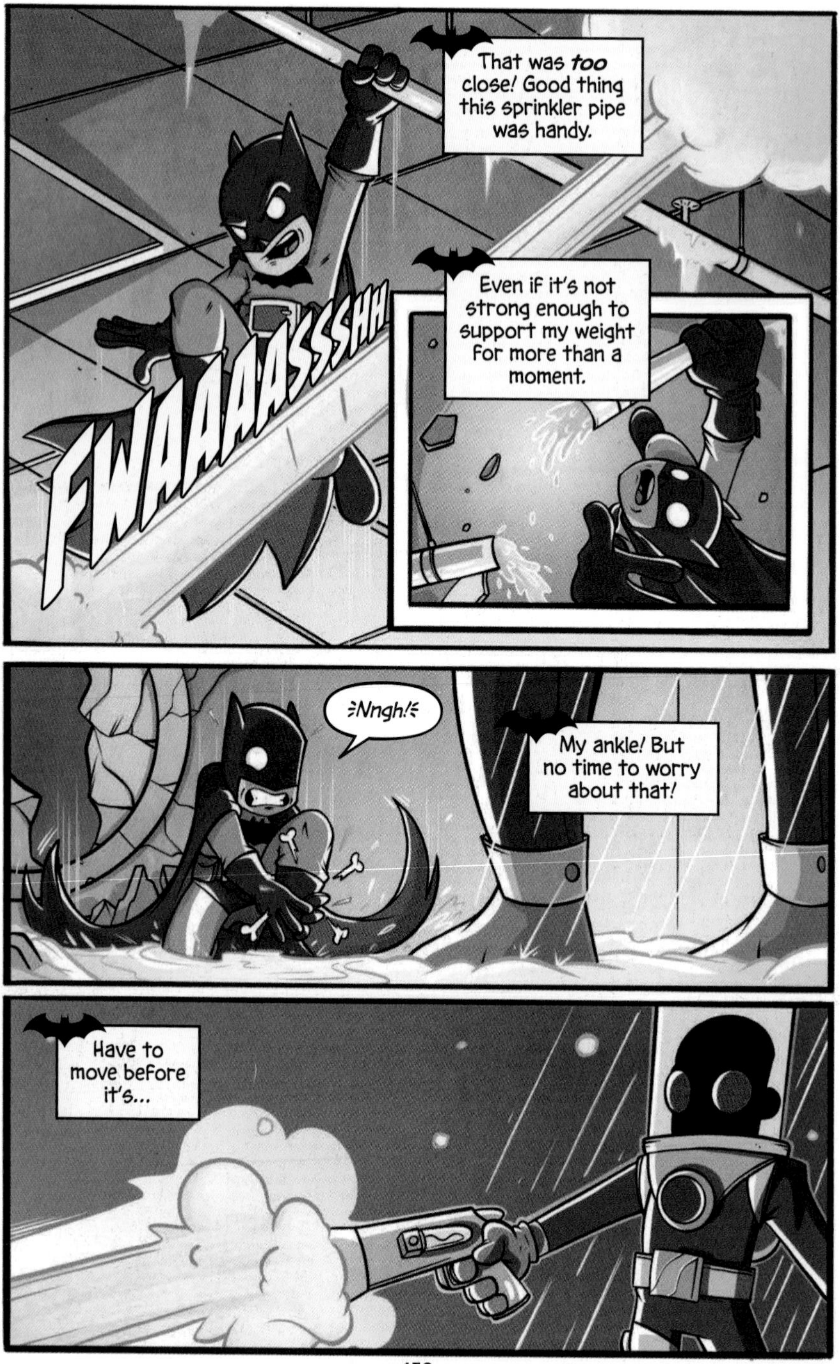
That was *too* close! Good thing this sprinkler pipe was handy.
FWAAAASSSHH
Even if it's not strong enough to support my weight for more than a moment.
Nngh!
My ankle! But no time to worry about that!
Have to move before it's...

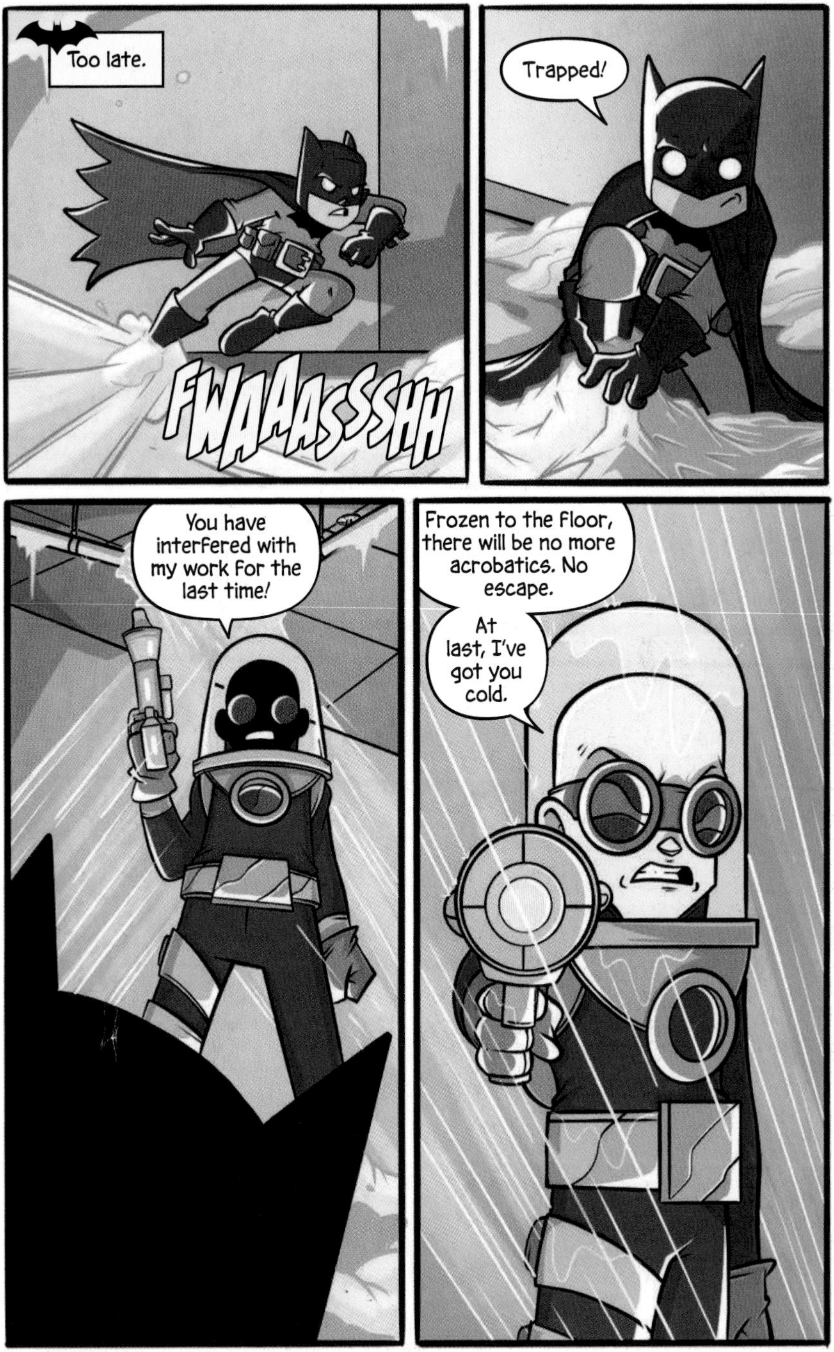
Too late.
FWAAASSSHH
Trapped!
You have interfered with my work for the last time!
Frozen to the floor, there will be no more acrobatics. No escape.
At last, I've got you cold.

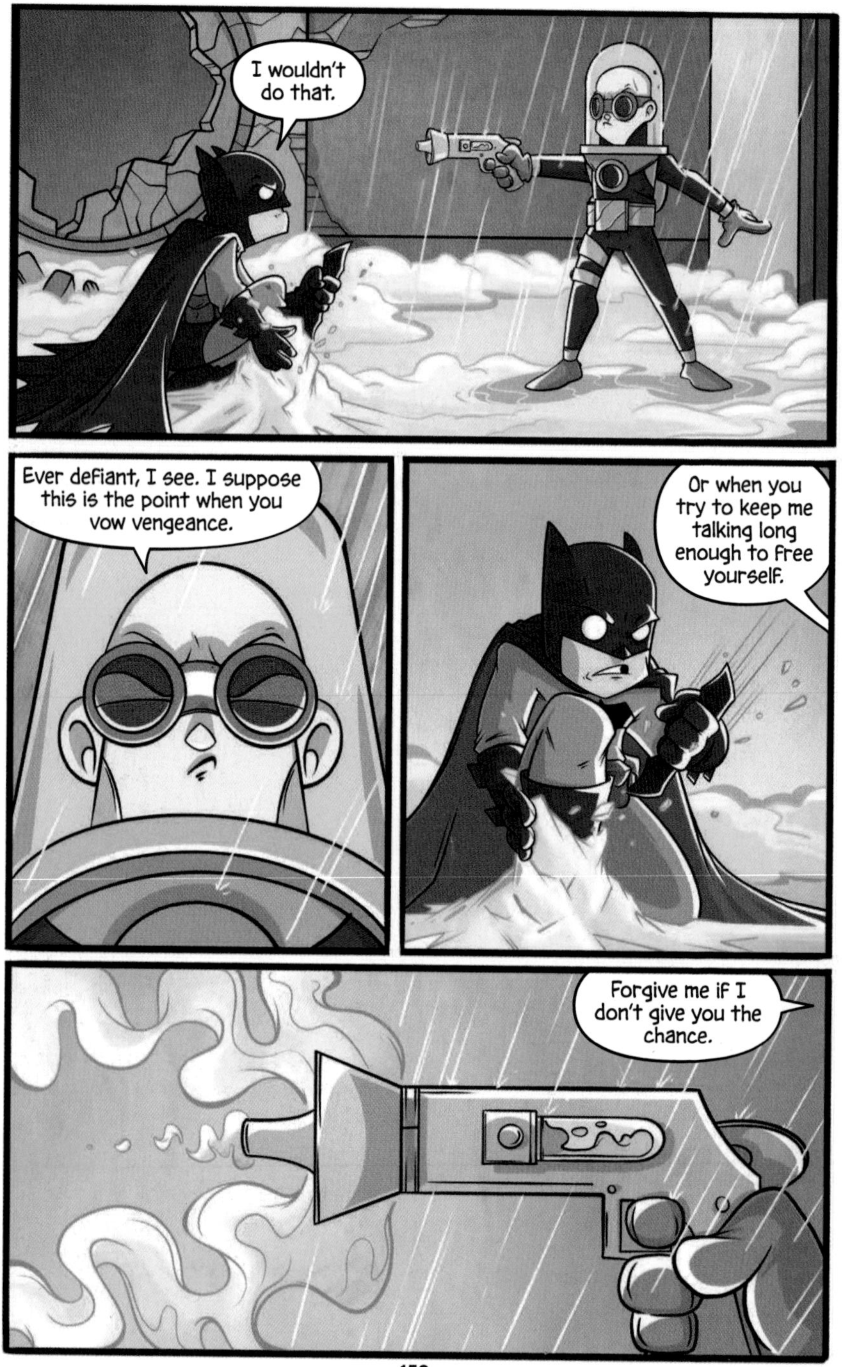
I wouldn't do that.
Ever defiant, I see. I suppose this is the point when you vow vengeance.
Or when you try to keep me talking long enough to free yourself.
Forgive me if I don't give you the chance.

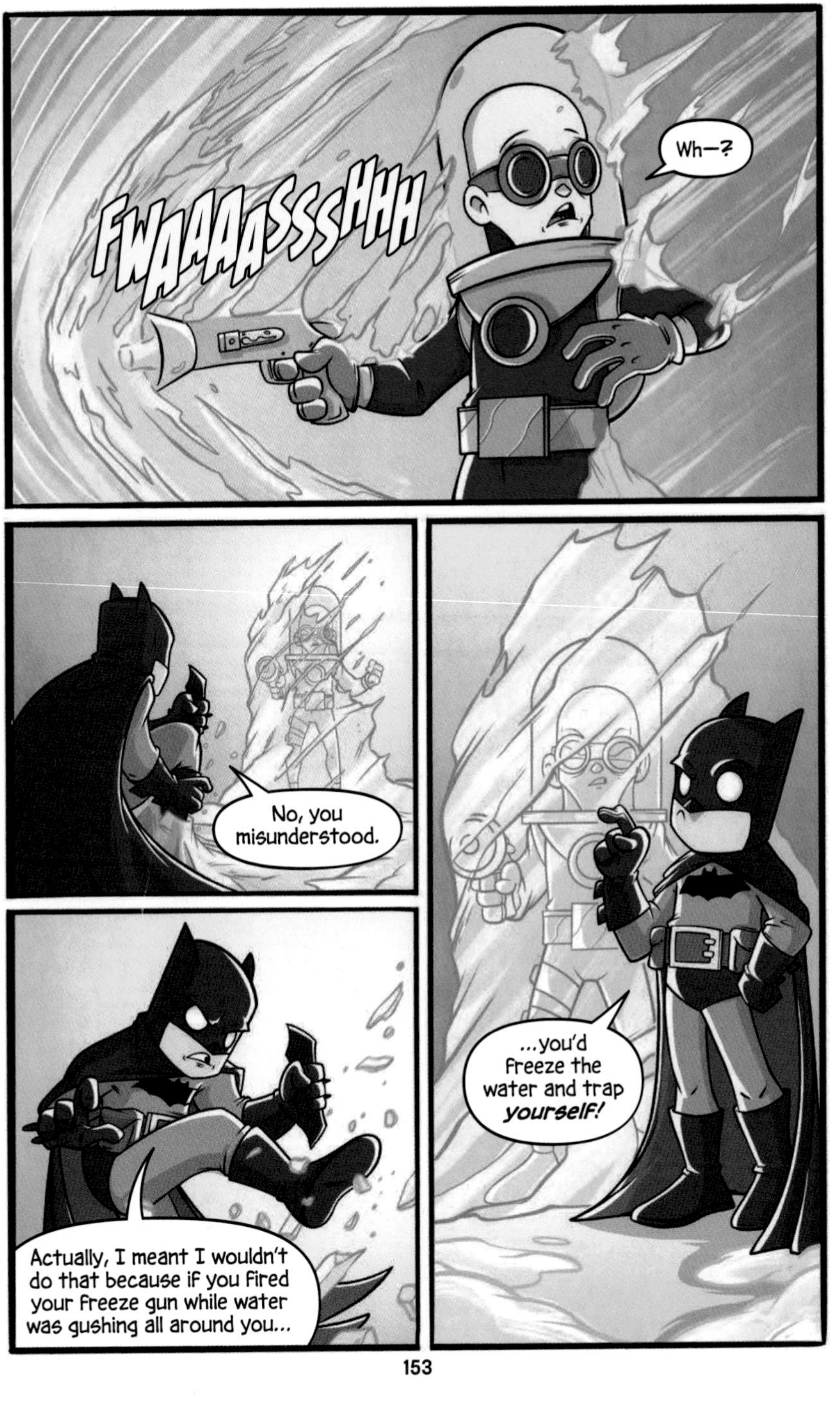
FWAAAASSSHHH
Wh—?
No, you misunderstood.
Actually, I meant I wouldn't do that because if you fired your freeze gun while water was gushing all around you...
...you'd freeze the water and trap *yourself!*

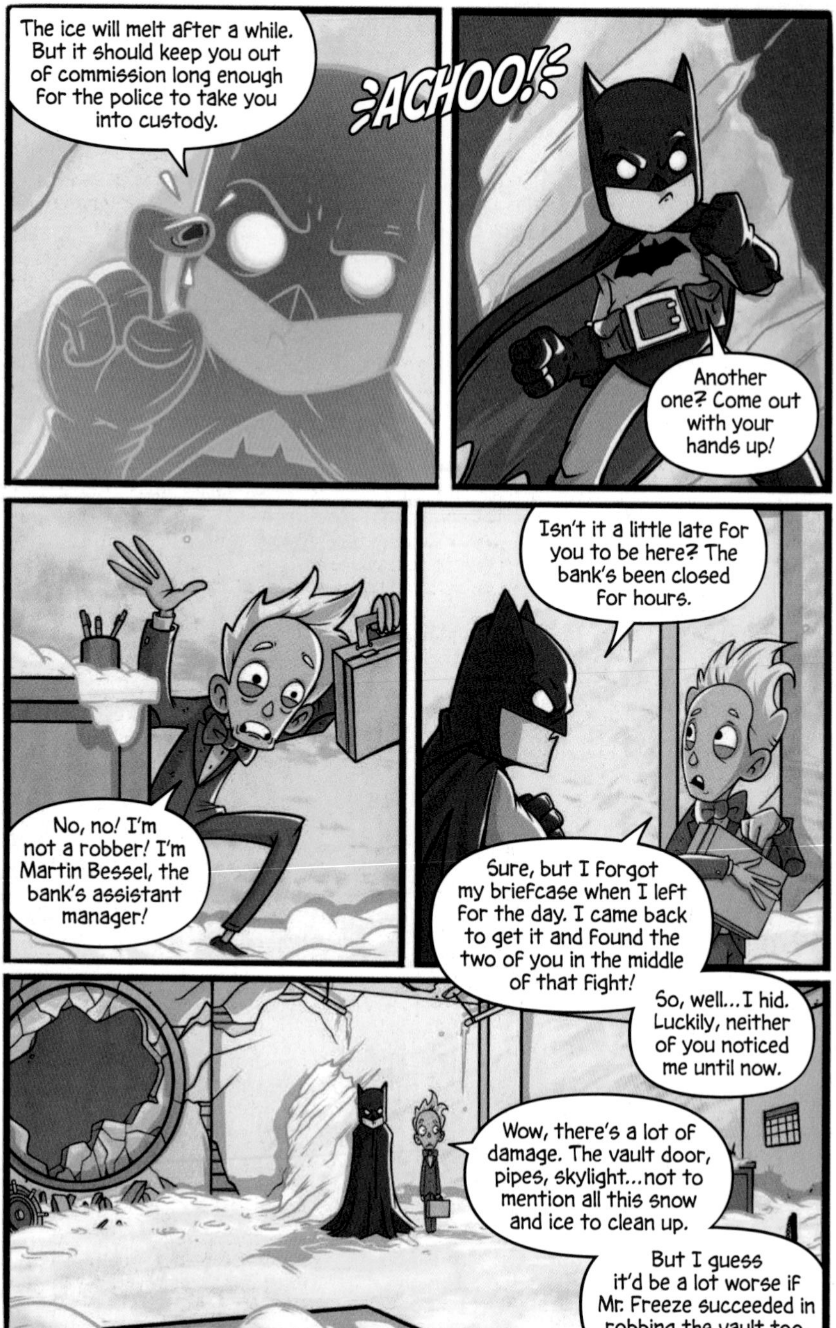
The ice will melt after a while. But it should keep you out of commission long enough for the police to take you into custody.
ACHOO!
Another one? Come out with your hands up!
Isn't it a little late for you to be here? The bank's been closed for hours.
No, no! I'm not a robber! I'm Martin Bessel, the bank's assistant manager!
Sure, but I forgot my briefcase when I left for the day. I came back to get it and found the two of you in the middle of that fight!
So, well...I hid. Luckily, neither of you noticed me until now.
Wow, there's a lot of damage. The vault door, pipes, skylight...not to mention all this snow and ice to clean up.
But I guess it'd be a lot worse if Mr. Freeze succeeded in robbing the vault too.

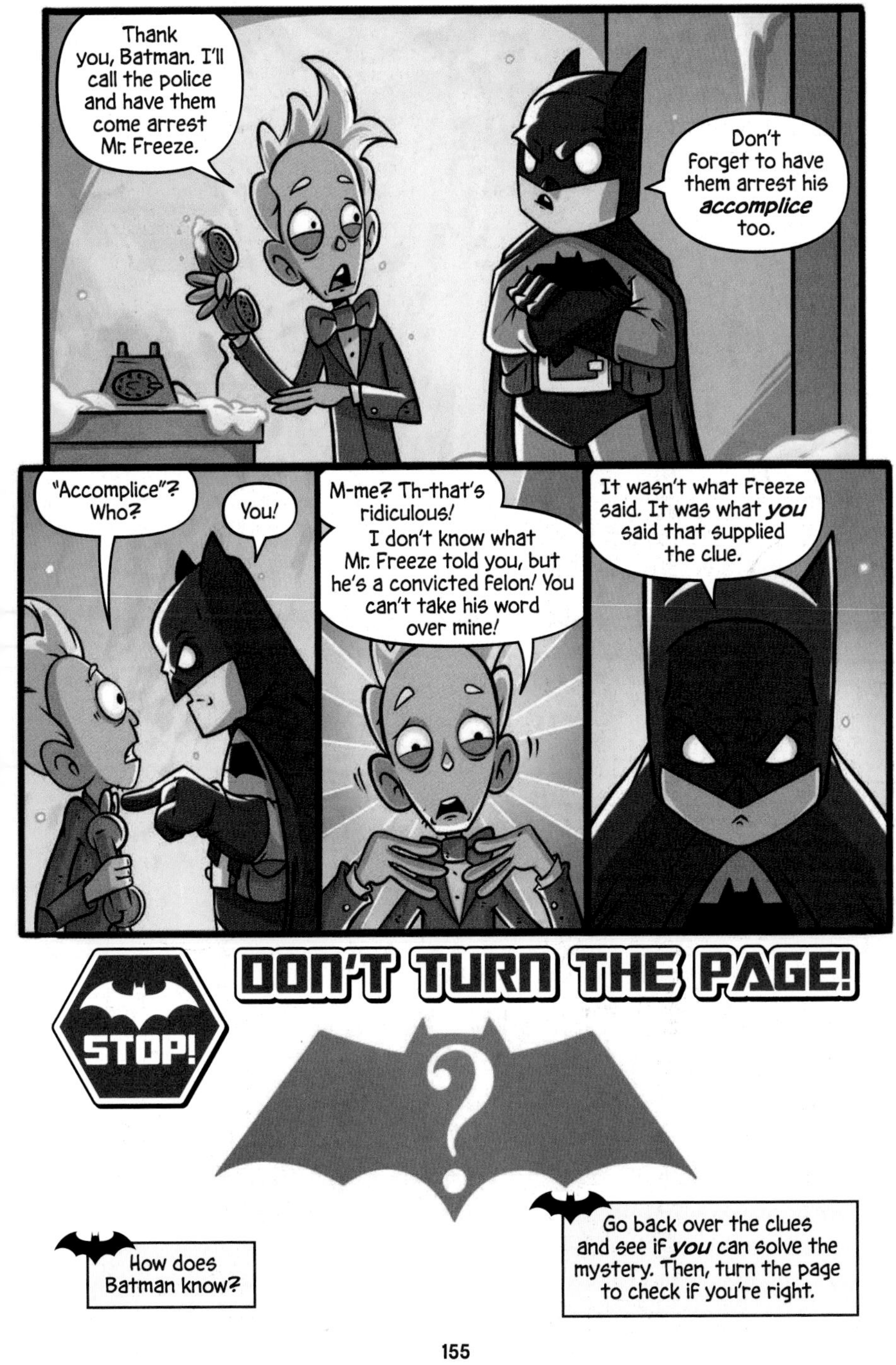
Thank you, Batman. I'll call the police and have them come arrest Mr. Freeze.
Don't forget to have them arrest his *accomplice* too.
"Accomplice"? Who?
You!
M-me? Th-that's ridiculous! I don't know what Mr. Freeze told you, but he's a convicted felon! You can't take his word over mine!
It wasn't what Freeze said. It was what *you* said that supplied the clue.

STOP!

DON'T TURN THE PAGE!

How does Batman know?

Go back over the clues and see if *you* can solve the mystery. Then, turn the page to check if you're right.

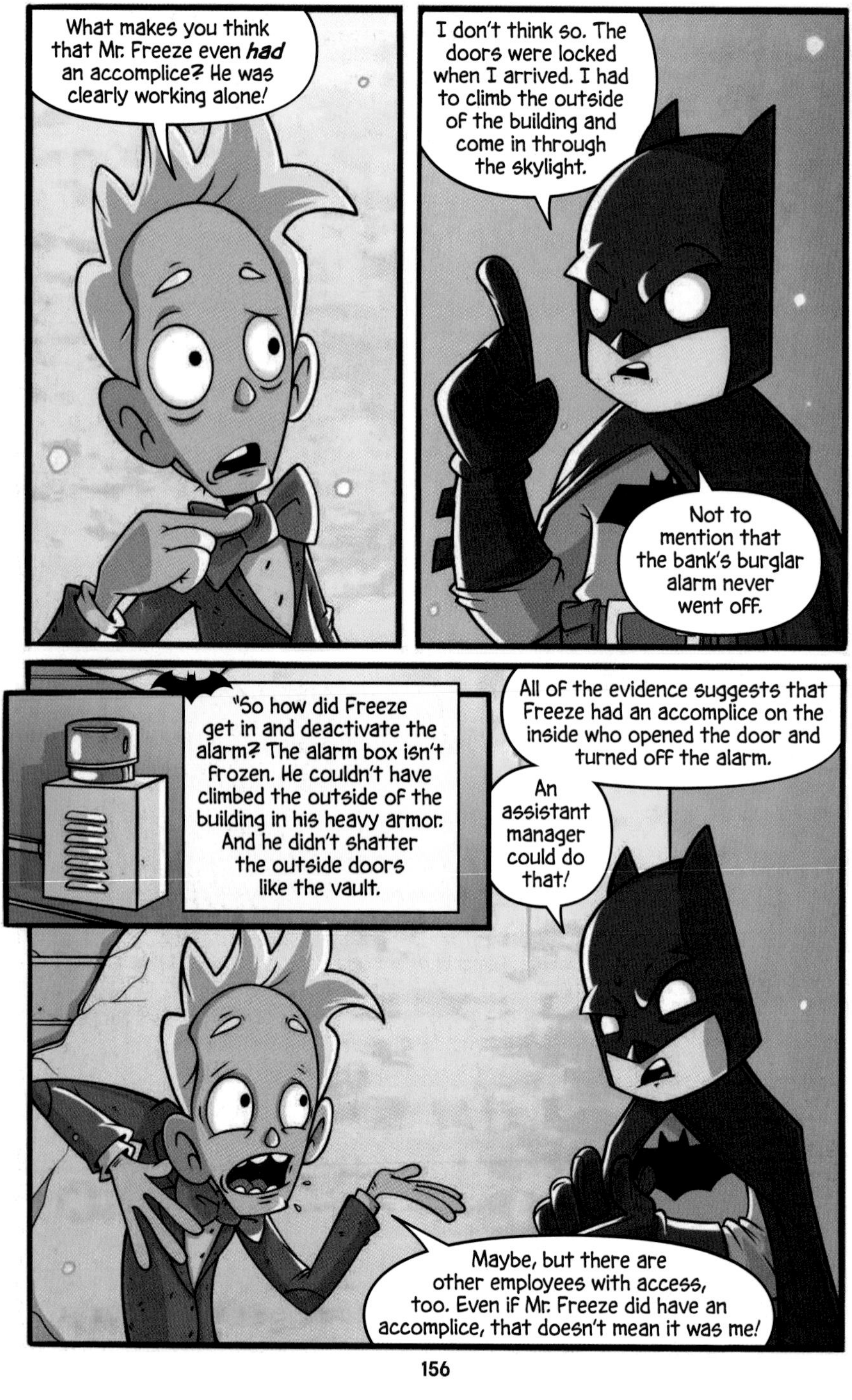
What makes you think that Mr. Freeze even ***had*** an accomplice? He was clearly working alone!
I don't think so. The doors were locked when I arrived. I had to climb the outside of the building and come in through the skylight.
Not to mention that the bank's burglar alarm never went off.
"So how did Freeze get in and deactivate the alarm? The alarm box isn't frozen. He couldn't have climbed the outside of the building in his heavy armor. And he didn't shatter the outside doors like the vault.
All of the evidence suggests that Freeze had an accomplice on the inside who opened the door and turned off the alarm.
An assistant manager could do that!
Maybe, but there are other employees with access, too. Even if Mr. Freeze did have an accomplice, that doesn't mean it was me!

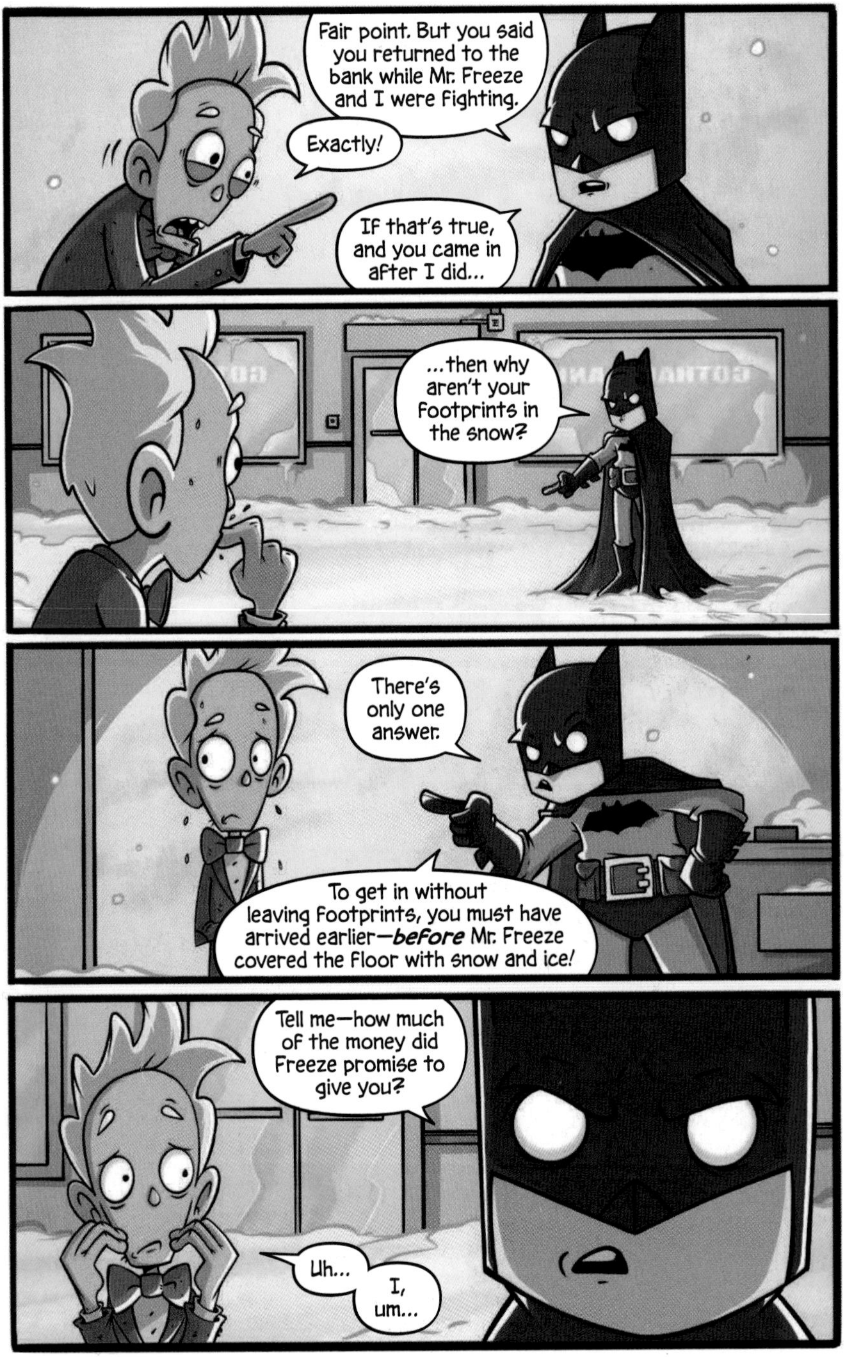
Fair point. But you said you returned to the bank while Mr. Freeze and I were fighting.
Exactly!
If that's true, and you came in after I did...
...then why aren't your footprints in the snow?
There's only one answer.
To get in without leaving footprints, you must have arrived earlier—*before* Mr. Freeze covered the floor with snow and ice!
Tell me—how much of the money did Freeze promise to give you?
Uh...
I, um...

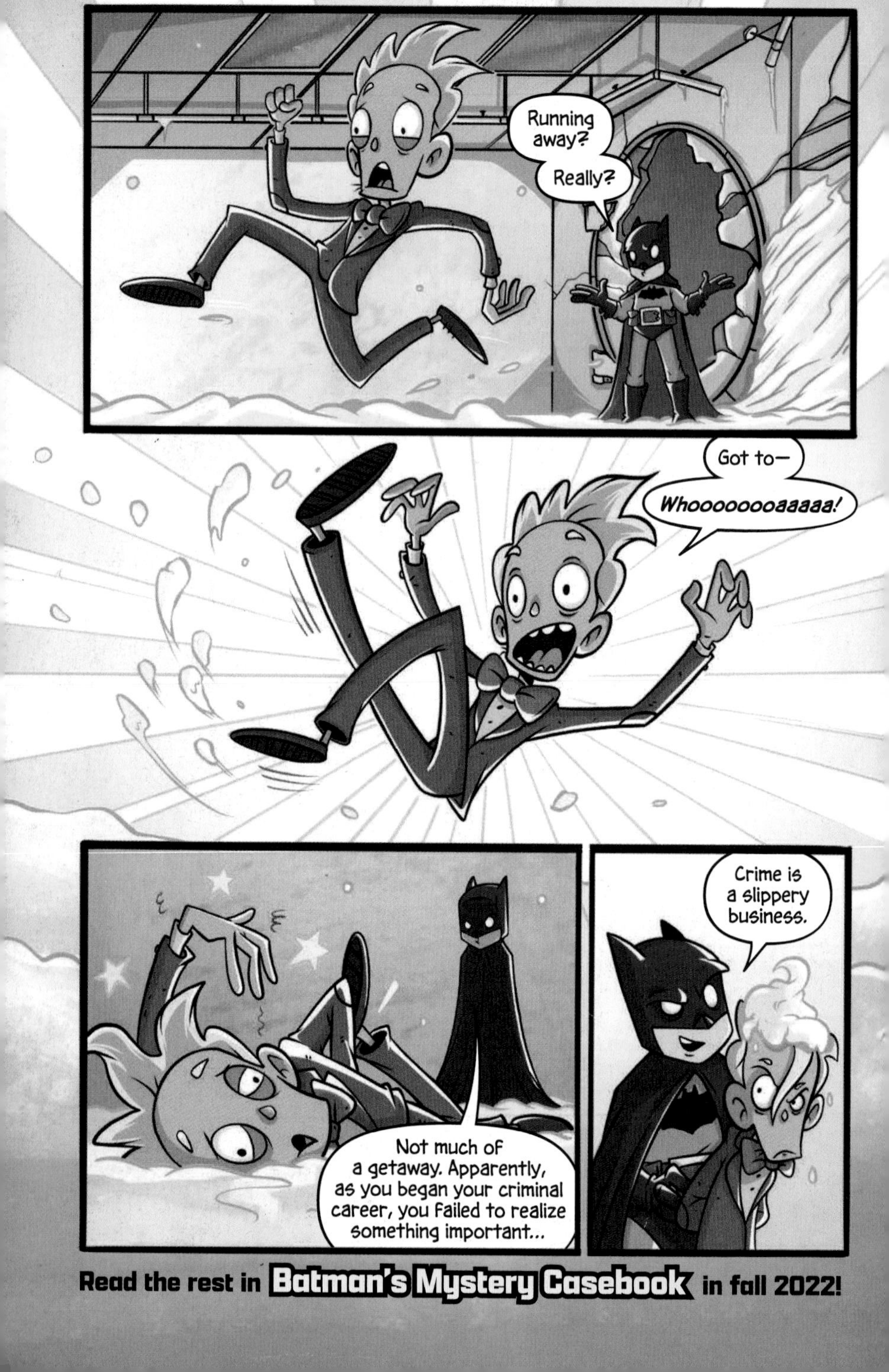
Running away?
Really?
Got to—
Whooooooooaaaaa!
Not much of a getaway. Apparently, as you began your criminal career, you failed to realize something important...
Crime is a slippery business.

Read the rest in Batman's Mystery Casebook in fall 2022!

STILL LOOKING FOR MORE? TRY THESE GRAPHIC NOVELS!

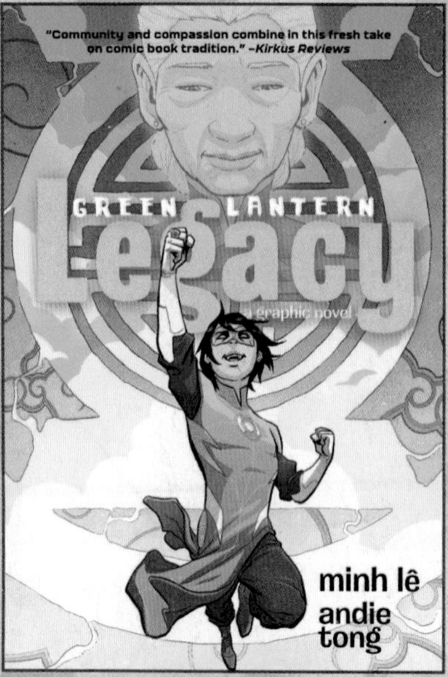
"Community and compassion combine in this fresh take on comic book tradition." –Kirkus Reviews
GREEN LANTERN
Legacy
a graphic novel
minh lê
andie tong

Green Lantern: Legacy
Minh Lê, Andie Tong
ISBN-13: 978-1-4012-8355-1

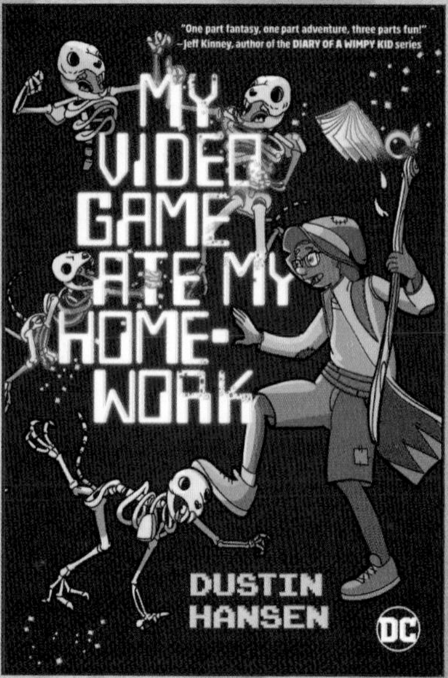
"One part fantasy, one part adventure, three parts fun!" –Jeff Kinney, author of the DIARY OF A WIMPY KID series
MY VIDEO GAME ATE MY HOME-WORK
DUSTIN HANSEN
DC

My Video Game Ate My Homework
Dustin Hansen
ISBN-13: 978-1-4012-9326-0

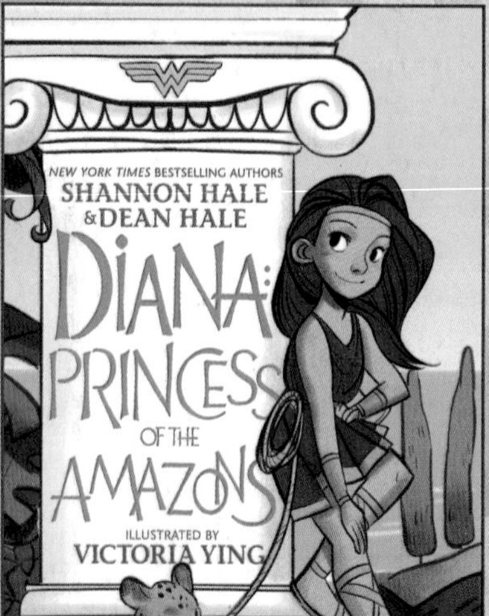
NEW YORK TIMES BESTSELLING AUTHORS
SHANNON HALE & DEAN HALE
DIANA: PRINCESS OF THE AMAZONS
ILLUSTRATED BY VICTORIA YING

Diana, Princess of the Amazons
Shannon Hale, Dean Hale, Victoria Ying
ISBN-13: 978-1-4012-9111-2

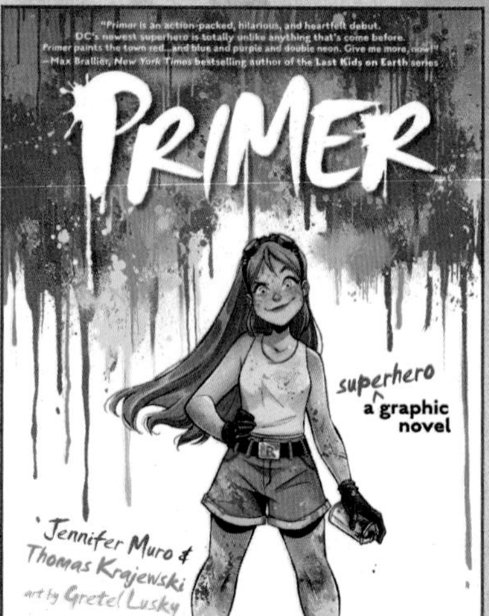
"Primer is an action-packed, hilarious, and heartfelt debut. DC's newest superhero is totally unlike anything that's come before. Primer paints the town red...and blue and purple and double neon. Give me more, now!" —Max Brallier, New York Times bestselling author of the Last Kids on Earth series
PRIMER
a superhero graphic novel
Jennifer Muro & Thomas Krajewski
art by Gretel Lusky

Primer
Jennifer Muro, Thomas Krajewski, Gretel Lusky
ISBN-13: 978-1-4012-9657-5